NYPHRON RISING

BY
MICHAEL J. SULLIVAN

RIDAN

To Robin, who breathed life into Amilia, gave comfort to Modina and saved two others from death.

To Steve Gillick my first sounding board.

And to the members of goodreads.com who supported the series and invited others to join the adventure.

A Ridan Publication

www.ridanpublishing.com
www.michaelsullivan-author.com
www.riyria.blogspot.com

Copyright © 2009 by Michael J. Sullivan
Cover Art and Map by Michael J. Sullivan

Editing by Robin Sullivan, Heather McBride, & Christine Cartwright

ISBN: 978-0-9796211-4-7

PRINTED IN THE UNITED STATES

First Printing: November 2009

CONTENTS

World Map of Elan

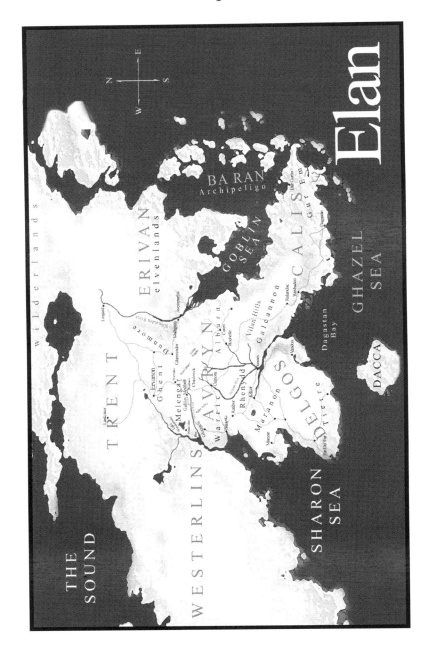

Detail Map of Avryn

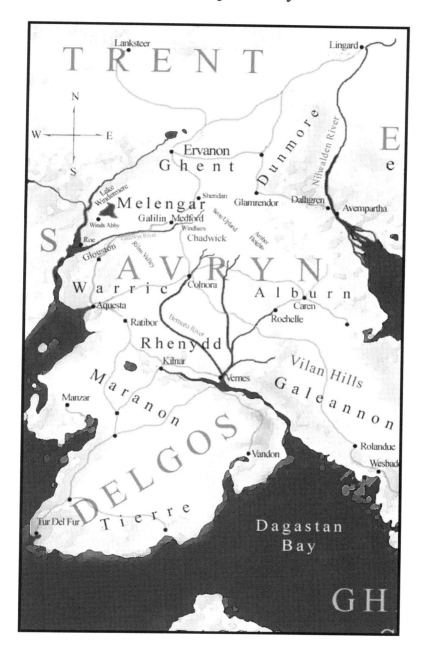

Nyphron
Rising

Chapter 1
THE EMPRESS

Amilia made the mistake of looking back into Edith Mon's eyes. She never meant to look up, never meant to raise her gaze from its place on the floor, but Edith startled her. The head maid would see it as defiance, a sign of rebellion in the ranks of the scullery. Amilia never looked in Edith's eyes before and for that brief instant, she wondered if a soul lurked behind them. If so, it must be cowering or dead and Amilia imagined it rotting like a late autumn apple—that would explain the smell. Edith had a sour scent, vaguely rancid as if something had gone bad.

"This 'ill be another tenent withheld from yer pay," the rotund woman said. "Yer diggin' quite a hole, ain't you?"

Edith was big, broad, and missing any sign of a neck. Her huge anvil of a head sat squarely on her shoulders. By contrast, Amilia barely existed. Small and pear-shaped with a plain face and long, lifeless hair—she was part of the crowd; one of the faces no one paused to consider—neither pretty nor grotesque enough to warrant a second glance. Unfortunately, her invisibility failed when it came to the palace's head maid, Edith Mon.

"I didn't break it." *Mistake number two*, Amilia thought to herself.

A meaty hand slapped her across the face, ringing her ears and watering her eyes. "Go on," Edith enticed with a sweet tone, and then whispered in her ear, "lie ta me again."

Gripping the washbasin to steady herself, Amilia felt the heat blossom on her cheek. Her gaze now followed Edith's hand and when it rose again, Amilia flinched. With a snicker, Edith ran her plump fingers through Amilia's hair.

"No tangles," Edith observed. "I can see how ya spend yer time, instead of doin' yer work. Ya hopin' ta catch the eye of the butcher? Maybe that saucy little man who delivers the wood? I saw ya talkin' ta him. Know what they sees when they looks at ya? They sees an ugly scullery maid is what. A wretched filthy guttersnipe who smells of lye and grease. They would rather pay fer a whore than get ya for nothin'. You'd be better off spendin' more time on yer tasks. If ya did, I wouldn't have ta beat ya so often."

Amilia felt Edith winding her hair, twisting and tightening it around her fist. "It's not like I enjoy hurtin' ya." She pulled until Amilia winced. "But ya have ta learn." Edith continued pulling Amilia's hair, forcing her head back until only the ceiling was visible. "Yer slow, stupid, and ugly. That's why yer still in the scullery. I can't make ya a laundry maid, much less a parlor or chambermaid. You'd embarrass me, understand?"

Amilia remained quiet.

"I said, do you understand?"

"Yes."

"Say yer sorry for chippin' the plate."

"I'm sorry for chipping the plate."

"And yer sorry for lyin' 'bout it?"

"Yes."

Edith roughly patted Amilia's burning cheek. "That's a good girl. I'll add the cost ta yer tally. Now as for punishment…" she let go of Amilia's hair and tore the scrub brush from her hand, measuring its weight. She usually used a belt—the brush would hurt more. Edith would drag her to the laundry, where the big cook could not see. The head cook took a liking to Amilia, and while Edith had every right to discipline her girls, Ibis would not stand for it in his kitchen. Amilia waited for a fat hand to grab her wrist, but instead Edith stroked her head. "Such long hair," she said at length. "It's your hair that's gettin' in yer way isn't it? It's makin' ya think too much of yerself. Well, I know just how to fix both problems. You're gonna look real pretty when I—"

The kitchen fell silent. Cora, who was incessantly plunging her butter churn, paused in mid-stroke. The cooks stopped chopping and even Nipper, who was stacking wood near the stoves, froze. Amilia followed their gaze to the stairs.

A noblewoman adorned in white velvet and satin glided down the steps and entered the steamy stench of the scullery. Piercing eyes and razor-thin lips stood out against a powdered face. The woman was tall and, unlike Amilia's hunched posture, stood as straight as a shaft of light. She moved immediately to the small table along the wall where the baker was preparing bread.

"Clear this," she ordered with the wave of her hand, speaking to no one in particular. The baker immediately scooped up his utensils and dough into his apron and hurried away. "Scrub it clean," the lady insisted.

Amilia felt the brush thrust back into her hand, and a push sent her stumbling forward. She did not look up, and went right to work making large swirls of flour-soaked film. Nipper was beside her in an instant with a bucket, and Vella arrived with a towel. Together they cleared the mess while the woman watched with disdain.

"Two chairs," the lady barked, and Nipper ran off to fetch them.

Uncertain what to do next, Amilia stood in place watching the lady holding the dripping brush at her side. When the noblewoman caught her staring, Amilia quickly looked down, and movement caught her eye. A small gray mouse froze beneath the baker's table, trying to conceal itself in the shadows. Taking a chance, it snatched a morsel of bread and disappeared through a small crack.

"What a miserable creature," she heard the lady say. Amilia thought she also saw the mouse, until she added. "You're making a filthy puddle on the floor. Go away."

Before retreating to her washbasin, Amilia attempted a pathetic curtsey. A flurry of orders erupted from the woman, each pronounced with perfect diction. Vella, Cora, and even Edith went about setting a table as if for a royal banquet. Vella draped a white tablecloth, and Edith started setting out silverware only to be shooed away as the woman carefully placed each piece herself. Soon the table was elegantly set for two, complete with multiple goblets and linen napkins.

Amilia could not imagine who could be dining there. No one would set a table for the servants and why would a noble come to the kitchen to eat?

"Here now, what's all this about?" Amilia heard the deep familiar voice of Ibis Thinly. The old sea cook was a large barrel-chested man with bright blue eyes and a thin beard that wreathed the line of his chin. He spent the morning meeting with farmers, yet he still wore his ever-present apron. The grease-stained wrap was his uniform, his mark of office. He barged into the kitchen like a bear returning to his cave to find mischief afoot. When he spotted the lady he stopped.

"I am Lady Constance," the noblewoman informed him. "In a moment I will be bringing the Empress Modina here. If you are the cook then prepare food." The lady paused a moment to study the table critically; she adjusted the position of a few items then turned and left.

"Leif, get a knife on that roasted lamb," Ibis shouted. "Cora, fetch cheese. Vella, get bread. Nipper, straighten that woodpile!"

"The empress!" Cora exclaimed as she raced for the pantry.

THE EMPRESS

"What's she doin' comin' here?" Leif asked. There was anger in his voice as if an unwelcome, no-account relative was dropping by and he was the inconvenienced lord of the manor.

Like everyone, Amilia had heard of the empress but never saw her—not even from a distance. Few had. She was coroneted in a private ceremony over half a year ago on Wintertide, and her arrival changed everything.

King Ethelred no longer wore his crown and was addressed as regent instead of Your Majesty. He still ruled over the castle, only now it was referred to as *the palace*. It was the other one, Regent Saldur, who made all the changes. Originally from Melengar, the old cleric took up residence, and set builders working day and night on the great hall and throne room. It was also Saldur who declared new rules that all of the servants had to follow.

The palace staff could no longer leave the grounds unless escorted by one of the new guards, and all outgoing letters were read and approved. This latter edict was hardly an issue, as few servants could write. The restriction on going outside the palace, however, was a hardship to almost everyone. Many with families in the city or surrounding farms chose to resign because they could no longer return home each night. Those remaining at the castle never heard from them again. Regent Saldur had successfully isolated the palace from the outside world, but inside, rumors and gossip ran wild. Speculations flourished in out-of-the-way corridors that giving notice was as unhealthy as attempting to sneak away.

The fact that no one ever saw the empress ignited its own set of speculations. Everyone knew she was the heir of the original legendary Emperor Novron and therefore a child of the god Maribor. This was proven when only she was able to slay the beast that slaughtered dozens of Elan's greatest knights. The fact that she was previously a farm girl from a small village confirmed that in the eyes of Maribor all were equal. Rumors concluded that she ascended to the state of a spiritual being. It was believed that only the regents and her personal secretary ever stood in her divine presence. That must be who the noblewoman was. The lady with the sour face and perfect speech was the Imperial Secretary to the Empress.

They soon had an array of the best food they could muster in a short time laid out on the table. Knob, the baker, and Leif, the butcher, disputed the placement of dishes, each wanting their wares in the center. "Cora," Ibis said, "put your pretty cake of cheese in the middle." This brought a smile and blush to the dairymaid's face and scowls from Leif and Knob.

Being a scullion, Amilia had no more part to play and returned to her dishes. Edith was chatting excitedly in the corner near the stack of oak kegs with the tapster and the cupbearer, and everyone was straightening their outfits and running fingers through their hair. Nipper was still sweeping when the lady returned. Once more, everyone stopped. She was leading a thin young girl by the wrist.

"Sit down," Lady Constance ordered in her brisk tone.

Everyone peered past the two women, trying to catch the first glimpse of their god-queen. Two well-armored guards emerged and took up positions on either side of the table. But no one else appeared.

Where is the empress?

"Modina, I said sit down," Lady Constance repeated.

Shock rippled through Amilia.

Modina? This waif of a child is the empress?

The girl did not appear to hear Lady Constance and stood limp with a blank expression. She looked to be a teenager, delicate and deathly thin. Once she might have been pretty, but what remained was an appalling sight. The girl's face was white as bone, her skin thin and stretched, revealing the detailed outline of her skull beneath. Her ragged blonde hair fell across her face. She wore only a thin white smock which added to the girl's ghostly appearance.

Lady Constance sighed and forced the girl into one of the chairs at the baker's table. Like a doll, the girl allowed herself to be moved. She said nothing and her eyes stared blankly.

"Place the napkin in your lap this way." Lady Constance carefully opened and laid the linen with deliberate movements. She waited, glaring at the empress who sat oblivious. "As empress, you will never serve yourself," Lady Constance went on. "You will wait as your servants fill your plate." Lady Constance looked around with irritation when her eyes found Amilia. "You—come here," she ordered. "Serve her eminence."

Amilia dropped the brush in the basin and, wiping her hands on her smock, rushed forward. She wanted to mention she had no experience with serving, but said nothing. Instead she focused on recalling the times she watched Leif cutting meat. Taking up the tongs and a knife she tried her best to imitate him. Leif always made it look effortless, but Amilia's fingers betrayed her and she fumbled miserably, managing only to place a few shredded bits of lamb on the girl's plate.

"Bread," Lady Constance snapped the word like a whip and Amilia sliced into the long twisted loaf, nearly cutting herself in the process.

"Now eat."

For a brief moment, Amilia thought this was another order for her and reached out in response. She caught herself and stood motionless, not certain if she was free to return to her dishes.

"Eat, I said." The Imperial Secretary glared at the girl who continued to stare blankly at the far wall.

"EAT DAMN YOU!" Lady Constance bellowed and everyone in the kitchen, including Edith Mon and Ibis Thinly jumped. She pounded the baker's table with her fist, knocking over the stemware and bouncing the knives against the plates. "EAT!" Lady Constance repeated and slapped the girl across the face. Her skin-wrapped skull rocked with the blow and came to rest on its own. The girl did not wince. She merely continued her stare, this time at a new wall.

In a fit of rage, the Imperial Secretary rose, knocking over her chair. She took one of the pieces of meat and tried to force it into the girl's mouth.

"What is going on?"

Lady Constance froze at the sound of the voice. An old white-haired man descended the steps into the scullery, his elegant purple robe and black cape looking out of place in the hot, messy kitchen. Amilia recognized Regent Saldur immediately.

"What in the world…" Saldur began, as he approached the table. He looked at the girl, then at the kitchen staff, and finally at Lady Constance, who at some point had dropped the meat. "What were you thinking…bringing her down here?"

"I—I thought if—"

Saldur held up his hand, silencing her, then slowly squeezed it into a fist. He clenched his jaw and drew a deep breath through his sharp nose. Once more, he focused on the girl. "Look at her. You were supposed to educate and train her. She's worse than ever!"

"I—I tried, but—"

"Shut up!" the regent snapped, still holding up his fist. No one in the kitchen moved. The only sound was the faint crackle of the fire in the ovens and the bubbling of broth in a pot. "If this is the result of an expert, we may as well try an amateur. They couldn't possibly do worse." The regent pointed at Amilia. "You! Congratulations, you are now the Imperial Secretary to the Empress." Turning his attention back to Lady Constance, he said, "And as for you—your services are no longer required. Guards, remove her ladyship."

Amilia saw Lady Constance falter. Her perfect posture evaporated as she cowered and walked backward, nearly falling over the upended chair. "No! Please, no," she cried as a palace guard gripped her arm and pulled her toward the back door. Another guard took her remaining arm. She grew frantic, pleading and struggling as they dragged her out.

THE EMPRESS

Amilia stood frozen in place holding the meat tongs and carving knife, trying to remember how to breathe. Once the pleas of Lady Constance faded, Regent Saldur turned to her, his face flushed red, his teeth revealed behind taunt lips. "Don't fail me," he told her and returned up the stairs, his cape whirling behind him.

Amilia looked back at the girl who continued to stare at the wall.

The mystery of why no one saw the empress was solved when a soldier escorted the girls to Modina's room. Amilia expected to travel to the eastern keep, home of the regents' offices and the royal residence. To her surprise, the guard remained on the service side and headed for a curved stair across from the laundry. Chambermaids used this stairwell to service rooms on the upper floors. But here, they went down.

Amilia did not question the guard, her thoughts preoccupied with the sword that hung at his side. His dark eyes were embedded in a stone face, and the top of her head reached the bottom of his chin. Each of his hands was the size of two of hers. He was not one of the guards that took Lady Constance away but Amilia knew he would not hesitate when the time came.

The air turned cool and damp as they descended into darkness cut only by three mounted lanterns. The last dripped wax from an unhinged faceplate. At the bottom of the stairs, a wooden door stood open leading to a tiny corridor with more doors on either side. In one room Amilia spotted several casks and a rack of bottles dressed in packs of straw. Large locks sealed two others and the third door stood open, revealing a small stone room empty except for a pile of straw and a wooden bucket. When they reached it, the soldier stood to one side, his back to the wall.

"I'm sorry…" Amilia began, confused. "I don't understand, I thought we were going to the empress' bed chamber?"

The guard nodded.

"Are you saying this is where her eminence sleeps?"

Again, the soldier nodded.

As Amilia stared in shock, Modina wandered forward into the room and curled up on the pile of straw. The guard closed the heavy door and began fitting a large lock through the latch.

"Wait," Amilia said, "you can't leave her here. Can't you see she's sick?"

The guard snapped the lock in place.

Amilia stared at the oak door.

How is this possible? She's the empress. She's the daughter of a god and the high priestess of the church.

"You keep the empress in an old cellar?"

"It's better than where she was," the soldier told her. He had not spoken until now, and his voice was not what she expected. Soft, sympathetic, and not much louder than a whisper—his tone disarmed her.

"Where was she?"

"I've said too much already."

"I can't just leave her in there. She doesn't even have a candle."

"My orders are to keep her here."

Amilia stared at him. She could not see his eyes. The visor of his helm and the way the shadows fell cast everything above his nose in darkness. "Fine," she said at last and walked out of the cellar.

She returned a moment later carrying the wax-laden lantern from the stairwell. "May I at least keep her company?"

"Are you sure?" he sounded surprised.

Amilia was not but nodded anyway. The guard opened the door.

The empress was lying huddled on the bed of straw, her eyes open, staring, but not seeing. Amilia spotted a blanket wadded up in the corner. She set the lantern on the floor, shook out the wool covering, and draped it over the girl, kneeling beside her.

"They don't treat you very well, do they?" she said, carefully brushing back the mass of hair that lay across Modina's face. The strands felt as stiff and brittle as the straw that littered it. "How old are you?"

The empress did not answer, nor did she stir at Amilia's touch. Lying on her side, the girl clutched her knees to her chest and pressed her cheek against the straw. She blinked occasionally and her chest rose and fell with each breath, but nothing more.

"Something bad happened, didn't it?" She ran her fingers lightly over Modina's bare arm. Amilia could circle the girl's wrist with her thumb and index finger with room to spare. "Look, I don't know how long I'm going to be here. I don't expect it will be too long. See, I'm not a noble lady. I'm just a girl who washes dishes. The regent says I'm supposed to educate and train you, but he made a mistake. I don't know how to do any of that." She petted her head and let her fingers run lightly over her hollow cheek, still blotchy from where Lady Constance struck her. "But I promise I won't ever hurt you."

Amilia sat for several minutes searching her mind for some way to reach the girl. "Can I tell you a secret? Now don't laugh…but… I'm really quite afraid of the dark. I know it's silly but I can't help myself. I've always been that way. My brothers tease me about it all the time. If you could chat with me a bit, maybe it would help me. What do you say?"

Still no reaction. Amilia sighed. "Well, tomorrow I'll bring some candles from my room. I have a whole bunch saved up. That will make things a bit nicer. You just try to rest now."

Amilia was not lying about her fear of the dark. But that night it had to stand in line behind a host of new fears as she struggled to find sleep huddled beside the empress.

NYPHRON RISING

The soldiers did not come for Amilia that night and she woke when breakfast was brought in, or rather skipped across the floor on a wooden plate that spun to a stop in the middle of the room. On it was a fist-sized chunk of meat, a wedge of cheese, and thick-crusted bread. It looked wonderful and was similar to Amilia's standard meals, courtesy of Ibis. Before coming to the palace, she never ate beef or venison, but now it was commonplace. Being friends with the head cook had other advantages as well. No one wanted to offend the man who controlled their diet so, with the exception of Edith Mon, Amilia was generally well treated. Amilia took a few bites and loudly voiced her appreciation. "This is sooooo good. Would you like some?"

The empress did not respond.

Amilia sighed. "No, I don't suppose you would. What would you like? I can get you whatever you want."

Amilia got to her feet, grabbed up the tray and waited. Nothing. After a few minutes, she rapped on the door and the same guard opened it.

"Excuse me, but I have to see about getting a proper meal for her eminence." The guard looked at the plate confused but stepped aside, leaving her to trot up the stairs.

The kitchen was still buzzing over the events of the previous night, but it stopped the moment Amilia entered the kitchen. "Sent ya back, did they?" Edith grinned. "Don't worry, I done saved yer pile of pots. And I haven't forgotten about that hair."

"Hush up, Edith," Ibis reprimanded with a scowl. Returning his attention to Amilia he said, "Are you alright? Did they send you back?"

"I'm fine, thank you, Ibis, and no I think I'm still the empress' secretary—whatever that means."

THE EMPRESS

"Good for you lassie," Ibis told her. He turned to Edith and added. "And I'd watch what you say now. Looks like you'll be washing that stack yourself." Edith turned and stalked off with a *humph*.

"So, my dear, what does bring you here?"

"I came about this food you sent to the empress."

Ibis looked wounded. "What's wrong with it?"

"Nothing, it's wonderful. I had some myself."

"Then I don't see—"

"Her eminence is sick. She can't eat this. When I didn't feel well my mother used to make me soup, a thin yellow broth that was easy to swallow. I was wondering, could you make something like that?"

"Sure," Ibis told her. "Soup is easy. Someone shoulda told me she was feeling poorly. I know exactly what to make. I call it Seasick Soup. It's the only thing the new lads kept down their first few days out. Leif, fetch me the big kettle."

Amilia spent the rest of the morning making trips back and forth to Modina's small cell. She removed all of her possessions from the dormitory: a spare dress, some underclothing, a night gown, a brush, and her treasured stash of nearly a dozen candles. From the linen supply she brought pillows, sheets, and blankets. She even snuck a pitcher, some mild soap, and a basin from an unoccupied guest room. Each time she passed, the guard gave her a small smile and shook his head in amusement.

After removing the old straw and bringing in fresh bundles from the stable, she went to Ibis to check on the soup. "Well, the next batch will be better, when I have more time, but this should put some wind in her sails."

Amilia returned to the cell and, setting down the steaming pot of soup, helped the empress to sit up. She took the first sip to check the temperature then lifted the spoon to Modina's lips. Most of the broth went down her chin and dripped onto the front of her smock.

"Okay, that was my fault. Next time I'll remember to bring one of those napkins that lady was all excited about." With her second spoonful, Amilia cupped her hand and caught most of the dribble. "Ah-ha!" she exclaimed. "I got some in. It's good, isn't it?" She tipped another spoonful and this time saw Modina swallow.

When the bowl was empty, Amilia guessed most of the soup was on the floor or soaked into Modina's clothes, but she was certain at least some got in. "There now, that must be a little better, don't you think? But I see I've made a terrible mess of you. What say we clean you up a bit, eh?" Amilia washed Modina and changed her into her own spare smock. The two girls were similar in height, however, Modina swam in the dress until Amilia fashioned a belt from a bit of twine.

Amilia continued to chatter while she made two make-shift beds with the straw and purloined blankets, pillows, and sheets. "I would have liked to bring us some mattresses but they were heavy. Besides I didn't want to risk too much attention. People were already giving me strange looks. I think these will do nicely, don't you?" Modina continued her blank stare. When everything was in order, Amilia sat Modina on her newly sheeted bed in the glow of a handful of cheery candles and began gently brushing her hair.

"So, how does one get to be empress anyway?" she asked. "They say you slew a monster that killed hundreds of knights. You know, you really don't look like the monster slaying type—no offense." Amilia paused and tilted her head. "Still not interested in talking? That's okay. You want to keep your past a secret. I understand. After all, we've only just met.

"So, let's see…what can I tell you about myself? Well first, I come from Tarin Vale. Do you know where that is? Probably not. It is a tiny village between here and Colnora. Just a little town people sometimes pass through on their way to more exciting places. Nothing much happens in Tarin. My father makes carriages and he is really good at it. Still, he doesn't make much money." She paused and studied the girl's face to try to determine if she heard any of what she was saying.

"What does your father do? I think I heard he was a farmer, is that right?"

Nothing.

"My da doesn't make much money. My mother says it's because he does *too good* of a job. He's pretty proud of his work, so he takes a long time. It can take him a whole year to make a carriage. That makes it hard because he only gets paid when it's done. What with buying the supplies and all, we sometimes run out of money.

"My mother does spinning and my brother cuts wood, but it never seems like enough. That's why I'm here, you see. I'm not a very good spinner but I can read and write." One side of the girl's head was now free of tangles and Amilia switched to the other.

"I can see you are impressed. It hasn't done me much good though, well except I guess it did get me a foot in the door, as it were.

"Hmm, what's that? You want to know where I learned to read and write? Oh, well thank you for asking. Devon taught me. He's a monk that came to Tarin Vale a few years ago," her voice lowered conspiratorially. "I liked him a lot and he was cute and smart—*very smart*. He read books and told me about faraway places and things that happened long ago. Devon thought either my dad or the head of his order would try to split us up, so he taught me so we could write each other. Devon was right of course. When my da found out he said, 'There's no future with a monk.' Devon was sent away and I cried for days."

Amilia paused to clear a particularly nasty snarl. She tried her best to be gentle, but was sure it caused the girl pain even if she did not show it. "That was a rough one," she said. "For a minute I thought you might have a sparrow hiding in there.

"Anyway, when Da found out I could read and write he was so proud. He bragged about me to everyone who came to the shop. One of his customers, Squire Jenkins Talbert, was impressed and said he could put in a good word for me here in Aquesta.

"Everyone was so excited when I was accepted. When I found out the job was just to wash dishes I didn't have the heart to tell my family, so I've not been home since. Now, of course, they won't let me go." Amilia sighed but then put on a bright smile. "But that's okay, because now I'm here with you."

There was a quiet knock and the guard stepped in. He took a minute to survey the changes in the cell and nodded his approval. His gaze shifted to Amilia and there was a distinct sadness in his eyes. "I'm sorry, Miss, but Regent Saldur has ordered me to bring you to him."

Amilia froze, then slowly put the brush down and with a trembling hand draped a blanket around the young girl's shoulder. She rose, kissed Modina on the cheek and in a quivering voice managed to whisper, "Goodbye."

Chapter 2
THE MESSENGER

He always feared he would die this way, alone on a remote stretch of road far from home. The forest pressed close from both sides, and his trained eyes recognized that the debris barring his path was not the innocent result of a weakened tree. He pulled on the reins, forcing his horse's head down. She snorted in frustration, fighting the bit—like him, she sensed danger.

He glanced behind and to either side scanning the trees standing in summer gowns of deep green. Nothing moved in the early morning stillness; nothing betrayed the tranquil facade except the pile before him. The deadfall was unnatural. Even from this distance, he saw the brightly colored pulp of fresh-cut wood—a barricade.

Thieves?

A band of highwaymen no doubt crouched under the cover of the forest watching, waiting for him to draw near. He tried to focus his thoughts as his horse panted beneath him. This was the shortest route north to the Galewyr River, and he was running out of time. Breckton was preparing to invade the Kingdom of Melengar, and he must deliver the dispatch before the knight launched the attack. His commander as well as the regents had personally expressed the importance of this mission before he embarked. They were counting on him—*she* was counting on him. Like thousands of others, he stood in the freezing square on Coronation Day just to catch a glimpse of Empress Modina. To their immense disappointment she never appeared. After many hours an announcement explained she was too consumed with the affairs of the New Empire. Ascended from the peasant class, the new ruler obviously had no time for frivolity.

He removed his cloak and tied it behind the saddle, revealing the gold crown on his tabard. They might let him pass. Surely they knew the Imperial Army was nearby, and Sir Breckton would not stand for the waylaying of an imperial messenger. Highwaymen might not fear that fool Earl Ballentyne, but even desperate men would think twice before offending Ballentyne's knight. Other commanders may ignore a bloodied or murdered dispatch rider, but Sir Breckton would take it as a personal assault on his honor, and insulting Breckton's honor was tantamount to suicide.

He refused to fail.

Brushing the hair from his eyes, he took a fresh grip on the reins and advanced cautiously. As he neared the barricade, he saw movement. Leaves quivered. A twig snapped. He pivoted his mount and prepared to bolt. He was a good rider—fast and agile. His horse was a well-bred three-year-old and once spurred, no one would catch them. He tensed in the saddle and leaned forward, preparing for the lurch, but the sight of imperial uniforms stopped him.

A pair of soldiers trudged to the road from the trees and grudgingly peered at him with the dull expression common to foot soldiers. They were dressed in red tabards emblazoned with the crest of Sir Breckton's command. As they approached, the larger one chewed a stalk of rye while the smaller man licked his fingers and wiped them on his uniform.

"You had me worried," the rider said with a mix of relief and irritation. "I thought you were highwaymen."

THE MESSENGER

The smaller one smiled. He took little care with his uniform. Two shoulder straps were unfastened, causing the leather tongues to stand up like tiny wings on his shoulders. "Did ya 'ear that, Will? He thoughts we was thieves. Not a bad idea, eh? We should cut us some purses—charge a toll as it were. At least we'd make a bit 'o coin standin' out 'ere all day. 'Course Breckton would skin us alive, if'n 'e 'eard."

The taller soldier, most likely a half-wit mute, nodded in silent agreement. At least he wore his uniform smartly. It fit him better and he took the time to wear it properly. Both uniforms were rumpled and stained from sleeping outdoors, but such was the life of an infantryman, and one of the many reasons he preferred being a courier.

"Clear this mess. I have an urgent dispatch. I need to get through to the Imperial Army command at once."

"Here now, we 'ave orders too, ya know? We're not ta let anyone pass," the smaller said as the larger strolled over and joined them.

"I am an imperial courier you fool!"

"Oh," the sentry responded with all the acumen of a wooden post, and glanced briefly at his partner, who maintained his dim expression. "Well, that's a different set of apples, now isn't it?" He petted the horse's neck. "That would explain the lather you've put on this 'ere girl, eh? She looks like she could use a drink. We got a bucket and there's a little stream just over—"

"I have no time for that. Just get that pile out of the road and be quick about it."

"Certainly, certainly. You don't 'ave ta be so rough. Just tell us the watchword and Will and me, we'll haul it outta yer way right fast," he said, as he dug for something caught in his teeth.

"Watchword?"

The soldier nodded. He pulled his finger out and sniffed at something with a sour look before giving it a flick. "You know, the password. We can't be lettin' no spies through 'ere. There's a war on after all."

"I've never heard of such a thing. I wasn't informed of any password."

"No?" The smaller soldier raised an eyebrow as he took hold of the horse's bridle.

"I spoke to the regents themselves and I—"

The larger of the two pulled him from his horse. He landed on his back, hitting the ground hard and banging his head. A jolt of pain momentarily blinded him. When he opened his eyes, he found the soldier straddling him with a blade to his throat.

"Who do you work for?" the large sentry growled.

"Whatcha doing, Will?" the smaller one asked still holding his horse.

"Trying to get this spy to talk, that's what."

"I—I'm not a spy. I'm an imperial courier. Let me go!"

"Will, our orders says nothin' about interrogatin' 'em. If'n they don't know the watchword, we cuts they's throats and tosses 'em in the river. Sir Breckton don't 'ave time ta deal with every fool we get on this 'ere road. Besides, who ya think 'e works for? The only ones fightin' us is Melengar, so 'e works for Melengar. Now slit 'is throat and I'll 'elp you drag 'im to the river as soon as I ties up this 'ere 'orse."

"But I *am* a courier!" he shouted.

"Sure ya is."

"I can prove it. I have dispatches for Sir Breckton in the saddlebag."

The two soldiers exchanged dubious looks. The smaller one shrugged. He reached into the horse's bags and proceeded to search. He pulled out a leather satchel and withdrew a wax-sealed parchment and promptly broke the seal, unfolded, and examined it.

"Well, if'n that don't beat all. Looks like 'e is telling the truth, Will. This 'ere looks like a real genuine dispatch for his lordship."

THE MESSENGER

"Oh?" the other asked as worry crossed his face.

"Sure looks that way. Better let 'im up."

The soldier sheathed his weapon and extended a hand to help him to his feet, his face downcast. "Ah—sorry about that. We were just following orders, you know?"

"When Sir Breckton sees this broken seal, he'll have your heads!" he said, shoving past the large sentry and snatching the document from the other.

"Us?" the smaller one laughed. "Like Will 'ere said, we was just followin' 'is orders. You were the one who failed ta get the watchword afore riding 'ere. Sir Breckton, 'e is a stickler for rules. 'E don't like it when 'is orders aren't followed. 'Course you'll most likely only lose a 'and or maybe an ear fer yer mistake. If'n I was you, I'd see if'n I could heat the wax up enough ta reseal it."

"That would ruin the impression."

"Ya could say it was hot and what with the sun on the pouch all day the wax melted in the saddlebag. Better than losing an 'and or an ear, I says. Besides, busy nobles like Breckton ain't gonna study the seal afore openin' an urgent dispatch, but 'e will notice if'n the seal is broken. That's fer sure."

The courier looked at the document flapping in the breeze and felt his stomach churn. He had no choice, but he would not do it here with these idiots watching. He remounted his horse.

"Clear the road!" he barked.

The two soldiers dragged the branches aside. He kicked his horse and raced her up the road.

Royce watched the courier ride out of sight before taking off his imperial uniform and turning to face Hadrian he said, "Well, that wasn't so hard."

"Will?" Hadrian asked as the two slipped into the forest.

Royce nodded. "Remember complaining yesterday that you'd rather be an actor? I was giving you a part: Will, the Imperial Checkpoint Sentry. I thought you did rather well with it."

"You know, you don't need to mock *all* my ideas." Hadrian frowned as he pulled his own tabard over his head. "Besides, I still think we should consider it. We could travel from town to town performing in dramatic plays, even a few comedies." Hadrian gave his smaller partner an appraising look. "Though maybe you should stick to drama—perhaps tragedies."

Royce glared back.

"What? I think I would make a superb actor. I see myself as a dashing leading man. We could definitely land parts in *The Crown Conspiracy*. I'll play the handsome swordsman that fights the villain, and you—well, you can be the other one."

They dodged branches while pulling off their coifs and gloves, rolling them in their tabards. Walking downhill, they reached one of the many small rivers that fed the great Galewyr where they found their horses still tied and enjoying the river grass. The animals lazily swished their tails, keeping the flies at bay.

"You worry me sometimes, Hadrian. You really do."

"Why not actors? It's safe. Might even be fun."

"It would be neither safe nor fun. Besides, actors have to travel and I'm content with the way things are. I get to stay near Gwen," Royce added.

"See, that's another reason. Why do you keep doing this? Honestly if I had what you do, I would never take another job."

Royce removed a pair of boots from a saddlebag. "We do it because it's what we're good at, and with the war Alric is willing to pay top fees for information."

Hadrian released a sarcastic snort. "Sure, top fees for us, but what about the other costs? Breckton might work for that idiot Ballentyne, but he's no fool himself. He'll certainly look at the seal and won't buy the story about it softening in the saddlebag."

"I know," Royce began, as he sat on a log exchanging the imperial boots for his own, "but after telling one lie, his second tale about sentries breaking the seal will sound even more outlandish, so they won't believe anything he says."

Hadrian paused in his own efforts to switch boots and scowled at his partner. "You realize they'll probably execute him for treason?"

Royce nodded. "Which will neatly eliminate the only witness."

"You see, that's exactly what I'm talking about," Hadrian sighed and shook his head.

Royce could see the familiar melancholy wash over his partner. It appeared too often lately. He could not fathom his friend's moodiness. These strange bouts of depression usually followed successes, and frequently led to a night of heavy drinking.

He wondered if Hadrian even cared about the money anymore. He took only what was needed for drinks and food and stored the rest. Royce could understand his friend's reaction if they were making a living by picking pockets or robbing homes, but they worked for the king now. It was almost too clean for Royce's taste. Hadrian had no real concept of filth. Unlike Royce, he had not grown up in the muddy streets of Ratibor.

He decided to try and reason with him. "Would you rather they find out and send a detachment to hunt us down?"

"No, I just hate being the cause of an innocent man's death."

"No one is innocent my friend. And you aren't the cause…you're more like…" he searched for words, "the grease beneath the skids."

"Thanks. I feel *so* much better."

Royce folded the uniform and, along with the boots, placed it neatly into his saddlebag. Hadrian still struggled to rid himself of the black boots that were too small. With a mighty tug he jerked the last one off and threw it down in frustration. He gathered it up and wrestled his uniform into the satchel. Cramming everything as deep as possible, he strapped the flap down and buckled it as tight as he could. He glared at the pack and sighed once more.

"You know, if you organized your pack a little better it wouldn't be so hard to fit all your gear," Royce said.

Hadrian looked at him with a puzzled expression. "What? Oh—no, I'm…it's not the gear."

"What is it then?" Royce pulled on his black cloak and adjusted the collar.

The fighter stroked his horse's neck. "I don't know," he replied mournfully. "It's just that—well—I thought by now I'd have done something more—with my life, I mean."

"Are you crazy? Most men work themselves to death on a small bit of land that isn't even theirs. You're free to do as you choose and go wherever you want."

"I know, but when I was young I used to think I was—well—special. I used to imagine that I would triumph in some great purpose, win the girl, and save the kingdom, but I suppose every boy feels that way."

"I didn't."

Hadrian scowled at him. "I just had this idea of who I would become, and being a worthless spy wasn't part of that plan."

"We're hardly worthless," Royce corrected him. "We've been making a good profit, especially lately."

"That's not the point. I was successful as a mercenary too. It's not about money. It's the fact that I survive like a leech."

"Why is this suddenly coming up now? For the first time in years, we're making good money with a steady stream of *respectable* jobs. We're in the employ of a king for Maribor's sake. We can actually sleep in the same bed two nights in a row and not worry about being arrested. Just last week I passed the captain of the city watch and he gave me a nod."

"It's not the amount of work; it's the *kind* of work. It's the fact that we're always lying. If that courier dies, it'll be our fault. Besides, it's not sudden. I've felt this way for years. Why do you think I'm always suggesting we do something else? Do you know why I broke the rules and took that job to steal Pickering's sword? The one that nearly got us executed?"

"For the unusual sum of money offered," Royce replied.

"No, that's why *you* took it. I wanted the job because it seemed like the right thing to do. For once I had the chance to help someone who really deserved to be helped, or so I thought at the time."

"And becoming an actor is the answer?"

Hadrian untied his horse. "No, but as an actor, I could at least *pretend* to be virtuous. I suppose I should just be happy to be alive, right?"

Royce did not answer. The nagging sensation was surfacing again. He hated keeping secrets from Hadrian and it weighed heavily on his conscience, which was amazing because he never knew he had one. Royce defined right and wrong by the moment. Right was what was best for him—wrong was everything else. He stole, lied, and even killed when necessary. This was his craft and he was good at it. There was no reason to apologize, no need to pause or reflect. The world was at war with him, and nothing was sacred.

Telling Hadrian what he learned ran too great a risk. Royce preferred his world constant, with each variable accounted for. Lines on maps were shifting daily and power slipped from one set of hands to another. Time flowed too fast and events were too unexpected. He felt like he was crossing a frozen lake in late spring. He tried to pick a safe path, but the surface cracked beneath his feet. Even so, there were some changes he could still control. He reminded himself that the secret he kept from Hadrian was for his friend's own good.

Climbing on Mouse, his short gray mare, Royce thought a moment. "We've been working pretty hard lately. Maybe we should take a break."

"I don't see how we can," Hadrian replied. "With the Imperial

Army preparing to invade Melengar, Alric is going to need us now more than ever."

"You'd think that wouldn't you? But you didn't read the dispatch."

Chapter 3
THE MIRACLE

The Princess Arista Essendon slouched on the carriage seat buffeted by every rut and hole in the road. Her neck was stiff from sleeping against the armrest and her head throbbed from the constant jostling. Rising with a yawn, she wiped her eyes and rubbed her face. An attempt to straighten her hair trapped her fingers in a mass of auburn knots.

The ambassadorial coach was showing the same wear as its passenger, having traveled too many miles over the last year. The roof leaked, the springs were worn, and the bench was becoming threadbare in places. The driver had orders to push hard to return to Medford by midday. He was making good time, but at the expense of hitting every rut and rock along the way. Drawing back the curtain, the morning sun flashed through gaps in the leafy wall of trees lining the road.

She was almost home.

Dirt, floating in the flickering light that revealed the interior of the coach, coated everything in a fine layer of dust. A discarded cheesecloth and several apple rinds covered a pile of parchments spilling from a stack on the opposite bench. Soiled footprints patterned the floor where a blanket, corset, and two dresses nested along with three shoes. She had no idea where the fourth was and only hoped it was in the carriage and not left in Lanksteer. Over the last six months, she felt as if she had left bits of herself all over Avryn.

Hilfred would have known where her shoe was.

She picked up her pearl-handled hairbrush and turned it over in her hands. Hilfred must have searched the wreckage for days. This one came from Tur Del Fur. Her father gave her a brush from every city he traveled to. He was a private man and saying "I love you" did not come easy, even to his own daughter. The brushes were his unspoken confessions. Once, she had dozens—now, this was the last. When her bedroom tower collapsed she lost them and it felt as if she lost her father all over again. Three weeks later this single brush appeared. It had to be Hilfred, but he never said a word or admitted a thing.

Hilfred had been her bodyguard for years, and now that he was gone she realized just how much she had depended on him, and took him for granted.

She had a new bodyguard now. Alric personally picked him from his own castle guards. His name began with a T—Tom, Tim, Travis—something like that. He stood on the wrong side of her, talked too much, laughed at his own jokes, and was always eating something. He was likely a brave and skilled soldier, but he was no Hilfred.

The last time she saw Hilfred was over a year ago in Dahlgren when he nearly died from the Gilarabrywn attack. It was the second time he suffered burns trying to save her. The first was when she was only twelve—the night the castle caught fire. Her mother and several others died, but a boy of fifteen, the son of a sergeant-at-arms, braved the inferno to pull her from her bed. At Arista's insistence, he went back for her mother. He never reached her, but nearly died trying. He suffered for months afterward, and Arista's father rewarded the boy by appointing him her bodyguard.

His wounds back then were nothing like what he suffered in Dahlgren. Healers had wrapped him from head to toe and he lay unconscious for days. When he woke, to her shock, he refused to see her. He left in the back of a wagon without saying goodbye, and at Hilfred's request, no one would tell her where he had gone. She could have pressed. She could have ordered the healers to talk. For months, she looked over her shoulder expecting to see him, waiting to hear the familiar clap of his sword against his thigh. She often wondered if she had done the right thing in letting him go. She sighed at yet another regret added to a pile that had been building over the last year.

Taking stock of the mess around her increased her melancholy. This is what came from refusing to have a handmaid along, but she could not imagine being cooped up in the carriage with anyone for so long. She picked up her dresses and laid them across the far seat. Spying a document crushed into a ball and hanging in the folds of the far window curtain, made her stomach churn with guilt. With a frown, she plucked the crumpled parchment and smoothed it out by pressing it in her lap.

It contained a list of kingdoms and provinces with a line slashed through each and the notation *IMP* scrawled beside them. Of course, the likes of Chadwick and King Ethelred were the first in line to kiss the empress' ring. She shook her head in disbelief. It happened over night. One day nothing, the next—*bang!* There was a New Empire and almost all of Warric and Rhenydd had joined. They pressured the small holdouts like Glouston, then invaded and swallowed them. Alburn caved in after a few threats. She ran her finger over the line indicating Dunmore. His Highness King Roswort graciously decided it was in his kingdom's best interest to accept the imperial offer of extended landholdings in return for joining the Empire. Arista would not be surprised if Roswort was promised Melengar as part of his payment.

It all happened so fast.

A year ago, the Empire was merely an idea. She had spent months as ambassador trying to strike alliances. Without support, without allies, Melengar could not hope to stand against the growing colossus.

How long do we have before the Empire marches north, before—

The carriage came to a sudden halt, throwing her forward, jerking the curtains, and creaking the tired springs. She looked out the window, puzzled. They were still on the old Steward's Road. The wall of trees had given way to an open field of flowers, which she knew placed them on the high meadow just a few miles outside Medford.

"What's going on?" she called out.

No response.

Where in Elan is Tim, or Ted, or whatever the blazes his name is?

She pulled the latch and, hiking up her skirt, pushed out the door. Warm sunlight met her, making her squint. Her legs were stiff and her back ached. At only twenty-six she already felt ancient. She slammed the carriage door and, holding a hand to protect her eyes, glared as best she could up at the silhouettes of the driver and groom. They glanced at her, but only briefly then looked back down the slope of the road ahead.

"Daniel! Why—" she started but stopped after seeing what they were looking at.

The high meadowlands just north of Medford provided an extensive view for several miles south. The land sloped gently down, revealing Melengar's capital city, Medford. She saw the spires of Essendon Castle and Mares Cathedral and farther out the Galewyr River marked the southern border of the kingdom. In the days when her mother and father were alive, the royal family would come here in the summer for picnics and enjoy the cool breeze and the view. Only today the view was quite different.

On the far bank, in the clear morning light, Arista saw rows and rows of canvas tents, hundreds of them, each flying the red-and-white flags of the Nyphron Imperial Empire.

"There's an army, Highness," Daniel found his voice. "An army is a stone's throw from Medford."

"Get me home, Daniel. Beat the horses if you must, but get me home!"

The carriage had barely stopped when Arista punched open the door, nearly hitting Tommy—or Terence, or whoever he was—in the face when he foolishly attempted to open it for her. The servants in the courtyard immediately stopped their early morning chores to bow reverently. Melissa prepared for the onslaught as soon as she spotted the coach. Unlike Tucker—or Tillman—the small redheaded maid had served Arista for years, and knew to expect a storm.

"How long has that army been there?" Arista barked at her even as she trotted up the stone steps.

"Nearly a week," Melissa replied, chasing after the princess and catching the traveling cloak as Arista discarded it.

"A week? Has there been fighting?"

"Yes, His Majesty launched an attack across the river just a few days ago."

"Alric attacked them? Across the river?"

"It didn't go well," Melissa replied in a lowered voice.

"I should think not! Was he drunk?"

Castle guards hastily pulled back the big oak doors, barely getting them open before the princess barreled through, her gown whipping behind her.

"Where are they?"

"In the War Room."

She stopped.

They stood in the northern foyer, a wide gallery of polished stone pillars, displayed suits of armor, and hallways that led to sweeping staircases.

"Missy, fetch my blue audience gown and shoes to go with it and prepare a basin of water—oh and send someone to bring me something to eat, I don't care what."

"Yes, Your Highness." Melissa made a curt bow and raced up the stairs.

"Your Highness," her bodyguard called chasing after her. "You almost lost me there."

"Imagine that. I'll just have to try harder next time."

Arista watched as her brother, King Alric, stood up from the great table. Normally this would require everyone else to stand as well, but Alric suspended that tradition inside the council chamber, as he had a habit of rising frequently and pacing during meetings.

"I don't understand it," he said, turning his back on all of them to begin his slow, familiar walk between the table and the window. As he moved, he stroked his short beard the way another man might wring his hands. Alric started the beard just before Arista left on her trip. It still had not filled in. She guessed he grew it to look more like their father. King Amrath had a dark, full beard, but Alric's light brown wisps only underscored his youth. He made matters worse by drawing attention to it with his constant stroking. Arista recalled how their father used to drum his fingers during state meetings. Under the weight of the crown, pressures must build up until action sought its own means of escape.

Her brother was two years her junior, and she knew he never expected to wear the crown so soon. For years she had heard Alric's plans to roam the wilds with his friend Mauvin Pickering. The two wanted to see the world and have grand adventures that would involve nameless women, too much wine, and too little sleep. They even hoped to find and explore the ancient ruins of Percepliquis. When he tired of the road, she suspected he would be happy to return home and marry a girl half his age and father several strong sons. Only then, as his temples grayed and all of life's other ambitions were accomplished, did he expect the crown would pass to him. All that changed the night their Uncle Percy arranged the assassination of their father and left him king.

"It could be a trick, Your Majesty," Lord Valin suggested. "A plan to catch you off your guard."

Lord Valin was an elderly knight with a bushy white beard known for his valor and courage, but never for his strategic skills.

"Lord Valin," Sir Ecton addressed the noble respectfully, "after our failure on the banks of the Galewyr, the Imperial Army can overrun Medford with ease, whether we are on or off our guard. We know it and they know it. Medford is their prize for the taking whenever they feel comfortable getting their feet wet."

Alric walked to the tall balcony window where the afternoon light spilled into the royal banquet hall of Essendon Castle. The hall served as the Royal War Room out of the need for a large space to conduct the defense of the kingdom. Where once festive tapestries hung, great maps now covered the walls, each slashed with red lines illustrating the tragic retreat of Melengar's armies.

"I just don't understand it," Alric repeated. "It's so peculiar. The Imperial Army outnumbers us ten to one. They have scores of heavy cavalry, siege weapons, and archers—everything they need. So why are they sitting across the river? Why stop now?"

"It makes no sense from a military stand point, sire," Sir Ecton said. He was Alric's chief general and field commander, a large powerful man with a fiery disposition. Ecton was also Count Pickering's most accomplished vassal, and regarded by many as the best knight in Melengar. "I would venture it is political," he continued. "It has been my experience that the most foolish decisions in combat are the result of political choices made by those with little to no field experience."

Earl Kendell, a pot-bellied fussy man who always dressed in a bright green tunic, glared at Ecton. "Careful with your tongue and consider your company!"

Ecton rose to his feet. "I held my tongue, and what was the result?"

"Sir Ecton!" Alric shouted, but his voice sounded high-pitched and feminine. "I am well aware of your opinion of my decision to attack the imperial encampment."

"It was insanity to attempt an assault across a river without even the possibility to flank," Ecton shot back.

"Nevertheless, it was my decision." Alric squeezed his hands into fists. "I felt it was…necessary."

"Necessary? Necessary!" Ecton spat the word as if it were a vile thing in his mouth. He looked like he was about to speak again but Count Pickering rose to his feet and Sir Ecton sat down.

Arista had seen this before. Too often Ecton looked to Count Pickering before acting on an order Alric gave. He was not the only one. It was clear that although her brother was king, Alric failed to earn the respect of his nobles, his army, or his people.

"Perhaps Ecton is right," the young Marquis Wymar spoke up. "About it being political, I mean," he added hastily. "We all know what a pompous fool the Earl of Chadwick is. Isn't it possible the earl ordered Breckton to hold the final attack until Archibald could arrive? It would certainly raise his standing in the imperial court to claim he personally led the assault that conquered Melengar for the New Empire."

"That would explain the delay in the attack," Pickering replied in his fatherly tone that she knew Alric despised. "But our scouts are reporting that large numbers of men are pulling out, and by all accounts are heading south."

"A feint perhaps?" Alric asked.

Pickering shook his head. "As Sir Ecton pointed out, there would be no need."

Several of the other advisers nodded thoughtfully.

"Something must be going on for the empress to recall her troops like this," Pickering said.

"But what?" Alric asked to no one in particular. "I wish I knew what kind of person she was. It's impossible to guess the actions of a total stranger." He turned to his sister. "Arista, you met Modina—spent time with her in Dahlgren. What is she like? Do you have any idea what would cause her to pull the army back?"

A memory flashed in Arista's mind of her and a young girl trapped at the top of a tower. The princess was frozen in fear but Thrace rummaged through a pile of debris and human limbs looking for a weapon to fight an invincible beast. Was it bravery or was she too naive to understand the futility? "The girl I knew as Thrace was a sweet, innocent child who wanted only the love of her father. The church may have changed her name to Modina, but I can't imagine they changed her. She did not order this invasion. She wouldn't want to rule her tiny village, much less conquer the world." Arista shook her head. "She is not our enemy."

"A crown can change a person," Sir Ecton said while glaring at Alric.

Arista rose. "It is more likely we are dealing with the church and a council of conservative Imperialists. I highly doubt a child from rural Dunmore could influence the archaic attitudes and inflexible opinions of so many stubborn minds who would strive to resist, rather than work with, a new ruler," she said, glaring at Ecton. From over the knight's shoulder she saw Alric cringe.

The door to the hall opened and Julian, the elderly Lord Chamberlain, entered. With a sweeping bow he tapped his staff of office twice on the tiled floor. "The Royal Protector, Royce Melborn, Your Majesty."

"Show him in immediately."

"Don't get your hopes too high," Pickering said to his king. "They're spies, not miracle workers."

"I pay them enough for miracles. I don't think it unreasonable to get what I pay for."

Alric employed numerous informants and scouts, but none were as effective as Riyria. Arista herself originally hired Royce and Hadrian to kidnap her brother the night their father was assassinated. Since then, their services had proved invaluable.

Royce entered the banquet hall alone. The small man with dark hair and dark eyes always dressed in layers of black. He wore a knee-length tunic and a long flowing cloak and, as always, showed no visible weapons. It was unlawful to carry a blade in the presence of the king, but given he and Hadrian had twice saved Alric's life, Arista surmised the royal guards did not thoroughly search him. She was certain Royce carried his white-bladed dagger and regarded the law as merely a suggestion.

Royce bowed before the assembly.

"Well?" her brother asked a bit too loudly, too desperately. "Did you discover anything?"

"Yes, Your Majesty," Royce replied, but his face remained so neutral that nothing more could be determined, for good or ill.

"Well, out with it. What did you find? Are they really leaving?"

"Sir Breckton has been ordered to withdraw all but a small containment force and march south immediately with the bulk of his army."

"So it really is true?" the Marquis Wymar said. "But why?"

"Yes, why?" Alric added.

"Because Rhenydd has been invaded by the Nationalists out of Delgos."

A look of surprise circulated the room.

"Degan Gaunt's rabble is invading Rhenydd?" Earl Kendell said in bewilderment.

"And doing quite well from the dispatch I read," Royce informed them. "Gaunt has led them up the coast, taking every village and town. He's managed to sack Kilnar and Vernes."

"He sacked Vernes?" Ecton asked shocked.

"That's a good-sized city," Wymar mentioned.

"It's also only a few miles from Ratibor," Pickering observed. "From there it's what—maybe a hard day's march to the imperial capital itself?"

"No wonder the Empire is recalling Breckton." Alric looked at the count. "What were you saying about miracles?"

"I can't believe you couldn't find anyone to ally with," Alric berated Arista as he collapsed on his throne. The two were alone in the reception hall, the most ornate room in the castle, which, along with the grand ballroom, banquet hall, and the foyer, were all that most people generally ever saw. Tolin the Great built the chamber to be intimidating. The three-story ceiling was an impressive sight and the observation balcony which circled the walls provided a magnificent view of the parquet floor inlaid with the royal falcon coat-of-arms. Double rows of twelve marble pillars formed a long gallery similar to that of a church, yet instead of an altar there was the dais. Built on seven pyramid-shaped steps sat the throne of Melengar—the only seat in the vast chamber. As children the throne had always appeared so impressive, but now with Alric slouched in it, Arista realized it was just a gaudy chair.

"I tried," she offered, sitting on the steps before the throne as she had once done with her father. "Everyone had already sworn allegiance to the New Empire." Arista gave her brother the demoralizing report on her last six months of failure.

"We're quite a pair, you and I. You've done little as ambassador and I nearly destroyed us with that attack across the river. Many of the nobles are being more vocal. Soon Pickering won't be able to control the likes of Ecton."

"I must admit I was shocked when I heard about your attack. What possessed you to do such a thing?" she asked.

"Royce and Hadrian had intercepted plans drafted by Breckton himself. He was about to launch a three-pronged assault. I had to make a preemptive strike. I was hoping to catch the Imperials by surprise."

"Well, it looks like it worked out after all. It delayed their attack just long enough."

"True, but what good will that do us if we can't find more help. What about Trent?"

"Well, they haven't said no, but they haven't said yes either. The church's influence has never been strong that far north, but they also don't have any ties to us. They are at least willing to wait and watch. They won't join us because they don't think we have a chance. But if we can show them some success they could be persuaded to side with us.

"Don't they realize the Empire will be after them next?"

"I said that, but…"

"But what?"

"They really weren't very amenable to what I had to say. The men of Lanksteer are brutish and backward. They respect only strength. I would have fared better if I'd beaten their king senseless." She hesitated. "I don't think they quite knew what to make of me."

"I should never have sent you," he said, running a hand over his face. "What was I thinking, making a woman an ambassador."

THE MIRACLE

His words felt like a slap. "I could have been disadvantaged in Trent, but in the rest of the kingdoms I don't think the fact I was a woman—"

"A witch then," Alric lashed out, "even worse. All those Warric and Alburn nobles are so devoted, and what do I do? I send them someone the church tried for witchcraft."

"I'm not a witch!" she snapped. "I wasn't convicted of anything, and everyone with a brain between their ears knows that trial was a fabrication of Braga and Saldur to get their hands on our throne."

"The truth doesn't matter. Everyone believes what the church tells them. They said you're a witch, so that makes it so. Look at Modina. The Patriarch claims she's the Heir of Novron, the descendant of the god Maribor and everyone believes. I should have never made an enemy of the church. But between Saldur's betrayal and their sentinels killing Fanen, I just couldn't bring myself to bend my knee.

"When I evicted the priests and forbade Deacon Thomas from preaching about what happened in Dahlgren, the people revolted. They set shops in Gentry Square on fire. I could see the flames from my window, for Maribor's sake. The whole city could have burned. They were calling for my head—people right in front of the castle burning stuffed images of me and shouting 'Death to the godless king!' I had to use the army to restore order. It's quiet now, but the people are restless." Alric reached up and pulled his crown off, turning the golden circlet over in his hands.

"I was in Caren at the court of King Armand when I heard about that," Arista said, shaking her head.

Alric laid the crown on the arm of the throne, closed his eyes, and softly banged his head against the back of the chair. "What are we going to do, Arista? The Imperials will return. As soon as they deal with Gaunt's rabble the army will come back." His eyes opened and his hand drifted absently toward his throat. "I suppose they'll hang me won't they, or do they use the axe on kings?" His tone was one of quiet acceptance, which surprised her.

The carefree boy she once knew was vanishing before her eyes. Even if the Empire failed and Melengar stood strong, Alric would never be the same. In many ways, their uncle had managed to kill him after all.

Alric looked at the crown sitting on the chair's arm. "I wonder what Father would do?"

"He never had anything like this to deal with. Not since Tolin defeated Lothomad at Drondil Fields has any monarch of Melengar faced invasion."

"Lucky me."

"Lucky us."

Alric nodded. "At least we've got some time now. That's something. What do you think of Pickering's idea to send the *Ellis Far* down the coast to Tur Del Fur and contact the Nationalist leader—this Gaunt fellow?"

"Honestly, I think establishing an alliance with Gaunt is our only hope. Isolated we don't stand a chance against the Empire," Arista agreed.

"But the Nationalists? Are they any better than the Imperials? They're as much opposed to monarchies as they are the Empire. They don't want to be ruled at all."

"Alone and surrounded by enemies is not the time to be choosy about your friends."

"We aren't completely alone," Alric corrected. "Marquis Lanaklin joined us."

"A lot of good that does. If we get more help like that we'll go broke just feeding them. Our only chance is to contact Degan Gaunt and form an alliance. If Delgos joins with us, that may be enough to persuade Trent to side in our favor. If that happens, we could deal a mortal blow to this new Nyphron Empire."

"Do you think Gaunt will agree?"

"Don't know why not," Arista said. "It is to our mutual benefit. I'm certain I can talk him into it, and I must say I'm looking forward to the trip. A rolling ocean is a welcome change from that carriage. While I'm away have someone work on it, or better yet order a new one. And put extra padding—"

"You aren't going," Alric told her as he put his crown back on.

"What's that?"

"I'm sending Linroy to meet with Gaunt."

"But I'm the ambassador and a member of the royal family. He can't negotiate a treaty or an alliance with—"

"Of course he can. Linroy is an experienced negotiator and statesman."

"He's the royal financier. That doesn't qualify him as a statesman."

"He's handled dozens of trade agreements," Alric interjected.

"The man's a bookkeeper!" she shouted rising to her feet.

"It may come as a surprise to you, but other people are capable of doing things too."

"But why?"

"Like you said, you're a member of the royal family." Alric looked away and his fingers reached up to stroke his beard. "Do you have any idea what kind of position it would put me in if you were captured? We're at war. I can't risk you being held for ransom."

She stared at him. "You're lying. This isn't about ransom. You think I can't do the job."

"Arista, it's my fault. I shouldn't have—"

"Shouldn't have what? Made your witch-sister ambassador?"

"Don't be that way."

"I'm sorry, Your Majesty, what way would you like me to be? How should I react to being told I'm worthless and an embarrassment and that I should go sit in my room and—"

"I didn't say any of that. Stop putting words in my mouth!"

"It's what you're thinking—it's what all of you think."

"Have you become clairvoyant now too?"

"Do you deny it?"

"Damn it, Arista, you were gone six months!" He struck the arm of the throne with his fist. The dull thud sounded loudly off the walls like a bass drum. "Six months, and not a single alliance. You barely got a maybe. That's a pretty poor showing. This meeting with Gaunt is too important. It could be our last chance."

She stood up. "Forgive me, Your Majesty. I apologize for being such an utter failure. May I please have your royal permission to be excused?"

"Arista, don't."

"Please, Your Majesty, my frail feminine constitution can't handle such a heated debate. I feel faint. Perhaps if I retire to my room I could brew a potion to make myself feel better. While I'm at it, perhaps I should enchant a broom to fly around the castle for fresh air."

She pivoted on her heel and marched out, slamming the great door behind her with a resounding *boom!*

She stood with her back against the door, waiting, wondering if Alric would chase after her.

Will he apologize and take back what he said and agree to let me go?

She listened for the sound of his heels on the parquet.

Silence.

She wished she did know magic—then no one could stop her from meeting with Gaunt. Alric was right, this was their last chance and she was not about to leave the fate of Melengar to Dillnard Linroy, statesman extraordinaire! Besides, she had failed and that made it her responsibility to correct.

She looked up to see Tim—or Tommy—leaning against the near wall, biting his fingernails. He glanced up at her and smiled. "I hope you're planning on heading to the kitchens, I'm starved—practically eating my fingers here," he chuckled.

THE MIRACLE

She pushed away from the door and quickly strode down the corridor. She almost did not see Mauvin Pickering sitting on the broad sill of the courtyard-facing window. Feet up, arms folded, back against the frame, he crouched in a shaft of sunlight like a cat. He was still wearing the black clothes of mourning.

"Troubles with His Majesty?" he asked.

"He's being an ass."

"What did he do this time?"

"Replaced me with that sniveling little wretch, Linroy. He's sending him on the *Ellis Far* in my place to contact Gaunt."

"Dillnard Linroy isn't a bad guy, he's—"

"Listen, I really don't want to hear how wonderful Linroy is at the moment. I'm right in the middle of hating him."

"Sorry."

She glanced at his side and he immediately turned his attention out the window.

"Still not wearing it?" she asked.

"It doesn't go with my ensemble, the silver hilt clashes with black."

"It's been over a year since Fanen died."

He turned back sharply. "Since he was killed by Luis Guy you mean."

Arista took a breath. She was not used to the new Mauvin. "Aren't you supposed to be Alric's bodyguard now? Isn't that hard to do without a sword?"

"Hasn't been a problem so far. You see, I have this plan. I sit here and watch the ducks in the courtyard—well I suppose it's not really so much a plan as a strategy really, or maybe it's more of a scheme. Anyway, this is the one place my father never thinks to look, so I can sit here all day and watch those ducks walking back and forth. There were six of them last year. Did you know that? Only five now. I can't figure out what happened to the other one. I keep looking for him, but I don't think he's coming back."

"It wasn't your fault," she told him gently.

Mauvin reached up and traced the lead edges of the window with his fingertips. "Yeah, it was."

She put her hand on his shoulder and gave a soft squeeze. She did not know what else to do. First her mother, then her father, Fanen and Hilfred—they were all gone. Mauvin was slipping away as well. The boy who loved his sword more than Wintertide presents, cake, or swimming on a hot day refused to touch it anymore. The eldest son of Count Pickering, who once challenged the sun to a duel because it rained on the day of a hunt, spent his days watching ducks.

"Doesn't matter," Mauvin remarked miserably. "The world is coming to an end anyway." He looked up at her. "You just said Alric is sending that bastard Linroy on the *Ellis Far*—he'll kill us all."

As hard as she tried not to, she could not help but laugh. She punched his shoulder, then gave him a peck on the cheek. "That's the spirit, Mauvin. Keep looking on the bright side."

She left him and continued down the hall, as she passed the office of the Lord Chamberlin the old man hurried out. "Your Highness?" he called, looking relieved. "The Royal Protector, Royce Melborn, is still waiting to see if there is something else needed of him. Apparently he and his partner are thinking of taking some time off, unless there is something pressing the king needs. Can I tell him he's excused?"

"Yes, of course, you—no wait." She cast a look at her bodyguard. "Tommy, you're right. I am hungry. Be a dear and fetch us both a plate of chicken or whatever you can find that's good in the kitchen, will you? I'll wait here."

"Sure, but my name is—"

"Hurry before I change my mind."

She waited until he was down the corridor then turned back to the Chamberlin. "Where did you say he was waiting?"

Chapter 4
THE NATURE OF RIGHT

The Rose & Thorn Tavern was mostly empty. Many of its patrons left Medford, fearful of the coming invasion. Those that remained were the indentured, infirmed, or those simply too poor or stubborn to leave. Royce found Hadrian sitting alone in the Diamond Room—his feet up on a spare chair, a pint of ale before him. Two empty mugs sat on the table, one lying on its side while Hadrian stared at it with a melancholy expression.

"Why didn't you come to the castle?" Royce asked.

"I knew you could handle it." He continued to stare at the mug, tilting his head slightly as he did.

"Looks like our break will have to be postponed," Royce told him, pulling over a chair and sitting down. "Alric has another job. He wants us to make contact with Gaunt and the Nationals. They're still working out the details. The princess is going to send a messenger here."

"Her Highness is back?"

"Got in this morning."

Royce reached into his vest, pulled out a bag and set it in front of Hadrian. "Here's your half. Have you ordered dinner yet?"

"I'm not going," Hadrian said, rocking the fallen mug with his thumb.

"Not going?"

"I can't keep doing this."

Royce rolled his eyes. "Now don't start that again. If you haven't noticed, there's a war going on. This is the best time to be in our business. Everyone needs information. Do you know how much money—"

"That's just it, Royce. There's a war on and what am I doing? I'm making a profit off it rather than fighting in it." Hadrian took another swallow of ale and set the mug back on the table a little too heavily, rattling its brothers. "I'm tired of collecting money for being dishonorable. It's not how I'm built."

Royce glanced around. Three men eating a meal looked over briefly, and then lost interest.

"They haven't all been just for money," Royce pointed out. "Thrace, for example."

Hadrian displayed a bitter smile. "And look how that turned out. She hired us to save her father. Seen him lately, have you?"

"We were hired to obtain a sword to slay a beast. She got the sword. The beast was slain. We did our job."

"The man is dead."

"And Thrace, who was nothing but a poor farm girl, is now empress. If only all our jobs ended so well for our clients."

"You think so, Royce? You really think Thrace is happy? See, I'm thinking she'd rather have her father than an imperial throne, but maybe that's just me." Hadrian took another swallow and wiped his mouth with his sleeve.

They sat in silence for a moment. Royce watched his friend staring at a distant point beyond focus.

"So, you want to fight in this war, is that it?"

THE NATURE OF RIGHT

"It would be better than sitting on the sidelines like scavengers feeding off the wounded."

"Okay, so tell me, for which side will you be fighting?"

"Alric's a good king."

"Alric? Alric's a boy still fighting with the ghost of his father. After his defeat at the Galewyr his nobles look to Count Pickering instead of him. Pickering has his hands full dealing with Alric's mistakes, like the riots here in Medford. How long before Pickering tires of Alric's incompetence and decides Mauvin would be better suited to the throne?"

"Pickering would never turn on Alric," Hadrian said.

"No? You've seen it happen plenty of times before."

Hadrian remained silent.

"Oh hell, forget about Pickering and Alric. Melengar is already at war with the Empire. Have you forgotten who the empress is? If you fought with Alric and he prevailed, how will you feel the day poor Thrace is hanged in the Royal Square in Aquesta? Would that satisfy your need for an honorable cause?"

Hadrian's face had turned hard, his jaw clenched stiffly.

"There are no honorable causes. There is no good or evil. Evil is only what we call those who oppose us."

Royce took out his dagger and drove it into the table where it stood upright. "Look at the blade. Is it bright or dark?"

Hadrian narrowed his eyes suspiciously. The brilliant surface of Alverstone was dazzling as it reflected the candlelight. "Bright."

Royce nodded.

"Now move your head over here and look from my perspective."

Hadrian leaned over, putting his head on the opposite side of the blade where the shadow made it black as chimney soot.

"It's the same dagger," Royce explained, "but from where you sat it was light while I saw it as dark. So who is right?"

"Neither of us," Hadrian said.

"No," Royce said. "that's the mistake people always make, and they make it because they can't grasp the truth."

"Which is?"

"That we are both right. One truth doesn't refute another. Truth doesn't lie in the object, but in how we see it."

Hadrian looked at the dagger then back at Royce.

"There are times when you are brilliant, Royce, and then there are times when I haven't a clue as to what you're babbling about."

Royce's expression turned to frustration as he pulled his dagger from the table and sat back down. "In the twelve years we've been together, I've never once asked you to do anything I wouldn't do, or didn't do with you. I've never lied or misled you. I've never abandoned or betrayed you. Name a single noble you even suspect you could say the same about twelve years from now."

"Can I get another round here?" Hadrian shouted.

Royce sighed. "So you're just going to sit here and drink?"

"That's my plan at present. I'm making it up as I go."

Royce stared at his friend a moment longer then finally stood up. "I'm going to Gwen's."

"Listen," Hadrian stopped him. "I'm sorry about this. I guess I can't explain it. I don't have any metaphors with daggers I can use to express how I feel. I just know I can't keep doing what I've been doing anymore. I've tried to find meaning in it. I've tried to pretend we achieved some greater good, but in the end, I have to be honest with myself. I'm not a thief, and I'm not a spy. So I know what I'm not, I just wish I knew what I am. That probably doesn't make much sense to you, does it?"

"Do me a favor at least." Royce purposely ignored the question, noticing how the little silver chain Hadrian wore peeked out from under his collar. "Since you're going to be here anyway, keep an eye out for the messenger from the castle while I'm at Gwen's. I'll be back in an hour or so."

The Nature of Right

Hadrian nodded.

"Give Gwen my love, will ya?"

"Sure," Royce said, heading for the door feeling that miserable sensation creeping in, the dull weight. He paused and looked back.

It won't help to tell him. It will just make matters worse.

It had only been a day and a half but Royce found himself desperate to see Gwen. While Medford House was always open, it did not do much business until after dark. During the day Gwen encouraged the girls to use their free time learning to sew or spin, skills they could use for coin in their old age.

All the girls at the brothel, better known as just *The House,* knew and liked Royce. When he came in they smiled or waved, but no one said a word. They knew he enjoyed surprising Gwen. Tonight, they pointed toward the parlor where she was concentrating on a pile of parchments, a quill pen in hand and her register open. She immediately abandoned it all when he walked through the door. She sprang from her chair and ran to him with a smile so broad her face could hardly contain it and an embrace so tight he could barely breathe.

"What's wrong?" she whispered, pulling back and looking into his eyes.

Royce marveled at Gwen's ability to read him. He refused to answer, preferring instead to look at her, drinking her in. She had a lovely face, her dark skin and emerald eyes so familiar yet mysterious. In all his life and all his travels he had never met anyone like her.

Gwen provided use of a private room at The Rose and Thorn, where he and Hadrian had conducted business, and she never blinked at the risks. They no longer used it. Royce was too concerned that Sentinel Luis Guy might track them there. Still, Gwen continued banking their money and watching out for them just as she had done from the start.

They met twelve years ago, the night soldiers filled the streets and two strangers staggered into the Lower Quarter, covered in their own blood. Royce still remembered how Gwen appeared as a hazy figure to his clouding eyes. "I've got you, you'll be alright now," she told him before he passed out. He never understood what motivated her to take them in when everyone else had the good sense to close their doors. When he woke, she was giving orders to her girls like a general marshalling troops. She sheltered them from the mystified authorities and nursed them back to health. She pulled strings and made deals to ensure no one talked. As soon as they were able they left, but he always found himself returning.

He was crushed the day she refused to see him. It didn't take long to discover why. Clients often abused prostitutes, and Medford House was no exception. It did not matter if he was a gentleman or a thug, the town sheriff never wasted his time on complaints by whores. In Gwen's case the attacker had been a powerful noble. He had beaten her so badly she didn't want anyone to see.

Two days later, the noble was dead. His body hung in the center of Gentry Square. City authorities closed Medford House and arrested the prostitutes. They were told to identify the killer or face execution themselves. To everyone's surprise, the women spent only one night in jail. The next day Medford House reopened and the Sheriff of Medford himself delivered a public apology for their arrest, adding that swift punishment would follow any future abuse regardless of rank. From then on Medford House prospered from unprecedented protection. Royce never spoke of the incident, and Gwen never brought it up, but she knew just as she knew he was part elven before he told her.

When he returned from Avempartha last summer, he decided to reveal his secret to her, to be completely open and honest. Royce never told anyone about his heritage, not even Hadrian. He expected she would hate him, if not for being a miserable *mir*, then certainly for deceiving her. He took Gwen for a walk down the bank of the Galewyr, away from people to lessen the embarrassment of her outrage. He braced himself, said the words, and waited for her to hit him. He would let her. She could scratch his eyes out if she wanted. He owed her that much.

"Of course you're elven." She touched his hand kindly. "Was it a secret?"

How she knew, she never explained. He was so overwhelmed he never asked. Gwen just had a way of always knowing his heart.

"What is it?" she asked again.

"Why haven't you packed?"

Gwen paused and smiled. That was her way of letting him know he would not get away with it. "Because there is no need, the Imperial Army isn't attacking us."

Royce raised an eyebrow. "The king himself has his things packed and his horse at the ready to evacuate the city on a moment's notice, but you know better?"

She nodded.

"And how is that?"

"If there was the slightest chance that Medford was in danger, you wouldn't be here asking me why I haven't packed. I'd be on Mouse's back holding on for dear life as you spurred her into a run."

"Still," he said, "I'd feel better if you moved to the monastery."

"I can't leave my girls."

"Take them with you. Myron has plenty of room."

"You want me to take whores to live in a monastery with monks?"

"I want you to be safe; besides, Magnus and Albert are there too, and I can guarantee you *they're* not monks."

"I'll consider it." She smiled at him. "But you're leaving on another mission so it can wait until you get back."

"How do you know these things?" he asked amazed. "Alric ought to hire you instead of us."

"I'm from Calis. It's in our blood," she told him with a wink. "When do you leave?"

"Soon, tonight perhaps. I left Hadrian at The Rose and Thorn to watch for a messenger."

"Have you decided to tell Hadrian yet?"

For the first time he looked away.

"Oh, so that's it. Don't you think you should?"

"No, just because a lunatic wizard—" he paused. "Listen, if I tell him what I saw he'll only get himself killed. If Hadrian were a moth, he'd fly into every flame he could find. If I tell him, his reason will disappear. He'll sacrifice himself if necessary, and for what? Even if it's true, all that stuff with the heir happened centuries ago and has nothing to do with him. And there's no reason to think that Esrahaddon wasn't just—wizards toy with people, okay? It's what they do. He tells me to keep quiet, makes a big stink about how I have to take this secret to my grave. But you know damn well he expects me to tell Hadrian. I don't like being used and I won't let Hadrian get himself killed at the whim of some wizard and his agendas."

Gwen said nothing but looked at him with a knowing smile.

"What?"

"Sounds like you are trying to convince yourself and you're not doing very well. I think it might help if you consider you're one kind of person and Hadrian is another. You are trying to look out for him, but you're using *cat's eyes*."

"I'm doing what?"

Gwen looked at Royce, puzzled for a moment, then chuckled quietly. "Oh, I suppose that must be a common saying only in Calis. Okay, let's say you're a cat and Hadrian's a dog and you want to make him happy. You give him a dead mouse and are surprised when he isn't thrilled. The problem is that you need to see the world through the eyes of a dog to understand what's best for him. If you did, you would see that a nice juicy bone would be a better choice, even though to a cat it's not very appealing."

"So you think I should let Hadrian go off and get himself killed?"

"I'm saying that for Hadrian, maybe fighting—even dying—for something or someone may be the same as a bone to a dog. Besides, you have to ask yourself, is keeping quiet really for his sake—or yours?"

"First daggers, now dogs and cats," Royce muttered.

"What?"

"Nothing." He let his hands run through her hair. "How did you get so wise?"

"Wise?" She looked at him and laughed. "I'm a thirty-four-year-old prostitute in love with a professional criminal. How wise can I possibly be?"

"If you don't know, perhaps you should try seeing with my eyes."

He kissed her warmly, pulling her tight. He recalled what Hadrian had said and wondered if he was being stupid for not settling down with Gwen. He noticed for some time a growing pain whenever he said goodbye and a misery that dogged him whenever he left. Royce never meant for it to happen. He always tried to keep her at a distance for her own good as well as his. His life was dangerous and only possible so long as he had no ties, nothing others could use against him.

Winters had caused him to crack. Deep snows and brutal cold kept team Riyria, idle in Medford for months. Huddled before the warmth of hearth fires through the long dark nights, they grew close. Casual chats turned into long intimate conversations; conversations changed to embraces and confessions. It was impossible to resist her open kindness and generosity. She was so unlike anyone, an enigma that flew in the face of all he had come to expect from the world. She made no demands and asked for nothing but his happiness.

It was Gwen who led to his and Hadrian's longest imprisonment six years ago. It was in the spring, and they received a job sending them all the way to Alburn. The thought of leaving her dragged on him like a weight. On top of everything, Gwen was sick. She had a spring flu and looked miserable. She pretended it was nothing, trying to be brave to make it easier on him, but she looked pale. He almost did not go, but she insisted. He could still remember her face as he left her with that brave little smile that quivered oh so slightly at the edges.

The job went bad. His concentration suffered, mistakes were made, and they were left rotting in the dungeons under Caren. All he could do was sit and think about Gwen and whether she was all right. As the months stretched out, he realized that if he survived he had to end their relationship. He resolved never to see her again, for both of their sakes, but the moment he returned, the moment he saw her again, felt her hands and smelled her hair, he knew it was impossible. Since that time, his feelings only increased. Even now, the thought of leaving her, even for a week, was agony.

Hadrian was right. He should quit and take her away somewhere, perhaps get a small bit of land where they could raise a family. Somewhere quiet where no one knew Gwen as a prostitute or himself as a thief. They could even go to Avempartha, that ancient citadel of his people. The tower stood vacant and would likely remain that way indefinitely, far beyond the reaches of anyone who did not know its secrets. The thought was appealing but he pushed it back, telling himself he would revisit it soon. For now, he had people waiting, which brought his mind back to Hadrian.

"I suppose I could look into Esrahaddon's story. Hadrian would be a fool for dedicating his life to someone else's dream, but at least I'd know it was genuine and not some kind of wizard's trick."

"How can you find out?"

"Hadrian grew up in Hintindar. If his father was a Teshlor Knight, maybe he left behind some indication. At least then I would have someone else's word instead of just Esrahaddon's. Our job is taking us south. I could make a stop in Hintindar and see if I can find something out. By the way," he told her gently, "I'll be gone a good deal longer than I have been. I want you to know so you don't worry needlessly."

"I never worry about you," she told him.

Royce's face reflected his pain.

Gwen smiled. "I *know* you will return safely."

"And how do you know this?"

"I've seen your hands."

Royce looked at her confused.

"I've read your palms, Royce," she told him without a trace of humor. "Or have you forgotten I also make a living as a fortune teller?"

Royce had not forgotten, but assumed it was just a way of swindling the superstitious. Not until that moment did he realize how inconsistent it would be for Gwen to deceive people.

"You have a long life ahead of you," she went on. "Too long— that was one of the clues that you weren't completely human."

"So I have nothing to worry about in my future?"

Gwen's smile faded abruptly.

"What is it?"

"Nothing."

"Tell me," he persisted, gently lifting her chin until she met his eyes.

"It's just that—you need to watch out for Hadrian."

"Did you look at his palms too?"

"No," she said, "but your lifeline shows a fork, a point of decision. You will head either into darkness and despair or virtue and light. This decision will be precipitated by a traumatic event."

"What kind of event?"

"The death of the one you love the most."

"Shouldn't you be worried about yourself then?"

Gwen smiled warmly at him. "If only that were so, I'd die a happy woman. Royce, I'm serious about Hadrian. Please watch out for him. I think he needs you now more than ever. And I'm frightened for you if something were to happen to him."

When Royce returned to the Rose and Thorn, he found Hadrian still seated at the same table only he was no longer alone. Beside him sat a small figure hooded in a dark cloak. Hadrian sat comfortably. Either the person sitting next to him was safe, or he was too drunk to care.

"Take it up with Royce when he gets here," Hadrian was saying. "Ah!" He looked up. "Perfect timing."

"Are you from—" Royce stopped as he sat down and saw the face beneath the hood.

"I do believe that is the first time I've ever surprised you, Royce," the Princess Arista said.

"Oh no, that's not true," Hadrian chuckled. "You caught him way off guard when we were hanging in your dungeon and you asked us to kidnap your brother. That was *much* more unpredictable, trust me."

Royce was not pleased with the idea of meeting the princess in the open tavern room, and Hadrian was speaking far too loudly for his liking. Luckily, the room was empty. Most of the limited clientele preferred to cluster around the bar, where the door hung open to admit the cool summer breeze.

THE NATURE OF RIGHT

"That seems a lifetime ago," Arista replied, thoughtfully.

"She has a job for you, Royce," Hadrian told him.

"For *us*, you mean."

"I told you." Hadrian looked at him, but allowed a glance at the princess as well. "I'm retired."

Royce ignored him. "What's been decided?"

"Alric wants to make contact with Gaunt and his Nationals," Arista began. "He feels, as the rest of us do, that if we can coordinate our efforts we can create a formidable assault. Also, an alliance with the Nationalists could very well be the advantage we need to persuade Trent to enter the war on our side."

"That's fine," Royce replied. "I expected as much, but did you have to deliver this information yourself? Don't you trust your messengers?"

"One can never be too careful. Besides, I'm coming with you."

"What?" Royce asked, stunned.

Hadrian burst into laughter. "I knew you'd love that part," he said, grinning with the delight of a man blessed with immunity.

"I am the Ambassador of Melengar, and this is a diplomatic mission. Events are transpiring rapidly and negotiations may need to be altered to suit the situation. I have to go because neither of you can speak for the kingdom. I can't trust anyone, not even you two, with such an important mission. This meeting will likely determine whether or not Melengar survives another year. I hope you understand the necessity of having me along."

Royce considered the proposal for a few minutes. "You and your brother understand that I cannot guarantee your safety?"

She nodded.

"You also understand that between now and the time we reach Gaunt, you will be required to obey Hadrian and myself and will be provided no special treatment because of your station?"

"I expect none. However, it must also be understood that I am

Alric's representative and as such speak with his voice. So where safety and methods are concerned you are granted authority and I will follow your direction, but as far as overall mission goals are concerned I reserve the right to redirect, or extend the mission if necessary."

"And do you also possess the power to guarantee additional payment for additional services?"

"I do."

"I now pronounce you client and escort," Hadrian said with a grin.

"As for you," Royce told him, "you'd better have some coffee."

"I'm not going, Royce."

"What's this all about?" Arista asked.

Royce scowled and shook his head at her.

"Don't shut her up," Hadrian said. He turned to the princess and added, "I have officially resigned from Riyria. We are divorced. Royce is single now."

"Really?" Arista said. "What will you do?"

"He's going to sober up and get his gear."

"Royce, listen to me. I mean it. I'm not going. There is nothing you can say to change my mind."

"Yes, there is."

"What, have you come up with another fancy philosophical argument? It's not going to work. I told you I'm done. It's over. Look at my face. I'm not kidding. I've had it." Hadrian looked suspiciously at his partner.

Royce simply looked back with a smug expression. At last Hadrian asked, "Okay, what is it? I'm curious now. What do you think you could possibly say to change my mind?"

Royce hesitated a moment, glancing uncomfortably at Arista, then sighed. "Because, I am asking you to—as a favor. After this mission, if you still feel the same, I won't fight you and we can part as friends. But I am asking you now—as my friend—to please come with me just one last time."

Just then, the barmaid arrived at the table.

"Another round, Hadrian?"

Hadrian did not look at her, but continued to stare at Royce and sighed.

"Apparently not. I guess I'll take a cup of coffee, strong and black."

Chapter 5
SHERIDAN

Trapped in her long dress and riding cloak, Arista baked as the heat of summer arrived early in the day. Making matters worse, Royce insisted she travel with her hood up. She wondered at its value, as she guessed she was just as conspicuous riding so heavily bundled as she would be if riding naked. Her clothes stuck to her skin and it was difficult to breathe, but she said nothing.

Royce rode slightly ahead on his gray mare that, to Arista's surprise, they called Mouse. A cute name—not at all what she expected. As always, Royce was dressed in black and grays, seemingly oblivious to the heat. His eyes scanned the horizon and forest eaves. Perhaps his elven blood made him less susceptible to the hardships of weather. Even a year later, she still marveled at his mixed race.

Why had I never noticed?

Hadrian followed half a length behind and on her right—exactly where Hilfred used to position himself. It gave her a familiar feeling of safety and security. She glanced back at him and smiled under her hood. He was not immune to the heat. His brow was covered in sweat and his shirt clung to his chest. His collar lay open, his sleeves rolled up revealing strong arms.

SHERIDAN

A noticeable silence marked their travel. Perhaps it was the heat or a desire to avoid prying ears, but the lack of conversation denied her a natural venue to question their direction. After slipping out of Medford before sunrise, they had traveled north across fields and deer paths into the highlands before swinging east and catching the road. Arista understood the need for secrecy, and a roundabout course would help confuse any would-be spies, but instead of heading south, Royce led them north, which made no sense at all. She had held her tongue as hours passed and they continued to ride out of Melengar and into Ghent. She was certain Royce took this route for a reason. She had agreed to follow their leadership and it would not do to question his judgment so early in their trip.

Arista was back in the high meadowlands where only the day before she caught her first sight of the imperial troops gathered against Melengar. A flurry of activity was now underway on the far side of the Galewyr as the army packed up. Tents collapsed, wagons lined up, and masses of men started forming columns. She was fascinated by the sheer number, and guessed there could be more imperial soldiers than citizens remaining in the city of Medford.

The meadowlands gave way to forest and the view disappeared behind the crest. The shade brought little relief from the heat.

If only it would rain.

The sky was overcast but rain was not certain. It was, of course, possible to *make* it rain.

Arista recalled at least two ways. One involved an elaborate brewing of compounds and burning the mixture out of doors. This method should result in precipitation within a day, but was not entirely reliable and failed more often than it succeeded. The other was more advanced and instantaneous, requiring great skill and knowledge. It could be accomplished with only hand movements, a focused mind, and words. The first she learned as part of her studies at Sheridan University, where the entire class performed the technique without producing a single drop. The latter Esrahaddon tried to teach her, but because the church amputated his hands he could not demonstrate the complex finger movements. This, of course, was the major obstacle in studying with him. Arista was nearly certain she would never learn anything until, almost by accident, she made a guard sneeze.

It was an odd sensation, feeling the power of the Art for the first time, like flipping a tiny lever and sliding a gear into place. She succeeded, not due to Esrahaddon's instructions, but rather because she was fed up with him. It was during a state dinner and to alleviate her boredom Arista was running Esrahaddon's instructions through her head. She purposely ignored his directions and tried something on her own. It felt easier, simpler. When she finally found the right combination of movements and sounds, it was like plucking the perfect note of music at exactly the right time.

That sneeze, along with a short-lived curse placed on Countess Amril, were her only magical successes during her apprenticeship with Esrahaddon. She had tried and failed the rain spell hundreds of times. Then her father was murdered and she never tried again. She was too busy helping Alric with their kingdom to waste time on childish games. She glanced skyward.

What else do I have to do?

She recalled the instructions, and letting the reins hang limp on her horse's neck, she practiced the delicate weaving patterns in the air. The incantation she recalled easily enough, but the motions were all wrong. She could feel the awkwardness in the movements. There needed to be a pattern to the motion—a rhythm, a pace. She tried different variations and discovered she could tell which motions felt right and which felt wrong. It was like fitting puzzle pieces together while blindfolded, or working out the notes of a melody by ear. She would simply guess at each note, until by sheer chance, she hit upon the right one, then adding it to the whole she moved on to the next.

SHERIDAN

It was tedious, but it kept her mind occupied. She caught a curious glance from Hadrian but she did not explain, nor did he ask.

Arista continued to work at the motions as the miles passed until, mercifully, it began to rain on its own. She looked up to let the cool droplets hit her face and she wondered if it was boredom that prompted her recollection of her magical studies, or was it because they had steered off the Imperial Highway and were now on the road to Sheridan University.

Sheridan was for the sons of merchants and scribes, those needing to know mathematics and writing, not for the nobility, and certainly not for future rulers. What use would a king have for mathematics? What good would come from philosophy? For that, he had advisers. All he needed to know was how to swing a sword, the proper tactics of military maneuvers, and the hearts of men. School could not teach these things. It was rare for a prince or duke's son to attend the university, much less a princess.

Arista spent some of her happiest years within the sheltered valley of Sheridan. Here the world opened up to her. Here she escaped the suffocating vacuum of courtly life where her only purpose was the same as the statues, another adornment for the castle halls and eventually a commodity—married for the benefit of the kingdom.

Her father was not at all pleased with his daughter's abnormal interest in books, but he never forbade her. She kept her reading habit discreet, which caused her to spend more and more time alone. She would steal books from the scribe's collection, or scrolls from the clergy. Most often she *borrowed* books from Bishop Saldur, who often left behind stacks of them after visits with her father. She spent hours reading in the sanctuary of her tower. They took her away to far off lands, where for a time she was happy. They filled her head with ideas; thoughts of a greater world, of a life beyond the halls, of a life lived bravely, heroically. It was through these borrowed books that she learned of the university and later of Gutaria Prison.

She remembered asking her father permission to attend the university. At first, he adamantly refused and laughed, patting her head. She cried herself to sleep feeling trapped. All her ideas and ambitions sealed forever in a permanent prison. When her father changed his mind the next day, it never occurred to her to ask him why.

What are we doing here?

It irked her not knowing—patience was a virtue she still wrestled with. As they descended into the university's vale, she felt a modest inquiry would not hurt. She opened her mouth, but Hadrian beat her to it.

"Why are we going to Sheridan?" he asked, trotting up closer to Royce.

"Information," Royce replied in his normal curt manner that betrayed nothing else.

"It's your party. I'm just along for the ride."

No, no, no, she thought, *ask more.* Arista waited. Hadrian let his horse drift back. This was her opening, she had to say something. "Did you know I attended school there? You should speak to the Master of Lore, Arcadius," she offered. "The Chancellor is a pawn of the church, but Arcadius can be trusted. He's a wizard and used to be my professor. He'll know, or be able to find out, whatever it is you're interested in."

That was perfect. She straightened up in her saddle, pleased with herself. Common politeness would demand Royce reveal his intentions now that she showed an interest, some knowledge on the subject, and an offer to help. She waited. Nothing. The silence returned.

I should have asked a question. Something to force him to respond. Damn.

Gritting her teeth, she slumped forward in frustration. She considered pressing further, but the moment had passed and now it would be difficult to say anything without sounding critical. Being an ambassador taught her the value of timing, to be conscious of other people's dignity and authority. Being born a princess, it was a lesson not easily learned. She opted for silence, listening to the rain drum on her hood and the horses plodding through the mud as they descended into the valley.

The stone statue of Glenmorgan stood in the center of the university holding a book in one hand and a sword in the other. Walkways, benches, trees, and flowers surrounded the statue on all sides as did numerous school buildings. A growing enrollment required the addition of several lecture halls and dormitories with each reflecting the architectural styles of their time. In the gray sheets of rain, the university looked like a mirage, a whimsical, romantic dream conceived in the mind of a man who spent his entire life at war. That an institution of pure learning existed in a world of brutish ignorance was more than a dream, it was a miracle, a testament to the wisdom of Glenmorgan.

Glenmorgan intended the school to educate laymen at a time when hardly any but ecclesiastics could read. Its success was unprecedented. Sheridan achieved eminence above every other seat of learning, winning the praises of patriarchs, kings, and sages. Early on, Sheridan also established itself as a center for lively controversy, with scholars involved in religious and political disputes. Handel of Roe, a Master of Sheridan, campaigned for Ghent's recognition of the newly established Republic of Delgos against the wishes of the Nyphron Church. The school was also decidedly Royalist in the civil wars following the Steward's Reign, which came as an embarrassment to the church that had retained control of Ghent. The humiliation led to the heresy trials of the three masters Cranston, Landoner, and Widley, all burned at the stake on the Sheridan commons.

NYPHRON RISING

This quieted the school's political voice for more than a century until Edmund Hall, Professor of Geometry and Lore at Sheridan, claimed to use clues gleaned from ancient texts to locate the ruins of Percepliquis. He disappeared for a year and returned with books and tablets revealing arts and sciences long lost spurring an interest in all things imperial. At this time, a greater orthodoxy had emerged within the church and it outlawed owning or obtaining holy relics, as all artifacts from the ancient Empire were deemed. They arrested Hall and locked him in Ervanon's Crown Tower along with his notes and maps. The church later declared that Hall never found the city and that the books were clever fakes, but no one ever heard from Edmund Hall again.

The tradition of Cranston, Landoner, Widley, and Hall was embodied in the present Master of Lore—Arcadius Vintarus Latimer. Arista's old magic teacher never appeared to notice the boundaries of good taste, much less those of political or religious significance. Chancellor Lambert was the school's head because the church found his political leanings satisfactory to the task, but Arcadius was its undisputed heart and soul.

"Should I take you to Master Arcadius?" Arista asked after they left their horses in the charge of the stable warden. "He really is very smart and trustworthy."

Royce nodded and she promptly led them through the now driving rain into Glen Hall, as most students referred to the original Grand Imperial College building in deference to Glenmorgan. An elaborate cathedral-like edifice embodied much of the grandeur of the Steward's Reign sadly missing from the other university buildings. Neither Royce nor Hadrian said a word as they followed her up the stairs to the second floor, shaking out their travel cloaks and the water from their hair. It was quiet inside, the air stuffy and hot. Because several people could easily recognize her, Arista remained in the confines of her hood.

SHERIDAN

"So as you can see, it would be possible to turn lead into gold, but it would require more than the gold's resulting worth to make the transformation permanent, thus causing the process to be entirely futile at least using this method."

Arista heard Arcadius' familiar voice booming as they approached the lecture hall.

"Of course, there are some who take advantage of the temporary transformation to dupe the unwary, creating a very realistic fool's gold that hours later reveals itself to be lead."

The lecture room was lined with tiers of seats all filled with identically gowned students. At the podium stood the lore master, a thin elderly man with a blue robe, white beard, and spectacles perched on the end of his nose.

"The danger here, of course, is that once the ruse has been discovered, the victim is often more than mildly unhappy about it." This comment drew laughter from the students. "Before you put too much thought into the idea of amassing a fortune based on illusionary gold, you should know that it has been tried. This crime—and it *is* a crime—usually results in the victim taking out his anger on the perpetrator of the hoax in the form of a rather unceremonious execution. This is why you don't see your Master of Lore traveling about in an eight-horse carriage with an entourage of retainers and dressing in the finest silks from Vandon."

More laughter.

It was unclear whether the lecture was at an end or if Arcadius spotted them on the rise and cut the class short. The lore master closed his instruction for the day with reminders about homework and dates of exams. As most of the students filed out, a few gathered around their professor with questions, which he patiently addressed.

"Give me a chance to introduce you," Arista said as they descended the tiers. "I know Arcadius looks a little...odd, but he's really very intelligent."

"…and the frog exploded, didn't it?" the wizard was saying to a young man wearing a depressed expression.

"Made quite a mess too, sir," his companion offered.

"Yes, they usually do," Arcadius sympathized.

The lad sighed. "I don't understand. I mixed the nitric acid, the sulfuric acid, and the glycerin and fed it to him. He seemed fine. Just as you said in class the blackmuck frog's stomach held the mixture, but then when he hopped…" The boy's shoulders slumped while his friend mimicked the impression of an explosion.

The lore master chuckled. "Next time, dissect the frog first and remove the stomach. There's a lot less chance of it jumping then. Now run along and clean up the library before Master Falquin gets back."

The two boys scampered off. Royce closed the door to the lecture hall after them, at which point the princess felt it safe to take off her cloak.

"Princess Arista!" Arcadius exclaimed in delight walking toward her with his arms wide. The two exchanged a fond embrace. "Your Highness, what a wonderful surprise! Let me look at you." He stepped back, still holding her hands. "A bit disheveled, soaking wet, and tracking mud into my classroom. How nice. It is as if you are a student here again."

"Master Arcadius," the princess began formally, "allow me to introduce Royce Melborn and Hadrian Blackwater. They have some questions for you."

"Oh?" he said, eyeing the two curiously. "This sounds serious."

"It is," Hadrian replied. He took a moment to search the room for any remaining students while Royce locked the doors.

Arista saw the puzzled expression on her instructor's face and clarified. "You have to understand they are cautious people by trade."

"I can see that. So I am to be interrogated, is that it?" the headmaster asked, accusingly.

"No," she said. "I just think they want to ask a few questions."

"And if I don't answer? Will they beat me until I talk?"

"Of course not!"

"Are you so sure? You said that you *think* they are here to ask questions. But I think they are here to kill me. Isn't that right?"

"The fact is you know too much," Royce told the wizard, his tone turning abruptly vicious. He reached into his cloak, drawing out his dagger as he advanced on Arcadius. "It's time we silenced you permanently."

"Royce!" Arista shouted, shocked. She turned to Hadrian, who sat relaxed in the front row of the lecture hall, casually eating an apple plucked from the lore master's table. "Hadrian, do something," she pleaded.

The old man shuffled backward trying to put more distance between himself and Royce. Hadrian did not respond, eating the apple like a man without a worry in the world.

"Royce! Hadrian!" Arista screamed at them. She could not believe what she was seeing.

"Sorry, princess," Hadrian finally spoke, "but this old man has caused us a great deal of trouble in the past, and Royce is not one to forgive debts easily. You might want to close your eyes."

"She should leave," Royce said. "Even if she doesn't look she'll hear the screams."

"You're not going to be quick then?" the old man whispered.

Hadrian sighed. "I'm not cleaning the mess up this time."

"But you can't! I—I—" Arista stood frozen in terror.

Royce closed the distance between him and Arcadius in a sudden rush.

"Wait," the wizard's voice quivered as he held up a hand to ward him off, "I think I am entitled to ask at least one question before I am butchered."

"What is it?" Royce asked, menacingly, his dagger raised and gleaming.

"How is your lovely Gwen doing?"

"She's fine," Royce replied, lowering his blade. "She told me to be certain to tell you she sends her love."

Arista glared at each of them. "But what—I—you know each other?"

Arcadius chuckled as Hadrian and Royce snickered sheepishly. "I'm sorry, my dear." The professor held up his hands and cringed slightly. "I just couldn't resist. An old man has so few opportunities to be whimsical. Yes, I have known these two surly characters most of their lives. I knew Hadrian's father before Hadrian was born and I met Royce when he was…" the lore master paused briefly, "well, younger than he is today."

Hadrian, still chewing, looked up at her. "Arcadius introduced Royce and me and gave us our first few jobs together."

"And you've been inseparable ever since." The wizard smiled. "It was a sound pairing. You have been a good influence on each other. Left on your own the two of you would have fallen into ruin."

There was a noticeable exchange of glances between the two. "You only say that because you don't know what we've been up to," Hadrian mentioned.

"Don't assume too much." Arcadius shook a menacing finger at him. "I keep tabs on you. So what brings you here?"

"Just a few questions I thought you would be able to shed some light on," Royce told him. "Why don't we talk in your study while Hadrian and Arista settle in and get out of their wet things? Is it alright if we spend the night here?"

"Certainly, I'll have dinner brought up, although you picked a bad day; the kitchen is serving meat pies." He made a grimace.

Arista stood stiffly, feeling her heart still racing. She narrowed her eyes and glared. "I hate all of you."

SHERIDAN

Barrels, bottles, flasks, exotic instruments, jars containing bits of animals swimming in foul-smelling liquids, and a vast array of other oddities cluttered the small office and spilled out into the hallway. Shelves of web-covered books lined the walls. Aquariums displayed living reptiles and fish. Cages stacked to the ceiling housed pigeons, mice, moles, raccoons, and rabbits, filling the cramped office with the sounds of chirps, chatters, and squeaks as well as a musky scent of books, beeswax, spices, and animal dung.

"You cleaned up," Royce said with feigned surprise as he entered carefully stepping over the books and boxes scattered on the floor.

"Quiet you," the wizard scolded, looking over the top of his glasses, which rested at the end of his nose. "You hardly ever visit anymore, and you don't need to be impertinent when you do."

Royce closed the door and slid the bolt, which drew another look from the wizard.

Royce pulled an amulet on a thin chain from his cloak. "What can you tell me about this?"

Arcadius took the jewelry from him. He moved to his desk, where he held it near the flame of a candle. He looked at it only briefly then lifted his spectacles. "This is Hadrian's medallion. The one his father gave him when he turned thirteen. Are you trying to test me for senility?"

"Did you know Esrahaddon made it?"

"Did he?"

"He says he did. I had a long chat with the wizard in Dahlgren. According to him, nine hundred years ago the church instigated the coup against the emperor. He insists he remained loyal and made two amulets giving one to the emperor's son and the other to his bodyguard. He sent them into hiding while he stayed behind. The amulets are supposed to be enchanted so only Esrahaddon could find them. When Arista and I were with him in Avempartha, he conjured images of those wearing these necklaces."

"And you saw Hadrian?"

Royce nodded.

"As the guardian or the heir?"

"Guardian."

"And the heir?"

"Blonde hair, blue eyes, no one I recognized."

"I see," Arcadius said. "But you haven't told Hadrian what you saw."

"What makes you say that?"

The wizard let the amulet and the chain fall into the palm of his hand. "You're here alone."

Royce nodded. "Hadrian's been moody lately. If I tell him, he'll want to fulfill his destiny—go find this long-lost heir and be his whipping boy. He won't even question it because he'll want it to be true, but I don't think it is. I think Esrahaddon is up to something. I don't want either of us to be pawns in his effort to bring his choice for emperor to the throne."

"You think Esrahaddon is lying? That he conjured false images to manipulate you?"

"That's what I came here to find out. Is it even possible to make enchanted amulets? If you can, is it possible to locate the wearers by magic? And you knew Hadrian's father, did he ever say anything to you about being the guardian to the Heir of Novron?"

Arcadius turned the amulet over in his hand. "*I* don't have the Art to enchant objects to resist magic, nor can I use magic to seek people, but a lot was lost when the Old Empire crumbled. Preserving him in that prison for nearly a thousand years makes Esrahaddon unique in his knowledge, so I can't intelligently say what is or isn't possible. As for Danbury Blackwater I don't recall him ever telling me he was the Guardian of the Heir. That isn't the kind of thing I would likely forget."

"So, I am right. This is all a lie."

"It may not be a lie, per se. You realize it's possible—even likely—that Danbury could have the amulet and not be involved. Nine hundred years is a long time to expect an heirloom to stay in the possession of one family. The odds are heavily against it. Personal effects are lost every day. This is made of silver and in a moment of desperation a poor man, convinced that it was all a myth, could be tempted to sell it for food. Moreover, what should happen if the owner died—killed in an accident—and this medallion taken from the dead body and sold? This has likely passed through hundreds of hands before ever reaching Danbury. So Esrahaddon may be sincere and still be wrong.

"Even if Danbury was the descendant of the Teshlor, he might not have known any more than Hadrian does. His father, or his father before him, could have failed to mention it because it didn't matter anymore. The line of the heir may have died out, or the two became separated centuries ago."

"Is that what you think?"

Arcadius took off his glasses and wiped them.

"For centuries people have searched for the descendants of Emperor Nareion and no one has ever found them. The Empire itself searched for Nareion's son Nevrik with the power of great wizards and questing knights at a time when they could identify him by sight. They failed—unless you accept the recent declaration that they found the heir in the form of this farm girl from Dahlgren."

"Thrace is not the heir," Royce said, simply. "The church orchestrated that whole incident as theatrics to anoint their choice for ruler. They botched the job and she accidentally caught the prize."

The wizard nodded. "So I think common sense decrees that an heir no longer exists…if he ever existed to begin with. Unless…" he trailed off.

"Unless what?"

"Nothing." Arcadius shook his head.

Royce intensified his stare until the wizard relented.

"Just supposition really, but, well—it just seems too romantic, that the heir and a bodyguard could have lived all alone on the run for so long, managing to hide while the entire world hunted them."

"What are you suggesting?" Royce asked.

"After the emperor's death, when Jerish and Nevrik fled, wouldn't Jerish have had friends? Wouldn't there have been hundreds of people loyal to the emperor's son willing to help conceal him? Support him? Organize an attempt to put him back on the throne? Of course this organization would have to act in secrecy, given that the bulk of the dying Empire was in control of the church."

"Are you saying such a group exists?" Royce asked.

Arcadius shrugged. "I am only speculating here."

"You're more than speculating. What do you know?"

"Well, I have come across some odd references in various texts that refer to a group known only as the Theorem Eldership. I first discovered them in a bit of historical text from 2465, about the time of the Steward's Reign of Glenmorgan the Second. Some priest who noted them only as a secret heretical sect mentioned the Theorem Eldership in an official report. Of course at that time anyone who opposed the church was considered heretical, so I didn't give it much thought. Then I spotted another reference to the same group in a very old letter sent from Lord Darius Seret to Patriarch Venlin dating back to within the first sixty years after the death of Emperor Nareion."

"Lord Seret?" Royce asked. "As in the Knights of Novron Seret?"

"Indeed," Arcadius said. "The duke was commanded by the Patriarch to locate the whereabouts of Emperor Nareion's missing son Nevrik, so the duke formed an elite band of knights who swore an oath to find the heir. It wasn't until a hundred years after the death of Darius that the knights adopted the official name, the Order of Seret Knights, which later shortened out of convenience. Quite ironic actually as their responsibilities and influence broadened dramatically. You would hardly know it as the seret work mostly in secret—hidden so they can perform their duties invisibly. To this end, they still report directly to the Patriarch. It is really a matter of perceptive logic. Given there is a pseudo-invisible order of knights that seek to hunt down the heir, is it so impossible another unseen group is protecting him?"

Arcadius stood up and, with no trouble navigating his way through the room's debris, reached the far wall. There a slate hung and with a bit of chalk he wrote:

Theorem Eldership

Then he crossed out each letter and underneath wrote:

Shield the Emperor

He returned to his desk and sat down.

"If you decide to search for the heir," Arcadius told Royce in a grave tone, "be very careful. This is not some bit of jewelry you seek and he may be protected and hunted by men who will sacrifice their lives and use any means against you. If any of this is true, then I fear you will be entering into a world of shadows and lies where a silent, secret war has been waging for nearly a thousand years. There will be no honor and no quarter given. It is a place where people disappear without a trace and martyrs thrive. No price will be too great, no sacrifice too awful. What is at stake in this struggle—at least in their eyes—is the future of Elan.

Nyphron Rising

ꬓ

The number of students at Sheridan always diminished in summer, so Arcadius arranged for them to sleep in the vacated top floor known as Glen's Attic. The fourth floor dormitory in Glen Hall lacked even a single window and was oven-hot in summer. Home to the sons of affluent farmers, the upper dorm was deserted this time of year as students returned home to tend crops. This left the entire loft to them. It was one long room with a slanted ceiling so shallow even Arista had to watch her head or risk hitting a rafter. Cots jutted out from the wall where the ceiling met the floor, each nothing more than a straw mattress. Personal belongings were absent, but every inch of wood was etched with a mosaic of names, phrases, or drawings—seven centuries of student memoirs.

Arista and Hadrian worked at drying their wet gear. They laid everything made of cloth across the floor and damp stains spread across the ancient timbers. Everything was soaked and smelled of horse.

"I'll get a drying line up," Hadrian told her. "We can use the blankets to create a bit of privacy for you at the same time." He gave her a quizzical look.

"What?"

He shook his head. "I've just never seen a soaking-wet princess before. You sure you want to do this? It's not too late, we can still head back to Medford and—"

"I'll be fine." She headed for the stairs.

"Where are you going?"

"To bring up the rest of the bags."

"It's probably still raining and I can get those just as soon—"

Arista interrupted him, "You have ropes to tie and, as you pointed out, I'm already soaked." She descended the steps. Her shoes squished and her wet dress hung with added weight.

SHERIDAN

No one thinks I can do it.

She led a pampered life. She knew that. She was no fool, but neither was she made of porcelain. How much fortitude did it take to live like a peasant? She was the daughter of King Amrath Essendon, Princess of Melengar—she could rise to any occasion. They all had her so well defined, but she was not like Lenare Pickering. She did not sit all day considering which dress went best with her golden locks. Arista stroked her still dripping head, and felt her flat tangled hair. Lenare would have fainted by now.

Outside the rain had stopped, which left the air filled with the earthy smell of grass, mud, and worms. Everything glistened, and breezes touched off showers beneath trees. She forgot her cloak. It lay four flights up. She was going only a short distance and would be quick, but by the time she reached the carriage house, she regretted her decision. Three gown-draped students stood in the shadows talking about the new horses.

"They're from Melengar," the tallest said with the confident, superior tone of a young noble speaking to lesser men. "You can tell by the Medford brand on that one."

"So Lane, you think Melengar has fallen already?" the shortest of them asked.

"Of course, I'll wager Breckton took it last night or maybe early this morning. It's about a day's ride from Medford, and that's why the owners of these horses are here. They're probably refugees, cowards fleeing like rats from a sinking ship."

"Deserters?"

"Maybe," Lane replied.

"If Melengar really did fall last night, it might have been the king himself who fled," the short one speculated.

"Don't be a rube!" the second tallest told him. "A king would never ride on nags like these."

"Don't be too sure about that." Lane came to the little one's defense. "Alric isn't a *real* king. They say he and his witch sister killed their father and stole the throne just as he was about to name Percy Braga his successor. I even heard that Alric has taken his sister as his mistress, and there's talk of her becoming queen."

"That's disgusting!"

"The church would never allow that," said the other.

"Alric kicked the church out of Melengar months ago because he knew it would try to stop him," Lane explained. "You have to understand that the Melengarians aren't civilized people. They're still mostly barbarians and slip further back into their tribal roots every year. Without the church to watch over them, they'll be drinking the blood of virgins and praying to Oberlin before the year is out. They allow elves to run free in their cities. Did you know that?"

Arista could not see their faces as she stood beyond the doorway, careful to keep herself hidden.

"So perhaps this *is* the nag the king of Melengar escaped on. He could be staying in one of the dorm rooms right now, plotting his next move."

"Do you think Chancellor Lambert knows?"

"I doubt it," Lane replied. "I don't think a good man like Lambert would allow a menace like Alric to stay here."

"Should we tell him?"

"Why don't you tell him, Hinkle?" Lane said to the short fellow.

"Why me? You should do it. After all you're the one that noticed them."

"Me? I don't have time. Lady Chastelin sent me another letter today and I need to work on my reply lest she drives a dagger into her chest for fear I have forgotten her."

"Don't look at me," said the remaining one. "I'll admit it, Lambert scares me."

The others laughed.

"No, I'm serious. He scares the wax out of me. He had me in his office last semester because of that rabid rat stunt Jason pulled. I'd rather he'd just cane me."

Together they walked off, continuing their chatter, only now it drifted to Lady Chastelin as doubts of her devotion to Lane arose.

Arista waited a moment until she was certain they were gone then found the bags near the saddles and stuffed one under her arm. She grabbed the other two and quickly, but carefully, returned across the commons and slipped back up the stairs of Glen Hall.

Hadrian was not in the loft when she returned but he had the lines up and blankets hung dividing the room. She slipped through the makeshift curtain and began the miserable task of stringing out her wet things. She changed into her nightgown and robe. They were near the center of her bag and only slightly damp. Then she began throwing the rest of her clothes over the lines. Hadrian returned with a bucket of water and paused when he spotted Arista brazenly displaying her petticoats and corset. She felt her face flush as she imagined what he was thinking. She traveled unescorted with two men, was bedding down in the same room—albeit a large and segmented hall—and now she displayed her underwear for them to see. She was surprised they had not questioned her more intently. It would eventually come up, she knew. Royce was not the type to miss such an obvious breech of protocol as a maiden princess being ordered to travel alone in the company of two rogues, no matter how highly esteemed by the crown. As for her clothes, there was no other way or place to dry them safely, so it was this or wear them wet in the morning. There was no sense being prissy about it.

Royce entered the dorm as she finished her work. He was wearing his cloak with the hood up. It dripped a puddle on the floor.

"We'll be leaving well before dawn," he pronounced.

"Is something wrong?" Hadrian asked.

"I found a few students snooping around the carriage house when I made my rounds."

"He does that," Hadrian explained. "Sort of an obsession he has. Can't sleep otherwise."

"You were there?"

Royce nodded. "They won't be troubling us anymore."

Arista felt the blood drain from her face. "You…you killed them?" she asked in a whisper. As she said it, she felt sick. A few minutes earlier, listening to their horrible discussion, she found herself wishing them harm, but she did not mean it. They were little more than children. She knew, however, that Royce might not see it that way. She had come to realize that for him, a threat was a threat no matter the package.

"I considered it." No tone of sarcasm tempered his words. "If they had turned left toward the Chancellor's residence instead of right toward the dormitories…but they didn't. They went straight to their rooms. Nevertheless, we will not be waiting until morning. We'll be leaving in a few hours, that way even if they do start a rumor about horses from Melengar, we will be long gone by the time it reaches the right ears. The Empire's spies will assume we are heading to Trent to beg their aid. We'll need to get you a new mount though before heading to Colnora."

"If we are leaving as soon as that, I should go see Arcadius about that meal he promised," Hadrian said.

"No!" Arista told him hastily. They looked at her, surprised. She smiled, embarrassed at her outburst. "I'll go. It will give you two a chance to change out of your wet things without me here." Before they could say anything, she slipped out and down the hallway to the stairs.

It had been nearly a year since that morning on the bank of the Nidwalden River when Esrahaddon put a question in her head. The wizard had admitted using her to orchestrate the murder of her father to facilitate his escape, but he also suggested there was more to the story. This could be her only chance to speak with Arcadius. She took a right at the bottom of the stairs and hurried to his study.

SHERIDAN

Arcadius sat on a stool at a small wooden desk on the far side of the room, studying a page of a massive tome. Beside him was a brazier of hot coals and an odd contraption she had never seen before—a brown liquid hung suspended above the heat of the brazier in a glass vial, as a steady stream of bubbles rose from a small stone immersed in the liquid. The steamy vapors rose through a series of glass tubes and passed through another glass container filled with salt crystals. From the end of that tube a clear fluid slowly dripped into a small flask. A yellow liquid also hung suspended above the flask, and through a valve one yellow drop fell for each clear one. As these two liquids mixed, white smoke silently rose into the air. Occasionally he adjusted a valve, added salt, or pumped bellows, causing the charcoal to glow red hot. At her entrance, Arcadius looked up.

He removed his glasses, wiped them with a rag from the desk, and put them back on. He peered at her through squinting eyes.

"Ah, my dear, come in." Then, as if remembering something important, he hastily twisted one of the valves. A large puff of smoke billowed up, causing several of the animals in the room to chatter. The stone fell to the bottom of the flask, where it lay quietly. The animals calmed down, and the elderly Master of Lore turned and smiled at Arista, motioning for her to join him.

This was no easy feat. Arista searched for open floor to step on and, finding little, grabbed the hem of her robe and opted to step on the sturdiest looking objects in the shortest path to the desk.

The wizard waited patiently with a cheery smile. His high rosy cheeks causing the edges of his eyes to wrinkle like a bed sheet held in a fist.

"You know," he began, as she made the perilous crossing, "I always find it interesting what paths my students take to reach me. Some are direct, while others take more of a roundabout approach. Some end up getting lost in the clutter and others find the journey too much trouble and give up altogether, never reaching me."

Arista was certain he implied more than he said, but she had neither the time nor inclination to explore it further. Instead, she replied, "Perhaps if you straightened up a bit you wouldn't lose so many students."

The wizard tilted his head. "I suppose you're right, but where would be the fun in that?"

Arista stepped over the rabbit cage, around the large pestle and mortar, and stood before the desk on a closed cover of a book no less than three feet in height and two in width.

The lore master looked down at her feet, pursed his lips, and nodded his approval. "That's Glenmorgan the Second's biography, easily seven hundred years old."

Arista looked alarmed.

"Not to worry, not to worry," he told her, chuckling to himself. "It's a terrible book written by church propagandists. The perfect platform for you to stand on, don't you think?"

Arista opened her mouth, thought about what she was going to say, and then closed it again.

The wizard chuckled once more. "Ah yes, they've gone and made an ambassador out of you, haven't they? You've learned to think before you speak. I suppose that's good. Now tell me, what brings you to my office at this hour? If it's about dinner, I apologize for the delay, but the stoves were out and I needed to fetch a boy to get them fired again. I also had to drag the cook away from a card game, which he wasn't at all pleased about. But a meal is being prepared as we speak and I will have it brought up the moment it is finished."

"It's not that Master—"

He put up a hand to stop her. "You are no longer a student here. You are a princess and Ambassador of Melengar. If you call me Arcadius, I won't call you Your Highness, agreed?" The grin of his was just too infectious to fight. She nodded and smiled in return.

"Arcadius," she began again, "I've had something on my mind

and I've been meaning to visit you for some time, but so much has been happening. First there was Fanen's funeral. Then, of course, Tomas arrived in Melengar."

"Oh yes, the Wandering Deacon of Dahlgren. He came here as well preaching that a young girl named Thrace is the Heir of Novron. He sounded very sincere. Even I was inclined to believe him."

"A lot of people did and that's part of the reason Melengar's fate is so precarious now."

Arista stopped. There was someone at the door, a pretty girl, perhaps six years old. Long dark hair spilled over her shoulders, her hands clasped together holding a length of thin rope that she played with, spinning it in circles.

"Ah, there you are. Good," the wizard told the girl, who stared apprehensively at Arista. "I was hoping you'd turn up soon. He's starting to cause a fuss. It's as if he can tell time." Arcadius glanced at Arista. "Oh, forgive me. I neglected to introduce you. Arista, this is Mercy."

"How do you do?" Arista asked.

The little girl said nothing.

"You must forgive her. She is a bit shy with strangers."

"A bit young for Sheridan, isn't she?"

Arcadius smiled. "Mercy is my ward. Her mother asked me to watch over her for awhile until her situation improved. Until then I try my best to educate her, but as I learned with you, young ladies can be most willful." He turned to the girl. "Go right ahead, dear. Take Mr. Rings outside with you before he rips up his cage again."

The girl moved across the room's debris as nimble as a cat and removed a thin raccoon from his cage. He was a baby by the look of it, and she carried him out the door, giggling as Mr. Rings sniffed her ear.

"She's cute," Arista said.

"Indeed she is. Now you said you had something on your mind?"

Arista nodded and considered her words. The question Esrahaddon planted she now presented to her old teacher. "Arcadius, who approved my entrance into Sheridan?"

The lore master raised a bristled eyebrow. "Ah," he said. "You know, I always wondered why you never asked before. You are perhaps the only female to attend Sheridan University in its seven hundred year history, and certainly the only one to study the arcane arts at all, but you never questioned it once."

Arista's posture tightened. "I am questioning it now."

"Indeed...indeed," the wizard replied. He sat back, removed his glasses, and rubbed his nose briefly. "I was visited by the Chancellor of the School, Ignatius Lambert, and asked if I would be willing to accept a gifted young lady into my instructions on Arcane Theory. This surprised me you see, because I didn't teach a class on Arcane Theory. I wanted to. I requested to have it added to the curriculum many times, but was always turned down by the school's patrons. It seemed they didn't feel that teaching magic was a respectable pursuit. Magic uses power not connected to a spiritual devotion to Maribor and Novron. At best it was subversive and possibly outright evil in their minds. The fact that I practiced the arcane arts at all has always been an embarrassment."

"Why haven't they replaced you?"

"It could be that my reputation as the most-learned wizard in Avryn lends such prestige to this school that they allow me my hobbies. Or it may be that anyone who has tried to force my resignation has been turned into the various toads, squirrels, and rabbits you see about you."

He appeared so serious that Arista looked around the room at the various cages and aquariums, at which point the wizard began to chuckle.

She scowled at him. Which only made him laugh harder.

"As I was saying," Arcadius went on when he had once again gained control of himself. "Ignatius was in one sentence offering me my desire to teach magic if I was willing to accept you as a student. Perhaps he thought I would refuse. Little did he know that unlike the rest of them, I harbor no prejudices concerning women. Knowledge is knowledge, and the chance to be able to instruct and enlighten a princess—a potential leader—with the power to help shape the world around us was not a deterrent at all, but rather a bonus."

"So you're saying I was allowed entrance because of a plan of the school's headmaster that backfired?"

"Not at all, that is merely how it happened, not why. *Why* is a much more important question. You see, School Chancellor Ignatius Lambert was not alone in my office that morning. With him was another man. He remained silent and stood over there just behind and to the left of you, where the birdcage is now, of course, the cage wasn't there then. Instead, he chose to stand on a discarded old coat and a dagger. As I mentioned, it is always interesting to see the paths people take when they enter this office, and where they choose to stand."

"Who was he?"

"Percy Braga, the Archduke of Melengar."

"So it *was* Uncle Percy."

"He certainly was involved, but even an archduke of Melengar wasn't likely to have influence over those running Sheridan University especially on a matter as volatile as teaching magic to young noble ladies. Sheridan is in the ecclesiastical realm of Ghent, where secular lords have no sway. There was, however, another man with them. He never entered my office but stood in the doorway, in the shadows."

"Could you tell who it was?"

"Oh, yes." Arcadius smiled. "These are reading glasses, my dear. I can see long distances just fine, but then I can see that is a common mistake people make."

"Who was it then?"

"A close friend of your family, I believe. It was Bishop Maurice

Saldur, of Medford's Mares Cathedral of Novron, but you probably knew that, didn't you?"

Good to his word, Arcadius sent steaming meat pies and red wine. Arista recalled the pies from her days as a student. They were never very good, even fresh. Usually made from the worst cuts of pork because the school saved lamb for the holidays. The pies were heavy on onions and carrots and thin on gravy and meat. Students actually gambled on how many paltry shreds of pork they found in their pie—a mere five stood as the record. Despite complaints, the other students wolfed down their meals, but she never did. Most of the other students' indignation she guessed was only bluster—they likely ate no better at home. Arista, however, was accustomed to three or four different meats roasted on the bone, several varieties of cheese, freshly baked breads, and whatever fruits were in season. To get her through the week, she had servants bring survival packages which she kept in her room.

"You could have mentioned that you knew Arcadius," Arista told them as they sat down together at the common table, an old bit of furniture defaced like everything else. It wobbled enough to make her glad the wine was in a jug with cups instead of a bottle and stemmed glasses.

"And ruin the fun?" Hadrian replied with a handsome grin. "So Arcadius was your professor here?"

"One of them. The curriculum requires that you take several classes learning different subjects from the various teachers. Master Arcadius was my favorite. He was the only one to teach magic."

"So you learned magic from Arcadius as well as Esrahaddon?" Royce asked, digging into his pie.

Arista nodded, poking her pie with a knife and letting the steam out.

"That must have been interesting. I am guessing their teaching styles were a bit different."

"Like night and day." She took a sip of wine. "Arcadius was formal in his lessons. He followed a structured course using books and lecturing very professorially, as you saw this evening. His style made the lessons seem right and proper, despite the stigma associated with them. Esrahaddon was haphazard and seemed to teach whatever came to mind, and often had trouble explaining things. Arcadius is clearly the better teacher, but…" She paused.

"But?" Royce asked.

"Well, don't tell Arcadius," she said, conspiratorially, "but Esrahaddon seems to be the more skilled and knowledgeable. Arcadius is the expert on the history of magic, but Esrahaddon *is* the history, if you follow me."

She took a bite of pie and got a mouthful of onions and burnt crust.

"Having learned from both, doesn't that make you the third most skilled mage in Avryn?"

Arista smirked bitterly and washed the mouthful down with more wine. While she suspected Royce was correct, she had only cast two spells since leaving their tutelage.

"Arcadius taught me many important lessons. Yet his classes concerned themselves with using knowledge as a means to broaden his students' understanding of their world. It's his way to get them thinking in new directions, to perceive what is around them in terms that are more sensible. Of course, this didn't make his students happy. We all wanted the secrets to power, the tools to reshape the world to our liking. Arcadius doesn't really give answers, but rather forces his students to ask questions.

"For instance he once asked us what makes noble blood different from a commoner's blood. We pricked our fingers and ran tests and as it turns out there is no detectable difference. This led to a fight on the commons between a wealthy merchant's son and the son of a low-ranking baron. Master Arcadius was reprimanded and the merchant's son was whipped."

Hadrian finished eating, and Royce was more than halfway through his pie, but the thief left his wine untouched, grimacing after the first sip. Arista chanced another bite and caught a mushy carrot, still more onions, and a soggy bit of crust. She swallowed with a sour look.

"Not a fan of pie?" Hadrian asked.

She shook her head. "You can have it if you like." She slid it over.

"So how was it studying with Esrahaddon?"

"He was a completely different story," she went on after another mouthful of wine. "When I couldn't get what I wanted from Arcadius, I went to him. You see, all of Arcadius' teachings involve elaborate preparations, alchemic recipes that are used to trigger the release of nature's powers and incantations to focus it. He also stressed observation and experimentation to tap the power of the natural world. But while Arcadius relied on manual techniques to derive power from the elements, Esrahaddon explained how the same energy can be summoned though more subtle enticement using only motion, harmonic sound, and the power of the mind.

"The problem was Esrahaddon's technique focused on hand movements, which explains why the church cut his off. He tried to talk me through the motions, but without the ability to demonstrate it was very frustrating. Because subtle differences can separate success from failure, it was hopeless. All I ever managed to do was make a man sneeze, oh and once I cursed the Countess Amril with boils." Hadrian poured out the last of the wine in his and Arista's glass after Royce waved him off. "Arcadius was angry when he found out about the curse and lectured me for hours. He was always against using magic for personal gain or for the betterment of a just a few. He often said, 'Don't waste energy to treat a single plague victim, instead search to eliminate the illness and save thousands.'

"So yes, you are right. I am likely the most-tutored mage in all of Avryn, yet I would be hard-pressed to do much more than make a person sneeze."

"And you can do that just with hand movements?" Royce asked, skeptically.

"Would you like a demonstration?"

"Sure, try it on Hadrian."

"Ah no, let's not," Hadrian protested. "I don't want to be accidently turned into a toad or rabbit or something. Didn't you learn anything else?"

"Well, he tried to teach me how to boil water, but I never got it to work. I was close, but always missing something and he—" she trailed off.

"What?" Hadrian asked.

She shrugged. "I don't know. It's just that I was practicing gestures on the ride here and I—" She squinted in concentration as she ran through the motions in her mind. They should be the same. Both the rain and the boiling spell contained the same element—water. The same motion should be found in each. Just thinking about it made her heart quicken.

That is it, isn't it? That is the missing piece.

If she had the rest of the spell right, then all she need do was… She looked around for the bucket that Hadrian had brought up. She closed her eyes and took several deep breaths. Boiling water, while harder than making a person sneeze, was a short, simple incantation and one she attempted without success hundreds of times. She cleared her mind, relaxed, then reached out, sensing the room—the light and heat emanating from the candles, the force of the wind above the roof, the dripping of water from their wet clothes. She opened her eyes and focused on the bucket and the water inside.

Lukewarm, it lay quiet, sleeping. She felt its place in the world, part of the whole, waiting for a change, wanting to please.

Arista began to hum, letting the sounds follow the rhythm that spoke to the water. She sensed its attention. Her voice rose, speaking the few short words in a melody of a song. She raised a single hand and made the motions, only this time she added a simple sweep of her thumb. It felt perfect—the hole that evaded her in the past. She closed her hand into a fist and squeezed. The moment she did she could feel the heat, and across the room steam rose.

Hadrian stood up, took two steps, and then stopped. "It's bubbling," he said, his voice expressing his amazement.

"So are our clothes." Royce pointed to the wet clothing hanging on the line, which were beginning to hiss as steam rose from them.

"Oops." Arista opened her hand abruptly. The wash water stopped boiling, and the clothes quieted.

"By Mar, that's unbelievable." Hadrian stood grinning. "You really did it."

Royce remained silent, staring at the steaming clothes.

"I know. Can you believe it?" she said.

"What else can you do?"

"Let's not find out," Royce interrupted. "It's getting late and we'll be leaving in just a few hours, so we should get to sleep."

"Killjoy," Hadrian replied. "But he's probably right. Let's turn in."

Arista nodded and walked behind the wall of blankets and only then allowed herself a smile.

It worked! It really worked.

Lying on the little cot not bothering with a blanket she stared at the ceiling, listening to the thieves moving about.

"You have to admit that was impressive." She heard Hadrian say.

If Royce made a reply, she did not hear it. She scared him. The expression on his face had said more than words ever could. Lying there looking up at the rafters, she realized she had seen that look before. The day Arcadius reprimanded her. She was leaving his office when he stopped her. "I never taught curses in this class, boils or otherwise. Did you cause them by mixing a draught that she drank?"

"No," she recalled saying. "It was a verbal curse."

His eyes widened and his mouth gaped, but he said nothing more. At the time, she thought his look was amazement and pride in a student exceeding expectations. Looking back, Arista realized she only saw what she wanted to see.

Chapter 6
THE WORD

As Amilia watched, the playful flicker of candlelight caught the attention of the empress, briefly replacing her blank stare.

Is that a sign?

Amilia often played this game with herself, looking for any improvement. A month passed since Saldur summoned her to his office to explain her duties. She knew she could never do half of what he wanted, but his main concern was the empress' health. She did look better. Even in this faint light, Amilia could see the change. Her cheeks were no longer hollow, her skin no longer stretched. The empress was now eating some vegetables and even bits of meat hidden in the soup, yet Amilia feared the progress was too slow.

Modina still had not said a word—at least, not while awake. Often, when the empress was sleeping she mumbled, moaned, and tossed about restlessly. Upon awakening, the girl cried, tears running down her cheeks. Amilia held her, stroked her hair, and tried to keep her warm, but the empress never acknowledged her presence.

Amilia continued to tell Modina stories to pass the time, hoping it would help. After telling her everything she could think of about her family, she moved on to fairytales from her childhood. There was Gronbach, the evil dwarf who kidnapped a milkmaid and imprisoned her in his subterranean lair. The maiden solved the riddle of the three boxes, snipped off his beard, and escaped.

She even recounted scary stories told by her brothers in the dark of the carriage workshop. She knew they were purposefully trying to frighten her, and even now they gave Amilia chills. But anything was worth a try to snap Modina back to land of the living. The most disturbing of these was about elves who put their victims to sleep with music before eating them.

When she ran out of fairytales, she turned to ones remembered from church like the epic tale of how, in their hour of greatest need, Maribor sent the divine Novron to save mankind wielding the wondrous Rhelacan to defeat the elves.

Thinking Modina would like the similarities to her own life, Amilia told the romantic account of the farmer's daughter Persephone, whom Novron took to be his queen. When she refused to leave her simple village, he built the great imperial capital right there and named the city Percepliquis after her.

"So what story shall we have this evening?" Amilia asked as the two girls lay across from one another, bathed in the light of the candles. "How about *Kile and the White Feather*? Our monsieur used it from time to time when he wanted to make a point about penance and redemption. Have you heard that one? Do you like it? I do.

"Well, you see, the father of the gods, Erebus, had three sons Ferrol, Drome, and Maribor; the gods of elves, dwarfs, and men. He also had a daughter Muriel, who was, of course, the loveliest being ever created and had dominion over all the plants and animals. Well, one night Erebus became drunk and raped his own daughter. In anger, her brothers attacked their father and tried to kill him, but of course, gods can't die."

Amilia saw the candles flicker from a draft. It was always colder at night and, getting up, she brought them both another blanket.

"So, where was I? Oh yes, racked with guilt and grief Erebus returned to Muriel and begged her forgiveness. She was moved by her father's remorse, but still could not look at him. He begged, pleading for her to name a punishment. She needed time to let the fear and pain pass so she told him, 'Go to Elan to live. Not as a god, but as a man to learn humiliation.' To repent for his misdeeds, she charged him with doing good works. Erebus did as she requested and took the name of Kile. It is said that to this day, he walks the world of men, working miracles. For each act that pleases her, she bestows upon him a white feather from her magnificent robe, which he keeps in a pouch forever by his side. Muriel decreed that when the day came when all the feathers were bestowed, she would call her father home and forgive him. It is said when all the gods are reunited, all will be made right and the world will transform into a paradise."

This really was one of Amilia's favorite stories and she told it hoping for miraculous results. Perhaps the father of the gods would hear her and come to their aid. Amilia waited. Nothing happened. The walls were the same cold stone, the flickering flames the only light. She sighed. "Well, maybe we'll just have to make our own miracles," she told Modina as she blew out all but a single candle then closed her eyes to sleep.

Amilia woke with a new-found purpose. She resolved to free Modina from her room, if only for a short while. The cell reeked of urine and mildew that lingered even after scrubbing and fresh straw. She wanted to take her outside, but knew that was asking too much. She was certain Lady Constance was dragged away because of Modina's failing health, not because she took her from her cell. Whatever the consequences, she had to try.

Amilia changed both herself and Modina into their day clothing and, taking her gently by the hand, led her to the door and knocked. When it opened, she faced the guard straight and tall and announced. "I'm taking the empress to the kitchen for her meal. I was appointed the Imperial Secretary by Regent Saldur himself, and I'm responsible for her care. She can't remain in this filthy cell. It's killing her."

She waited.

He would refuse and she would argue. She tried to organize her rebuttals: noxious vapors, the healing power of fresh air, the fact that they would kill her if the empress did not show improvement. Why that last one would persuade him she had not worked out, but it was one of the thoughts pressing on her mind.

The guard looked from Amilia to Modina and back to Amilia again. She was shocked when he nodded and stepped aside. Amilia hesitated—she had not considered the possibility he would relent. She led the empress up the steps while the soldier followed behind.

She made no announcement like Lady Constance. She simply walked in with the empress in tow, bringing the kitchen once more to a halt. Everyone stared. No one said a word.

"The empress would like her meal," Amilia told Ibis, who nodded. "Could you please put some extra bread at the bottom of the bowl, and could she get some fruit today?"

"Aye, aye," the big man acknowledged. "Leif, get on it. Nipper, go to the storage and bring up some of those berries. The rest of you, back to work. Nothing to see here."

Nipper bolted outside, leaving the door open. Red, one of the huntsman's old dogs, wandered in. Modina dropped Amilia's hand.

"Leif, get that animal out of here," Ibis ordered.

"Wait," Amilia said. Everyone watched as the empress knelt down next to the elkhound. The dog in turn nuzzled her.

Red was old, his muzzle had gone gray, and his eyes clouded with blindness. Why the huntsman kept him was a mystery, as all he did was sleep in the courtyard and beg for handouts from the kitchen.

Few took notice of his familiar presence, but he commanded the empress' attention. She scratched behind his ears and stroked his fur.

"I guess Red gets to stay." Ibis chuckled. "Dog's got important friends."

Edith Mon entered the kitchen, halting abruptly at the sight of Amilia and the empress. She pursed her lips, narrowed her eyes, and without a word pivoted and exited the way she came.

Amidst the sound of pounding hammers, Regent Maurice Saldur strode through the palace reception hall where artisans were busy at work. A year ago this was King Ethelred's castle, the stark stone fortress of Avryn's most powerful monarch. Since the coronation of the empress, it became the Imperial Palace of the Nyphron Empire and the home of the Daughter of Maribor. Saldur insisted on the renovations: A grand new foyer complete with the crown seal etched in white marble on the floor, several massive chandeliers to lighten the dark interior, a wider ornate balcony from which her eminence could wave to her adoring people, and of course a complete rework of the throne room.

Ethelred and the chancellor balked at the expense. The new throne cost almost as much as a warship, but they did not understand the importance of impressions the way he did. He had an illiterate, nearly comatose child for an empress, and the only thing preventing disaster was that no one knew. How much silk, gold, and marble did it take to blind the world? More than he had access to he was certain, but he would do what he could.

These last few weeks, Saldur felt as if he were balancing on his head while standing on a stool with one leg missing, strapped to the back of a runaway horse. The Empire went up practically overnight like a barn-raising. Centuries of planning had finally coalesced, but as with everything, there were mistakes, errors, and circumstances for which they could not possibly account.

The whole fiasco in Dahlgren was only the start. The moment they declared the establishment of the New Empire, Glouston went into open revolt. Alburn decided to haggle over terms, and, of course, there was Melengar. The humiliation was beyond words. Every other Avryn kingdom fell in step as planned, all except his. He was Bishop of Melengar and close personal adviser to the king and later his son, and yet Melengar remained independent. It was only Saldur's clever solution to the Dahlgren problem that kept him from fading into obscurity. He drew victory from ashes, and for that the Patriarch appointed him the church's representative, making him co-regent alongside Ethelred.

The old king of Warric maintained the existing systems, but Saldur was the architect of the new world order. His vision would define the lives of thousands for centuries to come. It was a tremendous opportunity, yet he felt as if he was rolling a massive boulder up a hill. If he should trip or stumble, the rock would roll back and crush him and everything else with it.

When he reached his office, he found Luis Guy waiting. The church sentinel had just arrived, hopefully with good news. The Knight of Nyphron waited near the window, as straight and impeccable as ever. He stood looking out at some distant point with his hands clasped behind his back. As usual, he wore the black and scarlet of his order, each line clean, his beard neatly trimmed.

"I assume you've heard," Saldur said, closing the door behind him and ignoring any greeting. Guy was not the type to bother with pleasantries—something Saldur appreciated about the man. Over the last several months, he had seen little of Guy, who the Patriarch kept occupied searching for the real Heir of Novron and the wizard Esrahaddon. This was also to his liking, as Guy could be a formidable rival and his travels kept the sentinel from the center of power. Strangely, Guy appeared to have little interest in carving out a place for himself in the New Empire—something else to be grateful for.

"About the Nationalists? Of course," Guy responded, turning away from the window.

"And?"

"And what?"

"And I would like to know what—" Saldur halted when he noticed another man in the room.

The office was comfortable in size, large enough to accommodate a desk, bookshelves, and a table with a chessboard between two soft chairs where the stranger sat.

"Oh, yes." Guy motioned to the man. "This is Merrick Marius. Merrick meet Bishop—forgive me—*Regent* Saldur."

"So this is him," Saldur muttered annoyed the man did not rise.

He remained sitting comfortably, leaning back with casual indifference, staring in a manner too direct, too brazen. Merrick wore a thigh-length coat of dark red suede—an awful shade Saldur thought—the color of dried blood. His hair was short; his face pale, and aside from his coat, his attire was simple and unadorned.

"Not very impressive, are you?" Saldur observed.

The man smiled at this. "Do you play chess, your grace?"

Saldur's eyebrows rose and he glanced at Guy. This was his man after all. Guy was the one who dug him up, unearthing him from the fetid streets, and praised his talents. The sentinel said nothing and showed no outward sign of outrage or discontent with his pet.

"I am running an Empire, young man," Saldur replied, dismissively. "I don't have time for games."

"How strange," Merrick said. "I've never thought of chess as a game. To me it is more of a religion really. Every aspect of life, distilled into sixteen pieces within sixty-four black and white squares, which from a distance actually appear gray. Of course, there are more than a mere sixty-four squares. The smaller squares taken in even numbers form larger ones, creating a total of two-hundred and four. Most people miss that. They see only the obvious. Few have the intelligence to look deeper to see the patterns hidden within patterns. That's part of the beauty of chess—it is much more than it first appears, more complicated, more complex. The world at your fingertips, so manageable, so defined. It has such simple rules, a near infinite number of possible paths, but only three outcomes.

"I've heard some clergy base sermons on the game, explaining the hierarchy of pieces and how they represent the classes of society. They correlate the rules of movement to the duties that each man performs in his service to Maribor. Have you ever done that, your grace?" Merrick asked but did not wait for an answer. "Amazing idea, isn't it?" He leaned over the board, his eyes searching the field of black and white.

"The bishop is an interesting piece." He plucked one off the board and held it in his hand, rolling the polished stone figure back and forth across his open palm. "It is not a very well-designed piece, not as pretty perhaps as say the knight. It is often overlooked, hiding in the corners appearing so innocent, so disarming. But it is able to sweep the length of the board at sharp unexpected angles, often with devastating results. I've always thought that bishops were underutilized through a lack of appreciation for their talents. I suppose I am unusual in this respect, but then I'm not the type of person to judge the value of a piece based on how it looks."

"You think you're a very clever fellow, don't you?" Saldur challenged.

"No, your grace," Merrick replied. "Clever is the man who makes a fortune selling dried up cows, explaining how it saves the farmers the trouble of getting up every morning to milk them. I am not clever—I'm a genius."

At this, Guy decided to interject, "Regent, at our last meeting I mentioned a solution to the Nationalist problem. He sits before you. Mister Marius has everything worked out. He merely needs approval from the regents."

"And certain assurances of payment," Merrick added.

"You can't be serious." Saldur whirled on Guy. "The Nationalists are sweeping north on a rampage. They've taken Kilnar. They are only miles from Ratibor. They will be marching on this palace by Wintertide. What I need are ideas, alternatives, solutions—not some irreverent popinjay!"

"You have some interesting ideas, your grace," Merrick told Saldur, his voice calm and casual as if he had not heard a word. "I like your views on a central government. The benefits of standardizations in trade, laws, farming, even the widths of roads are excellent. It shows clarity of thought that I would not expect from an elderly church bishop."

"How do you know anything of my—"

Merrick raised his hand to halt the regent. "I should explain right away that how I obtain information is confidential and not open for discussion. The fact is, I know it—what's more, I like it. I can see the potential in this New Empire you are struggling to erect. It may well be exactly what the world needs to get beyond the petty warfare that weakens our nations and mires the common man in hopeless poverty. At present, however, this is still a dream. That is where I come in. I only wish you came to me earlier. I could have saved you that embarrassing and now burdensome problem of her eminence."

"That was the result of an unfortunate error on the part of my predecessor, the archbishop. Something he paid for with his life. I was the one who salvaged the situation."

"Yes, I know. Some idiot named Rufus was supposed to slay the mythical beast and thereby prove he was the fabled Heir of Novron, the descendent of the god Maribor himself. Only instead, Rufus was devoured and the beast laid waste to everything in the vicinity. Everything, except a young girl who somehow managed to slay it, and in front of a church deacon no less—oops. But you're right. That wasn't your fault. You were the smart one with the brilliant idea to use her as a puppet—a girl so bereft from losing everything and everyone that she went mad. Your solution is to hide her in the depths of the palace and hope no one notices. In the meantime, you and Ethelred run a military campaign to take over all of Avryn, sending your best troops north to invade Melengar just as the Nationalists invade from the south. Brilliant. I must say, with things so well in hand it is a wonder I was contacted at all."

"I am not amused," Saldur told him.

"Nor should you be, for at this moment King Alric of Melengar is setting into motion plans to form an alliance with the Nationalists, trapping you in a two-front war, and bringing Trent into the conflict on their side."

"You know this?"

"It is what I would do. And with the wealth of Delgos and the might of Trent, your fledgling Empire, with its insane empress, will crumble as quickly as it rose."

"More impressed now?" Guy asked.

"And what would you have us do to stave off this impending cataclysm?"

Merrick smiled. "Pay me."

The grand exalted Empress Modina Novronian, ruler of Avryn, and high priestess of the Church of Nyphron, sat sprawled on the floor feeding her bowl of soup to Red, who expressed his gratitude by drooling on her dress. He rested his head on her lap and slapped his tail against the stone, his tongue sliding lazily in and out. The empress curled up beside the dog and laid her head on the animal's side. Amilia smiled, it was encouraging to see Modina interact with something, anything.

"Get that disgusting animal out of here and get her off the floor!"

Amilia jumped and looked up horrified to see Regent Saldur enter the kitchen with Edith Mon at his side, wearing a sinister smile. Amilia could not move. Several scullery maids rushed to the empress' side and gently pulled her to her feet.

"The very idea," he continued to shout as the maids busied themselves smoothing out Modina's dress. "You," the regent growled pointing at Amilia, "this is your doing. I should have known. What was I expecting when I put a common street urchin in charge of...of..." he trailed off, looking at Modina with an exasperated expression. "At least your predecessors didn't have her groveling with animals!"

"Your grace, Amilia was—" Ibis Thinly began.

"Shut up, you oaf!" Saldur snapped at the stocky cook, and then returned his attention to Amilia. "Your service to the empress has ended, as well as your employment at this palace."

Saldur motioned to the empress' guard, and then said, "Take her out of my sight." The guard approached Amilia, unable to meet her eyes.

Amilia breathed in short, stifled gasps and realized she was trembling as the soldier approached. Not normally given to crying, Amilia could not help it, and tears began streaming down her cheeks.

"No," Modina said.

Spoken with no force, barely above a whisper, the single word cast a spell on the room. One of the cooking staff dropped a metal pot that rang loudly on the stone floor. They all stared. The regent turned in surprise, and then began to circle the empress, studying her with interest. The girl had a focused, challenging look as she glared at Saldur. The regent glanced from Amilia to Modina several times. He cocked his head from side to side as if trying to work out a puzzle. The guard stood by awkwardly.

At length, Saldur put him at ease. "As the empress commands," Saldur said without taking his eyes off Modina. "It seems that I may have been a bit premature in my assessment of…" Saldur glance at Amilia, annoyed. "What's your name?"

"A—Amilia."

He nodded as if approving the correct answer. "Your techniques are unusual, but certainly one can't argue with results."

Saldur looked back at Modina as she stood within the circle of maids who parted at his approach. He circled her. "She does look better, doesn't she? Color's improved. There's…" he motioned toward her face, "a fullness to her cheeks." His head was nodding. He crossed his arms and with a final nod of approval said, "Very well, you can keep the position, as it seems to please her eminence."

The regent turned and headed out of the scullery. He paused at the doorway to look over his shoulder saying, "You know—I was really starting to believe she was mute."

Chapter 7
THE JEWEL

Arista always thought of herself as an experienced equestrian. Most ladies never even sat in a saddle, but she had ridden since childhood. The nobles mocked, and her father scolded, but nothing could dissuade her. She loved the freedom of the wind in her hair and her heart pounding with the beat of the hooves. Before setting out, she looked forward to impressing the thieves with her vast knowledge in horsemanship. She knew they would be awed by her skill.

She was wrong.

In Sheridan, Royce found her a spirited brown bay mare to replace her exquisite palfrey. Since setting out he forced them over rough ground, fording streams, jumping logs, and dodging low branches—often at a trot. Clutching white-knuckled to the saddle, she used all her skills and strength just to remain on the horse's back. Gone were her illusions of being praised as a skilled rider, and all that remained was the hope of making it through the day without the humiliation—not to mention the physical pain of falling.

They rode south after leaving the university, following trails only Royce could find. Before dawn they crossed the narrow headwaters of the Galewyr and proceeded up the embankment on the far side. Briars and thickets lashed at them. Unseen dips caught the horses by surprise, and Arista cried out once when her mount made an unexpected lunge across a washed-out gap. Their silence added to her humiliation. If she were a man they would have commented.

They climbed steadily, reaching such a steep angle that their mounts panted for air in loud snorts and on occasion uttered deep grunts as they struggled to scramble up the dewy slope. At last they crested the hill, and Arista found herself greeting a chilly dawn atop the wind-swept Senon Upland.

The Senon was a high, barren plateau of exposed rock and scrub bushes with expansive views on all sides. The horses' hooves clacked loudly on the barefaced granite until Royce brought them to a stop. His cloak fluttered with the morning breeze. To the east, the sunrise peered at them over the mist-covered forests of Dunmore. From this height, the vast wood appeared like a hazy blue lake as it fell away below them, racing toward the dazzling sun. Arista knew that beyond it lay the Nidwalden River, the Parthalorenon Falls, and the tower of Avempartha. Royce stared east for several minutes, and she wondered if his elven eyes could see that tiny pinnacle of his people in the distance.

In front of them and to the southwest lay the Warric province of Chadwick. Like everything else west of the ridge, it remained submerged in darkness. Down in the deep rolling valley, the predawn sky would only now be separating from the dark horizon. It would have appeared peaceful, a world tucked in bed before the first cock's crow, except for the hundreds of lights flickering like tiny fireflies.

"Breckton's camp," Hadrian said. "The Northern Imperial Army is not making very good time it seems."

"We'll descend before Amber Heights and rejoin the road well past Breckton," Royce explained. "How long do you figure before they reach Colnora?"

Hadrian rubbed the growing stubble of his beard. "Another three, maybe four, days. An army that size moves at a snail's pace, and I am guessing Breckton isn't pleased with his orders. He's likely dragging his feet hoping they'll be rescinded."

"You sound as if you know him," she said.

"I never met the man, but I fought under his father's banner. I've also fought against him when I served in the ranks of King Armand's army in Alburn."

"How many armies have you served in?"

Hadrian shrugged. "Too many."

They pushed on, traversing the crest into the face of a fierce wind that tugged at her clothes and caused her eyes to water. Arista kept her head down and watched her horse's hooves pick a path across the cracked slabs of lichen-covered rock. She clutched her cloak tight about her neck as the damp of the previous day's rain and sweat conspired with the wind to make her shiver. When they plunged back into the trees the slow descent began. Once more the animals struggled. This time Arista bent backward, nearly to her horse's flanks to keep her balance.

It was mercifully cooler than the day before, though the pace was faster. Finally, several hours after midday they stopped on the bank of a small stream, where the horses gorged themselves on cool water and river grass. Royce and Hadrian grabbed packs and gathered wood. Exhausted, Arista as much fell as sat down. Her legs and backside ached. There were insects and twigs in her hair and a dusting of dirt covering her gown. Her eyes stared at nothing, losing their focus as her mind stalled, numb from fatigue.

What have I gotten myself into? Am I up to this?

They were below the Galewyr, in imperial territory. She had thrown herself into the fire, perhaps foolishly. Alric would be furious when he found her missing, and she could just imagine what Ecton would say. If they caught her—she stopped herself.

THE JEWEL

This is not helping.

She turned her attention to her escorts.

Like the hours on horseback, Royce and Hadrian remained quiet. Hadrian unsaddled the horses and gave them a light brushing while Royce set up a small cook fire. It was entertaining to watch. Without a word, they would toss tools and bags back and forth. Hadrian blindly threw a hatchet over his shoulder and Royce caught it just in time to begin breaking up branches for the fire. Just as Royce finished the fire, Hadrian had a pot of water ready to place on it. For Arista, who lived her life in public among squabbling nobles and chattering castle staffs, such silence was strange.

Hadrian chopped carrots and dropped them into the dented, blackened pot on the coals. "Are you ready to eat the best meal you've ever had, Highness?"

She wanted to laugh, but did not have the strength. Instead, she said, "There are three chefs and eighteen cooks back at Essendon Castle that would take exception to that remark. They spend their whole lives perfecting elaborate dishes. You would be amazed at the feasts I've attended, filled with everything from exotic spices to ice sculptures. I highly doubt you'll be able to surpass them."

Hadrian smirked. "That might be," he replied, struggling to cut chunks of dry, brine-encrusted pork into bite-sized cubes, "but I guarantee this meal will put them all to shame."

Arista removed the pearl-handled hairbrush from a pouch that hung at her side and tried in vain to untangle her hair. She eventually gave up and sat watching Hadrian drop wretched-looking meat into the bubbling pot. Ash and bits of twigs thrown up by the cracking fire landed into the mix.

"Master chef, debris is getting in your pot."

Hadrian grinned. "Always happens. Can't help it. Just be careful not to bite down too hard on anything or you might crack a tooth."

"Wonderful," she told him, then turned her attention to Royce who was busy checking the horses' hooves. "We've come a long way today, haven't we? I don't think I've ever traveled so far so quickly. You keep a cruel pace."

"That first part was over rough ground," Royce mentioned. "We'll cover a lot more miles after we eat."

"After we eat?" Arista felt her heart sink. "We aren't stopping for the day?"

Royce glanced up at the sky. "It's hours until nightfall."

They mean for me to get back into the saddle?

She did not know if she could stand, much less ride. Virtually every muscle in her body was in pain. They could entertain any thoughts they may, but she would not travel any farther that day. There was no reason to move this fast, or over such rough ground. Why Royce was taking such a difficult course she did not understand.

She watched as Hadrian dished out the disgusting soup he had concocted into a tin cup and held it out to her. There was an oily film across the top through which green meat bobbed, everything seasoned with bits of dirt and tree bark. Most assuredly, it was the worst thing anyone ever presented her to eat. Arista held the hot cup between her hands, grimacing and wishing she had eaten more of the meat pie back in Sheridan.

"Is this a…stew?" she asked.

Royce laughed quietly. "He likes to call it that."

"It's a dish I learned from Thrace," Hadrian explained with a reminiscent look on his face. "She's a much better cook than I am. She did this thing with the meat that—well, anyway, no it's not stew. It's really just boiled salt-pork and vegetables. You don't get a broth, but it takes away the rancid taste of the salt and softens the meat. And it's hot. Trust me, you're going to love it."

Arista closed her eyes and lifted the cup to her lips. The steamy smell was wonderful. Before she realized it, she devoured the entire thing, eating so quickly she burned her tongue. A moment later, she was scraping the bottom with a bit of hard bread. She looked for more and was disappointed to see Hadrian already cleaning the pot. Lying in the grass she let out a sigh as the warmth of the meal coursed through her body.

"So much for ice sculptures." Hadrian chuckled.

Despite her earlier reluctance, she found new strength after eating. The next leg of the trip was over level ground along the relative ease of a deer trail. Royce drove them as fast as the terrain allowed, never pausing or consulting a map.

After many hours Arista had no idea where they were, nor did she care. The food faded into memory and she found herself once more near collapse. She rode bent over, resting on the horse's neck and drifting in and out of sleep. She could not discern between dream and reality and would wake in a panic, certain she was falling. Finally they stopped.

Everything was dark and cold. The ground was wet and she stood shivering once more. Her guides went back into their silent actions. This time, to Arista's immense disappointment, no fire was made and instead of a hot meal they handed her strips of smoked meat, raw carrots, an onion quarter, and a triangle of hard, dry bread. She sat on the wet grass, feeling the moisture soak into her skirt and dampening her legs as she devoured the meal without a thought.

"Shouldn't we get a shelter up?" she asked, hopefully.

Royce looked up at the stars. "It looks clear."

"But…" She was shocked when he spread out a cloth on the grass.

They mean to sleep right here—on the ground without even a tent!

Arista had three handmaids that dressed and undressed her daily. They bathed her and brushed her hair. Servants fluffed pillows and brought warm milk at bedtime. They tended the fireplace in shifts, quietly adding logs throughout the night. Sleeping in her carriage was a hardship; sleeping on that ghastly cot in the dorm a torment—this was insane! Even peasants had hovels.

Arista wrapped her cloak tight against the night's chill.

Will I even get a blanket?

Tired beyond memory, she got on her hands and knees and feebly brushed a small pile of dead leaves together to act as a mattress. Lying down, she felt them crunch and crinkle beneath her.

"Hold on," Hadrian said, carrying over a bundle. He unrolled a canvas tarp. "I really need to make more of these. The pitch will keep the damp from soaking through." He handed her a blanket as well. "Oh, there's a nice little clearing just beyond those trees, just in case you need it."

Why in the world would I need a—

"Oh," she said and managed a nod. Surely they would come upon a town soon. She could wait.

"Good night, Highness."

She did not reply as Hadrian went a few paces away and assembled his own bed from pine boughs. Without a tent, there was no choice but to sleep in her dress, which left her trapped in a tight corset. Arista spread out the tarp, removed her shoes, and lay down pulling the thin blanket up to her chin. Though utterly miserable, she stubbornly refused to show it. After all, common women lived every day under similar conditions—so could she. The argument was noble, but gave little comfort.

The instant she closed her eyes she heard the faint buzzing. Blinded by darkness, the sound was unmistakable—a horde of mosquitoes descended. Feeling one on her cheek, she slapped at it and pulled the blanket over her head, exposing her feet. Curling into a ball, she buried herself under the thin wool shield. Her tight corset made breathing a challenge and the musty smell of the blanket, long steeped in horse sweat, nauseated her. Arista's frustration overflowed and tears slipped from her tightly squeezed eyes.

THE JEWEL

What was I thinking coming out here? I can't do this. Oh Dear Maribor, what a fool I am. I always think I can do anything. I thought I could ride a horse—what a joke. I thought I was brave—look at me. I think I know better than anyone—I'm an idiot!

What a disappointment she was to those that loved her. She should have listened to her father and served the kingdom by marrying a powerful prince. Now, tarnished with the stain of witchery, no one would have her. Alric stuck his neck out and gave her a chance to be an ambassador. Her failure doomed the kingdom. Now this trip—this horrible trip was just one more mistake, one more colossal error.

I'll go home tomorrow. I'll ask Royce to take me back to Medford and I'll formally resign as ambassador. I'll stay in my tower and rot until the Empire takes me to the gallows.

Tears ran down her cheeks as she lay smothered by more than just the blanket until, mercifully in the cold unforgiving night, she fell asleep.

The songs of birds woke her.

Arista opened her eyes to sunlight cascading through the green canopy of leafy trees. Butterflies danced in brilliant shafts of golden light. The beams revealed a tranquil pond so placid it appeared as if a patch of sky had fallen. A delicate white mist hovered over the pool's mirrored surface like a scene from a fairy story. Circled by sun-dappled trees, cattails, and flowers, the pool was perfect—the most beautiful thing she had ever seen.

Where'd that come from?

Royce and Hadrian still slept under rumpled blankets leaving her alone with the vision. She got up quietly fearful of shattering the fragile beauty. Walking barefoot to the water's edge, she caught the warmth of the sun melting the night's chill. She stretched, feeling the unexpected pride in the ache of a well-worked muscle. Crouching, Arista scooped a handful of water and gently rinsed away the stiff tears of the night before. In the middle of the pond, a fish jumped. She saw it only briefly, flashing silver then disappearing with a *plop!* Another followed and, delighted by the display, Arista stared in anticipation for the next leap, grinning like a child at a puppet show.

The mist burned away before sounds from the camp caught her attention, and Arista walked over to find the clearing Hadrian mentioned. She returned to camp, brushed out her hair, and ate the cold pork breakfast waiting for her. When finished, she folded the blankets and rolled up the tarps, then stowed the food and refilled the water pouches. Arista mounted her mare, deciding at that moment to name her Mystic. It was only after Royce led them out of the little glade that she realized no one had spoken a word all morning.

They reached the road almost immediately, which explained the lack of a fire the night before and the unusual way Royce and Hadrian were dressed—in doublets and hose. Hadrian's swords were also conspicuously missing, stowed somewhere out of sight. How Royce knew the road was nearby baffled her. As they traveled with the warm sun overhead and the birds singing in the trees, Arista could scarcely understand what troubled her the night before. She was still sore, but felt a satisfaction in the dull pain that owed nothing to being a princess.

They had not gone far when Royce brought Mouse to a stop. A troop of imperial soldiers came down the road escorting a line of four large grain wagons—tall, solid-sided boxes with flat bottoms. Riders immediately rode forward, bringing a cloud of dust in their wake. An intimidating officer in bright armor failed to give his name, but demanded theirs, as well as their destination and the reason for traveling. Soldiers of his vanguard swept around behind the three with spears at the ready, horses puffing and snorting.

THE JEWEL

"This is Mr. Everton of Windham Village and his wife, and I am his servant," Royce explained quickly as he politely dismounted and bowed. His tone and inflections were formal and excessive; his voice nasal and high-pitched. Arista was amazed how much like her fussy day-steward he sounded. "Mr. Everton was…I mean is…a respected merchant. We are on our way to Colnora, where Mrs. Everton has a brother whom they hope will provide temporary…err I mean…they will be visiting."

Before leaving The Rose & Thorn, Royce had coached Arista on this story and the part she would play. In the safety of the Medford tavern, it seemed like a plausible tale. But now that the moment had come and soldiers surrounded her, she doubted its chances of success. Her palms began to sweat and her stomach churned. Royce continued to play his part masterfully, supplying answers in his non-threatening effeminate voice. The responses were specific sounding, but vague on crucial details.

"It's *your* brother in Colnora?" the officer confronted Arista, his tenor harsh and abrasive. No one spoke to her in such a tone. Even when Braga had threatened her life, he had been more polite than this. She struggled to conceal her emotion.

"Yes," she said, simply. Arista was remembering Royce's instructions to keep her answers as short as possible and her face blank. She was certain the soldiers could hear the pounding of her heart.

"His name?"

"Vincent Stapleton," she answered quickly and confidently knowing the officer would be looking for hesitation.

"Where does he live?"

"Bridge Street, not far from the Hill District," she replied. This was a carefully rehearsed line. It would be typical for the wife of a prominent merchant to boast about how near the affluent section of the city her family lived.

Hadrian now played his part.

"Look here, I've had quite enough of you, and your Imperial Army. The truth of the matter is my estate has been overrun, used to quarter a bunch of brigands like you who I'm sure will destroy my furniture and soil the carpets. I have some questions of my own. Like when will I get my home back?" he bellowed angrily. "Is this the kind of thing a merchant can expect from the empress? King Ethelred never treated us like this! Who's going to pay for damages?"

To Arista's great relief, the officer changed his demeanor. Just as hoped, he avoided getting involved in complaints from evicted patrons and waved them on their way.

As the wagons passed, she was revolted by the sight visible through the bars on the rear gate. The wagons did not hold captured soldiers, but elves. Covered in filth, they were packed so tightly they were forced to stand, jostling into each other as the wagon dipped and bounced over the rutted road. There were females and children alongside the males, all slick with sweat from the heat. Arista heard muffled cries as the wagons crawled by at a turtle's pace. Some reached through the bars pleading for water and mercy. Arista was so sickened at the sight she forgot her fear that only a moment before consumed her. Then a sudden realization struck her—she looked for Royce.

He stood a few feet away on the roadside holding Mouse's bridle. Hadrian was at his side firmly gripping Royce's arm and whispering in his ear. Arista could not hear what was said, but guessed at the conversation. A few tense moments passed then they turned and continued toward Colnora.

The street below drifted into shadow as night settled in. Carriages raced to their destinations, noisily bouncing along the cobblestone.

THE JEWEL

Lamplighters made their rounds in zigzag patterns, moving from lamp to lamp. Lights flickered to life in windows of nearby buildings, and silhouettes passed like ghosts behind curtains. Shopkeepers closed their doors and shutters while cart vendors covered their wares and harnessed horses as another day's work ended.

"How long do you think?" Hadrian asked. He and Royce had donned their usual garb and Hadrian once more wore his swords. While she was used to seeing them this way, their change in appearance and Royce's constant vigilance at the window put her on edge.

"Soon," Royce replied, not altering his concentration on the street.

They waited together in the small room at the Regal Fox Inn, the least expensive of the five hotels in the affluent Hill District. When they arrived, Royce continued to pose as their servant by renting two rooms—one standard, the other small. He avoided inquiries about luggage and arrangements for dinner. The innkeeper did not pursue the matter.

Once upstairs, Royce insisted they all remain in the standard room together. Arista noticed a pause after Royce said this, as if he expected an argument. This amused her because the idea of sharing a comfortable room was infinitely better than any accommodations she had experienced so far. Still she had to admit, if only to herself, that a week ago she would have been appalled by the notion.

Even the standard room was luxurious by most boarding house standards. The beds were made of packed feather and covered in smooth, clean sheets, overstuffed pillows, and heavy quilts. There was a full-length mirror, large dresser, wardrobe, small writing table and chair, and an adjoining room for the wash basin and chamber pot. The room was equipped with a fireplace and lamps, but Royce left them unlit and darkness filled the room. The only light was from the outside streetlamps, which cast an oblong checkerboard image on the floor.

Now that they were off the road and in a more familiar setting, the princess gave into curiosity. "I don't understand. What are we doing here?"

"Waiting," Royce replied.

"For what?"

"We can't just ride into the Nationalists' camp. We need a go-between. Someone to set up a meeting," Hadrian told her. He sat at the writing desk across the room from her. In the growing darkness, he was fading into a dim ghostly outline.

"I didn't see you send any messages, did I miss something?"

"No, but the messages were delivered nonetheless," Royce mentioned.

"Royce is kind of a celebrity here," Hadrian told her. "When he comes to town—"

Royce coughed intentionally.

"Okay, maybe not a celebrity, but he's certainly well known. I'm sure talk started the moment he arrived."

"We wanted to be seen then?"

"Yes," Royce replied. "Unfortunately, the Diamond wasn't the only one watching the gate. Someone's watching our window."

"And he's not a Black Diamond?" Hadrian asked.

"Too clumsy. Has about the same talent for delicate work as a draft horse. The Diamond would laugh if he applied."

"Black Diamond is the thieves' guild?" she asked. They both nodded.

While supposedly a secret organization, the Diamond was nevertheless well known. Arista heard of it from time to time in court and at council meetings. They were always spoken about with disdain by haughty nobles, even though they often used their services. The black market was virtually controlled by the Diamond, who supplied practically any commodity for anyone willing to pay the price.

"Can he see you?"

"Not unless he's an elf."

Hadrian and Arista exchanged glances, wondering if he meant it as a joke.

Hadrian joined Royce at the window and looked out. "The one near the lamppost with his hand on his hilt? The guy shifting his weight back and forth? He's an imperial soldier, a veteran of the Vanguard Scout Brigade."

Royce looked at Hadrian surprised.

The light from the street spilled across Hadrian's face as he grinned. "The way he's shifting his weight is a technique taught to soldiers to keep from going footsore. That short sword is standard issue for a lightly armed scout and the gauntlet on his sword hand is an idiosyncrasy of King Ethelred, who insists all his troops wear them. Since Ethelred is now part of the Empire, the fellow below is Imperial."

"You weren't kidding about serving in a lot of armies, were you?" Arista asked.

Hadrian shrugged. "I was a mercenary. It's what I did. I served anywhere the pay was good." Hadrian took his seat back at the table. "I even commanded a few regiments. Got a medal once. But I would fight for one army only to find myself going against them a few years later. Killing old friends isn't fun. So I kept taking jobs farther away. Ended up deep in Calis fighting for Tenkin Warlords." Hadrian shook his head. "Guess you could say that was my low point. You really know you've—"

Hadrian was interrupted by a knock. Without a word, Royce crossed the room taking up position on one side of door while Hadrian carefully opened it. Outside a young boy stood dressed in the typical poor clothing of a waif.

"Evening, sirs. Your presence is requested in room twenty-three," he said cheerily, then touching his thumb to his brow he walked away.

"Leave her here?" Hadrian asked Royce.

Royce shook his head. "She comes along."

"Must you speak about me as if I'm not in the room?" Arista asked, but only with feigned irritation. She sensed the seriousness of the situation from the look on Royce's face and was not about to interfere. She was behind enemy lines. If caught, it was not certain what would happen. If she tried to claim a diplomatic status, it was doubtful the Empire would honor it. Ransoming Arista for Alric's compliance was not out of the question—nor was a public execution.

"We're just going to walk in?" Hadrian asked, skeptically.

"Yes, we need their help and when one goes begging it's best to knock on the front door."

They lodged in room nineteen, so it was a short trip down the hall and around a corner to room twenty-three, which was conveniently isolated. There were no other doors off this hall, only a stair that likely led to the street. Royce rapped twice, paused then added three more.

The door opened.

"Come in, Duster."

The room was a larger, more luxurious suite with a chandelier brightly lighting the interior. No beds were visible as they entered into a parlor. Against the far wall were two doors, which no doubt led to sleeping quarters. Dark green damask fabric adorned the walls and carpet covered the entire floor except for the area around the marble fireplace. Four tall windows decorated the outside wall, each shrouded with thick velvet curtains. Several ornate pieces of furniture lined the room. In the center stood a gaunt man with sunken cheeks and accusing eyes. Two more men stood slightly behind him while another two waited near the door.

"Everyone, please take a seat," the thin man told them. He remained standing until they all sat. "Duster, let me get right to the point. I made it clear on your last visit that you are not welcome here, did I not?"

Royce was silent.

"I was unusually patient then, but seeing as how you've returned, perhaps politeness is not the proper tack to take with you. Personally, I hold you in the highest regard, but as First Officer, I simply cannot allow you to blatantly walk into this city after having been warned." He paused, but when no reaction came from Royce, he continued. "Hadrian and the princess are welcome to leave. Point of fact, I must insist the lady leave, as the death of a noblewoman would make things awkward. Shall I assume Hadrian will refuse?"

Hadrian glanced at Royce, who did not return his look. The fighter shrugged. "I would hate to miss whatever show is about to start."

"In that case, Your Highness." The man made a sweeping hand motion toward the door. "If you will please return to your room."

"I'm staying," Arista said. It was only two words, but spoken with all the confidence of a princess accustomed to getting her way.

He narrowed his eyes at her.

"Shall I escort her, sir?" one of the men near the door offered with a menacing tone.

"Touch her and this meeting will end badly," Royce said barely above a whisper.

"Meeting?" The thin man laughed. "This is no meeting. This is retribution, and it will most assuredly end very badly."

He looked back at Arista. "I've heard about you. I'm pleased to see the rumors are true."

Arista had no idea what he meant, but did not like a thug *knowing* about her. She was even more disturbed by his approval.

"Nevertheless, my men *will* escort you." He clapped his hands and the two doors to the adjoining rooms opened, as did the one behind them leading to the hallway. Many well-armed men poured in.

"We are here to see the Jewel," Royce quietly said.

Immediately the thin man's expression changed. Arista watched as in an instant his face followed a path from confidence to confusion then suspicion and finally curiosity. He ran a boney hand through his thin blonde hair. "What makes you think the Jewel will see you?"

"Because there's profit in it for him."

"The Jewel is already very wealthy."

"It's not that kind of profit. Tell me, Price, how long have you had the new gate guards? The ones in the imperial uniforms. For that matter, when did Colnora get a gate? How many others like them are roaming the city?" Royce sat back and folded his hands across his lap. "I should have been stopped the moment I entered Colnora, and under farmer Oslow's field over two hours ago. Why the delay? Why are there no watches posted on the Arch or Bernum Bridge? Are you really getting that sloppy, Price? Or are the Imps running the show?"

It was the thin man's turn to remain silent.

"The Diamond can't be happy with the New Empire flexing their muscle. You used to have full reign and The Jewel his own fiefdom. But not anymore. Now he must share. The Diamond has been forced back into the shadows while the new landlord kicks up his heels in front of the fire in the house they built. Tell Cosmos I'm here to help with his little problem."

Price stared at Royce, and then his eyes drifted to Arista. He nodded and stood up. "You will, of course, remain here until I return."

"Why not?" Hadrian remarked, apparently undisturbed by the tension radiating in the room. "This is a whole lot better than our room. Are those walnuts over there?"

During the exchange and while Price was gone, Royce never moved. Four men who were the most menacing of those present watched him intently. There seemed to be a contest of wills going on, each waiting to see who would flinch first. Hadrian, in contrast, casually strode around the room, examining the various paintings and furnishings. He selected a chair with a padded footstool, put up his feet, and began eating from a bowl of fruits and nuts.

"This stuff is great," he said. "We didn't get anything like this in our room. Anyone else want some?" They ignored him. "Suit yourself." He popped another handful of walnuts into his mouth.

Finally, Price returned. He had been gone for quite awhile, or perhaps it just seemed that way to Arista as she quietly waited. The Jewel consented to the meeting.

A carriage waited for them in front of the Regal Fox. Arista was surprised when Royce and Hadrian surrendered their weapons before boarding. Price joined them in the carriage while two of the guild members sat up top with the driver. They rolled south two blocks then turned west and traveled farther up the hill, past the Tradesmen Arch toward Langdon Bridge. Through the open window, Arista could hear the metal rims of the coach and the horses' hooves clattering on the cobblestone. Across from her the glare of tavern lights crawled across Price's face who sat eyeing her with a malevolent smile. The man was all limbs with fingers too long and eyes sunk too deep.

"It would seem you are doing better these days, Duster," he said with his hands folded awkwardly in his lap, a jackal pretending to be civilized. "At least your clientele has improved." The Diamond's first officer smiled a toothy grin and nodded at Arista. "Although rumor has it Melengar might not be the best investment these days. No offense intended, Your Highness. The Diamond is as a whole—and I personally am—rooting for you, but as a businessman, one does have to face facts."

Arista presented him a pleasant smile. "The sun will rise tomorrow, Mr. Price. That is a fact. You have horrid breath and smell of horse manure. That is also a fact. Who will win this war, however, is still a matter of opinion, and I put no weight in yours."

Price raised his eyebrows.

"She's an ambassador and a woman," Hadrian told him. "You'd be cut less fencing with a Pickering, and stand a better chance of winning."

Price smiled and nodded. Arista was unsure whether it was in approval or resentment, such was the face of thieves. "Who exactly are we going to see, or is that a secret?"

"Cosmos Sebastian DeLur, the wealthiest merchant in Avryn," Royce replied. "Son of Cornelius DeLur of Delgos, who's probably the richest man alive. Between the two of them, the DeLur family controls most of the commerce and lends money to kings and commoners alike. He runs the Black Diamond and goes by the moniker of The Jewel."

Price's hands twitched slightly.

As they reached the summit of the hill itself, the carriage turned into a long private brick road that ascended Bernum Heights, a sharply rising bluff that overlooked the river below. Here sprawled the palatial DeLur estate. A massive gate wider than three city streets opened at their approach. Elegantly dressed guards stood rigid while a stuffy administrative clerk with white gloves and powdered wig marked their passing on a parchment. Then the carriage began its long serpentine ascent along a hedge and lantern-lined lane. Unexpected breaks in the foliage revealed glimpses of an elegant garden with elaborate sculpted fountains. At the top of the bluff stood a magnificent white marble mansion. Three stories in height, it was adorned with an eighteen-pillar colonnade forming a half-moon entrance illuminated by a massive chandelier suspended at its center. This estate was built to impress, but what caught Arista's attention was the huge bronze fountain of three nude women pouring pitchers of water into a pool.

A pair of gold doors was opened by two more impeccably dressed servants. Another man dressed in a long dark coat led the way into the vestibule filled with tapestries and more sculptures than Arista had ever seen in one place. They were led through an archway outside to an expansive patio. Ivy-covered lattices lined an open-air terrace decorated with a variety of unusual plants and two more fountains—once more of nude women, only these were much smaller and wrought of polished marble.

"Good evening, Your Highness, gentlemen. Welcome to my humble home."

Seated on a luxurious couch a large man greeted them. He was not tall but of amazing girth. He looked to be in his early fifties and well on his way to going bald. He tied what little hair he had left with a black silk ribbon and let it fall in a tail down his back. His chubby face remained youthful, showing lines of age only at the corners of his eyes when he smiled, as he was doing now. He dressed in a silk robe and held a glass of wine, which threatened to spill as he motioned them over.

"Duster, how long has it been, my old friend? I can see now that I should have made you First Officer when I had the chance. It would have saved so much trouble for the both of us. Alas, but I couldn't see it then. I hope we can put all that unpleasantness behind us now."

"My business was settled the day Hoyte died," Royce replied. "Judging from our reception, I would say it was the Diamond that was having trouble putting the past behind them."

"Quite right, quite right." Cosmos chuckled. Arista determined he was the kind of man who laughed the way other people twitched, stammered, or bit their nails. "You won't let me get away with anything will you? That's good. You keep me honest—well as honest as a man in my profession can be." He chuckled again. "It's that pesky legend that keeps the guild on edge. You're quite the boogieman. Not that Mr. Price here buys into any of that, you understand, but it is his responsibility to keep the organization running smoothly. Allowing you to stroll about town is like letting a man-eating tiger meander through a crowded tavern. As the tavern keeper, they expect me to maintain the peace."

Cosmos motioned toward Price with his goblet. "You knew Mr. Price only briefly when you were still with us, I think. A pity. You would like him if you met under different circumstances."

"Who said I didn't like him?"

Cosmos laughed. "You don't like anyone, Duster with the exception of Hadrian and Miss DeLancy, of course. There are only those you put up with and those you don't. By the mere fact that I am here I can at least deduce I am not on your short list."

"Short list?"

"I can't imagine your slate of targets stays full for very long."

"We both have lists. Names get added and names get erased all the time. It would appear Price added me to yours."

"Consider it erased, my friend. Now tell me what can I get you to drink? Montemorcey? You always had a fondness for the best. I have a vintage stock in the cellar. I'll have a couple bottles brought up."

"That'd be fine," Royce replied.

He gave a slight glance to his steward, who bowed abruptly and left. "I hope you don't mind meeting in my little garden. I do so love the night air." Closing his eyes and tilting his head up, he took a deep breath. "I don't manage to get out nearly as often as I would like. Now please sit and tell me about this offer you bring."

They each took seats opposite Cosmos on elaborate cushioned benches, the span between taken up by an ornate table whose legs were fashioned to look like powerful snakes, each different from the next, facing out with fanged mouths open. Behind them Arista could hear the gurgling of fountains and the late breeze shifting foliage. Below that, hidden from view by the balcony, was the deeper, menacing roar of the Bernum River.

THE JEWEL

"It's more of a proposition really," Royce replied. "The princess here has a problem you might be able to help with, and you have a problem she may be able to solve."

"Wonderful, wonderful. I like how this is starting. If you had said you were offering me the chance of a lifetime, I would have been doubtful, but arrangements of mutual benefit shows you are being straight forward. I like that, but you were always blunt, weren't you, Duster? You could afford to lay your cards on the table because you always had such excellent cards."

A servant with white gloves identical to those worn by the gate clerk arrived and silently poured the wine then withdrew to a respectful distance. Cosmos waited politely for them each to take a taste.

"Montemorcey is one of the finest vineyards in existence, and my cellar has some of their very best."

Royce nodded his praise. Hadrian sniffed the dark red liquid skeptically then swallowed the contents in a single mouthful. "Not bad for old grape juice."

Cosmos laughed once more. "Not a wine drinker. I should have known. Wine is no potable for a warrior. Gibbons, bring Hadrian a pull from the Oak Cask and leave the head on it. That should be more to your liking. Now, Duster, tell me about our mutual problems?"

"Your problem is obvious. You don't like this New Empire crowding you."

"Indeed I do not. They're everywhere and spreading. For each one you see in uniform you can expect three more you don't. Tavern keepers and blacksmiths are secretly working for the imperials passing information. It is impossible to run a proper guild as extensive and elaborate as the Black Diamond in such a restrictive environment. There is even evidence they have spies in the Diamond itself, which is most unsettling."

"I also happen to know that Degan Gaunt is your boy."

"Well, not mine per se."

"Your father's then. Gaunt is supported by Delgos, Tur Del Fur is the capital of Delgos, and your father is the ruler of Tur Del Fur."

Cosmos laughed again. "No, not the ruler. Delgos is a republic, remember. He is but one of a triumvirate of businessmen elected to lead the government."

"Ah-huh."

"You don't sound convinced."

"It doesn't matter. The DeLurs are backing Gaunt in the hopes of breaking the Empire, so something that might help Gaunt would help you as well."

"True, true, and what are you bringing me?"

"An alliance with Melengar, the princess here is empowered to negotiate on behalf of her brother."

"Word has it Melengar is helpless and about to fall to Ballentyne's Northern Imperial Army."

"Word is mistaken. The empress recalled the Northern Army to deal with the Nationalists. We passed it near Fallen Mire. Only a token force remains to watch the Galewyr River. The army moves slowly but it will reach Aquesta before Gaunt does. That will tip the scales in favor of the Empire."

"What are you suggesting?"

Royce looked at Arista, indicating that she should speak now.

Arista set down her glass and gathered her thoughts as best she could. She was still befuddled from the day's ride and now the wine on an empty stomach caused her head to fog. She took a short breath and focused.

"Melengar still has a defensive force," the princess began. "If we used it to attack across the river and broke through into Chadwick, there would be nothing to stop us from sweeping across into Glouston. Once there, the Marquis Lanaklin could raise an army from his loyal subjects and together we could march on Colnora. We can catch the Empire in a vice with Melengar pushing from the north and the Nationalists from the south. The Empire would have to either recommit the Northern Army, leaving the capital to Gaunt, or let us sweep across northern Warric unopposed."

Cosmos said nothing, but there was a smile on his face. He took a drink of his wine and sat back to consider their words.

"All we need you to do," Royce spoke again, "is to set up a meeting between Gaunt and the princess."

"Once a formal agreement is struck between the Nationalists and Melengar," Arista explained. "I can take that to Trent. With the Nationalists on Aquesta's doorstep and my brother ravaging northern Warric, Trent will be more than happy to join us. And with their help, the Empire will be swept back into history, where it belongs."

"You paint a lovely picture, Your Highness," Cosmos said. "But is it possible for Melengar to break out of Medford? Will Lanaklin be able to raise a force quickly enough to fend off any counter attack the Empire sends? I suspect you would say yes to both, but without the conviction that comes from knowing. Fortunately, these are not my concerns so much as they are yours. I will contact Gaunt's people and arrange a meeting. It will take a few days, however, and in the meantime it is not safe for you to stay in Colnora."

"What do you mean?" Royce asked.

"As I said, I fear it is possible the guild has been compromised. Mr. Price tells me imperial scouts were on hand when you passed through the gate, so it would only be wishful thinking to suppose your visit here was not observed. Given the situation, it will not take a genius to determine what is happening. The next logical step will be to eliminate the threat. And, Duster, you're not the only Diamond alumnus passing through Warric."

Royce's eyes narrowed as he stared at Cosmos and studied the fat man carefully. Cosmos said nothing more on the subject, and strangely, Royce did not inquire further.

"We'll leave immediately," Royce said abruptly. "We'll head south into Rhenydd, which will carry us closer to Gaunt. I'll expect you to contact us with the meeting's place and time in three days. If by the morning of the fourth day we don't hear from you, we'll find our own way to Gaunt."

"If you don't hear from me by then, things will be very bad indeed," Cosmos assured them. "Gibbons, see that they have whatever is needed for travel. Price, arrange for them to slip out of town unnoticed, and get that message to Gaunt's people. Will you need to send a message back to Medford?" Cosmos asked the princess.

She hesitated briefly. "Not until I've reached an agreement with Gaunt. Alric knows the tentative plan and has already begun preparing the invasion."

"Excellent," Cosmos said, standing up and draining his glass. "What a pleasure it is working with professionals. Good luck to all of you and may fortune smile upon us. Just remember to watch your back, Duster. Some ghosts never die."

"Your horses and gear will be taken to Finlin's Windmills by morning," Price told them as he rapidly led them out through the rear of the patio. His long gangly legs gave him the appearance of a wayward scarecrow fleeing across a field. Noticing Arista had trouble keeping up he paused for her to catch her breath. "However, you three will be leaving by boat down the Bernum tonight."

"There'll be a watch on the Langdon and the South Bridge," Royce reminded him.

"Armed with crossbows and hot pitch, I imagine," Price replied, grinning. His face looked even more skull-like in the darkness. "But no worries, arrangements have been made."

THE JEWEL

The Bernum started as a series of tiny creeks that cascaded from Amber Heights and the Senon Upland. They converged, creating a swift-flowing river that cut through a limestone canyon, forming a deep gorge. Eventually it spilled over Amber Falls. The drop took the fight out of the water and from there on the river flowed calmly through the remaining ravine that divided the city. This put Colnora at the navigable headwater of the Bernum—the last stop for goods coming up the river, and a gateway for anyone traveling to Dagastan Bay.

After Arista regained herself, Price resumed rushing them along at a storm's pace. They ducked through a narrow ivy-covered archway and passed a wooden gate that brought them to the rear of the estate. A short stone wall, only a little above waist high, guarded the drop to the river gorge. Looking down, all she could see was darkness, but across the expanse she could make out points of light and the silhouette of buildings. Price directed them to an opening and the start of a long wooden staircase.

"Our neighbor, Bocant the pork mogul, has his six-oxen hoist," Price said, motioning to the next mansion over. Arista could just make out a series of cables and pulleys connected to a large metal box. Two lanterns, one hung at the top and another at the bottom, revealed the extent of the drop, which appeared to be more than a hundred feet. "But we have to make-do with our more traditional, albeit more dangerous, route. Try not to fall. The steps are steep and it's a long way down."

The stairs were indeed frightening—a plummeting zigzag of planks and weathered beams bolted to the cliff's face. It looked like a diabolical puzzle of wood and rusting metal, which quaked and groaned the moment they stepped on it. Arista was certain she felt it sway. Memories of a collapsing tower while she clutched on to Royce flooded back to her. Taking a deep breath, she gripped the handrail with a sweaty palm and descended, sandwiched between Royce and Hadrian.

A narrow dock sat at the bottom and a shallow-draft rowboat banged dully against it with the river's swells. A lantern mounted on the bow illuminated the area with a yellow flicker.

"Put that damn light out you fools!" Price snapped at the two men readying the craft.

A quick hand snuffed out the lantern and Arista's eyes adjusted to the moonlight. From previous trips to Colnora she knew that the river was as congested as Main Street on Hospitality Row during the day, but in the dark it lay empty the vast array of watercraft bobbing at various piers.

When the last of the supplies were aboard, Price returned their weapons. Hadrian strapped his on and Royce's white-bladed dagger disappeared into the folds of his cloak. "In you go," Price told them, putting one foot on the gunwale to steady the boat. A stocky boatman, naked to the waist, stood in the center of the skiff and directed them to their seats.

"Which one of ya might be handy with a tiller?" he asked.

"Etcher," Price said, "why don't you take the tiller?"

"I'm no good with a boat," the wiry youth with a thin mustache and goatee replied as he adjusted the lay of the gear.

"I'll take the rudder," Hadrian said.

"And grateful I am to you, sir," the boatman greeted him cheerily. "Name's Wally…you shouldn't need to use it much. I can steer fine with just the oars, but in the current it's sometimes best not ta paddle a'tall. All ya needs to do is keep her in the center of the river."

Hadrian nodded. "I can do that."

"But of course you can, sir."

Royce held Arista's hand as she stepped aboard and found a seat beside Hadrian on a shelf of worn planking. Royce followed her and took up position near the bow next to Etcher.

"When did you order the supplies brought down?" Royce asked Price, who still stood with his foot on the rail.

"Before returning to pick you up at the Regal Fox. I like to stay ahead of things." He winked. "Duster, you might remember Etcher here from the Langdon Bridge last time you were in Colnora. Don't hold that against him. Etcher volunteered to get you safely to the mills when no one else cared for the idea. Now off you go." Price untied the bowline and shoved them out into the black water.

"Stow those lines, Mr. Etcher sir," Wally said as he waited until they cleared the dock before locking the two long oars into place. With each stroke the oars creaked quietly and the skiff glided into the river's current.

The boatman sat backward as he pulled on the oars. Little effort was required as the current propelled them downstream. Wally pulled on one side or the other, correcting their course as needed. Occasionally he stroked both together to keep them moving slightly faster than the water's flow.

"Blast," Wally cursed softly.

"What is it?" Hadrian asked.

"The lantern went out on the Bocant dock. I use it to steer by. Just my luck, any other night they leave it on. They use that hoisting contraption to unload boats. Sometimes the barges are late rounding the point, and in the darkness that lantern is their marker. They never know when the barges will arrive, so they usually just leave it on all night and—oh wait, it's back. Must have just blown out or something."

"Quiet down," Etcher hissed from the bow. "This is no pleasure cruise. You're being paid to row, not be a river guide."

Royce peered into their dark wake. "Is it normal for small boats to be on the river at night?"

"Not unless you're smuggling," Wally said in a coy tone that made Arista wonder if he had firsthand experience.

"If you don't keep your traps shut someone will notice us," Etcher growled.

"Too late," Royce replied.

"What's that?"

"Behind us, there's at least one boat following."

Arista looked, but could see nothing except the line the moon drew on the black surface of the water.

"You've got a fine pair of eyes, you do," Wally said.

"You're the one that saw them," Royce replied. "The light on the dock didn't go out. The other boat blocked it when they passed in your line of sight."

"How many?" Hadrian asked.

"Six, and they're in a wherry."

"They'll be able to catch us then, won't they?" Arista questioned.

Hadrian nodded. "They race wherries down the Galewyr and here on the Bernum for prize money. No one races skiffs."

Despite this, Wally stroked noticeably harder and, combined with the current, the skiff moved along at a brisk pace, raising a breeze in their faces.

"Langdon Bridge approaching," Etcher announced.

Arista saw it towering above them as they rushed toward it. Massive pillars of stone blocks formed the arches supporting the bridge whose broad span straddled the river eight stories above. She could barely make out the curved heads of the decorative swan-shaped streetlamps that lit the bridge, creating a line of lights against the starry sky.

"There are men up there," Royce said, "and Price wasn't kidding about them having crossbows."

Wally glanced over his shoulder and peered up at the bridge before regarding Royce curiously. "What are ya, part owl?"

"Stop paddling and shut up!" Etcher ordered and Wally pulled his oars out of the water.

They floated silently, propelled by the river's current. Aided by the swan lights, the men on the span soon became visible even to

Arista. A dark boat on a black river would be hard to spot, but not impossible. The skiff started to rotate sideways as the current pushed the stern. A nod from Wally prompted Hadrian to compensate with the tiller and the boat straightened.

Light exploded into the night sky. A bright orange and yellow glow spilled onto the bridge from somewhere on the left bank. A warehouse was on fire. It burst into flame, spewing sparks skyward like a cyclone of fireflies. Silhouetted figures ran the length of the bridge and harsh shouts cut the stillness of the night.

"Now paddle!" Etcher ordered, and Wally put his back into it.

Arista used the opportunity to glance aft and now she also saw the wherry illuminated by the fire from above. It was a good fifteen-feet in length and she guessed barely four-feet across. Four men sat in two side-by-side pairs each manning an oar. Besides the oarsmen there was a man sitting in the stern and another at the bow with a grappling hook.

"I think they mean to board us," Arista whispered.

"No," Royce said. "They're waiting."

"For what?"

"I'm not sure, but I don't intend to find out. Give us as much distance as you can, Wally."

"Slide over, pal. Let me give you a hand," Hadrian told the boatman as he took up a seat beside him. "Arista, take the tiller."

The princess replaced Hadrian, grabbing hold of the wooden handle. She had no idea what to do with it and opted for keeping it centered. Hadrian rolled up his sleeves and, bracing his feet against the toggles, took one of the oars. Royce slipped off his cloak and boots and dropped them onto the floor of the boat.

"Don't do anything stupid," Etcher told him. "We've still got another bridge to clear."

"Just make sure you get them past the South Bridge and we'll be fine," Royce said. "Now, gentlemen if you could put a little distance between us."

"On three," Wally announced and they began stroking together, pulling hard and fast so that the bow noticeably rose and a wake began to froth. Caught by surprise, Etcher stumbled backward and nearly fell.

"What the blazes are—" Etcher started when Royce leapt over the gunwale and disappeared. "Damn fool. What does he expect us to do, wait for him?"

"Don't worry about Royce," Hadrian replied, as he and Wally stroked in unison. To Arista, the wherry did seem to drop farther back but perhaps that was only wishful thinking.

"South Bridge," Etcher whispered.

As they approached, Arista saw another fire blazing. This time it was a boat dock burning like well-aged kindling. The old South Bridge that marked the city's boundary was not nearly as high as the Langdon, and Arista could easily see the guards.

"They aren't going for it this time," Hadrian said. "They're staying at their posts."

"Quiet. We might slip by," Etcher whispered.

With oars held high, they all sat as still as statues. Arista found herself in command of the skiff as it floated along in the current. She quickly learned how the rudder affected the boat. The results felt backward to her, pulling right made the bow swing left. Terrified of making a mistake, she concentrated on keeping the boat centered and straight. Up ahead, something odd was being lowered from the bridge. It looked like cobwebs or tree branches dangling. She was going to steer around it when she realized it stretched the entire span.

"They draped a net!" Etcher said a little too loudly.

Wally and Hadrian back paddled, but the river's current was the victor and the skiff flowed helplessly into the fishnet. The boat rotated, pinning it sideways. Water frothed along the length threatening to tip them.

THE JEWEL

"Shore your boat and don't move from it!" A shout echoed down from above.

A lantern lowered from the bridge revealed their struggles to free themselves from the mesh. Etcher, Wally, and Hadrian slashed at the netting with knives, but before they could clear it, two imperial soldiers descended and took up position on the bank. Each was armed with a crossbow.

"Stop now or we'll kill you where you stand," the nearest soldier ordered with a harsh, anxious voice. Hadrian nodded and the three dropped their knives.

Arista could not take her eyes off the crossbows. She knew those weapons. She had seen Essendon soldiers practicing with them in the yard. They pierced old helms placed on dummies filled with straw, leaving huge holes through the heavy metal. These were close enough for her to see the sharp iron heads of the bolts—the power to pierce armor held in check by a small trigger and pointed directly at them.

Wally and Hadrian maneuvered the boat to the bank and one by one they exited, Hadrian offering Arista his hand as she climbed out. They stood side by side, Arista and Hadrian in front, Wally and Etcher behind.

"Remove your weapons," one of the soldiers ordered, motioning toward Hadrian. Hadrian paused, his eyes shifting between the two bowmen before slipping off his swords. One of the soldiers approached while the other stayed back, maintaining a clear line of sight.

"What are your names?" the foremost soldier asked.

No one answered.

The lead guard took another step forward and intently studied Arista. "Well, well, well," he said. "Look what we have here, Jus. We done caught ourselves a fine fish we have."

"Who is it?" Jus asked.

"This here is that Princess of Melengar, the one they say is a witch."

"How do you know?"

"I recognize her. I was in Medford the year she was on trial for killing her father."

"What's she doing here, ya think?"

"Don't know…what are you doing here?"

She said nothing, her eyes locked on the massive bolt heads. Made of heavy iron, the point looked sharp. Knight killers, Sir Ecton called them.

What will they do to me?

"The captain will find out," the soldier said. "I recognize these two as well." He motioned to Wally and Etcher. "I seen 'em around the city afore."

"'Course you have," Wally spoke up. "I've piloted this river for years. We weren't doing nothin' wrong."

"If you've been on this river afore, then you knows we don't allow transports at night."

Wally did not say anything.

"I don't know that one though, what's yer name?"

"Hadrian," he said, taking the opportunity to step forward as if to shake hands.

"Back! Back!" the guard shouted, bringing his bow to bear at Hadrian's chest. Hadrian immediately stopped. "Take one more step and I'll punch a hole clear through you!"

"So what's your plan?" Hadrian asked.

"You and your pals just sit tight. We sent a runner to fetch a patrol. We'll take you over to see the captain. He'll know what to do with the likes of you."

"I hope we don't have to wait long," Hadrian told them. "This damp night air isn't good. You could catch a cold. Looks like you have already. What do you think, Arista?"

"I ain't got no cold."

"Are you sure? Your eyes and nose look red. Arista, you agree with me, don't you?"

"What?" Arista said, still captivated by the crossbows. She could feel her heart hammering in her chest and barely heard Hadrian addressing her.

"I bet you two been coughing and sneezing all night, haven't you?" Hadrian continued. "Nothing worse than a summer cold. Right, Arista?"

Arista was dumbfounded by Hadrian's blathering and his obsession with the health of the two soldiers. She felt obligated to say something. "I—I suppose."

"Sneezing, that's the worst. I hate to *sneeze*."

Arista gasped.

"Just shut up," the soldier ordered. Without taking his eyes off Hadrian, he called to Jus behind him. "See anyone coming yet?"

"Not yet," Jus replied. "All of them off dealing with that fire I 'spect."

Arista never tried this under pressure before. Closing her eyes, she fought to remember the concentration technique Esrahaddon taught her. She took deep breaths, cleared her mind, and tried to calm herself. Arista focused on the sounds around her—the river lapping against the boat, the wind blowing through the trees, and the chirping of the frogs and crickets. Then slowly, one by one, she blocked each out. Opening her eyes she stared at the soldiers. She saw them in detail now, the three-day-old whiskers on their faces, their rumpled tabards, even the rusted links in their hauberks. Their eyes showed their nervous excitement and Arista thought she even caught the musky odor of their bodies. Breathing rhythmically, she focused on their noses as she began to hum then mutter. Her voice slowly rose as if in song.

"I said no—" The soldier stopped suddenly, wrinkling his nose. His eyes began to water and he shook his head in irritation. "I said no—" he began again and stopped once more, gasping for air.

At the same time, Jus was having similar problems and the louder Arista's voice rose, the greater their struggle. Raising her hand, she moved her fingers as if writing in the air.

"I—said—I—I—"

Arista made a sharp clipping motion with her hand and both of them abruptly sneezed in unison.

In that instant, Hadrian lunged forward and broke the closest guard's leg with a single kick to his knee. He pulled the screaming guard in front of him just as the other fired. The crossbow bolt caught the soldier square in the chest, piercing the metal ringlets of his halberd and staggering both of them backward. Letting the dead man fall, Hadrian picked up his bow as the other guard turned to flee. *Snap!* The bow launched the bolt. The impact made a deep resonating *thwack!* and drove the remaining guard to the ground, where he lay dead.

Hadrian dropped the bow. "Let's move!"

They jumped back in the skiff just as the wherry approached.

It came out of the darkness, its long pointed shape no longer slicing through the water. Instead, it drifted aimlessly, helpless to the whims of the current. As it approached, it became apparent why. The wherry was empty, even the oars were gone. As the boat passed by, a dark figure crawled out of the water.

"Why have you stopped?" Royce admonished, wiping his wet hair away from his face. "I would have caught up." Spotting the bodies halted his need for explanation.

Hadrian pushed the boat into the river, leaping in at the last instant. From above they could hear men's voices. They finished cutting loose the net and once free, slipped clear of the bridge. The

The Jewel

current, combined with Wally and Hadrian pulling hard on the oars, sent them flying downriver in the dark of night, leaving the city of Colnora behind them.

Chapter 8
HINTINDAR

Arista woke feeling disoriented and confused. She had been dreaming about riding in her carriage. She sat across from both Sauly and Esrahaddon. Only, in her dream, Esrahaddon had hands and Sauly was wearing his bishop's robes. They were trying to pour brandy from a flask into a cup and were discussing something—a heated argument, but she could not recall it.

A bright light hurt her eyes, and her back ached from sleeping on something hard. She blinked, squinted, and looked around. Her memory returned as she realized she was still in the skiff coasting down the Bernum River. Her left foot was asleep, and dragging it from under a bag started the sensation of pins and needles. The morning sun shone brightly. The limestone cliffs were gone, replaced by sloping farmlands. On either side of the river stretched lovely green fields swaying gently in the soft breeze. The tall spiked grass might have been wheat, although it could just as easily have been barley. Here the river was wider and moved slower. There was hardly any current, and Wally was back to rowing.

"Morning, my lady," he greeted her.

"Morning," Hadrian said from his seat at the tiller.

"I guess I dozed off," she replied, pulling herself up and adjusting her gown. "Did anyone else get any sleep?"

"I'll sleep when I get downriver," Wally replied, hauling on the oars, rocking back then sitting up again. The paddle blades dripped and plunged. "After I drop you fine folks off, I'll head down to Evlin, catch a nap and a meal, then try to pick up some travelers or freight to take back up. No sense fighting this current for nothing."

Arista looked toward Hadrian.

"Some," he told her. "Royce and I took turns."

Her hair was lose and falling in her face. Her blue satin ribbon had been lost somewhere during the night's ride from Sheridan. Since then she had been using a bit of rawhide provided by Hadrian. Even that was missing now, and she poked about her hair and found it caught in a tangle. While she worked to free it she said. "You should have woken me. I would have taken a shift at the tiller."

"We actually considered it when you started to snore."

"I don't snore!"

"I beg to differ," Hadrian chided while chewing.

She looked around the skiff as each of them, even Etcher, nodded. Her face flushed with embarrassment.

Hadrian chuckled. "Don't worry about it, you can't be held accountable for what you do in your sleep."

"Still," she said, "it's not very lady-like."

"Well, if that's all you're worried about, you can forget it," Hadrian informed her with a wicked smirk. "We lost all illusions of you being prissy back in Sheridan."

How much better it was when they were silent.

"That's a compliment," he added hastily.

"You don't 'ave much luck with the ladies do you, sir?" Wally asked, pausing briefly and letting the paddles hang out like wings, leaving a tiny trail of droplets on the smooth surface of the river. "I mean with compliments like that, an' all."

Hadrian frowned at him then turned back to her with a concerned expression. "I really did mean it as a compliment. I've never met a lady who would—well, without complaining you've been—" he paused in frustration, then added, "that little trick you managed back there was really great."

Hadrian only brought up the sneezing spell to try and smooth things over, but she had to admit a sense of pride that she had finally contributed something of value to their trip. "It was the first practical application of hand magic I've ever performed."

"I really wasn't sure you could do it," Hadrian said.

"Who would have thought such a silly thing would come in handy?"

"Travel with us long enough and you'll see we can find a use for just about anything." Hadrian extended his hand. "Cheese?" he asked. "It's really quite good."

Arista took the cheese and offered him a smile, but was disappointed he did not see it. His eyes had moved to the riverbank, and her smile faded as she ate self-consciously.

Wally continued to paddle in even strokes and the world passed slowly by. They rounded bend after bend, skirting a fallen tree then a sandy point. It took Arista nearly an hour with her brush to finally work all the knots out of her hair. She retied its length with the rawhide into a respectable ponytail. Eventually a gap opened in the river reeds to reveal a small sandy bank that showed signs of previous boat landings.

"Put in here," Etcher ordered, and Wally deftly spun the boat to land beneath the shadow of a massive willow tree. Etcher leapt out and tied the bowline. "This is our stop. Let's get the gear off."

"Not yet," Royce said. "You want to check the mill sails first?"

"Oh yeah," Etcher nodded looking a little embarrassed and a tad irritated. "Wait here," he said, before trotting up the grassy slope.

"Sails?" Hadrian asked.

"Just over this rise is the millwright Ethan Finlin's windmill,"

Royce explained. "Finlin is a member of the Diamond. His windmill is used to store smuggled goods and also serves as a signal that can be seen from the far hills. If the mill's sails are spinning, then all is clear. If furled, then there's trouble. The position of the locked sails indicates different things. If straight up and down like a ship's mast, it means he needs help. If the sails are cockeyed, it means stay away. There are other signals as well, but I am sure they've changed since I was a member."

"All clear," Etcher notified them as he strode back down the hill.

They each took a pack, waved goodbye to Wally, and climbed up the slope.

Finlin's Mill was a tall weathered tower that sat high on the crest of a grassy knoll. The windmill's cap rotated and currently faced into the wind, which blew steadily from the northeast. Its giant sails of cloth-covered wooden frames rotated slowly, creaking as they turned the great mill's shaft. Around the windmill were several smaller buildings, storage sheds, and wagons. The place was quiet and absent of customers.

They found their horses, as well as an extra one for Etcher, along with their gear in a nearby barn. Finlin briefly stuck his nose out of the mill and waved. They waved back, and Royce had a short talk with Etcher as Hadrian saddled their animals and loaded the supplies. Arista threw her own saddle on her mare, which garnered a smile from Hadrian.

"Saddle your own horse often, do you?" he asked as she reached under the horse's belly for the cinch. The metal ring at the end of the wide band swung back and forth, making catching it a challenge without crawling under the animal.

"I'm a princess, not an invalid."

She caught the cinch and looped the leather strap through it, tying what she thought was a fine knot, exactly like the one she used to tie her hair.

"Can I make one minor suggestion?"

She looked up. "Of course."

"You need to tie it tighter and use a flat knot."

"That's two suggestions. Thanks, but I think it will be fine."

He reached up and pulled on the saddle's horn. The saddle easily slid off and came to rest between the horse's legs.

"But it *was* tight."

"I'm sure it was." Hadrian pulled the saddle back up and undid the knot. "People think horses are stupid—dumb animals they call them, but they're not. This one, for instance, just out-smarted the Princess of Melengar." He pulled the saddle off, folded the blanket over, and returned the saddle to the animal's back. "You see, horses don't like to have a saddle bound around their chest any more than I suspect you enjoy being trussed up in a corset. The looser the better, they figure, because they don't really mind if you slide off." He looped the leather strap through the ring in the cinch and pulled it tight. "So what she's doing right now is holding her breath, expanding her chest and waiting for me to tie the saddle on. When she exhales, it will be loose. Thing is, I know this. I also know she can't hold her breath forever." He waited with two hands on the strap and the moment the mare exhaled he pulled, gaining a full four inches. "See?"

She watched as he looped the strap across then through and down, making a flat knot that laid comfortably against the horse's side. "Okay, I admit it. This is the first time I've saddled a horse," she confessed.

"And you're doing wonderfully," he mocked.

"You are aware I can have you imprisoned for life, right?"

Royce and Etcher entered the barn. The younger thief grabbed his horse and left without a word. "Friendly sorts, those Diamonds are," Hadrian observed.

"Cosmos seemed friendly," Arista pointed out.

"Too friendly. It's how you might expect a spider to talk to a fly as he wraps him up."

HINTINDAR

"What an interesting metaphor," Arista noted. "You could have a future in politics, Hadrian."

The fighter glanced at Royce. "We never considered that as one of the options."

"I'm not sure how it differs from acting."

"He never likes my ideas," Hadrian told her, then turned his attention back to Royce. "Where to now?"

"Hintindar," Royce replied.

"Hintindar? Are you serious?"

"It's out-of-the-way and a good place to disappear for awhile. Problem?"

Hadrian narrowed his eyes. "You know darn well there's a problem."

"What's wrong?" Arista asked.

"I was born in Hintindar."

"I've already told Etcher that's where we will wait for him," Royce said. "Nothing we can do about it now."

"But Hintindar is just a tiny manorial village—some farms and trade shops, there's no place to stay."

"Even better. After Colnora, lodging in a public house might not be too smart. There must be a few people there that still know you. I'm sure someone will lend a hand and put us up for awhile. We need to go somewhere off the beaten track."

"You don't honestly think anyone is still following us. I know the Empire would want to stop Arista from reaching Gaunt, but I doubt anybody recognized her in Colnora—at least no one still alive."

Royce did not answer.

"Royce?"

"I'm just playing it safe," he snapped.

"Royce? What did Cosmos mean back there about you not being the only ex-Diamond in Warric? What was that talk of ghosts all about?" Royce remained silent. Hadrian glared at him. "I came along as a favor to you, but if you're going to keep secrets…"

Royce relented. "It's probably nothing, but then again—Merrick could be after us."

Hadrian lost his look of irritation, and replied with a simple, "Oh."

"Anyone going to tell me who Merrick is?" Arista asked. "Or why Hadrian doesn't want to go home?"

"I didn't leave under the best of circumstances," Hadrian answered, "and haven't been back in a long time."

"And Merrick?"

"Merrick Marius, also known as Cutter, was Royce's friend once. They were members of the Diamond together, but they…" He glanced at Royce. "Well, let's just say they had a falling out."

"So?"

Hadrian waited for Royce to speak, and when he did not, answered for him. "It's a long story, but the gist of the matter is that Merrick and Royce seriously don't get along." He paused then added. "Merrick is an awful lot like Royce."

Arista continued to stare at Hadrian until the revelation dawned on her.

"Still, that doesn't mean Merrick is after us," Hadrian went on. "It's been a long time, right? Why would he bother with you now?"

"He's working for the Empire," Royce said. "That's what Cosmos meant. And if there's an imperial mole in the Diamond, Merrick knows all about us by now. Even if there isn't a spy, Merrick could still find out about us from the Diamond. There are plenty who think of him as a hero for sending me to Manzant. I'm the evil one in their eyes."

"You were in Manzant?" Arista asked, stunned.

"It's not something he likes to talk about," Hadrian again answered for him. "So if Merrick is after us, what do we do?"

"What we always do," Royce replied, "only better."

HINTINDAR

The village of Hintindar lay nestled in a small sheltered river valley surrounded by gentle hills. A patchwork of six cultivated fields, outlined by hedgerows and majestic stands of oak and ash, decorated the landscape in a crop mosaic. Horizontal lines of mounded green marked three of the fields with furrows, sown in strips, to hold the runoff. Animals grazed in the fourth field and the fifth was cut for hay. The last field lay fallow. Young women were in the fields cutting flax and stuffing it in sacks thrown over their shoulders while men weeded crops and threw up hay.

The center of the village clustered along the main road near a little river, a tributary of the Bernum. Wood, stone, and wattle and daub buildings with shake or grass-thatched roofs lined the road, beginning just past the wooden bridge and ending halfway up the hillside toward the manor house. Between them were a variety of shops. Smoke rose from buildings, the blackest of which came from the smithy. Their horses announced their arrival with a loud hollow *clop clip clop* as they crossed the bridge. Heads turned, each villager nudging the next, fingers pointing in their direction. Those they passed stopped what they were doing to follow, keeping a safe distance.

"Good afternoon," Hadrian offered, but no one replied. No one smiled.

Some whispered in the shelter of doorways. Mothers pulled children inside and men picked up pitchforks or an axe.

"This is where *you* grew up?" Arista whispered to Hadrian. "Somehow it seems more like how I would imagine Royce's hometown to be."

This brought a look from the thief.

"They don't get too many travelers here," Hadrian explained.

"I can see why."

They passed the mill, where a great wooden wheel turned with the power of the river. The town also had a leatherworker's shop, candlemaker, weaver, and even a shoemaker. They were halfway up the road when they reached the brewer.

A heavyset matron with gray hair and a hooked nose worked outside beside a large boiling vat next to a stand of large wooden casks. She watched their slow approach then walked to the middle of the road, wiping her hands on a soiled rag.

"That'll be fer 'enuf," she told them with a heavy south-province accent.

She wore a stained apron tied around her shapeless dress and a kerchief tied over her head. Her feet were bare and her face covered in dirt and sweat.

They reined their horses and she eyed each one carefully.

"Who are ya and what's your business 'ere? And be quick afore the hue and cry is called and yer carried ta the bailiff. We don't stand troublemakers here."

"Hue and cry?" Arista softly asked.

Hadrian looked over. "It's an alarm that everyone in the village responds to. Not a pretty sight." His eyes narrowed as he studied the woman. Then he slowly dismounted.

The woman took a step back and grabbed hold of a mallet used to tap the kegs. "I said I'd call the hue and cry and I meant it!"

Hadrian handed his reins to Royce and walked over to her. "If I remember correctly *you* were the biggest troublemaker in the village, Armigil, and in close to twenty years it doesn't seem much has changed."

The woman looked surprised, then suspicious. "Haddy?" she said in disbelief. "That can't be, can it?"

Hadrian chuckled. "No one's called me Haddy in years."

"Dear Maribor, 'ow you've grown, lad!" When the shock wore

off she set the mallet down and turned to the spectators now lining the road. "This 'ere is Haddy Blackwater, the son of Danbury the smithy, come back 'ome."

"How are you, Armigil?" Hadrian said with a broad smile, stepping forward to greet her.

She replied by making a fist and punching him hard in the jaw. She had put all her weight into it and winced, shaking her hand in pain. "Oww! Damned if ya 'avent got a 'ard bloody jaw!"

"Why did you hit me?" Hadrian held his chin, stunned.

"That's fer runnin' out on yer father and leaving 'im to die alone. I've been waiting ta do that fer nearly twenty years."

Hadrian licked blood from his lip and scowled.

"Oh get over it, ya baby! An' ya better keep yer eyes out fer more round 'ere. Danbury was a damn fine man and ya broke his 'eart the day ya left."

Hadrian continued to massage his jaw.

Armigil rolled her eyes. "Come 'ere," she ordered and grabbed hold of his face. Hadrian flinched as she examined him. "Yer fine, for Maribor's sake. 'Onestly, I thought yer father made ya tougher than that. If I 'ad a sword in me 'and yer shoulders would 'ave less of a burden to carry and the wee ones would 'ave a new ball to kick around, eh? 'Ere, let me get you a mug 'a ale. This batch came of age this morning. That'll take the sting out of a warm welcome it will."

She walked to a large cask, filled a wooden cup with a dark amber draught, and handed it to him. Hadrian looked at the drink dubiously. "How many times have you filtered this?"

"Three," she said, unconvincingly.

"Has his lordship's taster passed this?"

"'Acourse not ya dern fool, I just told ya it got done fermenting this morning. Brewed it day afore yesterday I did, a nice two days in the keg. Most of the sediment ought ta 'ave settled and it should 'ave a nice kick by now."

"Just don't want to get you into trouble."

"I ain't selling it to ya, now am I? So drink it and shut up or I'll 'it ya again for being daft."

"Haddy? Is it really you?" A thin man, about Hadrian's age, approached and pushed back the people milling about. He had shoulder-length blonde hair, a soft doughy face and was dressed in a worn gray tunic and a faded green cowl. His feet were wrapped in cloth up to his knees. A light brown dust covered him as if he had been burrowing through a sand hill.

"Dunstan?"

The man nodded and the two embraced, clapping each other on the shoulders. Wherever Hadrian patted Dunstan, a puff of brown powder arose leaving the two in a little cloud.

"You used to live here?" A little girl from the gathering crowd asked, and Hadrian nodded. This touched off a wave of conversations among those gathering in the street. More people rushed over and Hadrian was enveloped in their midst. Eventually he was able to get a word in and motioned toward Royce and Arista.

"Everyone, this is my friend Mr. Everton and his wife, Erma."

Arista and Royce exchanged glances.

"Vince, Erma, this is the village brew mistress, Armigil, and Dunstan here is the baker's son."

"Just the baker, Haddy, Dad's been dead five years now."

"Oh—sorry to hear that Dun. I have nothing but fond memories of trying to steal bread from his ovens."

Dunstan looked at Royce. "Haddy and I were best friends when he lived here—until he disappeared," he said with a note of bitterness.

"Will I have to endure a swing from you too?" Hadrian feigned fear.

"You should, but I remember all too well the last time I fought you."

Hadrian grinned wickedly as Dunstan scowled back.

"If my foot hadn't slipped…" Dunstan began, then the two

broke into spontaneous laughter at a joke no one else appeared to understand.

"It's good to have you back, Haddy," he said sincerely. He watched Hadrian take a swallow of beer then to Armigil he said, "I don't think it fair that Haddy gets a free pint and I don't."

"Let me give ya a bloody lip and ya can 'ave one too." She smiled at him.

"Break it up! Break it up!" bellowed a large muscular man, making his way through the crowd. He had a bull neck, full dark beard, and balding head. "Back to work all of ya!"

The crowd groaned in displeasure, but quickly quieted down as two horsemen approached. They rode down the hill coming from the manor at a trot.

"What's going on here?" the lead rider asked, reining his horse. He was a middle-aged man with weary eyes and a strong chin. He dressed in light tailored linens common to a favored servant and on his chest was an embroidered crest of crossed daggers in gold threading.

"Strangers, sir," the loud bull-necked man replied.

"They ain't strangers, sir," Armigil spoke up. "This 'ere's Haddy Blackwater, son of the old village smith—come fer a visit."

"Thank you, Armigil," he said. "But I wasn't speaking to you, I was addressing the reeve." He looked down at the bearded man. "Well, Osgar, out with it."

The burly man shrugged his shoulders and stroked his beard, looking uncomfortable. "She might be right, sir. I haven't had a chance to ask, what with getting the villeins back to work and all."

"Very well Osgar, see that they do return to work, or I'll have you in stocks by nightfall."

"Yes, sir, right away, sir." He turned bellowing at the villagers until they moved off. Only Armigil and Dunstan remained quietly behind.

"Are you the son of the old smithy?" the rider asked.

"I am," Hadrian replied. "And you are?"

"I am his lordship's bailiff. It is my duty to keep order in this village and I don't appreciate you disrupting the villein's work."

"My apologies, sir." Hadrian nodded respectfully. "I didn't mean—"

"If you're the smithy's son, where have you been?" The other rider spoke this time. Much younger looking, he was better dressed than the bailiff, wearing a tunic of velvet and linen. His legs were covered in opaque hose and his feet in leather shoes with brass buckles. "Are you aware of the penalty for leaving the village without permission?"

"I am the son of a freeman, not a villein," Hadrian declared. "And who might you be?"

The rider sneered at Hadrian. "I am the Imperial Envoy to this village, and you would be wise to watch the tone of your voice. Freemen can lose that privilege easily."

"Again, my apologies," Hadrian said. "I am only here to visit my father's grave. He died while I was away."

The envoy's eyes scanned Royce and Arista then settled on Hadrian looking him over carefully. "Three swords?" he asked the bailiff. "In this time of war an able-bodied man like this should be in the army fighting for the empress. He's likely a deserter, or a rogue. Arrest him, Siward, and take his associates in for questioning. If he hasn't committed any crimes, he will be properly pressed into the Imperial Army."

The bailiff looked at the envoy with annoyance. "I don't take my orders from you, Luret. You forget that all too frequently. If you have a problem, take it up with the steward. I'm certain he will speak to his lordship the moment he returns from loyal service to the Empire. In the meantime, I will administer this village as best I can for my lord—not for you."

Luret jerked himself upright in indignation. "As Imperial Envoy I am addressed as, *Your Excellency.* And you should understand that my authority comes directly from the empress."

"I don't care if it comes from the good lord Maribor himself. Unless his lordship, or the steward in his absence, orders me otherwise, I only have to put up with you. I don't have to take orders from you."

"We'll see about that." The envoy spun and spurred his horse back toward the manor, kicking up a cloud of dust.

The bailiff shook his head with irritation, waiting for the dust to settle.

"Don't worry," he told them. "The steward won't listen to him. Danbury Blackwater was a good man. If you're anything like him, you'll find me a friend. If not, you had best make your stay here as short as possible. Keep out of trouble. Don't interfere with the villein's work, and stay away from Luret."

"Thank you, sir," Hadrian said.

The bailiff then looked around the village in irritation. "Armigil, where did the reeve get off to?"

"Went to the east field I think, sir. There is a team 'e 'as working on drainage up thata way."

The bailiff sighed. "I need him to get more men working on bringing in the hay. Rain's coming and it will ruin what's been cut if he doesn't."

"I'll tell 'im, sir, if 'e comes back this way."

"Thank you, Armigil."

"Sir?" She tapped off a pint of beer and handed it up to him. "While you're 'ere, sir?" He took one swallow then poured the rest out and tossed her back the cup.

"A little weak," he said. "Set your price at two copper tenents a pint."

"But, sir! It's got good flavor. Let me ask three at least."

He sighed. "Why must you always be so damn stubborn? Let it

be three, but make them brimming pints. Mind you, if I hear one complaint, I'll fine you a silver and you can take your case to the Steward's Court."

"Thank you, sir," she said, smiling.

"Good day to you all." He nodded and trotted off toward the east.

They watched him go, and then Dunstan started chuckling. "A fine welcome home you've had so far—a belt in the mouth and threat of arrest."

"Actually, outside the fact that everything looks a lot smaller, not much has changed here," Hadrian observed. "Just some new faces— a few buildings, and, of course, the envoy."

"He's only been here a week," Dunstan said, "and I'm sure the bailiff and the steward will be happy when he leaves. He travels a circuit covering a number of villages in the area and has been showing up here every couple of months since the Empire annexed Rhenydd. No one likes him, for obvious reasons. He's yet to meet Lord Baldwin face to face. Most of us think Baldwin purposely avoids being here when the envoy comes. So Luret's list of complaints keeps getting longer and longer and the steward just keeps writing them down."

"So are you really here just to see your father's grave? I thought you were coming back to stay."

"Sorry, Dun, but we're just passing through."

"In that case, we had best make the most of it. What say you, Armigil? Roll a keg into my kitchen and I'll supply the bread and stools for toasts to Danbury and a proper welcome for Haddy?"

"'E don't deserve it. But I think I 'ave a keg round 'ere that is bound ta go bad if'n I don't get rid of it."

"Hobbie!" Dunstan shouted up the street to a young man at the livery. "Can you find a place for these horses?"

Dunstan and Hadrian helped Armigil roll a small barrel to the bakery. As they did, Royce and Arista walked their animals over to the stables. The boy cleared three stalls then ran off with a bucket to fetch water.

"Do you think the envoy will be a problem?" Arista asked Royce once Hobbie left.

"Don't know," he said, untying his pack from the saddle. "Hopefully we won't be here long enough to find out."

"How long will we be here?"

"Cosmos will move fast. Just a night or two, I imagine." He threw his bag over his shoulder and crossed to Hadrian's horse. "Have you decided what you'll say to Gaunt when you meet him? I hear he hates nobility, so I wouldn't start by asking him to kiss your ring or anything."

She pulled her own gear off Mystic, and then holding out her hands wiggled her bare fingers. "Actually, I thought I'd ask him to kidnap my brother." She smiled. "It worked for you. And if I can gain the trust and aid of a Royce Melborn, how hard can it be to win over a Degan Gaunt?"

They carried the gear across the street to the little whitewashed shop with the signboard portraying a loaf of bread. Inside a huge brick oven and a large wooden table dominated the space. The comforting scent of bread and wood smoke filled the air, and Arista was surprised the bakery wasn't broiling. The wattle and daub walls, and the good-sized windows, managed to keep the room comfortable. As Arista and Royce entered, they were introduced to Arbor, Dunstan's wife and a host of other people whose names Arista struggled to remember.

Once word spread, freemen, farmers, and other merchants dropped by, grabbing a pint and helping themselves to a hunk of dark bread. There was Algar the woodworker, Harbert the Tailor, and his wife Hester. Hadrian introduced Wilfred the carter, and explained how he used to rent his little wagon four times every year to travel to Ratibor to buy iron ingots for his father's smithy. There were plenty of stories of the skinny kid with pimples who used to swing a hammer beside his father. Most remembered Danbury with kindness, and there were many toasts to his good name.

Just as the bailiff predicted, it started to rain and soon the villeins, released from work due to weather, dropped by to join the gathering. They slipped in, quietly shaking off the wetness. Each got a bit of bread, a pint to drink, and a spot to sit on the floor. Some brought steaming crocks of vegetable pottage, cheese, and cabbage for everyone to share. Even Osgar the reeve pressed himself inside and was welcomed to share the community meal. The sky darkened, the wind whipped up, and Dunstan finally closed the shutters as outside the rain poured.

They all wanted to know what had happened to Haddy. Where he had gone; what he had done. Most of them spent their whole lives in Hintindar, barely crossing the river. In the case of the villeins, they were bound to the land and by law could not leave. For them, generations passed without ever setting foot beyond the valley.

Hadrian kept them entertained with stories of his travels. Arista was curious to hear of adventurous tales he and Royce had over the years, but none of those came out. Instead, he told harmless stories of distant lands. Everyone was spellbound to hear about the far east, where the Calian people interbred with the Ba Ran Ghazel to produce the half-goblin Tenkin. Children gathered close to the skirts of their mothers when he spoke about the Oberdaza—Tenkin who worshiped the dark god Oberlin and blended Calian traditions with Ghazel magic. Even Arista was captivated by his stories of far off Dagastan, so few people had ever traveled there.

With Hadrian the center of attention, few took notice of Arista, which was fine with her. She was happy just to be off her horse and in a safe place. The tension melted away from her.

The hot bread and fresh brewed beer were wonderful. She was comfortable for the first time in days and reveled in the camaraderie of the bakery. She drank pints of beer until she lost track of just how many she had. Outside night fell and the rain continued. They lit candles, giving the room an even friendlier charm. The beer was infecting the group with mirth, and soon they were singing loudly. She did not know the words, but found herself rocking with the rhythm, humming the chorus, and clapping her hands. Someone told a bawdy joke and the room burst into laughter.

"Where are you from?" It was the third time the question was asked, but the first time Arista realized it was addressed to her. Arbor, the baker's wife, sat beside her. She was a petite woman with a plain face and short-cropped hair.

"I'm sorry," Arista apologized. "I'm not accustomed to beer. The bailiff said it was weak, but I think I would take exception to that."

"From yer mouth ta 'is ears darling!" Armigil said loudly from across the room. Arista wondered how she heard from so far away, especially when she thought she had spoken so softly.

Arista remembered Arbor had asked her a question. "Oh—right, ah…Colnora," the princess said at length. "My husband and I live in Colnora. Well, actually we are staying with my brother now because we were evicted from our home in Windham Village by the Northern Imperial Army. That's up in Warric you know—Windham Village I mean, not the army. Of course it could be—the army I mean this time—not the village—because they could be there. Does that answer your question?"

The room was spinning slowly and it gave Arista the feeling she was falling, though she knew she was sitting still. The whole sensation made it difficult for her to concentrate.

"You were evicted? How awful." Arbor looked stricken.

"Well, yes, but it's not that great of a hardship really, my brother has a very nice place in the Hill District in Colnora. He's quite well off, you know?" she whispered this last part into her ear. At least she thought she did, but Arbor pulled back sharply.

"Oh really? You come from a wealthy family?" Arbor asked,

rubbing her ear. "I thought you did. I was admiring your dress. It's very beautiful."

"This? Ha!" She pulled at the material of her skirt. "I got this old rag from one of my servants who herself was ready to throw it out. You should see my gowns. Now those are something, but yes, we're very wealthy, my brother has a virtual *army* of servants," she said, and burst out laughing.

"Erma?" Someone said from behind her.

"What does your brother do?" Arbor asked.

"Hmm? Do? Oh, he doesn't *do* anything."

"He doesn't work?"

"Erma, *dear*?"

"My brother? He calls it work, but it's nothing like what *you* people do. Did you know I slept on the ground just two nights ago? Not indoors either, but out in the woods. My brother never did that. I can tell you. You probably have, haven't you? But he hasn't. No, he gets his money from taxes. That's how all kings get their money. Well, some can get it from conquest. Glenmorgan got *loads* from conquest, but not Alric. He's never been to war—until now, of course, and he's not doing well at all, I can tell you."

"ERMA!" Arista looked up to see Royce standing over her his face stern.

"Why are you calling me that?"

"I think my wife has had a little too much to drink," he said to the rest of them.

Arista looked around to see several faces smirking in an effort to suppress laughter.

"Is there anywhere I can take her to sleep it off?"

Immediately several people offered the use of their homes, some even the use of their bed saying they would sleep on the floor.

"Spend the night here," Dunstan said. "It's raining out. Do you really want to wander around out there in the dark? You can actually make a fine bed out of the flour sacks in the storeroom."

"How would you know that, Dun?" Hadrian asked, chuckling. "The wife's kicked you out a few times?" This brought a roar of laughter from the crowd.

"Haddy, *you*, my friend, can sleep in the rain."

"Come along, wife." Royce pulled Arista to her feet.

Arista looked up at him and winked. "Oh right, sorry. Forgot who I was."

"Don't apologize 'oney," Armigil told her. "That's why we're drinking in the first place. Ya just got there quicker than the rest 'o us, is all."

The next morning, Arista woke up alone and could not decide which hurt more, her head from the drink, or her back from the lumpy flour bags. Her mouth was dry, her tongue coated in some disgusting film. She was pleased to discover someone had the foresight to drop her saddlebags beside her. She pulled them open and grimaced. Everything inside smelled of horse sweat and mildew. She only brought three dresses: the one worn through the rain was a wrinkled mess, the stunning silver receiving gown she planned to wear when she met Degan Gaunt, and the one she presently wore. Surprisingly, the silver gown was holding up remarkably well and was barely even wrinkled. She brought it hoping to impress Gaunt, but recalling her conversation with Royce and how the Nationalist leader felt about royalty, she realized it was a poor choice. She would have been much better off with something simpler. It would at least have given her something decent to change into. Pulling off her dirt-stained garment she removed her corset and pulled on the dress she wore in Sheridan.

She stepped out of the storeroom and found Arbor hard at work kneading dough surrounded by dozens of cloth-covered baskets.

Villagers entered and set either a bag of flour or a sackcloth of dough on the counter along with a few copper coins. Arbor gave them an estimated pickup time of either midday or early evening.

"You do this every day?" Arista asked.

Arbor nodded with sweat glistening on her brow as she used the huge wooden paddle to slide another loaf into the glowing oven. "Normally Dun is more helpful, but he's off with your husband and Haddy this morning. It's a rare thing, so I'm happy to let him enjoy the visit. They are down at the smithy if you're interested, or would you rather have a bite to eat?"

Arista's stomach twisted. "No, thank you. I think I'll wait a bit longer."

Arbor worked with a skilled hand born of hundreds, perhaps thousands of repetitions. *How does she do it?* She knew the baker's wife got up every morning repeating the same actions as the day before. *Where is the challenge?* Arista was certain Arbor could not read and probably had few possessions, yet she seemed happy. She and Dunstan had a pleasant home and, compared to those toiling in the fields, her work was relatively easy. Dunstan seemed a kind and decent man and their neighbors were good friendly folk. While not terribly exciting, it was nonetheless a safe comfortable life, and Arista felt a twinge of envy.

"What's it like to be wealthy?"

"Hmm? Oh—well, actually, it makes life easier, but perhaps not as rewarding."

"But you travel and can see the world. Your clothing is so fine and you ride horses! I'll bet you've even ridden in a carriage, haven't you?"

Arista snorted. "Yes, I have certainly ridden in a carriage."

"And been to balls in castles where musicians play and the ladies are all dressed up in embroidered gowns of velvet?"

"Silk, actually."

"Silk? I've heard of that, but never seen it. What's it like?"

"I can show you." Arista went back into the storeroom and returned with the silver gown.

At the sight of the dress, Arbor gasped, her eyes wide. "I've never seen anything so beautiful. It's like—it's like…" Arista waited but Arbor never found her words. Finally she said, "May I touch it?"

Arista hesitated, looking first at Arbor then at the dress.

"That's okay," Arbor said quickly with an understanding smile. She looked at her hands. "I would ruin it."

"No, no," Arista told her. "I wasn't thinking that at all." She looked down at the dress in her arms once more. "What I was thinking was it was stupid for me to have brought this. I don't think I will have a chance to wear it, and it is taking up so much space in my pack. I was wondering—would you like to have it?"

Arbor looked like she was going to faint. She shook her head adamantly, her eyes wide as if with terror. "No, I—I couldn't."

"Why not? We're about the same size. I think you'd look beautiful in it."

A self-conscious laugh escaped Arbor and she covered her face with her hands, leaving flour on the tip of her nose. "Oh, I'd be a sight wouldn't I? Walking up and down Hintindar in *that*. It is awfully nice of you, but I don't go to grand balls or ride in carriages."

"Maybe one day you will, and then you will be happy you have it. In the meantime, if you ever have a bad day, you can put it on and perhaps it will make you feel better."

Arbor laughed again, only now there were tears in her eyes.

"Take it—really—you'd be doing me a favor. I do need the space." She held out the dress. Arbor reached toward it and gasped at the sight of her hands. She ran off and scrubbed them red, before taking the dress in her quivering arms, cradling it as if it were a child.

"I promise to keep it safe for you. Come back and pick it up any time, alright?"

"Of course," Arista replied, smiling. "Oh, and one more thing."

Arista handed her the corset. "If you would be so kind, I never wish to see this thing again."

Arbor carefully laid the dress down and put her arms around Arista hugging her close as she whispered, "Thank you."

When Arista stepped out of the bakery into the sleepy village her head throbbed, jolted by the brilliant sunlight. She shaded her eyes and spotted Armigil working in front of her shop stoking logs under her massive cooker.

"Morning, Erma," she called to her. "You look a might pale, lassie."

"It's your fault," Arista growled.

Armigil chuckled. "I try my best. I do indeed."

Arista shuffled over. "Can you direct me to the well?"

"Up the road four 'ouses, you'll find it in front of the smithy."

"Thank you."

Following the unmistakable clanging of a metal hammer, Arista found Royce and Hadrian under the sun canopy in the smithy's yard watching another man beating a bit of molten metal on an anvil. He was muscular and completely bald-headed, with a bushy brown moustache. If he was in the bakery last night, Arista did not remember. Beside him was a barrel of water, and not far away was the well where a full bucket rested on its edge.

The bald man dropped the hot metal into his barrel, where it hissed. "Your father taught me that," the man said. "He was a fine smith—the finest."

Hadrian nodded and recited, "Choke the hammer after stroke, grip it high when drilling die."

This brought laughter from the smith. "I learned that one too. Mr. Blackwater was always making up rhymes."

"So this is where you were born?" Arista asked, dipping a community cup into the bucket of water and taking a seat on the bench beside the well.

"Not exactly," Hadrian replied. "I lived and worked here, I was actually born across the street there at Gerty and Abelard's home." He pointed at a tiny wattle and daub hovel without even a chimney. "Gerty was the midwife back then. My father kept pestering her so much that she took mum to her house and Da had to wait outside in the rain during a terrible thunderstorm, or so I was told."

Hadrian motioned to the smith. "This is Grimbald, he appreciced to my father sometime after I left—does a good job too."

"You inherited the smithy from Danbury?" Royce asked.

"No, Lord Baldwin owns the smithy. Danbury rented from him just as I do. I pay ten pieces of silver a year and in return for charcoal I do work for the manor at no cost."

Royce nodded. "What about personal belongings? What became of Danbury's things?"

Grimbald raised a suspicious eyebrow. "He left me his tools and if'n you're after them you'll have to fight me before the steward in the manor court."

Hadrian raised his hands and shook his head calming the burly man. "No, no, I'm not here after anything. His tools are in good hands."

Grimbald relaxed a bit. "Ah, okay, good then. I do have something for you, though. When Danbury died, he made a list of all his things and who they should go to. Almost everyone in the village got a little something. I didn't even know the man could write until I saw him scribbling it. There was a letter and instructions to give it to his son, if he ever returned. I read it, but it didn't make much sense. I kept it though."

Grimbald set down his hammer and ducked inside the shop, emerging a few minutes later with the letter.

Hadrian took the folded parchment and without opening it stuffed the note into his shirt pocket and walked away.

"What's going on?" Arista asked Royce. "He didn't even read it."

"He's in one of his moods," Royce told her. "He'll mope for awhile. Maybe get drunk. He'll be fine tomorrow."

"But why?"

Royce shrugged. "Just the way he is lately. It's nothing really."

Arista watched Hadrian disappear around the side of the candlemaker's shop. Picking up the hem of her dress, she chased after him. When she rounded the corner, she found him seated on a fence rail, his head in his hands. He glanced up.

Is that annoyance or embarrassment on his face?

Biting her lip she hesitated, then walked over and sat beside him. "Are you alright?" she asked.

He nodded in reply but said nothing. They sat in silence for awhile.

"I used to hate this village," he offered at length, his tone distant and his eyes searching the side of the shop. "It was always so small." He lowered his head again.

She waited.

Does he expect me to say something now?

From down the street she heard the rhythmic hammering of metal as Grimbald resumed his work, the blows marking the passage of time. She pretended to straighten her skirt, wondering if it would be better if she left.

"The last time I saw my father we had a terrible fight," Hadrian said without looking up.

"What about?" Arista gently asked.

"I wanted to join Lord Baldwin's men-at-arms. I wanted to be a soldier. He wanted me to be a blacksmith." Hadrian scuffed the dirt with his boot. "I wanted to see the world, have adventures—be a hero. He wanted to chain me to that anvil. And I couldn't understand it. I was good with a sword, he saw to that. He trained me every day. When I couldn't lift the sword anymore, he just made me switch arms. Why'd he do that if he wanted me to be a smith?"

A vision swept back to her of two faces in Avempartha—the heir she did not recognize—but Hadrian's face was unmistakable as the guardian.

Royce didn't tell him? Should I?

"When I told him my plans to leave, he was furious. He said he didn't train me to gain fame or money. That my skills were meant for *greater things*, but he wouldn't say what they were.

"The night I left, we had words—lots of them—and none of them good. I called him a fool. I might even have said he was a coward. I don't remember. I was seventeen. I ran away and did just what he didn't want me to. I was gonna show him—prove the old man wrong. Only he wasn't. It's taken me this long to figure that out. Now it's too late."

"You never came back?"

Hadrian shook his head. "By the time I returned from Calis, I heard he'd died. I didn't see any point in returning." He pulled the letter out. "Now there's this." He shook the parchment in his fingers.

"Don't you want to know what it says?"

"I'm afraid to find out." He continued to stare at the letter as if it were a living thing.

She placed a hand on his arm and gave a soft squeeze. She did not know what else to do. She felt useless. Women were supposed to be comforting, consoling, nurturing, but she did not know how. She felt awful for him, and her inability to do anything to help just made her feel worse.

Hadrian stood up. With a deep breath he opened the letter and began reading. Arista waited. Slowly he lowered his hand holding the letter at his side.

"What does it say?"

Hadrian held out the letter, letting it slip from his fingers. Before she could take it, the parchment drifted to the ground at her feet. As she bent to pick it up, Hadrian walked away.

Arista rejoined Royce back at the well.

"What was in the letter?" he asked. She held it out to Royce who carefully read it. "What was his reaction?"

"Not good. He walked off. I think he wants to be alone. You never told him, did you?"

Royce continued to study the letter.

"I can't believe you never told him. I mean, I know Esrahaddon told us not to but I guess I just expected that you would anyway."

"I don't trust that wizard. I don't want me or Hadrian wrapped up in his little schemes. I could care less who the guardian is, or the heir for that matter. Maybe it *was* a mistake coming here."

"You came here on purpose? You mean this had nothing to do with—you came here for proof, didn't you?"

"I wanted something to confirm Esrahaddon's claim. I really didn't expect to find anything."

"He just told me his father trained him night and day in sword fighting and said his skills were *for greater things*. Sounds like proof to me. You know, you would have discovered that if you had just talked to him. He deserves the truth and when he gets back, one of us needs to tell him."

Royce nodded, carefully refolding the letter. "I'll talk to him."

Chapter 9
THE GUARDIAN

The oak clenched the earth with a massive hand of gnarled roots unchanged by time. In the village, houses were lost to fires. New homes were built to accommodate growing families and barns were raised on once vacant land, but on this hill time stood as still as the depths of Gutaria Prison. Standing beneath its leaves, Hadrian felt young again.

It was at this tree that Haddy first kissed Arbor, the shoemaker's daughter. He and Dunstan competed for her favor for years, but Haddy kissed her first. That's what started the fight. Dun knew better. He had seen Haddy spar with his father and witnessed Haddy beat the old reeve for whipping Willie, a villein friend of theirs. The reeve was too embarrassed to report to the bailiff that a fourteen-year-old boy bested him. Haddy's skill was no secret to Dunstan, but rage overcame reason.

When Dunstan found out about Arbor he charged at Haddy, who instinctually sidestepped and threw him to the ground. Misfortune landed Dun's head on a fieldstone. He lay unconscious with blood running from his nose and ears. Horrified, Haddy carried him back to the village, convinced he just killed his best friend. Dun recovered, but Haddy never did. He never spoke to Arbor again. Three days later, the boy known as Haddy was gone for good.

Hadrian slumped to the ground and sat in the shade of the tree with his back to the old oak's trunk. As a boy, this is where he always came to think. From here, he could see the whole village below and the hills beyond—hills that had called to him, and a horizon that whispered of adventure and glory.

Royce and Arista would be wondering where he went. It was not like him to be self-indulgent on the job. *The job!* He unconsciously shook his head. It was Royce's job not his. He kept his bargain, and all that remained was for Arista to reach the rendezvous. When she did, that would end the assignment and his career in the world of intrigue. Strange how the end brought him back to the beginning. Coming full circle could be a sign for him to make a fresh start.

He could see the smithy near the center of the village. It was easy to pick out by the black smoke rising. He had worked those bellows for hours each day. He remembered the sound and the ache in his arms. It was a time when all he knew of the world stopped at this tree, and Hadrian could not help but wonder how his life might have been if he had stayed. One thing was certain; he would have more calluses and less blood on his hands.

Would I have married Arbor? Have children of my own? A stout, strong son who would complain about working the bellows and come to this tree to kiss his first girl? Could I have found contentment making ploughshares and watching Da smile as he taught his grandson fencing, like a commoner's version of the Pickerings? If I had stayed, at this very moment, would I be sitting here thinking of my happy family below? Would Da have died in peace?

He sighed heavily. Regret was a curse without a cure, except to forget. He closed his eyes. He did not want to think. He fell asleep to the sound of songbirds and woke to the thunder of horses' hooves.

The Guardian

It was almost dark and Royce was worried. Once more, they enjoyed the hospitality of the Bakers. Arbor was making a dinner of pottage while Dunstan ran a delivery of loaves to the manor. Arista offered assistance, but appeared more a hindrance than a help. Arbor did not seem to mind. The two were inside chatting and laughing while Royce stood outside, watching the road with an uneasy feeling.

The village felt different to him. The evening had an edge, a tension to the air. Somewhere in the distance, a dog barked. He felt a nervous energy in the trees and an apprehension rising from the earth and rock. Before Avempartha, he considered it intuition, now he wondered. Elves drew power from nature. They understood the river's voice and the chatter of the leaves.

Had that passed to me?

He stood motionless, his eyes panning the road, shops, houses, and the dark places between. He was hoping to spot Hadrian returning, but felt something else.

"The cabbage goes in last," Arbor was telling Arista, her voice muffled by walls. "And cut it up into smaller pieces than that. Here let me show you."

"Sorry," Arista said. "I don't have a lot of experience in a kitchen."

"It must be wonderful to have servants. Dun could never make that much money here. There aren't enough people to buy his bread."

Royce focused on the street. The sun had set and the twilight haze had begun to mask the village. He was looking at the candlemaker's shop when he spotted movement by the livery. When he looked closer, nothing was there. It could have been Hobbie coming to check the animals, but the fact that the image vanished so quickly made him think otherwise.

Royce slipped into the shadows behind Armigil's brew shop and crept toward the livery. He entered from the rear, climbing to the loft. A fresh pile of hay cushioned his movements and muted his approach. In the dark, he could clearly see the back of a figure standing by the doorway, peering at the street.

"Move and die," Royce whispered softly in his ear. The man froze.

"Duster?"

Royce turned the man to face him. "Etcher, what are you doing here?"

"The meeting has been set. I've been sent to fetch you."

"That was fast."

"We got word back this morning and I rode hard to get here. The meeting is set for tonight at the ruins of Amberton Lee. We need to get going if we are going to make it in time."

"We can't leave right now. Hadrian is missing."

"We can't wait. Gaunt's people are suspicious—they think it could be an imperial trap. They'll back off if we don't stick to the plan. We need to leave now or the opportunity will pass."

Royce silently cursed to himself. It was his own fault for not chasing after Hadrian this afternoon. He almost had. Now there was no telling where he was. Etcher was right—the mission had to come first. He would leave word for Hadrian with the Bakers and get the princess to her meeting with Gaunt.

The moist, steamy smell of the boiling cabbage and wood smoke filled the bakery. The candles Arista lit flickered with the opening of the door. Arbor was stirring the pot while Arista set the table. Both looked up startled.

"Hadrian hasn't shown?"

"No," Arista replied.

"We need to get going," Royce told her.

"Now? But what about Hadrian?"

"He'll have to catch up. Get your things."

Arista hesitated only a moment, and then crossed to the flour storage to gather her bags.

"Can't you even stay for dinner?" Arbor asked. "It's almost ready."

"We need to get moving, we have a—" Royce stopped as he heard the noisy approach of a horse and cart being driven fast down the road. It stopped just out front, so close they could hear the driver pull the hand-break. Dunstan came through the door a moment later.

"Hadrian's been arrested!" he announced hurriedly, and then he pointed at Royce and Arista. "The steward ordered your arrests as well."

"Their arrests?" Arbor said shocked. "But why?"

"The bailiff was wrong. It looks like Luret has more influence than he thought," Royce muttered. "Let's get the horses."

"His lordship's soldiers were just behind me as I started down the hill. They will be here in minutes," Dunstan said.

"My horse is down by the river," Etcher said. "It can carry two."

Royce was thinking quickly, calculating risk and outcome. "You take her to the rendezvous on your horse then," he told Etcher. "I'll see what I can do to help Hadrian. With any luck, we'll catch up to you. If we don't, it shouldn't matter." He looked at Arista. "From what I've heard of your *contact*, he will see to your safety even if he ultimately declines your offer."

"Don't worry about me." The princess rushed toward the door with her bags. "I'll be fine, just see that Hadrian is okay." Taking a bag and the princess' hand, Etcher pulled her out into the night and dodged into the shadows of the buildings.

Royce followed them out, caught hold of the eaves, and climbed up on the Bakers' shake roof, where he crouched in the shadow of the chimney, listening. From the direction of the manor, he watched half a dozen men with torches moving fast down the main street. They stopped first at the livery then went to the Bakers.

"Where are the strangers that rode in with the old blacksmith's son?" a loud voice he had not heard before demanded.

"They left hours ago," Dunstan replied.

Royce heard a grunt and a crash followed by a scream from Arbor and the sound of furniture falling over.

"Their horses are still in the livery. We saw you race from the manor to warn them! Now where are they?"

"Leave him alone!" Arbor shouted. "They ran out when they heard you coming. We don't know where. They didn't tell us anything."

"If you're lying, you'll be arrested for treason and hanged, do you understand?"

There was a brief silence.

"Fan out in pairs. You two cover the bridge. You and you search the fields and you two start going door to door. Until further notice, all citizens of Hintindar are to remain in their homes. Arrest anyone outside. Now move!"

The men scattered out of the bakery in all directions, marked conveniently by their flaming torches, leaving Royce to watch them scurrying about. He glanced across the fields. It was dark. Etcher would have no trouble avoiding the foot search. Once they reached his horse, they would be gone. Arista was safely on her way, his job done. All he had to worry about now was Hadrian.

The manor house's jail was less a dungeon and more an old well. Forced to descend by a rope, Hadrian was left trapped at the bottom.

THE GUARDIAN

He waited in silence, looking up at the stars. The rising moon cast a shaft of pale light that descended the wall, marking the slow passage of the night.

Cold spring water seeped in through the walls, leaving them damp and creating a shallow pool at the base. With his feet tiring, Hadrian eventually sat in the cold puddle. Jagged rocks hidden under the water added to his misery. In time, he was forced to stand again to fight the cold.

The moonlight was more than halfway down the wall when Hadrian heard voices and movement from above. Dark silhouettes appeared and the iron grate scraped as it slid clear. A rope lowered and Hadrian thought they had reconsidered. He stood up to take hold of it, but stopped when he saw another figure coming down.

"In ya go," someone at the top ordered and laughed, his voice echoed. "We keep all our rats down there!"

The figure was nimble and descended quickly.

"Royce?" Hadrian asked. "They—they *captured you*?"

The rope flew up and the grate slid back.

"More or less," he replied, glancing around. "Not much on accommodations, are they?"

"I can't believe they caught you."

"It wasn't as easy as you'd think. They aren't very bright." Royce reached out and let his fingers run over the glistening walls. "Was this just a well that went dry?"

"Hintindar doesn't have much need for a big prison." Hadrian shook his head. "So you *let* them capture you?"

"Ingenious don't you think?"

"Oh—brilliant."

"I figured it was the easiest way to find you." Royce shuffled his feet in the water, grimacing. "So what's your excuse? Did they come for you with an army of twenty heavily armored men?"

"They caught me sleeping."

Royce shot him a skeptical look.

"Let's just say I was put in a position where I'd have to kill people and I chose not to. This is my home, remember. I don't want to be known as a killer here."

"So it *is* good I didn't slit throats. I'm smarter than I thought."

"Oh yes, I can see the genius in your plan." Hadrian looked up. "How do you suggest we get out now?"

"Eventually, Luret will haul us out and hand us over to a press gang just as he threatened. We'll serve in the Imperial Army for a few days, learn what we can, and then slip away. We can report what we discover to Alric for an added bonus."

"What about Arista?"

"She's safely on her way to the rendezvous with Gaunt. Etcher arrived just before dark and I sent her with him. She'll likely stay with Gaunt, sending dispatches back to Melengar via messengers until Alric's forces join with the Nationalists."

"And if Gaunt turns her down?"

"It's in Gaunt's best interest to see to her safety. It's not like he's going to turn her over to the Empire. She'll probably end up returning to Melengar by sea. Actually, it's better we aren't with her. If Merrick *is* out there, I am sure he'll be more interested in me than her. So that job is complete."

"I guess there is that to be thankful for at least."

Royce chuckled.

"What?"

"I'm just thinking about Merrick. He'll have no idea where I am now. My disappearance will drive him crazy."

Hadrian sat down.

"Isn't that water cold?" Royce asked, watching him and making an unpleasant face.

He nodded. "And the bottom has sharp rocks coated in a disgusting slime."

Royce looked up at the opening once more then gritted his teeth and slowly eased himself down across from Hadrian. "Oh yeah, real comfortable."

They sat in silence for a few minutes, listening to the breeze flutter across the grating. It made a humming noise when it blew just right. Occasionally a droplet of water would drip into the pool with a surprisingly loud *plop!* magnified by the stone.

"You realize that with this job over, I am officially retired."

"I assumed as much." Royce fished beneath him, withdrew a rock, and tossed it aside.

"I was thinking of returning here. Maybe Grimbald could use a hand, or Armigil. She's getting older now and probably would welcome a partner. Those barrels can be heavy and brewing beer has its perks."

Moonlight revealed Royce's face. He looked tense.

"I know you're not happy with this, but I really need a change. I'm not saying I'll stay here. I probably won't, but it's a start. I consider it practice for a peaceful life."

"And that's what you want, a peaceful life? No more dreams of glory?"

"That's all they were, Royce, just dreams. It's time I faced that and got on with my life."

Royce sighed. "I have something to tell you. I should have told you a long time ago, but—I guess I was afraid you'd do something foolish." He paused. "No, that's not true either. It's just taken me awhile to see that you have the right to know."

"Know what?"

Royce looked around him. "I never thought I'd be telling you in a place like this, but I have to admit it could be a benefit that they took your weapons." He pulled out Danbury's letter.

"How do you have that?" Hadrian asked.

"From Arista."

"Didn't they take it when they grabbed you?"

"Are you kidding? I practically had to remind them to take my dagger. They don't seem too accustomed to thieves, much less ones that turn themselves in." Royce handed the note to Hadrian. "What did you think of when you read this?"

"That my father died filled with pain and regret. He believed the words of a selfish seventeen-year-old that he was a coward and wasted his life. It's bad enough I left him, but I had to paint that stain on him before leaving."

"Hadrian, I don't think this letter had anything to do with your leaving. I think it is due to your heritage. I think your father was trying to tell you something about your past."

"What are you saying?"

"I'm saying your father had a secret—a big secret."

"How would you know? You never met my father. You're not making any sense."

Royce sighed. "Last year in Avempartha, Esrahaddon was using a spell to find the heir."

"I remember, you told me that before."

"But I didn't tell you everything. The spell didn't find the heir exactly, but rather magical amulets worn by him and his guardian. Esrahaddon made the necklaces so he could locate the wearers and prevent other wizards from finding them. As I said, I didn't recognize the face of the heir."

"And this is important why?"

"I didn't know, at least not for certain, not really. I always thought Esra was using us. That's mainly why I never told you. I wanted to be sure it was true, that's why I asked you to come and why I led us here."

Royce paused a moment then asked, "Where did you get that necklace, the amulet you wear under your shirt?"

"I told you, my father…"

Hadrian paused, staring at Royce, his hand unconsciously rising to his neck to feel the necklace.

"I didn't recognize the heir…but I did recognize the guardian. Your father had a secret Hadrian—a *big* secret."

Hadrian continued to stare back at Royce. His mind flashed back to his youth, to his gray-haired father spending day after day toiling humbly on the anvil and forge making harrows and ploughshares. He recalled Danbury growling at him to clean the shop.

"No," Hadrian said. "My father was a blacksmith."

"How many blacksmiths teach their sons ancient Teshlor combat skills, most of which have been lost for centuries? Where did you get that big spadone sword you've carried on your back since I first met you? Was that your father's too?"

He slowly nodded and felt a chill raise the hairs on his arms. He never told Royce about that. He never told anyone. He took the sword the night he left. He needed his own blade. Da often had several weapons in his shop, but taking them would cost his father money. Instead, he took the only weapon he felt his father would not miss. Da kept the spadone hidden in a small compartment under the shop's fifth floorboard. Hadrian remembered Danbury taking it out only once. It was a long time ago when his mother was still alive. He was very young and could barely remember it. His mother was asleep and he was supposed to be too, but something woke him. He crawled out of bed and found his father in the shop. Da had been drinking Armigil's ale and was sitting on the floor in the glow of the forge. In his hands, he cradled the huge two-handed sword, talking to it as if it was a person. He was crying. In seventeen years of living with the man, Hadrian only saw him cry that one time.

"I want you to do me a favor. Read this again, only this time pretend you hadn't run away. Read it as if you and your father were on great terms and that he was proud of you."

Hadrian held the parchment up to the moonlight and read it again.

Haddy,

I hope this letter will find you. It is important that you know there was a reason why you should never use the training for money or fame. I should have told you the truth, but my pain was too great. I can admit to you now I am ashamed of my life, ashamed of what I failed to do. I suppose you were right. I am a coward. I let everyone down. I hope you can forgive me, but I can never forgive myself.

Love Da

Before you were born, the year ninety-two
Lost what was precious, and that what was new.
The blink of an eye, the beat of a heart
Out went the candle, and guilt was my part.

A king and his knight, went hunting a boar
A rat and his friends, were hunting for lore.
Together they fought, till one was alive
The knight sadly wept, No king had survived.

The answers to riddles, to secrets and more
Are found in the middle of Legends and Lore.
Seek out the answer, and learn if you can
The face of regret, the life of a man.

"You realize a spadone is a knight's weapon?" Royce asked.

Hadrian nodded.

"And yours is a very old sword, isn't it?"

Hadrian nodded again.

"I would venture to guess it's about nine hundred years old. I think you are the descendent of Jerish, the Guardian of the Heir," Royce told him. "Although maybe not literally. The way I heard it, the heir has a direct bloodline but the guardian just needed to pass down his skills. The next in line didn't need to be his son, although I guess it's possible."

Hadrian stared at Royce. He did not know how to feel about this. Part of him was excited, thrilled, vindicated, and part of him was certain Royce was insane.

"And you kept this from me?" Hadrian asked, astonished.

"I didn't want to tell you until I knew for sure. I thought Esrahaddon might be playing us."

"Don't you think I would have thought of that too? What do you take me for? Have you worked with me for twelve years because you think I'm stupid? How conceited can you be? You can't trust me to make my own decisions, so you make them for me?"

"I'm telling you now, aren't I?"

"It took you a whole damn year, Royce!" Hadrian shouted at him. "Didn't you think I'd find this important? When I told you I was miserable because I felt my life lacked purpose—that I wanted a cause worth fighting for—you didn't think that protecting the heir qualified?" Hadrian shook his head in disbelief. "You stuck-up, manipulative, lying—"

"I *never* lied to you!"

"No, you just concealed the truth, which to me is a lie, but in *your* twisted little mind is a virtue!"

"I knew you were going to take it this way," Royce said in a superior tone.

"How else would you expect me to take it? Gee pal, thanks for thinking so little of me that you couldn't tell me the truth about my own life?"

"That's not the reason I didn't tell you," Royce snapped.

"You just said it was!"

"I know I did!"

"So you're lying to me again?"

"Call me a liar one more time—"

"And what? What? You going to fight me?"

"It's dark in here."

"But there's no room for you to hide. You're only a threat until I get my hands on you. I just need to grab your spindly little neck. For all your quickness, once I get a grip on you it's all over."

Without warning, cold water poured down on them. Looking up they could see silhouetted figures.

"You boys, be quiet down there!" shouted a voice. "His Excellency wants a word with you."

One head disappeared from view and another replaced it at the opening's edge.

"I am Luret, the Imperial Envoy of Her Eminence the Grand Imperial Empress Modina Novronian. Because of your involvement in escorting a member of the royal court of Melengar to Her Majesty's enemy, the Nationalists, the two of you are hereby charged with espionage and hitherto will be put to death by hanging in three days' time. Should, however, you wish to attempt to rescind that sentence to life in prison, I would be willing to do so under the condition that you reveal to me the whereabouts of the Princess Arista Essendon of Melengar."

Neither said a word.

"Tell me where she is, or you will be hanged as soon as the village carpenter can build a proper gallows."

Again they were silent.

"Very well, perhaps a day or two rotting in there will change your mind." He turned away and spoke to the jailor. "No food or water. It might help to loosen their tongues, besides there's really no sense in wasting it."

They waited in silence as the figures above moved away.

"How does he know?" Hadrian whispered.

A ghastly look stole over Royce's face.

"What is it?"

"Etcher. He's the mole in the Diamond."

Royce kicked the wall causing a splash. "How could I have been so blind!? He was the one who lit the lamp on the river alerting the wherry behind us. The only reason he never thought to check the mill's sails was because it didn't matter to him. I bet he never even told Price where we were, so there would be no way for the Diamond to find us. There must be an ambush waiting at Amberton Lee, or somewhere along the way."

"But why take her there? Why not just turn Arista over to Luret?"

"I'd wager this is Merrick's game. He doesn't want some imperial clown like Luret getting the prize. She's a commodity which can be sold to the Empire, or ransomed to Melengar for a profit. If Luret grabs her he gets nothing,"

"So why tell Luret about us at all?"

"Insurance. With the manor officials after us, we'd be pressed for time and wouldn't question Etcher's story. I'm sure it was to hasten our departure and have us unprepared, but it turned out even better because you were captured and I decided to stay behind to help you."

"And you sent Arista off alone with Etcher."

"She's on her way to Merrick, or Guy, or both. Maybe they'll keep her and demand Alric surrender Medford. He won't, of course. Pickering won't let him."

"I can't believe Alric sent her in the first place. What an idiot!

Why didn't he pick a representative outside the royal court? Why did he have to send *her?*"

"He didn't send her," Royce said. "I doubt anyone in Medford has a clue where she is. She did this on her own."

"What?"

"She arrived at The Rose & Thorn unescorted. Have you *ever* seen her go anywhere without a bodyguard?"

"So why did you—"

"Because I needed an excuse to bring you here, to find out if what Esrahaddon showed me was true."

"So this is *my* fault?" Hadrian asked.

"No, it's everyone's fault: you for pushing so hard to retire, me for not telling you the truth, Arista for being reckless, even your father for never having told you who you really were."

They sat in silence a moment.

"So what do we do now?" Hadrian said at last. "Your original plan isn't going to work so well anymore."

"Why do I always have to come up with the plans, Mr. I'm-not-so-stupid?"

"Because, when it comes to deciding how I should live my own life—I should be the one to choose—but when getting out of a prison, even as pathetic as it is, that's more your area of expertise."

Royce sighed and began to look around at the walls.

"By the way," Hadrian began, "what was the *real* reason you didn't tell me?"

"Huh?"

"A bit ago you said—"

"Oh," Royce continued to study the walls. He seemed a little too preoccupied by them. Just as Hadrian was sure he would not answer, Royce said, "I didn't want you to leave."

Hadrian almost laughed at the comment, thinking it was a joke, and then nearly bit his tongue. It was hard to think of Royce as anything but callous. Then he realized Royce never had a family and precious few friends. He grew up an orphan on the streets of Ratibor, stealing his food and clothes and likely receiving his share of beatings for it. He probably joined the Diamond as much from a desire to belong as a means to profit. After only a few short years they betrayed him. Hadrian realized at that moment Royce did not see him just as his partner, but his family. Along with Gwen and perhaps Arcadius, they were the only ones he had.

"You ready?" Royce asked.

"For what?"

"Turn around, let's go back to back and link arms."

"You're kidding. We aren't going to do that again, are we?" Hadrian said miserably. "I've been sitting in cold water for hours. I'll cramp."

"You know another way to get up there?" Royce asked, and Hadrian shook his head. Royce looked up. "It isn't even as high as the last time and it's narrower so it will be easier. Stand up and stretch a second. You'll be fine."

"What if the guard is up there with a stick to poke us with?"

"Do you want to get out of here or not?"

Hadrian took a deep breath. "I'm still mad at you," he said, turning and linking arms back to back with Royce.

"Yeah well, I'm not too happy with me either right now."

They began pushing against each other as they walked up the walls of the pit. Immediately Hadrian's legs began to protest the effort, but the strain on his legs was taken up some by the tight linking of their arms and the stiff leverage it provided.

"Push harder against me," Royce told him.

"I don't want to crush you."

"I'm fine just lean back more."

Initially the movement was clumsy and the exertion immense, but soon they fell into a rhythm.

"Step," Royce whispered. The pressure exerted against each other was sufficient to keep them pinned.

"Step." They slid another foot up, scraping over the stony sides.

The water running down the walls gave birth to a slippery slime and Hadrian carefully placed his feet on the drier bricks and used the cracks for traction. Royce was infinitely better at this sort of thing, and likely impatient with their progress. Hadrian was far less comfortable and often pushed too hard. His legs were longer and stronger and he had to keep remembering to relax.

They finally rose above the level of the slime to where the rock was dry, and moved with more confidence. They were now high enough that a fall would break bones. He started to perspire with the exertion and his skin was slicked with sweat. A droplet cascaded down his face and hung dangling on the tip of his nose. Above he could see the grate growing larger, still a maddening distance away.

What if we can't make it? How can we get back down besides falling?

Hadrian had to push the thought out of his mind and concentrate. Nothing good would come from anticipating failure. Instead, he forced himself to think of Arista riding to her death or capture. They had to make it up—and quickly—before his legs lost all of their strength. Already they shook from fatigue, buckling under the strain.

As they neared the top, Royce stopped calling steps. Hadrian kept his eyes on the wall where he placed his feet, but felt Royce tilting his head back peering up. "Stop," he whispered. Panting for air they steadied themselves, unlinked arms, and grabbed the grating. Letting their tortured legs fall loose, they hung for a minute. The release of the strain was wonderful, and Hadrian closed his eyes with pleasure as he gently swayed.

"Good news and bad news," Royce said. "No guards, but it's locked."

"You can do something about that, right?"

"Just give me a second."

He could feel Royce shifting around behind him. "Got it." There was another brief pause and Hadrian's fingers were starting to hurt. "Okay, we'll slide it to your left, ready? Feet up."

Lighter than Hadrian expected, they slid the grate clear of the opening and in one fluid movement hauled themselves out. Rolling on the damp grass of the manor's lawn, they lay for a second catching their breath. They were alone in a darkened corner of the manor's courtyard.

"Weapons?" Hadrian asked.

"I'll check the house. You see about getting horses."

"Don't kill anyone," Hadrian mentioned.

"I'll try not to, but if I see Luret—"

"Oh yeah, kill him."

Hadrian worked his way carefully toward the courtyard stable. The horses made a sudden start at his approach, snorting and bumping loudly into the stall dividers. He grabbed the first saddle and bridle he found and discovered they were familiar. Arista's bay mare, his horse, and Mouse were corralled with the rest.

"Easy girl," Hadrian whispered softly as he threw the blankets on two of them. He buckled the last bridle around Mouse's neck when Royce came in carrying a bundle of swords.

"Your weapons, sir knight."

"Luret?" Hadrian asked, strapping his swords on.

Royce made a disappointed sound. "Didn't see him. Didn't see hardly anyone. These country folk go to bed early."

"We're a simple lot."

"Mouse?" Royce muttered. "I just can't seem to get rid of this horse, can I?"

Arista discovered riding on the back of a horse was significantly less comfortable than riding in a saddle. Etcher added to her misery by keeping the horse at a trot. The hammering to Arista's body caused her head to ache. She asked for him to slow down, but was ignored. Before long, the animal slowed to a walk on its own. It frothed and Arista could feel its sweat soaking her gown. Etcher kicked the beast until it started again. When the horse once more returned to a walk, the thief resorted to whipping it with the ends of the reins. He missed and struck Arista hard across the thigh. She yelped, but that was also ignored. Eventually Etcher gave up and let the horse rest. She asked where they were going and why they needed to rush. Still, he said nothing—he never even turned his head. After a mile or two, he drove the animal into a trot once more. It was as if she was not there.

With each jarring clap on the horse's back Arista became increasingly aware of her vulnerability. She was alone with a strange man somewhere in the backwoods of Rhenydd, where any authority of law would seize her rather than him, regardless of what he did. All she knew about him—the only thing she could be certain of—was that he was morally dubious. While it was one thing to trust herself to Royce and Hadrian, it was quite another to leap onto the back of a horse with a stranger who took her off into the wilds. If she had time to think, she might have declined to go, but now it was too late. She rode trusting to the mercy of a dangerous man in a hostile land.

His silence did nothing to alleviate her fear. When it came to silence, Etcher put Royce to shame. He said nothing at all. The profession of thievery was not likely to attract gregarious types but Etcher seemed an extreme case. He even refused to look at her. This was perhaps better than other alternatives. A man such as Etcher was likely only acquainted with sun-baked, easy women in dirty dresses. How appealing must it be to have a young noblewoman clutching to him alone in the wilderness—and a royal princess at that.

If he attacks me, what can I do?

THE GUARDIAN

A good high-pitched scream would draw a dozen armed guards in Essendon castle, but since leaving Hintindar she had not seen a house or a light. Even if someone heard her she would probably spend her life in an imperial prison once her identity was discovered. He could do with her as he willed and when he was done he could kill her or hand her over to imperial authorities who would no doubt pay him for the service. No one would care if he delivered her bruised and bloodied. She regretted her fast escape without taking the time to think. She had nothing to defend herself with. Her small side pouch held only her father's hairbrush and a bit of coin. Her dagger was somewhere in the bundle of her bedding. How long would it take her to find it in the dark?

She sighed.

Why must I always focus on the negative? The man has done nothing at all. So he's quiet, so what? He's risking his own life smuggling me to this meeting. He's nervous, watchful, perhaps he's frightened too. Is it so odd he's not making small talk? I'm just scared, that's all. Everything looks bad when you're scared. Isn't it possible he's just shy around women? Cautious around noble ladies? Concerned anything he says or does could be misconstrued and lead to dangerous accusations? Obviously, he has good cause to be concerned. I've already practically convicted him of a host of crimes he hasn't had time to commit! Royce and Hadrian are honorable thieves, why not Etcher as well?

The trail disappeared entirely and they rode across unmarked fields of windswept grass. They seemed to be heading toward a vague and distant hill. She spotted some structures silhouetted against the pallid sky. They entered yet another forest this time through a narrow opening in the dense foliage. Here, Etcher was content to let the horse walk. It was quiet away from the wind. Fireflies blinked around them and Arista listened to the clacking steps of their mount.

We're on a road?

Too dark to see anything clearly, Arista recognized the sound of hooves on cobblestone.

NYPHRON RISING

Where are we?

When at last they cleared the trees she could see the slope of a bald hill where the remains of buildings sat. Giant stones spilled and scattered to the embrace of grass, forming dark heaped ruins of arched doorways and pylons of rock. Like grave markers they thrust skyward at neglected angles, the lingering cadavers and bleached bones of forgotten memories.

"What is this place?" Arista asked.

She heard a horse whinny and spotted the glow of a fire up the slope. Without a word Etcher kicked the horse once more into a trot. Arista took solace knowing the end of her ordeal was at hand.

Near the top, two men sat huddled amidst the ruins. A campfire flicked, sheltered from the wind by a corner section of weathered stone and rubble. One was hooded, the other hatless, and immediately Arista thought of Royce and Hadrian.

Had they somehow arrived ahead of us?

As they drew closer, Arista realized she was wrong. These men were younger, and both as large as, if not larger than, Hadrian. They stood at their approach and Arista saw dark shirts, leather tunics and broadswords hanging from thick belts.

"Running late," the hooded one said. "Thought you weren't going to make it."

"Are you Nationalists?" she asked.

The men hesitated. "Of course," the other replied.

They approached, and the hooded one helped her down from the horse. His hands were large and powerful. He showed no strain taking her weight. He had two days of beard and smelled of sour milk.

"Are one of you Degan Gaunt?"

"No," the hooded one replied. "He sent us ahead to see if you were who you said you were. Are you the Princess Arista Essendon of Melengar?"

THE GUARDIAN

She looked from one face to the next, all harsh expressions, even Etcher glared at her.

"Well, are you or aren't you?" He pressed, moving closer.

"Of course she is!" Etcher blurted out. "I have a long ride back so I want my payment, and don't try and cheat me."

"Payment?" Arista asked.

Etcher once more ignored her.

"I don't think we can pay you for delivery until we know it's her, and we certainly aren't taking *your* word for it. She could be a whore from the swill yards of Colnora that you washed and dressed up— and did a piss-poor job of it, at that."

"She's pretending to be a commoner and she's dirty on account of the ride here."

The hooded man advanced even closer to study her. She backed up instinctively but not fast enough as he grabbed her roughly at the chin and twisted her face from side to side.

Infuriated, she kicked at him and managed to strike his shin.

The man grunted and anger flashed in his eyes. "You bloody little bitch!" He struck her hard across the face with the flat of his hand.

The explosion of pain overwhelmed her. She found herself on her hands and knees gripping a spinning world with fists of grass. Her face ached, and her eyes watered.

The men laughed.

The humiliation was too much. "How dare you strike me!" she screamed.

"See," Etcher said pointing at her.

The hooded man nodded. "Alright, we'll pay you. Danny, give him twenty gold."

"Twenty? The sentinel agreed to fifty!" Etcher protested.

"Keep your mouth shut or it'll be ten."

Arista panted on the ground, her breath coming in short stifled gasps. She was scared and rapidly losing herself to panic. She needed to calm down—to think. Through bleary eyes, she looked to Etcher and his horse. There was no chance of grabbing it and riding away. His feet were in the stirrups and her weight could never pull him off.

"Guy won't appreciate you pocketing thirty of the gold he sent with you."

They laughed. "Who do you really think he'll believe? You or us?"

Arista considered the fire. She could try to run to it and grab a burning stick. No. She would never make the distance, and even if she did, what would a burning stick do against swords. They would only laugh at her.

"Take the twenty and keep your damn mouth shut, or you can ride away with nothing."

She could try running. It was downhill and in the dark she could—no, she was not fast enough and the hill was bare of cover. She would have to make it all the way to the forest before having the slightest hope of getting away and Etcher could ride after her and drag her back. Afterward they would beat and tie her, then all hope would be lost.

"Don't even think about it you little git," the hooded one was saying.

Etcher spat in anger. "Give me the twenty."

The hooded man tossed a pouch that jingled and Etcher caught it with a bitter look.

Arista started to cry. Time was running out. She was helpless and there was nothing at all she could do. For all her royal rank, she could not defend herself. Nor was her education in the art of magic any help. All she could do was make them sneeze and that was not going to save her this time.

Where are Royce and Hadrian? Where is Hilfred? How could I be so stupid, so reckless? Isn't there anyone to save me?

Not surprisingly, Etcher left without a word to her.

"So this is what a princess looks like?" the hooded one said.

"There's nothing special about you, is there? You look just as dirty as any wench I've had."

"I don't know," the other said. "She's better than I've seen. Throw me the rope over there. I wanna enjoy myself, not get scratched up."

She felt her blood go cold. Her body trembled, tears streamed down her cheeks as she watched the man set off to fetch the rope.

No man had ever touched her before. No one dared think in such terms. It would mean death in Melengar. She had no midnight rendezvous, no casual affairs, or castle romances. No boy ever chanced so much as a kiss, but now…she watched as the man with the stubble beard came at her with a length of twine.

If she had only learned something more useful than tickling noses and boiling water she could—

Arista stopped crying. She did not realize it but she had stopped breathing as well.

Can it work?

There was nothing else to try.

The man grinned expectantly as Arista closed her eyes and began to hum softly.

"Look at that. I think she likes the idea. She's serenading us."

"Maybe it's a noble ritual or something?"

Arista barely heard them. Once more using the concentration method Esrahaddon taught her she focused her mind. She listened to the breeze sway the grass, the buzz of the fireflies and mosquitoes, and the song of the crickets. She could feel the stars and sense the earth below. There was power there. She pulled it toward her, breathing it in, sucking it into her body, drawing it to her mind.

"How you want her?"

"Wrists behind the back works for me, but maybe we should ask her how *she* likes it?" They laughed again. "Never know what might tickle a royal's fancy."

She was muttering, forming the words, drawing in the power, giving it form. She focused elements, giving them purpose and direction. She built the incantation as she had before but now varied it. She pushed, altering the tone to shift the focus just enough.

The crickets stopped their song and the fireflies creased their mating flashes, even the gentle wind no longer blew. The only sound now was Arista's voice as it grew louder and louder.

Arista felt herself pulled to her feet as the man spun her and maneuvered her arms behind her back. She ignored him concentrating instead on moving her fingers as if she were playing an invisible musical instrument.

Just as she felt the rough scratchy rope touch her wrists, the men began to scream.

The ruins of Amberton Lee stood splintered on the hilltop. Pillars, broken steps of marble, and slab walls lay fractured and fallen. Only three trees stood near the summit of the barren hill and all of them dead leafless corpses like the rest of the ruins, still standing long after their time.

"There's a fire up there, but I only see Arista," Royce said.

"Bait?"

"Probably. Give me a head start, maybe I can free her before they know something is up. If nothing else, I should spring whatever trap is waiting and then hopefully you can rush in and save the day."

It bothered Royce how quiet the hill was. He could hear the distant snorting and hoofing of horses and the crackle of the campfire, but nothing else. They had raced as fast as their horses could manage, and still Royce was afraid they were too late. When riding, he was certain she was dead. Now he was confused. There was no doubt that the woman near the fire was Arista. So where was Etcher? Where were those they intended to meet?

THE GUARDIAN

He crept carefully, slipping nimbly around a holly tree and up the slope. Half-buried stones and tilted rocks lay hidden beneath grass and thorns, making the passage a challenge. He circled once and found no sentries or movement.

He climbed higher and happened upon two bodies. The men were dead, yet still warm to the touch, more than warm, they felt—hot. There were no wounds, no blood. Royce proceeded up the last of the hill, advancing on the flickering fire. The princess sat huddled near it quietly staring into the flames. She was alone and lacked even her travel bags.

"Arista?" he whispered.

She looked up lazily, drunkenly, as if her head weighed more than it should. The glow of the fire spilled across her face. Her eyes appeared red and swollen. A welt stood out on one of her cheeks.

"It's Royce. You alright?"

"Yes," she replied. Her voice was distant and weak.

"Are you alone?"

She nodded.

He stepped into the firelight and waited. Nothing happened. A light summer breeze gently brushed the hill's grass and breathed on the flames. Above them, the stars shone, muted only by the white moon that cast nighttime shadows. Arista sat with the stillness of a statue, except for the hairbrush she turned over and over in her hands. As tranquil as it appeared, Royce's senses were tense. This place made him uneasy. The odd marble blocks, toppled and broken rose out of the ground like teeth. Once more he wondered if somehow he was tapping into his elven heritage, sensing more than could be seen, feeling a memory lost in time.

He caught sight of movement down the slope and spotted Hadrian climbing toward them. He watched him pause for a moment near the bodies before continuing up.

"Where's Etcher?" Royce asked the princess.

"He left. He was paid by Luis Guy to bring me here, to deliver me to some men."

"Yeah. We found that out a bit late. Sorry."

The princess did not look well. She was too quiet. He expected anger or relief, but her stillness was eerie. Something happened—something bad. Besides the welt there was no other sign of abuse. Her clothes were fine. There were no rips or tears. He spotted several blades of dead grass and a brown leaf tangled in her hair.

"You alright?" Hadrian asked as he crested the hill. "Are you hurt?"

She shook her head and one of the bits of grass fell out.

Hadrian crouched down next to her. "Are you sure? What happened?"

Arista did not answer. She stared at the fire and started to rock.

"What happened to the men down on the hill?" Hadrian asked Royce.

"Wasn't me. They were dead when I found them. No wounds either."

"But how—"

"I killed them," Arista said.

They both turned and stared at her.

"You killed two Seret Knights?" Royce asked.

"Were they seret?" Arista muttered.

"They have broken crown rings," Royce explained. "There's no wound on either body. How did you kill them?"

She started trembling. Her breaths drawn in staggered bursts. Her hand went to her cheek rubbing it lightly with her fingertips. "They attacked me. I—I couldn't think of—I didn't know what to do. I was so scared. They were going to—and I was alone. I didn't have a choice. I didn't have a choice. I couldn't run. I couldn't fight. I couldn't hide. All I could do was make them sneeze and boil water. I didn't have a choice. It was all I could do."

She began sobbing. Hadrian tentatively reached toward her. She dropped the brush and took his hands squeezing them tightly. She pulled at him and he wrapped his arms around her while she buried her face into the folds of his shirt. He gently stroked her hair.

Hadrian looked up at Royce with a puzzled look and whispered, "She made them sneeze to death?"

"No," Royce said, glancing back over his shoulder in the direction of the bodies. "She boiled water."

"I didn't know—I didn't know if it would really work," she whispered between hitching breaths. "I—I had to change it. Switch it. Fill in the blanks. I was only guessing, but—but it felt right. The pieces fit. I felt them fit—I *made* them fit."

Arista lifted her head, wiped her eyes, and looked down the slope of the hill. "They screamed for a very long time. They were on the ground—writhing. I—I tried to stop it then, but I didn't know how and they just kept—they kept on screaming, their faces turning so red. They rolled around on the ground and clawed the dirt, they cried and their screams—they—they got quieter and quieter, then they didn't make any noise except—except they were hissing—hissing and I could see steam rising from their skin."

Tears continued to slip down her cheeks as she looked up at them. Hadrian wiped her face.

"I've never killed anyone before."

"It's okay," Hadrian told her, stroking the back of her head and clearing away the remainder of the grass and leaves. "You didn't want to do it."

"I know. It's just—just that I've never killed anyone before, and you didn't hear them. It's horrible, like part of me was dying with them. I don't know how you do it, Royce. I just don't know."

"You do it by realizing that if the situation was reversed and they succeeded, they wouldn't be crying."

Hadrian slipped a finger under her chin and tilted her face. He cleared the hair stuck to her cheeks and brushed his thumbs under her eyes. "It's okay, it wasn't your fault. You did what you had to. I'm just sorry I wasn't here for you."

Arista looked into his eyes for a moment then nodded and took a clear deep breath and wiped her nose. "I'm really ruining your impression of me, aren't I? I get drunk, I wolf down food, I think nothing of sharing a room with you, and now I…"

"You've nothing to be ashamed of," Hadrian told her. "I only wish more princesses were as worthy of their title as you."

Royce made another survey of the hill and a thorough check of the seret, their horses, and gear. He found symbol-emblazoned tunics, confirming their knightly identities, and a good-sized bag of gold, but no documents of any sort. He pulled the saddle and bridle off one horse and let it go.

"There's only the two?" Hadrian asked when he returned. "I would have expected more." He was stirring the coals of the fire with a stick, brightening the hilltop. Arista looked better. She was eating a bit of cheese, her face was washed, her hair brushed. She certainly was showing more resilience than he expected.

"Gives you a whole new respect for Etcher, doesn't it?" Royce said.

"How do you mean?"

"He never planned to bring all of us here, just her. He's a lot brighter than I gave him credit for."

"He wasn't too smart," Arista told them. "The seret cheated him out of thirty gold Luis Guy had promised."

"So this was Guy's operation, not Merrick's," Hadrian said.

"Not sure," Royce responded. "Seems too sophisticated for Guy, but Merrick's plans don't fail." He looked at the princess. "Of course, not even Merrick could have anticipated what she did."

Hadrian stood up and threw away the stick, then looked at the princess. "You gonna be okay? Can you ride?"

She nodded rapidly and followed it with a sniffle. "I was pretty scared—really missed you two. You have no idea—no idea how happy I am to see you again." She blew her nose.

"I get that from a lot of women," Hadrian replied, grinning. "But I will admit, you're the first princess."

She managed a slight smile. "So what do we do now? I haven't a clue where we are, and I'm pretty sure there isn't any meeting with Gaunt."

"There could be," Royce said. "But Cosmos doesn't know where we are to tell us. I'm sure Etcher never carried any message about Hintindar back to Colnora. I should have told Price before we left, but I didn't want to take chances. Just stupid really, I was being too cautious."

"Well, you know I'm not going to argue," Hadrian told him. "It was withholding information that got us into this."

Arista looked at Royce questioningly.

"I told him," Royce said.

"No bruises?" she asked. "Not even a black eye?"

"We never got that far, but maybe later when we have more time," Hadrian said. "Turned out we had to hurry to save a woman who didn't need saving."

"I'm real glad you did."

"We should head to Ratibor," Royce said. "We aren't too far. We can reestablish connection with the Diamond there."

"*Ratibor?*" Hadrian said suddenly.

"Yeah, you know, dirty, filthy rat hole—the capital of Rhenydd? We've seen where you grew up so we might as well stop by my hometown as well."

Hadrian started searching his clothing. "Hunting a boar," he exclaimed as he pulled out the note from his father. He rushed toward the firelight. "*A king and his knight went hunting a boar; a rat and his friends were hunting for lore.* A rat and a boar—Ratibor! The king and his knight are my father and the heir, who must have traveled to Ratibor and were attacked by lore hunters." Hadrian pointed over his shoulder in the direction of the dead men. "Seret."

"What's the rest of it?" Royce asked intrigued.

"*Together they fought, till one was alive; the knight sadly wept, no king had survived.*"

"So they fought, but only your father survived the battle and the heir was killed."

"No king had survived," Hadrian said. "An odd way to put that, isn't it? Why not say 'The king died'?"

"Because it doesn't rhyme?" Royce suggested.

"Good point."

"What comes next?" Arista asked.

"*The answers to riddles, to secrets and more, are found in the middle, of Legends and Lore.*"

"There's more to the story apparently," she said, "and you can find the answers in ancient lore? Maybe you need to talk to Arcadius again."

"I think not," Royce said. "There's a street in Ratibor called Legends Avenue and another named Lore Street."

"Do they intersect?"

Royce nodded. "Just a bit south of Central Square."

"And what's there?"

"A church, I think."

"Royce is right, we need to get to Ratibor," Hadrian announced. "You alright to ride, Arista?"

Arista stood up. "Trust me. I am more than ready to leave this place. When I—" She stopped herself. "When I used the Art, I sensed something unpleasant. It feels…"

"Haunted," Royce provided, and she nodded.

"What is this place?" Royce asked Hadrian.

"I don't know."

"It's only a few miles from where you grew up."

Hadrian shrugged. "Folks in Hintindar never talked about it much. There are a few ghost stories and rumors of goblins and ghouls that roam the woods, that kind of thing."

"Nothing about what it was?"

"There was a children's rhyme I remember, something like:

> *Ancient stones upon the Lee,*
> *dusts of memories gone we see.*
> *Once the center, once the all,*
> *lost forever, fall the wall.* "

"What's that supposed to mean?"

Hadrian shrugged again. "We used to sing it when playing Fall-the-Wall—it's a kids' game."

"I see," Royce lied.

"Whatever it was I don't like it," Arista declared.

Royce nodded. "It almost makes me look forward to Ratibor—almost."

Chapter 10
REWARDS

The midday bell rang and Amilia stopped, uncertain which way to go. As a kitchen servant, she was unfamiliar with areas reserved for nobles. On only rare occasions had she filled in for sick chambermaids servicing bedrooms on the third floor. She worked as fast as possible to finish before the guests returned. Working with a noble present was a nightmare. They usually ignored her, but she was terrified of drawing attention. Invisibility was her best defense and it was easy to remain unseen in the steam and bustle of the scullery. In the open corridors, anyone could notice her.

This time she had no choice. Saldur ordered her to his office. A soldier found her on the way to breakfast and told her to report to his grace at the midday bell. She lost her appetite and spent the rest of the morning speculating on what horrible fate awaited her.

The bell rang for the second time and Amilia began to panic. She visited the regent's office only once, and being under armed escort, the route was the last thing on her mind. She remembered going upstairs, but didn't recall the number of flights.

Oh why hadn't I left earlier?

She passed the Great Hall filled with long tables set with familiar plates and shining goblets that she had washed each day—old companions all. They were friends of a simpler time, when the world made sense. Back then she woke each morning knowing every day would be as the one before. Now each day was filled with the fear of being discovered a failure.

On the far side of the hall, men entered, dressed in embroidered clothing rich in colors—nobles. They took seats, talking loudly, laughing, rocking back in chairs and shouting for stewards to bring wine. She held the door for the server Bastion carrying a tray of steaming food. He smiled gratefully at her as he rushed by, wiping his forehead with his sleeve.

"How do I get to the regent's office?" she whispered.

Bastion did not pause as he hurried past but called back, "Go around the Reception Hall, through the Throne Room."

"Then what?"

"Just ask the clerk."

She headed down the corridor and around the curved wall of the Grand Stair toward the palace entrance. Workers propped the front doors open, granting entry to three stories of daylight that revealed the cloud of dust they were building. Sweat-oiled men hauled in timber, mortar, and stone. Teams cut wood and marble. Workers scrambled up and down willowy ladders while pulleys hoisted buckets to scaffold-perched masons. All of them working hard to reshape visitors' first impressions. She noticed with amazement that a wall had been moved and the ceiling was higher than the last time she was here. The entrance was now more expansive and impressive than the darkened chamber it once was.

"Excuse me?" She heard a voice call. Turning she saw a thin man standing in the open doorway to the courtyard. He hesitated on the steps, dodging the passing workers. "May I enter?" The man coughed, waving a handkerchief before his face.

Amilia looked at him and shrugged. "Why not, everyone else is."

He took several tentative steps, glancing up fearfully, his arms partially raised as if to ward off a blow. He stood only a few inches taller than Amilia, a pencil-thin, brittle-looking man wearing a powdered wig, a brilliant yellow tunic, and stripped orange britches.

"Good day to you, my lady," he greeted her with a bow as soon as he cleared the activity. "My name is Nimbus of Vernes and I have come to offer my services."

"Oh," she said with a blank stare. "I don't think—"

"Oh please, I beg of you, hear me out. I am a courtier formerly of King Fredrick and Queen Josephine of Galeannon. I am well versed in all courtly protocol, procedures, and correspondence. Prior to that, I was chamberlain to Duke Ibsen of Vernes, so I am capable of managing—" He paused. "Are you alright?"

Amilia swallowed. "I'm just in a hurry. I'm on my way to a very important meeting with the regent."

"Please forgive me then. It is just that—well, I've—" He slouched his shoulders and sighed. "I'm embarrassed to say that I am a refugee of the Nationalists' invasion and have nothing more than the clothes on my back and what little I have in this satchel. I've walked my way here and...I'm a bit hungry. I was hoping I could find employment at the palace court. I'm not suited for anything else," he said, dusting his shoulders clear of the snowy debris that drifted down from the scaffolds.

"I'm sorry to hear that, but I'm not—" She stopped when she saw his lip tremble. "How long has it been since you've eaten?"

"Quite some time, I'm afraid. I've actually lost track."

"Listen," she told him. "I can get you something to eat, but you have to wait until after my meeting."

She thought he would cry then as he bit his lip and nodded several times saying, "Thank you ever so much, my lady."

"Wait here. I'll be back soon...I hope."

She headed off, dodging the lathered men in leather aprons, and slipped past three others in robes holding measuring sticks like staffs and arguing over lines on huge parchments spread across a work table.

The Throne Room, which also showed signs of renovation, was nearly finished and only a few towers of scaffolding remained. The marble floor glistened with a luster, as did the mammoth pillars that held up the domed ceiling. Near the interior wall rose the dais upon which lay the golden imperial throne sculpted in the shape of a giant bird of prey. The wings spread into a vast circle of splayed feathers that formed the chair's back. She passed through the arcade behind it to the administration offices.

"What do you want?" The clerk asked Amilia. She never liked him. He had a face like a rodent with small eyes, large front teeth and a brief smattering of black hair on a pale, balding head. The little man sat behind a formidable desk, his fingers dyed black from ink.

"I am here to see Regent Saldur," she replied. "He sent for me."

"Upstairs, fourth floor," he said, dismissing her by looking back down at his parchments. On the second floor plaster covered the walls, on the third, paneling, and by the fourth, the paneling was a richly carved dark cherry wood. Lanterns became elegant chandeliers, a long red carpet ran the length of the corridor and glass windows let in light from outside. She recalled how out of place Saldur had seemed when he visited the kitchen. She looked down at her dirty smock and recognized the irony.

The door lay open and Regent Saldur stood before an arched window built from three of the largest pieces of glass she had ever seen. Bird song drifted in from the ward below as the regent read a parchment he held in the sunlight.

"You're late," he said without looking up.

"I'm sorry. I didn't know how to get here."

"Something you should understand, I am not interested in excuses or explanations. I am only interested in results. When I tell you to do something, I expect it will be done exactly as I dictate, not sooner, not later, not differently, but *exactly* how I specify, do you understand?"

"Yes, your grace." She felt considerably warmer than a moment ago.

The regent walked to his desk and laid the parchment on it. He placed his fingertips together, tapping them against one another while studying her. "What is your name again?"

"Amilia of Tarin Vale."

"Amilia—pretty name at least. Amilia, you impressed me. That is not easy to do. I appointed five separate women to the task of Imperial Secretary. Ladies of breeding, ladies of pedigree—you are the first to show an improvement in her eminence. You have also presented me with a unique problem. I can't have a common scullery maid working as the personal assistant to the empress. How will that look?" He took a seat behind his desk, brushing out the folds of his robe. "It is conceivable that the empress could have died if not for whatever magic you preformed. For this, you deserve a reward. I am bestowing on you the diplomatic rank equal to a baroness. From this moment on, you are to be known as Lady Amilia."

He dipped a quill into ink and scribbled his name. "Present this to the clerk downstairs and he will arrange for you to obtain the necessary material for a better—well, for a dress."

Amilia stared at him unable to move, taking shallow breaths not wanting to disturb anything. She was riding a wave of good fortune and feared the slightest movement could throw her into an unforgiving sea. He was not punishing her after all. The rest she could think about later.

"Have you nothing to say?"

Amilia hesitated. "Could the empress get a new dress as well?"

"You are now Lady Amilia, Imperial Secretary to Empress Modina

Novronian. You can take whatever measures you feel are necessary to ensure the well-being of the empress."

"Can I take her outside for walks?"

"No," he said curtly. He then softened his tone and added, "As we both know, Modina is not well. I personally feel she may never be. But it is imperative that her subjects believe they have a strong ruler. Through her name, Ethelred and I are doing great things for the people out there." He pointed at the window. "But we can't hope to succeed if they discover their beloved empress does not have her wits about her. It is a difficult task that Novron has laid before us, to build a better world while concealing the empress' incapacitation, which brings me to your first assignment."

Amilia blinked.

"Despite all my efforts, word is getting out that the empress is not well. Since the public has never seen her, there is a growing rumor that she doesn't exist. We need to calm the people's fear. To this end, it will be your task to prepare Modina to give a speech upon the Grand Balcony in three days' time."

"What?"

"Don't worry, it's only three sentences." He picked up the parchment he had been reading and held it out to her. "It should be a simple task. You got her to say one word now get her to say a few more. Have her memorize the speech and train her to deliver it—like an empress."

"But I—"

"Remember what I said about excuses. You are part of the nobility now, a person of privilege and power. I've given you means and with that comes responsibility. Now out with you. I have more work to do."

Taking the parchments, she turned and walked toward the door.

"And Lady Amilia, remember, there were five Imperial Secretaries before you, and all of them were noble as well."

෫

"Well, if that don't put a stiff wind in your main," Ibis declared, looking at the patent of nobility Amilia showed him. Most of the kitchen staff gathered around the cook as he held the parchment up, grinning.

"It's awfully pretty." Cora pointed out. "I love all the fancy writing."

"Never had a desire to read before," Ibis said. "But I sure wish I could now."

"May I?" Nimbus asked. He carefully wiped his hands on his handkerchief and reaching out, gently took the parchment. "It reads: *We, Modina, who is right wise empress, appointed to this task by the mercy of our Lord Maribor, through our Imperial Regents, Maurice Saldur and Lanis Ethelred decree that in recognition of faithful service and commission of charges found to our favor, that Amilia of Tarin Vale, daughter of Bartholomew the carriage maker, be raised from her current station and shall belong to the unquestionable nobles of the Novronian Empire and henceforth and forever be known as Lady Amilia of Tarin Vale.*" Nimbus looked up. "There is a good deal more concerning the limitations of familial inheritance and nobility rights, but that is the essence of the writ."

They all stared at the cornstalk of a man.

"This is Nimbus," Amilia introduced. "He's in need of a meal, and I was hoping you could give him a little something."

Ibis grinned and made a modest bow.

"Yer a lady now, Amilia. There isn't a person in this room who can say no to you. You hear that Edith?" he shouted at the head maid as she entered. "Our little Amilia is a noble lady now."

Edith stood where she was. "Says who?"

"The empress and Regent Saldur that's who. Says so right on this here parchment. Care to read it?"

Edith scowled.

Rewards

"Oh, that's right. You can't read any more than I can. Would you like *Lady* Amilia to read it to you? Or how about her personal steward here. He has a real nice reading voice."

Edith grabbed up a pile of linens from the bin and headed for the laundry, causing the cook to burst into laughter. "She's never given up spouting how you'd be back scrubbing dishes—or worse." Clapping his big hands he turned his attention to Nimbus. "So what would you like?"

"Anything actually," Nimbus replied, his hands quivering, shaking the parchment he still held. "After several days—shoe leather looks quite appetizing."

"Well, I'll get right on that then."

"Can we clear a place for Nimbus to sit?" Amilia asked, and immediately Cora and Nipper were cleaning off the baker's table and setting it just as they had before.

"Thank you," Amilia said. "You don't need to go to this much— but thank you everyone."

"Pardon me, milady," Nimbus addressed her. "If I may be so bold, it is not entirely proper for a lady of nobility to convey appreciation for services rendered by subordinates."

Amilia sat down beside him and sighed. She dropped her chin into her hands and grimaced. "I don't know how to be noble. I don't know anything, but I'm expected to teach Modina how to be an empress?" The contrast of fortune and pending disaster left her perplexed. "His grace might as well kill me now." She took the parchment from Nimbus and shook it in her hand. "At least now that I am noble I might get a quick beheading."

Leif delivered a plate of stew. Nimbus looked down at the bowl and the scattering of utensils arrayed around him. "The kitchen staff isn't very experienced in setting a table are they? He picked up a small, two-prong fork and shook his head. "This is a shellfish fork, and it should be on the left of my plate...assuming I was eating shellfish. What I don't have is a spoon."

Amilia felt stupid. "I don't think anyone here knows what a fork is." She looked down incredulously at the twisted spindle of wire. "Even the nobility don't use them. At least I've never washed one before."

"Depends on where you are. They are popular farther south."

"I'll get you a spoon." She started to get up when she felt his hand on hers.

"Again," he said, "forgive my forwardness, but a lady doesn't fetch flatware from the pantry. And you *are* the nobility. You there!" he shouted at Nipper as he flew by with a bucket. "Fetch a spoon for her ladyship."

"Right away," the boy replied, setting the bucket down and running to the pantry.

"See," he said, "it's not that hard. It just takes a bit of confidence and the right tone of voice."

Nipper returned with the spoon. It never touched the table. Nimbus took it right from his hand and began to eat. Despite his ravenous state he ate slowly, occasionally using one of the napkins that he placed neatly on his lap to dab the corners of his mouth. He sat straight in much the same way Lady Constance had—his chin up, his shoulders squared, his fingers placed precisely on the spoon. She had never seen anyone eat so…perfectly.

"You needn't stay here," he told her. "While I appreciate the company, I am certain you have more important things to attend to. I can find my way out when I am finished, but I do wish to thank you for this meal. You saved my life."

"I want you to work for me," she blurted out. "To help me teach Modina to act like an empress."

Nimbus paused with a spoonful halfway to his mouth.

"You know all about being noble. You even said you were a courtier. You know all the rules and stuff."

"Protocol and etiquette."

Rewards

"Yeah, those too. I don't know if I can arrange for you to be paid, but I might. The regent said I could take whatever steps necessary. Even if I can't, I can find you a place to sleep and see you get meals."

"At the moment, milady, that is a fortune and I would consider it an honor if I could assist her eminence in any way."

"Then it's settled. You are officially the…"

"Imperial Tutor to Her Eminence, the Empress Modina?" Nimbus supplied.

"Right. And our first job is to teach her to give a speech on the Grand Balcony in three days."

"That doesn't sound too hard. Has she done much public speaking?"

Amilia forced a smile. "A week ago she said the word, 'no.'"

Chapter 11
RATIBOR

Entering the city of Ratibor at night, Arista thought it the most filthy, wretched place she could ever imagine. Streets lay in random, confusing lines crisscrossing intersections as they ran off at various odd angles. Refuse was piled next to every building and narrow dirt thoroughfares were appalling mires of mud and manure. Wooden planks created a network of haphazard paths and bridges over the muck, forcing people to parade in lines like tightrope walkers. The houses and shops were as miserable as the roads. Constructed to fit in the spaces left by the street's odd, acute corners, buildings were shaped like wedges of cheese, giving the city a strange splintered appearance. The windows, shut tight against the reeking smell, were opaque with thick grime repeatedly splashed by passing wagons.

Ratibor reveled in its filth like a poor man was proud of calluses on his hands. She had heard of its reputation, but until experiencing it firsthand she didn't truly understand. It was a workingman's city, a struggling city, where no quarter was expected or given. Here, men bore poverty and misfortune as badges of honor, deriving dubious prestige from contests of woe over tankards of ale.

Idlers and vagabonds, hawkers and thieves moved along the plank ways, appearing and disappearing again into the shadows. There were children on the street—orphans by the look—ragged and pitiful waifs covered in filth, crouching under porches. Small families also moved amongst the crowds. Tradesmen with their wives and children carried bundles or wheeled over-filled carts, loaded with all of their worldly possessions. Each looked exhausted and destitute as they trudged through the city's maze.

The rain started not long after they left Amberton Lee and poured the entire trip. She was soaked through. Her hair lay matted to her face, her fingers pruned, and her hood collapsed about her head. Arista followed Royce as he led them through the labyrinth of muddy streets. The cool night wind blew the downpour in sheets, making her shiver. During the trip she looked forward to reaching the city. Although it was not what she expected, anything indoors would be welcomed.

"Care for a raincoat, mum?" A hawker asked, holding a garment up for Arista to see. "Only five silver!" he continued, as she showed no sign of slowing her horse. "How about a new hat?"

"Either of you gentlemen looking for companionship for the night?" called a destitute woman standing on a plank beneath the awning of a closed dry-goods shop. She flipped back her hair and smiled alluringly, revealing missing teeth.

"How about a nice bit of poultry for an evening meal?" another man asked, holding up a dead bird so thin and scraggly it was hardly recognizable as a chicken.

Arista shook her head, saying nothing except to urge her horse forward.

Signs were everywhere—nailed to porch beams or attached to tall stakes driven into the mud, they advertised things like: "*Ale, Cider, Mead, Wine, No Credit!*" and "*Three-day-old pork—cheap!*" But some were more ominous such as, "*Beggars will be jailed!*" and "*All elves entering the city must register at the sheriff's office.*" This last poster's paint was still bright.

Royce stopped at a public house with a signboard of a grotesque cackling face and the scripted epitaph, which read: The Laughing Gnome. The tavern stood three stories, a good-size even by Colnora's standards, yet people still struggled to squeeze in the front door. Inside the place smelled of damp clothes and wood smoke. A large crowd filled the common room such that Hadrian had to push his way through.

"We're looking for the proprietor," Royce told a young man carrying a tray.

"That would be Ayers. He's the gray-haired gent behind the bar."

"It's true I tell you!" A young man with fiery red hair was saying loudly as he stood in the center of the common room. To whom he was speaking, Arista was not certain. It appeared to be everyone. "My father was a Praleon Guard. He served on His Majesty's personal retinue for twenty years."

"What does that prove? Urith and the rest of them died in the fire. No one knows how it started."

"The fire was set by Androus!" shouted the red-haired youth with great conviction. Abruptly the room quieted. The young man was not content with this, however, and he took the stunned paused to press his point. "He betrayed the king, killed the royal family, and took the crown so he could hand the kingdom over to the empress. Good King Urith would never have accepted annexation into the Empire, and those loyal to his name shouldn't either."

The crowd burst into an uproar of angry shouts.

In the midst of this outburst, they reached the bar, where a handful of men stood watching the excitement with empty mugs in hand.

"Mr. Ayers?" Royce asked of a man and a boy as they struggled to hoist a fresh keg onto the rear dock.

"Who wants to know?" the man in a stained apron asked. A drop of sweat dangled from the tip of his red nose, his face flushed from exertion.

"We're looking to rent a pair of rooms."

"Not much luck of that, we're full up," Ayers replied, not pausing from his work. "Jimmy, jump up and shim it." The young lad, filthy with sweat and dirt, leapt up on the dock and pushed a wooden wedge under the keg, tilting it forward slightly.

"Do you know of availability elsewhere in the city?" Hadrian asked.

"Gonna be the same all over, friend. Every boarding house is full—refugees been coming in from the countryside for weeks."

"Refugees?"

"Yeah, the Nationalists have been marching up from the coast sacking towns. People been running ahead of them and most come here. Not that I mind—been great for business."

Ayers pulled a tap out of the old keg and hammered it into the face of the new barrel with a wooden mallet. He turned the spigot and drained a pint or two to clear the sediment, and then wiping his hands on his apron began filling the demands of his customers.

"Is there no place to find lodging for the night?"

"I can't say that, just no place I know of," Ayers replied, and finally took a moment to wipe a sleeve over his face and clear the drop from his nose. "Maybe some folks will rent a room in their houses, but all the inns and taverns are packed. I've even started to rent floor space."

"Is there any left?" Hadrian asked, hopefully.

"Any what?"

"Floor space? It's raining pretty hard out there."

Ayers lifted his head up and glanced around his tavern. "I've got space under the stairs that no one's taken yet. If you don't mind the people walking on top of you all night."

"It's better than the gutter," Hadrian said, shrugging at Royce and Arista. "Maybe tomorrow there will be a vacancy."

Ayers' face showed he doubted this. "If you want to stay it'll be forty-five silver."

"Forty-five?" Hadrian exclaimed stunned. "For space under the stairs? No wonder no one has taken it. A room at the Regal Fox in Colnora is only twenty!"

"Go there then, but if you want to stay here it will cost you forty-five silver—in tenents. I don't take those imperial notes they're passing now. It's your choice."

Hadrian scowled at Ayers but counted out the money just the same. "I hope that includes dinner."

Ayers' shook his head. "It doesn't."

They pushed and prodded their way through the crowd with their bags until they came to the wooden staircase. Beneath it, several people had discarded their wet cloaks on nail heads or on the empty kegs and crates stored there. They stacked the containers to make a cubby and threw the coats and cloaks on them. A few people shot them harsh looks—the owners of the cloaks no doubt—but no one said anything, as it appeared most understood the situation. Looking around, Arista saw others squatting in corners and along the edge of the big room. Some were families with children trying to sleep, their little heads resting on damp clothes. Mothers rubbed their backs and sung lullabies over the racket of loud voices, shifting wooden chairs, and the banging of pewter mugs. These were the lucky ones. She wondered about the families who could not afford floor space.

How many are cowering outside under a boardwalk or in a muddy alley somewhere in the rain?

As they settled, Arista noticed the noise of the inn was not simply the confusing sound of forty unrelated conversations, but rather one discussion voiced by several people with various opinions. From time to time one speaker would rise above the others to make a point, and then drown in the response from the crowd. The most vocal was the red-haired young man.

"No, he's not!" he shouted once more. "He's not a blood relative of Urith. He's the brother of Urith's second wife."

"And I suppose you think his first wife was murdered so he could be pushed into marrying Amiter, just so Androus could become duke?"

"That's exactly what I'm saying!" the youth declared. "Don't you see? They planned this for years, and not just here either. They did it in Alburn, Warric, they even tried it in Melengar, but they failed there. Did anyone see that play last year? You know—*The Crown Conspiracy*. It was based on real events. The children of Amrath outsmarted the conspirators. That's why Melengar hasn't fallen to the Empire. Don't you see? We're all the victims of a conspiracy. I've even heard that the empress might not exist. The whole story of the Heir of Novron is a sham, invented to placate the masses. Do you really think a farm girl could kill a great beast? It is men like Androus who control us—evil, corrupt murderous men without an ounce of royal blood in their veins, or honor in their hearts!"

"So what?" a fat man in a checked vest asked, defiantly. "What do we care who rules us? Our lot is always the same. You speak of matters between blue bloods. It doesn't affect us."

"You're wrong! How many men in this city were pressed into the army? How many are off to die for the empress? How many sons have gone to fight Melengar, who has never been our enemy? Now the Nationalists are coming. They are only a few miles south. They will sack this city just as they did Vernes, and why? Because we are now joined to the Empire. Do you think your sons, brothers and fathers would be off dying if Urith were still alive? Do you want to see Ratibor destroyed?"

"They won't destroy Ratibor!" the fat man shouted back. "You're just spouting rumors, trying to scare decent people and stir up trouble. Armies will fight, and maybe the city will change hands, but it won't affect *us*. We'll still be poor and still struggling to live as we always have. King Urith had his wars and Viceroy Androus will have his. We work, fight, and die under both of them. That's our lot and treasonous talk like this will only get people killed."

"They will burn the city," an older woman in a blue kerchief said suddenly. "Just as they burned Kilnar. I know. I was there. I saw them."

All eyes turned to her.

"That's not true! It can't be," the fat man protested. "It doesn't make sense. The Nationalists have no cause to burn the cities. They would want them intact."

"The Nationalists didn't burn it," she said. "The Empire did." This statement brought the room to stunned silence. "When the imperial government saw that the city would be lost, they ordered Kilnar to be torched to leave nothing for the Nationalists."

"It's true," a man seated with his family near the kitchen spoke up. "We lived in Vernes. I saw the city guards burning the shops and homes there too."

"The same will happen here." The youth caught the crowd's attention once more. "Unless we do something about it."

"What can we do?" a young mother asked.

"We can join the Nationalists. We can give the city to them before the viceroy has a chance to torch it."

"This is treason," the fat man accused. "You'll bring death to us all!"

"The Empire took Rhenydd through deceit, murder, and trickery. I don't speak treason. I speak loyalty—loyalty to the monarchy. To sit by and let the Empire rape this kingdom and burn this city *is* treason and what's more it's foolhardy cowardice!"

"Are you calling me a coward?"

"No, sir, I am calling you a fool *and* a coward."

The fat man stood up indignantly and drew a dagger from his belt. "I demand satisfaction."

RATIBOR

The youth stood and unsheathed a long sword. "As you wish."

"You would duel me sword against dagger and call me the coward?"

"I also called you a fool, and a fool it is who holds a dagger and challenges a man with a sword."

Several people in the room laughed at this, which only infuriated the fat man more. "Do you have no honor?"

"I'm but a poor soldier's son from in a destitute town. I can't afford honor." Again the crowd laughed. "I'm also a practical man who knows it's more important to win than to die—for honor is something that concerns only the living. But understand this, if you choose to fight me I'll kill you any way I can, the same as I'll try and save this city and its people any way I can. Honor and allegiance be damned!"

The crowd applauded now, much to the chagrin of the fat man. He stood red-faced for a moment then shoved his dagger back in his belt and abruptly stalked out the door into the rain.

"But how can we turn the city over to the Nationalists?" the old woman asked.

The youth turned to her. "If we raise a militia, we can raid the armory and storm the city garrison. After that, we'll arrest the viceroy. That will give us the city. The Imperial Army is camped a mile to the south, when the Nationalists attack they will expect to retreat to the safety of the city walls. But when they arrive, they will find the gates locked. In disarray and turmoil, they will rout and the Nationalists will destroy them. After that, we'll welcome the Nationalists in as allies. Given our assistance in helping them take the city, we can expect fair treatment and possibly even self-rule, as that is the Nationalists' creed.

"Imagine that," he said dreamily. "Ratibor, the whole city—the whole kingdom of Rhenydd—being run by a people's council just like Tur Del Fur!"

This clearly caught the imagination of many in the room.

"Craftsmen could own their own shops instead of renting. Farmers would own their land and be able to pass it tax-free to their sons. Merchants could set their own rates, and taxes wouldn't be used to pay for foreign wars but instead used to clean up this town. We could pave the roads, tear down the vacant buildings, and put all the people of the city to work doing it. We would elect our own sheriffs and bailiffs, but they would have little to do for what crime could there be in a free city? Freemen with their own property have no cause for crime."

"I would be willing to fight for that," a man seated with his family near the windows said.

"For paved roads—I would too," said the elderly woman.

"I'd like to own my own land," another said.

Others voiced their interest and soon the conversation turned more serious. As it did, the level of the voices dropped and men clustered together to speak in small groups.

"You're not from Rhenydd are you?" someone asked Arista.

The princess nearly jumped when she discovered a woman had slipped in beside her. She was not immediately certain that it was a woman, as she was oddly dressed in dark britches and a man's loose shirt. With short blonde hair and dappled freckles, Arista initially thought she was an adolescent boy, but her eyes gave her away. They were heavy and deep as if stolen from a much older person.

"No," Arista said apprehensively.

The woman studied her. Her old eyes slowly moving over her body as if memorizing every line of her figure and every crease in her dress. "You have an odd way about you. The way you walk, the way you sit. It is all very…*precise*, very—proper."

Arista was over being startled now and was just plain irritated. "You don't strike me as the kind of person who should accuse others of being odd," she replied.

"There!" the woman said excitedly and wagged a finger. "See? Anyone else would have called me a mannish little whore. You have manners. You speak in subtle innuendo like a—*princess.*"

"Who are you?" Hadrian abruptly intervened, moving between the two. Royce also appeared from the shadows behind the strange woman.

"Who are *you?*" she replied, saucily.

The door to The Laughing Gnome burst open and uniformed imperial guards poured in. Tables were turned over and drinks hit the floor. Customers nearest the door fell back in fear, cowering in the corners, or were pushed aside.

"Arrest everyone!" a man ordered in a booming voice. He was a big man with a potbelly, dark brows and sagging cheeks. He kept his weight on his heels and his thumbs in his belt as he glared at the crowd.

"What's this all about, Trenchon?" Ayers shouted from behind the bar.

"You would be smart to keep your hole shut, Ayers, or I'll close this tavern tonight and have you in stocks by morning—or worse. Harboring traitors and providing a meeting place for conspirators will buy you death at the post!"

"I didn't do nothing!" Ayers cried. "It was the kid. He's the one that started all the talk, and that woman from Kilnar. They're the ones. I just served drinks like every night. I'm not responsible for what customers say. I'm not involved in this. It was them and a few of the others who were going along with it."

"Take everyone in for questioning," Trenchon ordered. "We'll get to the bottom of this. I want the ring leaders!"

"This way," the mannish woman whispered. Grabbing Arista's arm she began to pull the princess away from the soldiers toward the kitchen.

Arista pulled back.

The woman sighed. "Unless you want to have a long talk with the viceroy about who you are and what you're doing here, you'll follow me now."

Arista looked at Royce who nodded, but there was concern on his face. They grabbed up their bags and followed.

Starting at the main entrance, the imperial soldiers began hauling people out into the rain and mud. Women screamed and children cried. Those who resisted were beaten and thrown out. Some near the rear door tried to run only to find more soldiers waiting.

The mannish woman plowed through the crowd into the tavern's kitchen, where a cook looked over surprised. "Best look out," their guide said. "Trenchon is looking to arrest everyone."

The cook dropped her ladle in shock as they pressed by her, heading to the walk-in pantry. Closing the door, the woman revealed a trapdoor in the pantry's floor. They climbed down a short wooden stair into The Laughing Gnome's wine cellar. Several dusty bottles lined the walls, as did casks of cheese and containers of butter. The woman took a lantern that hung from the ceiling, and closing the door above, led them behind the wine racks to the cellar's far wall. Here was a metal grate in the floor. She wedged a piece of old timber in the bars and pried it up.

"Inside, all of you," she ordered.

Above, they could still hear the screams and shouts, then the sound of heavy boots on the kitchen floor.

"Hurry!" she hissed.

Royce entered first, climbing down metal rungs that formed a ladder. He slipped down into darkness and Hadrian motioned for the princess to follow. She took a deep breath as if going underwater and climbed down.

The ladder continued far deeper than Arista would have expected and instead of the tight, cramped tunnel she anticipated, she found herself dropping into a large gallery. All was dark except around the lantern, and without pause or word of direction the woman set off walking. They had no choice but to follow her light.

They were in a sewer far larger and grander than Arista imagined possible after seeing the city above. Walls of brick and stone rose twelve feet to a roof of decorative mosaic tiles. Every few feet grates formed waterfalls that spilled from the ceiling, raining down with a deafening roar. Storm water formed a rushing river in the center of the tunnel that frothed and foamed as it churned around corners or broke upon dividers, spraying walls and staining them dark.

They chased the woman with the lantern as she moved quickly along the brick curb near the wall. Like ribs supporting the ceiling, thick stone archways jutted out at regular intervals, blocking their path. The woman skirted around these easily, but it was much harder for Arista in her gown to traverse the columns and keep her footing on the slick stone curb. Below her, the storm's runoff created a fast-flowing river of dirty water and debris that echoed in the chamber.

The corridor reached a four-way intersection. In the stone at the top corners were chiseled small notations. These read, "Honor Way" going one direction and "Herald's Street" going the other. The woman with the lantern never wavered and turned without a pause, leading them down Honor Way at a breakneck pace. Abruptly she stopped.

They stood on a curb beside the sewer river. It was like any other part of the corridor they had traveled, except perhaps it was a bit wider and quieter.

"Before we go further I must be certain," she began. "Allow me to make this easier by guessing the lady here is actually Princess Arista Essendon of Melengar. You are Hadrian Blackwater, and you are Duster, the famous Demon of Colnora. Am I correct?"

"That would make you a Diamond," Royce said.

"At your service." She smiled, and Arista thought how cat-like her face was in that she appeared both friendly and sinister at the same time. "You can call me Quartz."

"In that case, you can assume you are correct."

"Thanks for getting us out of there," Hadrian offered.

"No need to thank me, it's my job and in this particular case, my happy pleasure. We didn't know where you were since leaving Colnora, but I was hoping you would happen by this way. Now follow me."

Off she sprang again, and Arista once more struggled to follow.

"How is this here?" Hadrian asked from somewhere behind her. "This sewer is incredible but the city above has dirt roads."

"Ratibor wasn't always Ratibor," Quartz shouted back. "Once it was something bigger. All that's been forgotten—buried like this sewer under centuries of dirt and manure."

They moved on down the tunnel until they came to an alcove, little more than a recessed area surrounded by brick. Quartz leaned up against a wooden panel and gave a strong shove. The back shifted inward slightly. She put her fingers in the crack and slid the panel sideways, exposing a hidden tunnel. They entered and traveled up a short set of steps to a wooden door. There was light seeping around its cracks and voices on the far side. Quartz knocked and opened it revealing a large subterranean chamber filled with people.

Tables, chairs, desks, and bunk beds stacked four high filled the room lit by numerous candles that spilled a wealth of waxy tears. A fire burned in a blackened cooking hearth where a huge iron pot was suspended by a swivel arm. Several large chests lay open, displaying sorted contents of silverware, candlesticks, clothes, hats, cloaks, and even dresses. Still other chests held purses, shoes, and rope. At least one was partially filled with coins, mostly copper, but Arista spotted a few silver and an occasional gold tenent sparkling in the firelight. This last chest they closed the moment the door opened.

RATIBOR

A dozen people filled the room, all young thin predators, each dressed in odd assortments of clothing.

"Welcome to the Rat's Nest," Quartz told them. "Rats, let me introduce you to the three travelers from Colnora." Shoulders settled, hands pulled back from weapons, and Arista heard a number of exhales. "The older gent back there is Polish." Quartz pointed over some heads at a tall, thin man with a scraggly beard and drooping eyes sporting a tall black hat and a dramatic-looking cloak like something a bishop would wear. "He's our fearless leader."

This comment drew a round of laughter.

"Damn you, Quartz!" a young boy no older than twelve cursed her.

"Sorry, Carat," she told him. "They just walked into The Gnome while I was there."

"We heard the Imps just crashed The Gnome," Polish said.

"Aye, they did." Quartz gleamed.

Eyes left them and focused abruptly on Quartz, who allowed herself a dramatic pause as she took a seat on a soft, beat-up chair, throwing her legs over the arm in a cavalier fashion. She obviously enjoyed the attention as the members of the room gathered around her.

"Emery was speeching again," she began like a master storyteller to an anxious audience. "This time people were actually listening. He might have got something started, but he got under Laven's skin. Laven challenged him to a duel, but Emery says he'll fight sword to dagger, which really irks Laven and he storms out of The Gnome. Emery shoulda known to beat it then, but the dispute with Laven gets him in real good with the crowd see, so he keeps going."

Arista noticed the thieves hanging on every word. They were enthralled as Quartz added to her tale's drama with sweeping arm gestures.

"Laven, being the bastard that he is, goes to Bailiff Trenchon, right? And returns with the town garrison. They bust in and start arresting everyone for treason."

"What'd Ayers do?" Polish asked, excitedly.

"What could he do? He says, 'What's going on?' and they tell him to shut up, so he does."

"Anyone killed?" Carat asked.

"None that I saw, but I had to beat it out of there real quick like to save our guests here."

"Did they take Emery?"

"I suppose so, but I didn't see it."

Polish crossed the room to face them up close. He nodded as if in approval and pulled absently on his thin beard.

"Princess Arista," he said formally, and tipped his hat as he made a clumsy bow. "Please excuse the place. We don't often entertain guests of your stature here, and quite frankly, we didn't know when, or even if, you'd be coming."

"If we had known, we'd have at least washed the rats!" someone in the back shouted, bringing more laughter.

"Quiet, you reprobate. You must forgive them, my lady. They are the lowest form of degenerates and their lifestyle only aggravates their condition. I try to elevate them, but as you can see, I have been less than successful."

"That's because you're the biggest blackguard here, Polish," Quartz shot at him.

Polish ignored the comment and moved to face Royce.

"Duster?" he said, raising an eyebrow.

At the sound of the name, the whole room quieted and everyone pushed forward to get a better look.

"I thought he was bigger," someone said.

"That's not Duster," Carat declared, bravely stepping forward. "He's just an old man."

"Carat," Quartz said dismissively, "the cobbler's new puppy is old compared to you."

This brought forth more laughter and Carat kicked Quartz's feet off the chair's arm. "Shut up, freckle face."

"The lad makes a good point," Polish said.

"I don't have that many freckles," Quartz countered.

Polish rolled his eyes. "No, I meant just how do we really know this *is* Duster and the princess? Could be the Imps knew we were looking and are setting us up. Do you have any proof about who you are?"

As he said this, Arista noticed Polish let his hand drift casually to the long black dagger at his belt. Others in the room began to spread out, making slow but menacing movements. Only Quartz remained at ease on her chair.

Hadrian looked a bit concerned as Royce cast off his cloak, letting it fall to the floor. Eyes narrowed on him as they stared at the white-bladed dagger in his belt. Everyone waited anxiously for his next move. Royce surprised them by slowly unbuttoning his shirt and pulling it down to expose his left shoulder, revealing a scarred brand in the shape of an M. Polish leaned forward and studied the scar. "The Mark of Manzant," he said, and his expression changed to one of wonder. "Duster is the only living man known to escape that prison."

They all nodded and murmured in awed tones as Royce put his cloak back on.

"He still doesn't look like no monster to me," Carat said with disdain.

"That's only because you've never seen him first thing in the morning," Hadrian told him. "He's an absolute fiend until he's had breakfast."

This brought a chuckle from the Diamonds and a reluctant smile from Carat.

"Now that that's settled, can we get to business?" Royce asked. "You need to send word to the Jewel that Etcher is a traitor and find out if a meeting has been setup with Gaunt."

"All in good time," Polish said. "First we have a very important matter to settle."

"That's right." Quartz came to life and leapt to her feet, taking a seat at the main table. "Pay up people!"

There were irritated grumblings as the thieves reluctantly pulled out purses and counted coins. They each set stacks of silver in front of Quartz. Polish joined her and they started counting together.

"You too, Set," Quartz said. "You were down for half a stone."

When everyone was finished, Polish and Quartz divided the loot into two piles.

"And for being the one to find them?" she said, smiling at Polish.

Polish scowled and handed over a stack of silver to her, which she dropped into her own purse that was now bulging and so heavy she needed to use two hands to hold it.

"You bet we wouldn't make it here?" Arista asked.

"Most everyone did, yes," Polish replied, smiling.

"'Cept Polish and I," Quartz said happily. "Not that I thought you'd make it either, I just liked the odds and the chance for a big payoff if you did."

"Great minds, my dear," Polish told her as he also put his share away. "Great minds indeed."

Once his treasure was safely locked in a chest, Polish turned with a more serious look on his face. "Quartz, take Set and visit the Nationalists' camp. See if you can arrange a meeting. Take Degan Street, it will be the safest now."

"Not to mention poetic," Quartz said smiling at her own insight. She waved at Set who grabbed his cloak. "I know exactly how much is in my trunk," Quartz told everyone as she dropped her purse in a chest. "It had best be there when I come back or I'll make sure *everyone* pays."

No one scoffed or laughed. Apparently, when it came to money thieves did not make jokes.

"Yes, yes, now out with you two." Polish shooed them into the sewer, then turned to face the new guests. "Hmm, now what to do with you? We can't move around tonight with the city watch in a frenzy, besides the weather has been most unfriendly. Perhaps in the morning, we can find you a safe house, but for tonight I am afraid you will all have to stay here in our humble abode. As you can see, we don't have the finest accommodations for a princess."

"I'll be fine," she said.

Polish looked at her, surprised. "Are you sure you *are* a princess?"

"She's becoming more human every day," Hadrian said, smiling at her.

"You can sleep over here," Carat told them, bouncing on one of the bunks. "This is Quartz's bed and the one below is Set's. They'll be out all night."

"Thank you," Arista told him, taking a seat on the lower berth. "You're quite the gentleman."

Carat straightened up at the comment and puffed up his chest, smiling back at Arista fondly.

"He's a miserable thief, behind on his accounts is what he is," Polish admonished, pointing a finger. "You still owe me, remember?"

The boy's proud face dropped.

"I am surprised they already named a street after Degan Gaunt," Arista mentioned, changing the subject. "I had no idea he was that popular."

Several people snickered.

"You got it backward," an older man with a craggy face said.

"The street wasn't named after Gaunt," Polish explained. "Gaunt's mother named him after the street."

"Gaunt is from Ratibor?" Hadrian asked.

Polish looked at him as if he just questioned the existence of the sun. "Of course, he was just one of us until he went to sea as a young lad. They say he was captured by pirates and that's where his life changed and the legend began."

Hadrian turned to Royce. "See? Being raised in Ratibor isn't always such a bad thing."

"Duster is from Ratibor? Where 'bouts did you live?"

Royce kept his eyes on his pack. "Don't you think you should send someone with that message about Etcher back to Colnora? The Jewel will want to know about him immediately, and any delay could get people killed."

Polish wagged a finger at Royce. "I remember you, you know. We never met, but I was in the Diamond back when you were. You were quite the bigwig, telling everyone what to do." Polish allowed himself a snicker. "I suppose that's a hard habit to break, eh? Still, practice makes perfect," Polish turned away saying. "There are dry blankets here you can use. We'll see about better arrangements in the morning."

Royce and Hadrian rooted around in their bags. Arista watched them enviously. Etcher took her bundle with him. Maybe he wanted it as proof, or perhaps thought there could be something of value. In any case, he knew she would not need it. Most likely, he forgot her pack was still on the horse. The loss was not much, a mangled and dirty dress, her night gown and robe, her kris dagger, and a blanket. The only thing she still had with her was the only thing she cared about, the hairbrush from her father, which she took out and attempted to tame the mess that was her hair.

"You have such a way with people, Royce," Hadrian mentioned as he opened another pack.

Royce growled something Arista could not make out and seemed overly focused on his gear. "Where *did* you live, Royce?" Arista asked. "When you were here."

There was a long pause. Finally he replied, "This isn't the first time I've slept in these sewers."

RATIBOR

The sun had barely peeked over the horizon and already the air was hot, arriving with a stifling blanket of humidity. The rain stopped but clouds lingered, shrouding the sun in a milky haze. Puddles filled the streets, great pools of brown water, still as glass. A mongrel dog—thin and mangy—roamed the market sniffing garbage. Flushing a rat, the mutt chased it to the sewers. Having lost it, he lapped from the brown water then collapsed, panting. Insects appeared. Clouds of gnats formed over the larger puddles and biting flies circled the tethered horses. They fought them as best they could with a shake of their head, a stomp of their hooves, or a swish of their tail. Soon people appeared. Most were women clad in plain dresses. The few men were naked to the waist, and everyone went about barefoot, their legs caked with mud to their knees. They opened shops and stands displaying a meager assortment of fruits, eggs, vegetables, and some meat laid bare to the flies' delight.

Royce barely slept. Too wary to close his eyes for more than a few minutes at a time, he gave up rising sometime before dawn and made his way to the surface. He climbed on the bed of a wagon left abandoned in the mud and watched East End Square come alive. He had seen the sight before, only the faces were different. He hated this city. If it were a man, he would have slit its throat decades ago. The thought appealed to him as he stared at the muddy, puddle-filled square. Some problems were easily fixed by the draw of a knife, but others…

He was not alone.

Not long after first light, Royce spotted a boy lying under a cart in the mud, only his head visible above the ruts. For hours the two remained aware of each other, but neither acknowledged it. As the shops began to open the boy slipped from his muddy bed, crawled to one of the larger puddles, and washed some of the muck off. His hair remained caked with the gray clay, as he refused to submerge his head. Moving down the road, Royce saw he was nearly naked, and kept a small pouch tied around his neck. Royce knew the pouch held all of the boy's possessions. He imagined a small bit of glass for cutting, string, a smooth rock for hammering and breaking, and perhaps even a copper coin or two—it was a king's ransom that he would defend with his life, if it came to that.

The boy moved to an undisturbed puddle and drank deeply from the surface. Untouched rainwater was the best. Cleaner, fresher than well water, and much easier to get—much safer.

The boy kept a keen eye on him, constantly glancing over.

With his morning wash done, the lad crept around the cooper's shop, which was still closed. He hid himself between two tethered horses, rubbing their muddy legs. He glanced once more at Royce with an irritated look, and then threw a pebble in the direction of the grocer. Nothing happened. The boy searched for another, paused then threw again. This time the stone hit a pitcher of milk that toppled and spilled. The grocer howled in distress and rushed to save what she could. As she did, the boy made a dash to steal a small sour apple and an egg. He made a clean grab and was back around the corner of the cooper's barn before the grocer turned.

His chest heaved as he watched Royce. He paused only a moment then cracked the egg and spilled the gooey contents into his mouth swallowing with pleasure.

Over the waif's right shoulder, two figures approached. They were boys like him, but older and larger. One wore a pair of man's britches that extended to his ankles. The other wore a filthy tunic tied around his waist with a length of twine and a necklace made from a torn leather belt. The boy did not see them until it was too late. The two grabbed him by the hair and dragged him into the street, where they forced his face into the mud. The bigger boys wrenched the apple from his hand and ripped the pouch from his neck before letting go.

RATIBOR

Sputtering, gasping, and blind, the boy struggled to breathe. He came up swinging and found only air. The kid wearing the oversized britches kicked him in the stomach, crumpling the boy to his knees. The one wearing the tunic took a turn and kicked the boy once striking him in the side and landing him back in the mud. They laughed as they continued up Herald's Street, one holding the apple, the other swinging the neck pouch.

Royce watched the boy lying in the street. No one helped. No one noticed. Slowly the boy crawled back to his shelter beneath the wheel cart. Royce could hear him crying and cursing as he pounded his fist in the mud.

Feeling something on his cheek, Royce brushed away the wetness. He stood up, surprised his breathing was so shallow. He followed the plank walkway to the grocer, who smiled brightly at him.

"Terribly hot it is today, ain't it, sir?"

Royce ignored her. He picked out the largest, ripest apple he could find.

"Five copper if you please, sir."

Royce paid the woman without a word, then pulling a solid gold tenent from his pouch pressed it sideways into the fruit. He walked back across the square. This time he took a different path, one that passed by the cart the boy lie under and as he did, the apple slipped from his fingers and fell into the mud. He muttered a curse at his clumsiness, and continued his way up the street.

It was midmorning and the temperature turned oppressive. Arista was dressed in a hodge-podge of boyish clothes gleaned from the Diamond's stash. A shapeless cap hid most of her hair, a battered oversized tunic and torn trousers gave her the look of a hapless urchin. In Ratibor, this nearly guaranteed her invisibility. Hadrian guessed it was more comfortable than her heavy gown and cloak.

The three of them arrived at the intersection of Legends and Lore. There had been a brief discussion about leaving Arista in the Rat's Nest, but after Hintindar, Hadrian was reluctant to have her out of his sight.

The thoroughfares of the two streets formed one of the many acute angles so prevalent in the city. Here a pie shape church dominated. Made of stone, the building stood out among its wooden neighbors, a heavy, over-built structure more like a fortress than a place of worship.

"Why a Nyphron church of all things?" Hadrian asked as they reached the entrance. "Maybe we got it wrong. I don't even know what I'm looking for."

Royce nudged Hadrian and pointed at the corner stone. Chiseled into its face, the epitaph read:

ESTABLISHED 2992

"Before you were born, the year ninety-two," he whispered. "I doubt it's a coincidence."

"Churches keep accounts concerning births, marriages, and deaths in their community," Arista pointed out. "If there was a battle where people died, there could be a record."

Pulling on the thick oak doors, Hadrian found them locked. He knocked and when no response came, knocked again. He pounded with his fist and then just as Royce began looking for another way in, the door opened.

"I'm sorry, but services aren't until tomorrow," an elderly priest announced. He was dressed in the usual robes. He had a balding head and a wrinkled face that peered through the small crack of the barely opened door.

"That's okay, I'm not here for services," Hadrian replied. "I was hoping I could get a look at the church records."

"Records?"

Hadrian glanced at Arista. "I heard churches keep records on births and deaths."

"Oh yes, but why do you want to see them?"

"I'm trying to find out what happened to someone." The priest looked skeptical. "My father," he added.

Understanding washed over the priest's face and he beckoned them in.

As Hadrian expected, it was oppressively dark. Banks of candles burned on either side of the altar and at various points around the worship hall, each doing more to emphasize the darkness than provide illumination.

"We actually keep very good records here," the priest mentioned as he closed the door behind them. "By the way, I'm Monsignor Bartholomew. I am watching over the church while his reverence Bishop Talbert is away on pilgrimage to Ervanon. And you are?"

"Hadrian Blackwater." He gestured to Royce and Arista. "These are friends of mine."

"I see, then if you will please follow me," Bartholomew said.

Hadrian never spent much time in churches. The darkness, opulence, and staring eyes of the sculptures unnerved him. He was at home in a forest or field, a hovel or fortress, but the interior of a church always made him uneasy. This one had a vaulted ceiling supported by marble columns, and cinquefoil-shaped stonework and blind-tracery moldings common to all Nyphron churches. The altar itself was an ornately carved wooden cabinet with three broad doors and a blue-green marble top. His mind flashed back to a similar cabinet in Essendon Castle that concealed a dwarf waiting to accuse him and Royce of Amrath's death. That incident started his and Royce's longstanding employment with Medford's royal family.

On this one, more candles burned, and three large gilded tomes lay sealed. The sickly-sweet fragrance of salifan incense was strong. On the altar, stood the obligatory alabaster statue of Novron. As always, he knelt sword in hand while the god Maribor loomed over him placing a crown on his head, anointing his son the ruler of the world. All the churches Hadrian visited had one, each a replica of the original sculpture preserved in the Crown Tower of Ervanon. They only varied in size and material.

Taking a candle, the priest led them down a narrow curling stair. At the base, they stopped at a door, beside which hung an iron key on a peg. The priest lifted it off and twisted it in the large square lock until it clanked. The door creaked open and the priest replaced the key.

"Doesn't make much sense, does it? To keep the key there?" Royce pointed out.

The priest glanced back at it blankly. "It's heavy and I don't like carrying it."

"Why lock the door then?"

"Only way to keep it closed. And if left open the rats eat the parchments."

Inside, the cellar was half the size of the church above and divided in aisles of shelves that stretched to the ceiling filled with thick leather-bound books. The priest took a moment to light a lantern that hung near the door.

"They're all in chronological order," he told them as the lantern revealed a shallow ceiling and walls made of small stacked stones quite unlike the larger blocks and bricks used in the rest of the church.

"About what time period are you looking for? When did your father die?"

"Twenty-nine ninety-two."

The priest hesitated. "Ninety-two? That was forty-two years ago. You age remarkably well. How old were you then?"

"Very young."

The priest looked skeptical. "Well, I'm sorry. We have no records from ninety-two."

"The corner stone outside says this church was built then," Royce said.

"And yet we do not have the records for which you ask."

"Why is that?" Hadrian pressed.

The priest shrugged. "Maybe there was a fire."

"*Maybe* there was a fire? You don't know?"

"Our records cannot help you, so if you will please follow me, I will show you out."

The priest took a step toward the exit. Royce stepped in his path. "You're hiding something."

"I'm doing nothing of the sort. You asked to see records from ninety-two—there are none."

"The question is—why?"

"Any number of reasons. How should I know?"

"The same way you knew there aren't any records here for that date without even looking," Royce replied, his voice lowering. "You're lying to us, which again brings up the question of—why?"

"I am a monsieur; I don't appreciate being accused of lying in my own church."

"And I don't appreciate being lied to." He took a step forward.

"Neither do I," Bartholomew replied. "You're not looking for anyone's father. Do you think I'm a fool? Why are you back here? That business ended decades ago. Why are you still at it?"

Royce glanced at Hadrian. "We've never been here before."

The priest rolled his eyes. "You know what I mean. Why is the seret still digging this up? You're Sentinel Thranic aren't you?" he pointed at Royce. "Talbert told me about the interrogation you put him through—a bishop of the church! If only the Patriarch knew what his pets were up to, you would all be disbanded. Why do you still exist anyway? The Heir of Novron is on her throne, isn't she? Isn't that what we're all supposed to believe? At long last, you found the seed of Novron and all is finally right with the world. You people can't accept that your mandate is over, that we don't need you anymore—if we ever did."

"We aren't seret," Hadrian told him, "and my friend here is definitely not a sentinel."

"No? Talbert described him perfectly—small, wiry, frightening, *like Death himself*. But you must have shaved your beard."

"I'm not a sentinel," Royce told him.

"We're just trying to find out what happened here forty-two years ago," Hadrian explained. "And you're right. I'm not looking for a record of my father's death, because I know he didn't die here. But he was here."

The monsignor hesitated, looking at Hadrian and shooting furtive glances at Royce. "What was your father's name?" he asked at length.

"Danbury Blackwater."

The priest shook his head. "Never heard of him."

"But you know what happened," Royce said. "Why don't you just tell us?"

"Why don't you just get out of my church? I don't know who you are and I don't want to. What happened—happened. It's over. Nothing can change it. Just leave me alone."

"You were there," Arista muttered in revelation. "Forty years ago—you were there, weren't you?"

The monsignor glared at her, his teeth clenched. "Look through the stacks if you want," he told them in resignation. "I don't care; just lock up when you leave. And be sure to blow out the light."

"Wait," Hadrian spoke quickly as he fished his medallion out of his shirt and held it up toward the light. Bartholomew narrowed his eyes, and then stepped closer to examine it.

"Where did you get that?"

"My father left it to me. He also wrote me a poem, a sort of riddle I think. Maybe you can help explain it." Hadrian took out the parchment and passed it to the cleric.

RATIBOR

After reading he raised a hand to his face, covering his mouth. Hadrian noticed his fingers tremble. His other hand sought and found the wall and he leaned heavily against it. "You look like him," the priest told Hadrian. "I didn't notice it at first. It's been over forty years and I only knew him briefly, but that's his sword on your back. I should have recognized that if nothing else. I still see it so often in my nightmares."

"So you knew my father, you knew Danbury Blackwater?"

"His name was Tramus Dan. That's what he went by at least."

"Will you tell us what happened?"

He nodded. "There's no reason to keep it secret, except to protect myself, and perhaps it's time I faced my sins."

The monsignor looked at the open door to the stairs. "Let's close this." He stepped out then returned puzzled. "The key is gone."

"I've got it," Royce volunteered, revealing the iron key in his hand and, pulling the door shut, locked it from the inside. "I've never cared for rooms I can be locked in."

Bartholomew took a small stool from behind one of the stacks and perched himself on it. He sat bent over with his head between his knees as if he might be sick. They waited as the priest took several steadying breaths.

"It was forty-two years ago, next week in fact," he began, his head still down, his voice quiet. "I had been expecting them for days and was worried. I thought they had been discovered, but that wasn't it. They were traveling slowly because she was with child."

"Who was?" Hadrian asked.

The monsignor looked up confused. "Do you know the significance of that amulet you wear?"

"It once belonged to the Guardian of the Heir of Novron."

"Yes," the old man said simply. "Your father was the head of our order. A secret organization dedicated to protecting the descendants of Emperor Nareion."

"The Theorem Eldership," Royce said.

Bartholomew looked at him surprised. "Yes. Shopkeepers, tradesmen, farmers—people who preserved a dream handed down to them."

"But you're a priest in the Nyphron Church."

"Many of us were encouraged to take vows. Some even tried to join the seret. It was important to know what the church was doing, where they were looking. I was the only one in Ratibor to receive the would-be emperor and his guardian. The ranks of the Eldership had dwindled over the centuries. Few believed in it anymore. My parents raised me to be a Loyalist, to believe in the dream of seeing the heir of Nareion returned to an imperial throne, but I never expected it would happen. I often questioned if the heir even existed, if the stories were just a myth. You see, the Eldership only contacted members if needed. You had a few meetings and years could go by without a word. Even then, messages were only words of encouragement reminding us to stay strong. We never heard a thing about the heir. There were no plans to rise up, no news of sightings, victories, or defeats.

"I was only a boy, a young deacon, recently arrived in Ratibor assigned to the old South Square Church when my father sent a letter saying simply: *He is coming. Make preparations.* I didn't know what to think. It took several readings before I even understood what *he* meant. When I realized I was dumbstruck. The heir of Maribor was coming to Ratibor. I didn't know exactly what I should do, so I rented a room at the Bradford Boarding House and waited. I should have found a better place. I should have…" He paused for a moment, dropped his head again to look at the floor and took a breath.

"What happened?" Hadrian asked, keeping his voice calm, not wanting to do anything to stop the cleric from revealing his tale.

"They arrived late, around midnight because his wife was about to give birth and their travel was slow. His name was Naron and he traveled with his guardian, Tramus Dan and Dan's young apprentice, whose name I sadly can't recall. I saw them to their rooms at the boarding house and your father sent me in search of a midwife. I found a young girl and sent her ahead while I set out to find what supplies were needed.

"By the time I returned with my arms full, I saw a company of Seret Knights coming up the street, searching door to door. I was horrified. I had never seen seret in Ratibor. They reached the boarding house before I could.

"They found it locked and beat on the door. There was no answer. When they tried to break in your father refused them entry, and the fight began. I watched from across the street. It was the most amazing thing I ever saw. Your father and his apprentice stepped out and fought back to back, defending the entrance. Knight after knight died until as many as ten lay dead or wounded on the street, and then came a scream from inside. Some of the seret must have found a way into the building from the back.

"The apprentice ran inside, leaving your father alone at the door to face the remainder of the knights. There must have been a dozen or more but, wielding two swords in the shelter of the entrance, he kept them at bay. He held them off for what felt like an eternity, then Naron appeared at the doorway. He was mad with rage and drenched in blood. He pushed past Dan into the street. Your father tried to stop him, but Naron kept screaming, 'They killed her!' and threw himself into the crowd of knights, swinging his sword like a man possessed.

"Your father tried to reach Naron—to protect him. The seret surrounded Naron and I watched him butchered on their swords. I fell to my knees, the blankets, needle, and thread falling to the street. Your father, surrounded by his own set of knights, cried out and dropped his two swords. I thought they had stabbed him too.

I expected to see him fall, but instead he drew the spadone blade from his back. The bloodshed I witnessed up to that point did not compare to what followed. Tramus Dan, with that impossibly long sword, began cleaving the seret to pieces. Legs, arms, and heads—explosions of blood—even across Lore Street, I felt the spray carried on the wind like a fine mist on my face.

"When the last seret fell, Dan ran inside only to emerge a moment later with tears streaking down his cheeks. He went to Naron and cradled the heir, rocking him. I will admit I was too frightened to approach or even speak. Dan looked like Oberlin himself bathed slick from head to foot in blood, that sword still at his side, his body shaking as if he might explode. After a time, he gently laid Naron on the porch. A few of the knights were still alive, groaning, twitching. He picked up the sword again. It was as if he were chopping wood. Then he picked up his weapons and walked away.

"I was too scared to follow, too terrified to even stand up, and I did not dare approach the house. As time passed, others arrived and together we found the courage to enter. We found the younger swordsman—your father's apprentice—dead in the upper bedroom surrounded by several bodies of seret. In the bed was a woman stabbed to death, her newborn child murdered in her arms. I never saw or heard anything of your father again."

They sat in silence for a few minutes.

"It explains a lot I never understood about my father," Hadrian finally said. "He must have wandered to Hintindar after that and changed his name. Dan—bury. Even his name was a riddle. So the line of Novron is dead?"

The old priest said nothing at first. He sat perfectly still except for his lips that began to tremble. "It's all my fault. The seed of Maribor is gone. The tree, so carefully watered for centuries, has withered and died because of me. If only I had found a better safe house or if I had kept a better watch." He looked up, the light of the lantern glistened off tears. "The next day, more seret came and burned the boarding house to the ground. "I petitioned for this church to be built. The bishops never realized I was doing it as a testament—a monument to their memory. They thought I was honoring the fallen seret. So here I remained, upon their graves, guarding still. Yet now I protect not hope, but a memory, a dream that because of me, will never be."

At noon, the ringing of the town bell summoned the citizens to the Central Square. On their way back from the church Arista, Hadrian, and Royce entered the square barely able to see due to the gathered crowd. There they found twelve people locked in stocks. They each stood bent over with head and wrists locked, their feet and lower legs sunk deep in mud. Above each hung hastily scrawled signs with the word, *Conspirator* written on them. The young red-haired Emery was not in a stock, instead he hung by his wrists from a pole. Naked to the waist, his body covered in numerous dark bruises and abrasions. His left eye was puffed and sealed behind a purple bruise and his lower lip split and stained dark with dried blood. Next to him hung the older woman from The Laughing Gnome, the one who told of the Imperials burning Kilnar. Above both of them were signs reading, *Traitors*. Planks circled the prisoners, and around them paced the Sheriff of Ratibor. In his hands he held a short whip comprised of several strands knotted at the ends, which he wagged threateningly as he walked. The whole city garrison turned out to keep the angry crowd at bay. Archers were poised on roofs, and soldiers armed with shields and unsheathed swords threatened any who approached too close.

Many of the faces in the stocks were familiar to Arista from the night before. She was shocked to see mothers, who had sung their children to sleep, now locked in stocks beside their husbands, sobbing. The children reached out for their parents from the crowd. The treatment of the woman from Kilnar disturbed her the most. Her only crime was telling the truth and now she hung before the entire city, awaiting the whip. The sight was all the more terrifying knowing it could be her up there if Quartz had not intervened.

A regally dressed man in a judge's robe and a scribe approached the stocks. When they reached the center of the square, the scribe handed a parchment to the judge. The sheriff shouted for silence, then the judge held up the parchment and began to read.

"For the crimes of conspiracy against her royal eminence, the Empress Modina Novronian, against the Empire, against Maribor and all humanity; for slander against His Excellency the Empress' Imperial Viceroy; and for the general agitation of the lower classes to challenge their betters, it is hereby proclaimed good and right that punishment be laid immediately upon these criminals. Those guilty of conspiracy are hereby ordered to be flogged twenty lashes and spend one day in stocks, not to be released until sunset. Those guilty of treason will receive one hundred lashes and, if they remain alive, will be left hanging until they expire from want of food and water. Anyone attempting to help or lend comfort to any of these criminals will be likewise found guilty and receive similar punishment." He rolled up the parchment. "Sheriff Vigan, you may commence."

With that, he thrust the scroll into the hands of the scribe and promptly walked back the way he came. With a nod from the sheriff, a soldier approached the first stock and ripped open the back of the young mother's dress. From somewhere in the crowd Arista heard a child scream, yet without pause the sheriff swung his whip even as the poor woman cried for mercy. The knots bit into the pale skin of her back and she howled and danced in pain. Stroke after stroke fell with the scribe standing by keeping careful track. By the time it was done, her back was red and slick with blood. The sheriff took a break and handed the whip to a soldier, who performed similar punishment on her husband as the sheriff sat by leisurely drinking from a cup.

The crowd, already quiet, grew deadly still as they came to the woman from Kilnar who began screaming as they approached. The sheriff and his deputies took turns whipping her, as the day's heat made such work exhausting. The fatigue in their arms was evident by the wild swings that struck the woman high on her shoulders as well as low on her back, and even occasionally as low as her thighs. After the first thirty lashes, the woman stopped screaming and only whimpered softly. The whipping continued and by the time the scribe counted sixty the woman merely hung limp. A physician approached the post, lifted her head by her hair, and pronounced her dead. The scribe made a note of this. They did not remove her body.

The sheriff finally moved to Emery. The young man was not daunted after seeing the punishment carried out on the others, and made the bravest showing of all. He stood defiant as the soldier with the whip approached him.

"Killing me will not change the truth that Viceroy Androus is the real traitor and guilty of killing King Urith and the royal family!" he managed to shout before the first strokes of the whip silenced him. He did not cry out, but gritted his teeth and only dully grunted as the knots turned his back into a mass of blood and pulpy flesh. By the last stroke, he also hung limp and silent, but everyone could see him breathing. The physician indicated such to the scribe, who dutifully jotted it down.

"Those people didn't do anything," Arista said, as the crowd began to disperse. "They're innocent."

"You, of all people, know that isn't the point," Royce replied.

Arista whirled. She opened her mouth, hesitated, and then shut it.

"Alric had twelve people publicly flogged for inciting riots when the church was kicked out of Melengar," he reminded her. "How many of them were actually guilty of anything?"

"I'm sure that was necessary to keep the peace."

"The viceroy will tell you the same."

"This is different. Mothers weren't whipped before their children, and women weren't beaten to death before a crowd."

"True," Royce said. "It was only fathers, husbands, and sons who were whipped bloody and left scarred for life. I stand corrected, Melengar's compassion is astounding."

Arista glared at him, but could say nothing. As much as she hated it, as much as she hated him for pointing it out, she realized what Royce said was true.

"Don't punish yourself over it," Royce told her. "The powerful control the weak; the rich exploit the poor. It's the way it's always been and how it always will be. Just thank Maribor you were born both rich and powerful."

"But it's not right," she said, shaking her head.

"What does *right* have to do with it? With anything? Is it right that the wind blows or that the season's change? It's just the way the world is. If Alric hadn't flogged those people, maybe they would have succeeded in their revolt. Then you and Alric might have found yourselves beaten to death by a cheering crowd because they would hold the power and you two would be weak."

"Are you really that indifferent?" she asked.

"I like to think of it as practical, and living in Ratibor for any length of time has a tendency to make a person *very* practical." He glanced sympathetically at Hadrian, who had been quiet since leaving the church. "Compassion doesn't make house calls to the streets of Ratibor—now or forty years ago."

"Royce..." Hadrian said, then sighed, "I'm going to take a walk. I'll see you two back at the Nest in a little while."

"Are you alright?" Arista asked.

"Yeah," he said unconvincingly, and moved away with the crowd.

"I feel bad for him," she said.

"Best thing that could have happened. Hadrian needs to understand how the world really works and get over his childish affection for ideals. You see Emery up there? He's an idealist and that's what eventually happens to idealists, particularly those that have the misfortune of being born in Ratibor."

"But for a moment he might have changed the course of this city," Arista said.

"No, he would only have changed who was in power and who wasn't. The course would remain the same. Power rises to the top like cream and dominates the weak with cruelty disguised as—and often even believed to be—benevolence. When it comes to people, there is no other possibility. It's a natural occurrence like the weather, and you can't control either one."

Arista thought for a moment as her eyes glanced skyward, then said defiantly, "I wouldn't be so sure of that."

Chapter 12

MAKING IT RAIN

By the time Hadrian returned to the Rat's Nest, he could see Quartz had returned and there was trouble. Arista stood in the middle of the room with arms folded stubbornly, a determined look on her face. The rest watched her, happily entertained while Royce paced with a look of exasperation.

"Thank Maribor you're back!" Royce said. "She's driving me insane."

"What's going on?"

"We're going to take control of the city," Arista announced.

Hadrian raised an eyebrow. "What happened to the meeting with Gaunt?"

"Not going to happen," Quartz answered. "Gaunt's gone."

"Gone?"

"Officially, he's disappeared," Royce explained. "Likely he's dead or captured. I'm certain Merrick is behind this somehow. It feels like him. He stopped us from contacting Gaunt and used both sides as bait for the other. Brilliant, really. Degan went to meet with Arista just as Arista went to meet him and both walked into a trap. Arista avoided hers but it would appear that Gaunt was not so fortunate.

Making it Rain

The Nationalists are blaming Her Highness and Melengar, convinced that she's responsible. Even though the plan failed to catch the princess, there is no chance for an alliance. Definitely Merrick."

"Which is exactly why we need to prove ourselves to the Nationalists," Arista explained while Royce shook his head. She turned to face Hadrian. "If we take the city from the inside and hand it over to them, they'll trust us and we'll be able to get them to agree to an alliance. When you took this job I reserved the right to change the objectives, and I'm doing so now."

"And how *exactly* do we *take* the city?" Hadrian asked carefully, trying to keep his tone neutral. He was usually inclined to side with Royce, and at face value Arista's idea did seem more than a little insane. On the other hand, he knew Arista was no fool and Royce often made choices based solely on self-interest. Beyond all of that, he could not help but admire Arista, standing in a room full of thieves and opportunists proclaiming such a noble idea.

"Just like Emery said at The Laughing Gnome," Arista began. "We storm the armory. Take weapons and what armor we can find. Then attack the garrison. Once we defeat them, we seal the city gates."

"The garrison in Ratibor is made up of what?" Hadrian asked. "Fifty? Sixty experienced soldiers?"

"At least that," Royce muttered disdainfully.

"Going up against hastily armed tailors, bakers, and grocers? You'd need to have half the population of the city backing you," he pointed out.

"Even if you could raise a rabble, scores of people will die and the rest will break and run," Royce added.

"They won't run," Arista said. "There's no place for them to go. We're trapped in a walled city, there can be no retreat. Everyone will have to fight to the death. After this afternoon's demonstration of the Empire's cruelty, I don't think anyone will chance surrender."

Hadrian nodded. "But how do you expect to incite the city to fight for you? They don't even know you. You're not like Emery with life-long friends who will lay their lives on the line on your behalf. I doubt Polish here has a reputation that will elicit that kind of devotion—no offense."

Polish smiled at him. "You are quite right. The people rarely see me, and when they do I'm thought of as a despicable brigand—imagine that."

"That's why we need Emery," Arista said.

"The kid dying in the square?"

"You saw the way the people listened," she said earnestly. "They believe in him."

"Right up until they were flogged at his side," Royce put in.

Arista stood straighter and spoke in a louder voice, "And even when they did, did you see the anger in the faces of the people? In The Laughing Gnome, they already saw him as something of a hero—standing up for them against the Imperials. When they flogged him, when he faced death and yet stood by his convictions, it solidified their feelings for him. The Imperials left Emery to die today. When they did, they made him a martyr. Just imagine how people will feel if he survives? If he slipped out of their grasp just as everyone felt certain he was dead—it would be the spark that could ignite their hopes."

"He's probably already dead," Quartz said indifferently, as she cleaned her nails with a dagger.

Arista ignored her. "We'll steal Emery from the post, spread the news that he's alive and that he asks everyone to stand up with him and fight—to fight for the freedom he promised them."

Royce scoffed but Hadrian considered. He wanted to believe. He wanted to be swept along with her passion but his practical side, after waging dozens of battles, told him different. "It won't work," he stated. "Even if you managed to take the city, the Imperial Army will hear about it and take it back. A few hundred civilians could overwhelm the city garrison, but they aren't going to stop an army."

"That's why we have to coordinate our attack with the Nationalists. Remember Emery's plan. We'll shut the gates and lock them out. Then the Nationalists can crush them."

"And if you don't manage to close the gates in time? If the battle against the garrison doesn't go perfectly to plan?" Royce asked.

"It still won't matter," Arista said. "If the Nationalists attack Lord Dermont at the same time as we launch our rebellion, they won't have time to bother with us."

"Except the Nats won't attack without Gaunt," Quartz said. "That's the reason they are still out there. Well, that and the three hundred heavy cavalry Lord Dermont has. The Nats haven't ever faced an organized Imp army. Without Gaunt they have no one to lead them. They aren't disciplined troops. Just townsfolk and farmers Gaunt picked up along the way here. They'll run the moment they see armored knights."

"Who's in charge of Gaunt's army?" Hadrian asked. He had to admit Arista's plans were at least thought out.

"Some fat chap who goes by the name of Parker. Rumor has it he was a bookkeeper for a textile business. He used to be the Nat's quartermaster before Gaunt promoted him," Quartz said. "Not the brightest coin in the purse, if you understand me. Without Gaunt planning and leading the attack, the Nats don't stand a chance."

"You could do it," Arista said, looking squarely at Hadrian. "You've commanded men in battle before. You got a medal."

Hadrian rolled his eyes. "It wasn't as impressive as it sounds. It was only small regiments. Grendel's army was—well—in a word, pathetic. They refused to even wear helms because they didn't like the way their voices echoed in their heads."

"But you led them in battle?"

"Yes, but—"

"And did you win or lose?"

"We won but—"

"Against a larger or smaller force?"

Hadrian stood silent, a beaten look on his face.

Royce turned toward him. "Tell me you aren't considering this nonsense?"

Am I? But three hundred heavy cavalry!

Desperation slipped into Arista's voice, "Breckton's Northern Army is marching here. If the Nationalist Army doesn't attack now, the combined imperial forces will decimate them. That's what Lord Dermont is waiting for—that's his plan. If he sits and waits he will win, but if the Nationalists attack first, if he has no support, and nowhere to run…this may be our only chance. It's now or all will be lost.

"If the Nationalists are destroyed, nothing will stop the Empire. They'll retake and punish all of Rhenydd for its disobedience, and that will include Hintindar." She paused, letting him consider this. "Then they will take Melengar. After that, nothing will stop them from conquering Delgos, Trent, and Calis. The Empire will rule the world once more, but not like it once did. Instead of an enlightened rule uniting the people, it will be one of cruelty dividing them, headed not by a noble, benevolent emperor, but by a handful of greedy, power-hungry men who pull strings while hiding behind the shield of an innocent girl.

"And what about you, Royce?" She turned toward the thief. "Have you forgotten the wagons? What do you think the fate of those and others like them will be when the Empire rules all?

"Don't you see?" she addressed the entire room. "We either fight here and win or die trying, because there won't be anything left if we fail. This is the moment. This is the crucial point where the future of yet unborn generations will be decided either by our action or inaction. For centuries to come, people will look back at this time and rejoice at our courage, or curse our weakness." She looked directly at Royce now. "For we have the power. Here. Now. In this place. We have the power to alter the course of history and we will be forever damned should we not so much as try!"

She stopped talking. Exhausted and out of breath.

The room was silent.

To Hadrian's surprise, it was Royce who spoke first. "Making Emery disappear isn't the hard part. Keeping him hidden is the problem."

"They'll tear the city apart looking, that's certain," Polish said.

"Can we bring him here?" Arista asked.

Polish shook his head. "The Imps know about us. They leave us alone because we don't cause much trouble and they enjoy the black market we provide. No, they'll most certainly come down here looking. Besides, without orders from the Jewel or the First Officer, I couldn't expose our operation to that much risk."

"We need a safe house where the Imps won't dare look," Royce said. "Some place they won't even want to look. Is the city physician an Imperialist or a Loyalist?"

"He's a friend of Emery, if that's any indication," Quartz explained.

"Perfect. By the way, princess, conquering Ratibor wasn't in our contract. This will most certainly cost you extra."

"Just keep a tally," she replied, unable to suppress her smile.

"If this keeps up we're going to own Melengar," Hadrian mentioned.

"What's this *we* stuff?" Royce asked. "You're retired remember?"

"Oh? So *you'll* be leading the Nationalist advance will you?"

"Sixty, forty?" Royce proposed.

NYPHRON RISING

❧

Despite the recent rain, the public stable on Lords Row caught fire just after dark. More than two dozen horses ran through the streets. The city's inhabitants responded with a bucket brigade. Those unable to find a place in line stood in awe as the vast wooden building burned with flames reaching high into the night's sky.

With no chance of saving the stable, the town fought to save the butcher's shop next door. Men climbed on the roof, and braving the rain of sparks, soaked the shake shingles. Bucket after bucket doused the little shop as the butcher's wife watched terrified from the street, her face glowing with the horrific light. The town folk, and even some imperial guards, fought the fire for hours until at last, deprived of the shop next door, it burned itself out. The stable was gone. All that remained was charred and smoking rubble, but the butcher's shop survived with one blackened wall to mark its brush with disaster. The townsfolk, covered in soot and ash, congratulated themselves on a job well done. The Gnome filled with patrons toasting their success. They clapped their neighbors on the back, told jokes and stories of near-death.

No one noticed Emery Dorn was missing.

The next morning the city bell rang with the news. A stuffed dummy hung in his place. Guards swore they had not left their stations but had no explanation. Sheriff Vigan, the judge, and various other city officials were furious. They stood in Central Square, shouting and pointing fingers at the guards then at each other. Even Viceroy Androus interrupted his busy schedule to emerge from City Hall to personally view the scene.

By midmorning, The Gnome filled with gossipers and happy customers as if the town had declared a holiday, and Ayers was happily working up a sweat filling drinks.

"He was still breathing at sunset!" the cooper declared.

"He's definitely alive. Why free him if he was dead?" the grocer put forth.

"Who did it?"

"What makes you think *anyone* did it? That boy likely got away himself. Emery is a sly one, he is. We shoulda known the Imps couldn't kill the likes of him."

"He's likely down in the sewers."

"Naw, he's left the city, nothing for him here now."

"Knowing Emery, he's in the viceroy's house right now drinking the old man's brandy!"

This brought laughter to go with the round of ales Ayers dispensed. Ayers had his own thoughts on the matter—he guessed the guards freed him. Emery was a great talker. Ayers heard him giving speeches in The Gnome dozens of times and he always won over the crowd. It was easy to imagine the boy talking all night to those men set to watch him and turning them around. He wanted to mention it, but the keg was nearly empty and he was running low on mugs. He did not care much for the Imps personally, but they sure were great for business.

A loud banging at the tavern's entrance killed the laughter and people turned sharply. Ayers nearly dropped the keg he was lifting, certain the sheriff was leading another raid, but it was only Doctor Gerand.

He stood at the open door, hammering the frame with his shoe to get their attention. Everyone breathed again.

"Come in, Doctor!" Ayers shouted. "I'll have another keg brought up."

"Can't," he replied, "need to be keeping my distance from everyone for awhile. Just want to let people know to stay clear of the Dunlaps' house. They've got a case of pox there."

"Is it bad?" the grocer asked.

"Bad enough," the physician said.

"All these new immigrants from down south are bringing all kinds of sickness with them," Ayers complained.

"Aye, that's probably what did it," Doctor Gerand said. "Mrs. Dunlap took in a boarder a few days back, a refugee from Vernes. It was that fella who first come down with the pox. So don't be going near the Dunlaps' place until you hear it's safe from me, in fact, I'd steer clear of Benning Street altogether. I'm gonna see if I can get the sheriff to put up some signs and maybe a fence or something to let people know to keep out. Anyway, I'm just going around telling folks, and I would appreciate it if you helped me spread the word before this gets out of hand."

By noon, the city guard was turning everyone out of their houses and shops searching for the escaped traitor, and the very first place they looked was the Dunlaps' home. The five guards on duty the night Emery disappeared were forced to draw lots, and one lone soldier went in. He came out finding nothing but a couple of sick people, neither of whom were Emery. After making his report at a distance, he returned to the Dunlaps to remain under quarantine.

The soldiers then tore through The Laughing Gnome, the marketplace, the old church, and even the scribe's office, leaving them all a mess. Squads of soldiers entered the sewers and came up soaked. They did not find the escaped traitor, but they did find a couple of chests that some said were filled with stolen silver.

There was no sign of Emery Dorn.

By nightfall, a make-shift wooden fence stood across Benning Street and a large whitewashed sign read:

KEEP OUT!
Quarantined by order of the Viceroy!

Two days later, the soldier who searched the Dunlaps' house died. He was seen in the yard covered with puss-filled boils. The doctor dug a hole himself while people watched from a distance. After that, no one went near Benning Street.

The city officials and those at The Gnome concluded Emery left town or died—secretly buried somewhere.

Arista, Hadrian, and Royce waited silently just outside the entrance to the bedroom until the doctor finished. "I've taken the bandages off him," Doctor Gerand said. He was an elderly man with white hair, a hooknose, and bushy eyebrows that managed to look sad even when he smiled. "He's much better today. A whipping like he took," he paused, unsure how to explain, "well, you saw what it did to the poor lady that hung alongside him. He should have died, but he's young. He'll bounce back once he wakes up and starts eating. Of course, his back will be scarred for life and he'll never be as strong as he was—too much damage. The only concern I have is noxious humors causing an imbalance in his body, but honestly, that doesn't look like it will be a problem. Like I said, the boy is young and strong. Let him continue to rest and he should be fine."

They followed the doctor downstairs, escorting him to the front door of the Dunlaps' home where he bid them goodnight.

Pausing in the doorway he looked back. "Emery is a good lad. He was my son's best friend. Jimmy was taken into the Imperial Army and died in some battle up north." He paused a moment, glancing at the floor. "Watching Emery on that post was like losing him all over again. Whatever happens now, I just wanted to say thank you." With that, the doctor left.

Arista saw the inside of more commoners homes over the last week than she had in her entire life. After visiting with the Bakers of Hintindar, she assumed all families lived in identical houses, but the

Dunlaps' home was nothing like the Bakers. It was two stories with a solid wooden floor on both levels, the upper story creating a thick-beamed ceiling to the lower. While still modest and a bit cramped, it showed touches of care and a dash of prosperity that Hintindar lacked. The walls were painted and decorated with pretty designs of stars and flowers, and the wood surfaces were buffed and stained. Knickknacks of glazed pottery and woodcarvings lined shelves above the fireplace. Unlike Dunstan and Arbor's sparse home, the Dunlaps had a lot of furniture. Wooden chairs with straw seats circled the table. Another pair bookended a spinning wheel surrounded by several wicker baskets. Little tables held vases of flowers and on the wall hung a cabinet with small doors and knobs. Kept neat, clean, and orderly, it was a house loved by a woman whose husband was a good provider, but rarely home.

"Are you sure you don't want anything else?" Mrs. Dunlap asked, while clearing the dinner plates. She was an old, plump woman who always wore an apron and matching white scarf and had a habit of wringing her wrinkled hands.

"We're fine," Arista told her. "And thank you again for letting us use your home."

The old woman smiled. "It's not so much a risk as you might think. My husband has been dead six years now. He proudly served as His Majesty Urith's coachman. Did you know that?" Her eyes sparkled as she looked off as if seeing him once more. "He was a handsome man in his driver's coat and hat with that red plume and gold broach. Yes, sir, a mighty fine-looking man, proud to serve the king, and had for thirty years."

"Was he killed with the king?"

"Oh, no." She shook her head. "But he died soon after, of heartbreak I think. He was very close to the royal family. Drove them everywhere they went. They gave him gifts and called him by his given name. Once, during a storm, he even brought the princes here to spend the night. The little boys talked about it for weeks. We never had children of our own, you see, and I think Paul—that's my husband—I think he thought of the royals as his own boys. It devastated him when they died in that fire—that horrible fire. Emery's father died in it too, did you know that? He was one of the king's bodyguards. There was so much death that terrible, terrible night."

"Urith was a good king?" Hadrian asked.

She shrugged. "I'm just an old woman, what do I know? People complained about him all the time when he was alive. They complained about the high taxes, and some of the laws, and how he would live in a castle with sixty servants dining on deer, boar, and beef all at the same meal while people in the city were starving. I don't know that there is such a thing as a good king, perhaps there are just kings that are good enough." She looked at Arista and winked. "Perhaps what we need is less kings and more womenfolk running the show."

Mrs. Dunlap went back to the work of straightening as they sat at the round dining table.

"Well," Royce began, looking at Arista, "step one of your rebellion is complete. So now what?"

She thought a moment then said, "We'll need to circulate the story of Emery leading the coming attack. Play him up as a hero, a ghost that the Empire can't kill."

"I've heard talk like that around town already," Royce said. "You were right about that at least."

Arista smiled. Such a compliment from Royce was high praise.

"We need to use word of mouth," she continued, "to get the momentum for the revolt started. I want everyone to know it is coming. I want them to think of it as inevitable as the coming of dawn. I want them to believe it can't fail. I'll need leaders as well.

Hadrian, keep an eye out for reliable men who can help lead the battle. Men others listen to and respect. I'll also need you to devise a battle plan to take the armory and the garrison for me. Unlike my brother, I never studied the art of war. They made me learn needlepoint instead. Do you know how often I have used needlepoint?"

Hadrian chuckled.

"It's also imperative that we get word to Alric to start the invasion from the north. Even if we take the city, Breckton can wait us out unless Melengar applies pressure. I would suggest asking the Diamond to send the message, but given how reliable they were last time and how utterly important this is—Royce, I need to ask you to carry the message for me. If anyone can get through and bring back help, it's you."

Royce pursed his lips, thinking, and then nodded. "I'll talk to Polish just the same and see if I can get him to part with one or two of his men to accompany me. You should write three messages to Alric. Each of us will carry one and spilt up if there's trouble. Three people will increase the odds that at least one will make it. And don't neglect to write an additional letter explaining how this trip south was all your idea. I don't want to bear the brunt of his anger when he finds out where you went. Oh, and of course an explanation of the fees to be paid," he said with a wink.

Arista sighed. "He'll want to kill me."

"Not if you succeed in taking the city," Hadrian encouraged.

"Speaking of which, after you complete the battle plan for the garrison you'll need to see about reaching Gaunt's army and taking command of it. I'm not exactly sure how you're going to do that, but I'll write you a decree and declare you general-ambassador in proxy, granting you the power to speak on my behalf. I'll give you the rank of Auxiliary Marshall and the title of Lord. That might just impress them and at least give you the legal right to negotiate and the credentials to command."

"I doubt royal titles will impress Nationalists much," Hadrian said.

"Maybe not, but the threat of the Northern Imperial Army should give you a good deal of leverage. Desperate men might be willing to cling to an impressive title in the absence of anything else."

Hadrian chuckled again.

"What?" she asked.

"Oh, nothing," he said. "I was just thinking that for an ambassador, you're a very capable general."

"No you weren't," she told him bluntly. "You're thinking that I'm capable for a *woman*."

"That, too."

Arista smiled. "Well, it's lucky that I am, because so far I'm pretty lousy at being a woman. I honestly can't stand needlepoint."

"I suppose I should set out tonight for Melengar," Royce said. "Unless there's something else you need before I go?"

Arista shook her head.

"How about you?" he asked Hadrian. "Assuming you survive this stunt, what are you going to do now that you know the heir is dead?"

"Hang on, are you sure the heir is dead?" Arista broke in.

"You were there. You heard what Bartholomew said," Hadrian replied. "I don't think he was lying."

"I'm not saying that he was…it's just that…well Esrahaddon seemed pretty convinced the heir was still alive when he left Avempartha. And then there's the church. They're after Esra, expecting him to lead them to the *real* heir. They so much as told me that when I was at Ervanon last year. So why is everyone looking if he's dead."

"There's no telling what Esrahaddon is up to. As for the church, they pretended to look for the heir just as they are pretending they found the heir," Royce said.

"Perhaps, but there's still the image that we saw in the tower. He seemed like a living, breathing person to me."

Royce thought. "Maybe there was a previous wife, or even a prostitute."

"You're assuming the heir was a man," Arista pointed out. "It could have been the woman."

Royce nodded. "Good point."

Hadrian shook his head. "There couldn't have been another child. My father would have known and searched for him…or *her*. No, Danbury knew the line ended or he wouldn't have stayed in Hintindar."

He glanced at Royce then lowered his eyes. "In any case, if I survive I won't be returning to Riyria."

Royce nodded. "You'll probably get killed anyway. But…I suppose you're okay with that—as happy as a dog with a bone."

"How's that?"

"Nothing."

There was a pause then Hadrian said, "It's not completely hopeless. It's just that damn cavalry. They'll cut down the Nationalists in a heartbeat. If only it would rain again."

"Rain?" Arista asked.

"Charging horses carrying heavy armored knights need solid ground. After the last few days, the ground has already dried. If I could engage them over tilled rain-drenched farmland, the horses will mire themselves and Dermont would lose his best advantage. But the weather doesn't look like it's gonna cooperate."

"So you would prefer it to rain non-stop between now and the battle?" Arista asked.

"That would be one sweet miracle, but I don't expect we'll have that kind of luck."

"Perhaps luck isn't what we need." Arista smiled at him.

MAKING IT RAIN

◈

The Dunlap household was dark except for the single candle Arista carried up the steps to the second floor. She had said her goodbyes to Royce and Hadrian. Mrs. Dunlap went to bed hours ago and the house was quiet. It was the first time in ages she found herself alone.

How can this plan possibly work? Am I crazy?

She knew what her old handmaid, Bernice, would say. Then the old woman would offer her a gingerbread cookie as a consolation prize.

What will Alric say when Royce reaches him?

Even if she succeeded, he would be furious that she disobeyed him and went off without telling anyone. She pushed those thoughts away and would worry about all that later. They could hang her for treason if they wished, so long as Melengar was safe.

All estimates indicated Breckton would arrive in less than four days. She would have to control the city by then. She planned to launch the revolt in two days and hoped she had at least a few days to recover, pull in supplies from the surrounding farms, and set up some defenses.

Royce would get through with the message. If he could get to Alric quickly, and if her brother moved fast, Alric could attack across the Galewyr in just a few days, and it would only take two or three days for word to reach Aquesta. Hearing that Alric was invading from the north, Sir Breckton would receive new orders. She would need to hold him off at least that long. All this assumed they successfully took the city and defeated Lord Dermont's knights to the south.

Two days. How long did it normally take to plan a successful revolution?

Longer than two days, she was certain.

"Excuse me. Hello?"

NYPHRON RISING

Arista stopped as she passed the open door of Emery's bedroom. They put him in the small room at the top of the stairs, in the same bed where the princes of Rhenydd once slept on a stormy night. Emery had remained unconscious since they stole him from the post. She was surprised to see his eyes open and looking back at her, his hair pressed from sleep, a puzzled look on his face.

"How are you feeling?" she asked, softly.

"Terrible," he replied. "Who are you? And where am I?"

"My name is Arista and you're at the Dunlaps on Benning Street." She set the candle on the nightstand and sat on the edge of the bed.

"But I should be dead," he told her.

"Awfully sorry to disappoint, but I thought you would be more helpful alive." She smiled at him.

His brow furrowed. "Helpful with what?"

"Don't worry about that now. You need to sleep."

"No! Tell me. I won't be a party to the Imperialists, I tell you!"

"Settle down, of course not. We need your help taking the city back *from* the Imperialists."

Emery looked at her, stunned. His eyes shifted from side to side. "I don't understand."

"I heard your plan in The Laughing Gnome. It was a good one and we are going to do it in two days, so you need to rest and get your strength back."

"Who are *we*? Who are you? How did you manage this?"

Arista smiled. "Practice, I guess."

"Practice?"

"Let's just say this isn't the first time I've had to save a kingdom from a traitorous murderer out to steal the throne. It's okay; just go back to sleep it will—"

"Wait! You said your name was *Arista?*"

She nodded.

MAKING IT RAIN

"You're the princess of Melengar!"

She nodded again. "Yes."

" But…but how…why?" He started to push up on the bed with his hands and winced.

"Calm down," she told him firmly. "You need to rest. I mean it."

"I shouldn't be lying down in your presence!"

"You will if I tell you to, and I am telling you to."

"I—I just can't believe…why…why would you come here?"

"I'm here to help."

"You're amazing."

"And you are suffering from a flogging that would have killed any man with the good sense to know he should be dead. Now you need to go back to sleep this instant, and that's an order. Do you understand?"

"Yes, Your Majesty."

She smiled. "I am not a ruling queen, Emery, just a princess, my brother is the king."

Emery looked embarrassed. "Your Highness, then."

"I would prefer it if you just called me Arista."

Emery looked shocked.

"Go ahead, give it a try."

"It's not proper."

"And is it proper that you should deny a princess' request? Particularly one who saved your life?"

He shook his head slowly. "Arista," he said shyly.

She smiled at him and, on an impulse, leaned over and kissed him on the forehead. "Good night, Emery," she said, and stepped back out of the room.

She walked back down the steps through the dark house and out the front door. The night was still. Just as Hadrian had mentioned the sky was clear, showing a bountiful banquet of stars spilling like dust across the vast blackness. Benning Street, a short lane that dead-ended at the Dunlaps' carriage house, was empty.

It was unusual for Arista to be completely alone outdoors. Hilfred had always been her ever-present shadow. She missed him and yet it felt good to be on her own facing the night. It had only been a few days since she rode out of Medford, but she knew she was not the same person who left. She had always feared her life would be no more than that of a woman of privilege, helpless and confined. She escaped that fate and entered into the more prestigious, but equally restricted, role of ambassador, which was nothing more than a glorified messenger. Now, however, she felt for the first time she was finding her true calling.

She began to hum softly to herself. The spell she cast on the Seret Knights had worked, yet no one taught her how to do it. She invented the spell, drawing from a similar idea and her general knowledge of the Art.

That is what makes it an art.

There was indeed a gap in her education, but it was because what was missing could not be taught. Esrahaddon had not held back anything. The gap was the reality of magic. Instructors could teach the basic techniques and methods, but a mastery of mechanical knowledge can never make a person an artist. No one can teach creativity or invention. A spark needs to come from within. It must be something unique, something discovered by the individual, a leap of understanding, a burst of insight, the combining of common elements in an unexpected way.

Arista knew it to be true. She had known it since killing the knights. The knowledge both excited and terrified her. The horrible deaths of the seret only compounded that terrible realization. Now, however, standing alone in the yard under the blanket of stars and the stillness of the warm summer night, she embraced her understanding and it was thrilling. There was danger, of course, both intoxicating and alluring, and she struggled to contain her emotions. Recalling the death cries of the knights and the ghastly looks on their faces helped to ground her. She did not want to get lost in that power. In her mind's eye, the Art was a great beast, a dragon of limitless potential that yearned to be set free, but a mindless beast let loose upon the world would be a terrible thing. She understood the wisdom of Arcadius and the need to restrain the passion she now touched.

Arista set the candle down before her and cleared her mind to focus.

She reached out and pressed her fingers in the air as if gently touching the surface of an invisible object. Power vibrated like the strings of a harp as her humming became a chant. They were not the words that Esrahaddon had taught her. Nor was it an incantation from Arcadius. The words were her own. The fabric of the universe was at her fingertips, and she fought to control her excitement. She plucked the strings on her invisible harp. She could play individual notes or chords, melodies, rhythms, and a multitude of combinations of each. The possibilities of creation were astonishing and so numerous were the choices that she was equally overwhelmed. It would clearly take a lifetime, or more, to begin to grasp the potential she now felt. Tonight however, her path was simple and clear. A flick of her wrist and sweep of her fingers, almost as if she was motioning farewell, and at that moment the candle blew out.

A wind gusted. The dry soil of the street whirled into a dirt-devil. Old leaves and bits of grass buffeted about. The stars faded as thick full clouds crept across the sky. On a tin roof, she heard it. It sang on the metal, the chorus of her song, and then she felt the splatter of rain on her upturned and laughing face.

Chapter 13
MODINA

The ceiling of the Grand Imperial Throne Room was a dome painted robin's egg blue interspersed with white puffy clouds mimicking the sky on a gentle summer's day. The painting was heavy and uninspired, but Modina thought it was beautiful. She could not remember the last time she saw the real sky.

Her life since Dahlgren was a nightmare of vague unpleasant people and places she could not, and did not care to, remember. She had no idea how much time passed since the death of her father. It did not matter. Nothing did. Time was a concern of the living, and if she knew anything it was that she was dead. A ghost drifting dream-like, pushed along by unseen hands, hearing disembodied voices—but something had changed.

Amilia had come, and with her the haze and fog that she had been lost in for so long had begun to lift. She became aware of the world around her.

"Keep your head up, and don't look at them," Nimbus was telling her. "You are the empress and they are beneath you, contemptuous and not worthy of even the slightest glance from your imperial eyes. Back straight. Back straight."

MODINA

Modina, dressed in a formal gown of gold and white, stood on the imperial dais before an immense and gaudy throne. She scratched it once and discovered the gold was a thin veneer over dull metal. The dais itself was twelve feet from the ground with sheer sides except for where the half moon stairs provided access. The stairs were removable, allowing her to be set on display, the perfect unapproachable symbol of the New Empire.

Nimbus shook his head miserably. "It's not going to work; she's not listening."

"She's just not used to standing straight all the time," Amilia told him.

"Perhaps a stiff board sewn into her corset and laced tight?" a steward proposed timidly.

"Actually, that's not a bad idea," Amilia replied. She looked at Nimbus, "What do you think?"

"Better make it a *very* stiff board," Nimbus replied, sardonically.

They waved over the royal tailor and seamstress and an informal meeting ensued. They droned on about seams, stays, and ties while Modina looked down from above.

Can they see the pain in my face?

She did not think so. She did not see sympathy in their eyes, but awe—awe and admiration. They simultaneously marveled and quaked when in her presence. She heard them whisper about *the beast* she slew, and how she was the daughter of a god. To the thousands of soldiers, knights, and commoners she was something to worship.

Until recently, Modina had been oblivious to it all. Her mind shut in a dark hole where any attempt to think caused such anguish she recoiled back into the dull safety of the abyss. Time dulled the pain, and slowly the words of nearby conversations seeped in. She began to understand. According to what she overheard, she and her father were descendents of some legendary lost king. This was why only they could harm the beast. She had been anointed empress, but she was not certain what that meant. So far, it meant pain and isolation.

Nyphron Rising

Modina stared at those around her without emotion. She was no longer capable of feeling. There was no fear, anger, or hate, nor was there love or happiness. She was a ghost haunting her own body, watching the world with detached interest. Nothing that transpired around her held any importance—except Amilia.

Previously the people hovering around her were vague gray faces. They spoke to her of ridiculous notions the vast majority she could not begin to comprehend even if she wanted to. Amilia was different. When she spoke it was of things she understood. Amilia told stories of her family and reminded her of another girl—a girl named Thrace—who died and was just a ghost now. It was a painful memory, but Amilia managed to remind her about times before the darkness, before the pain, when there was still someone in the world that loved her.

When Saldur threatened to send Amilia away, she could see the terrible fear in the girl's eyes. She recognized that fear. Saldur's voice was the screech of the beast and at that moment, she awoke from her long dream. Her eyes focused, seeing clearly for the first time since that night. She would not allow the beast to win again.

Somewhere in the chamber, out of sight of the dais, a door slammed. The sound echoed around the marbled hall. Loud footsteps followed with an even louder conversation.

"I don't understand why I can't launch an attack against Alric on my own," the voice came from an agitated well-dressed man.

"Breckton's army will dispatch the Nationalists in no time then he can return to Melengar and you can have your prize, Archie." replied the voice of an older man. "Melengar isn't going anywhere, and it's not worth the risk."

The younger voice she did not recognize, but the older one she had heard many times before. They called him Regent Ethelred. The pair of nobles and their retinue came into view. Ethelred was dressed as she usually saw him—red velvet and gold silk. His thick mustache and beard betrayed his age, as both were going steadily gray.

The younger man walking beside him dressed in a stylish scarlet silk tunic with a high-ruffed collar, an elegant cape, and an extravagant plumed hat that matched the rest of his attire perfectly. Taller than the regent, his long auburn hair trailed down his back in a ponytail. They walked at the head of a group of six others: personal servants, stewards, and court officials. Four of the six Modina recognized, as she had seen the little parade before.

There was the court scribe, who went everywhere carrying a ledger. He was a plump man with long red cheeks and a balding head who always had a feathered quill behind each ear, making him look like a strange bird. His staunchly straight posture and odd strut reminded her of a quail parading through a field, and because she did not know the scribe's name, in her mind she dubbed him simply *The Quail*.

There was also Ethelred's valet, whom she labeled the *White Mouse,* as he was a thin, pale man with stark white hair whose fastidious pampering seemed rodent-like. She never heard him speak except to say "of course, my lord." He continuously flicked lint from Ethelred's clothes, and was always on hand to take a cloak or change the regent's footwear.

Then there was *The Candle* because he was a tall, thin man with wild red curly hair and a drooping mouth that sagged like tallow wax.

The last of the entourage was a soldier of some standing. He wore a uniform that had dozens of brightly colored ribbons pinned to it.

"I would appreciate you using a formal address when we are in public," Archie pointed out.

Ethelred turned as if surprised to see they were not alone in the hall.

"Oh," he said, quickly masking a smile. Then in a tone heavy with sarcasm proclaimed, "Forgive me, *Earl of Chadwick*," then added, "I didn't notice them. They are more like furniture to me. My point was, however, that we only suspect the extent of Melengar's weakness. Attacking them would introduce more headaches than it is worth. As it is, there is no chance Alric will attack us. He's a boy, but not so foolhardy as to provoke the destruction of his little kingdom."

"Is that…" Archibald stared up at Modina and stopped walking so that Ethelred lost track of him for a moment.

"The empress? Yes," Ethelred replied, his tone revealing a bit of his own irritation that the earl had apparently not heard what he just said.

"She's…she's…beautiful."

"Hmm? Yes, I suppose she is," Ethelred responded without looking. Instead, he turned to Amilia who, along with everyone else, was standing straight, her eyes looking at the floor. "Saldur tells me you're our little miracle worker. You got her eating, speaking and generally cooperating. I am pleased to hear it."

Amilia curtseyed in silence.

"She will be ready in time, correct? We can ill-afford another fiasco like the one we had at the coronation. She couldn't even make an appearance. You will see to that, won't you?"

"Yes, my lord." Amilia curtseyed again.

The Earl of Chadwick's eyes remained focused on Modina, and she found his expression surprising. She did not see the awe inspired look of the palace staff, nor the cold callous countenance of her handlers. His face bore a broad smile.

A soldier entered the hall, walking briskly toward them. The one with the pretty ribbons left the entourage and strode forward to intercept him. They spoke in whispers for a brief moment, and then the other soldier handed over some parchments. *Ribbon Man* opened and read them silently to himself before returning to Ethelred's side.

"What is it?"

Modina

"Your lordship, Admiral Gafton's blockade fleet succeeded in capturing the *Ellis Far*, a small sloop, off the coast of Melengar. On board they found parchments signed by King Alric granting the courier permission to negotiate with the full power of the Melengar crown. The courier and ship's captain were unfortunately killed in the action. The coxswain, however, was taken and persuaded to reveal the destination of the vessel as Tur Del Fur."

Ethelred nodded his understanding. "Trying to link up with the Nationalists, but that was expected. The sloop sailed from Roe then?"

"Yes."

"You're sure no other ship slipped past?"

"The reports indicate it was the only one."

While Ethelred and the soldier spoke and the rest of the hall remained still as statues, only the Earl of Chadwick was unaffected. Modina did not return his gaze, and it made her uncomfortable the way he stared at her.

He ascended the steps and knelt. "Your eminence," he said, gently taking her hand and kissing the ring she wore. "I am Archibald Ballentyne, twelfth Earl of Chadwick."

Modina said nothing.

"Archibald?" Ethelred's voice once more.

"Forgive my rude approach," the earl continued, "but I find I can't help myself. How strange it is that we haven't met before. I've been to Aquesta many times but never had the pleasure. Bad luck I suppose, I am certain you are very busy, and as I command a substantial army, I am busy as well. Recent events have seen fit to bring my command here. It is not something I was pleased with. That is until now. You see, I was doing very well conquering new lands for your growing Empire, and having to stop I considered unfortunate. But my regret has turned to one of genuine delight as I've been blessed to behold your splendor."

"Archie!" Ethelred had been calling out to him for some time, but it was not until he used that name that the well-dressed man's attention finally left her. "Stop with that foolishness, will you. We need to get to the meeting."

The earl frowned in irritation.

"Please forgive me, your eminence, but duty calls."

The moment the practice was over, they changed Modina back into her simple dress and she was escorted to her cell. She thought there was a time when two palace soldiers walked with her everywhere, but now there was only one. His name was Gerald. That was all she knew about him, which was strange because she saw him every day. Gerald escorted her wherever she went and stood guard outside her cell door. She assumed he took breaks, most likely late at night, but in the mornings when she and Amilia went to breakfast he was always there. She never heard him speak. They were quite a quiet pair.

When she reached the cell door, it was open, the dark interior waiting. He never forced her in. He never touched her. He merely stood patiently, taking up his post at the entrance. She hesitated before the threshold, and when she looked at Gerald he stared at the floor.

"Wait." Amilia trotted up the corridor toward them. "Her eminence is moving today."

Both Gerald and Modina looked puzzled.

"I've given up talking to the Lord Chamberlin," Amilia declared. She was speaking quickly and seemed to address them both at once. "Nimbus is right—I am the Secretary to the Empress after all." She focused on Gerald. "Please escort her eminence to her new bedroom on the east wing's fifth floor."

MODINA

The order was weak, not at all the voice of a noblewoman. It lacked the tenor of confidence, the power of arrogance. There was a space of time, a beat of uncertainty when no one moved and no one spoke. Committed now, Amilia remained awkwardly stiff facing Gerald. For the first time Modina noticed how large a man he was, the sword at his side, the castle guard uniform, every line straight, every bit of metal polished.

Gerald nodded, and moved aside.

"This way, your eminence," Amilia said, letting out a breath.

The three of them walked to the central stairs as Amilia continued to talk. "I got her eating, I got her to talk—I just want a better place for her to sleep. How can they argue? No one is even on the fifth floor."

As they reached the main hall they passed several surprised servants. One young woman stopped, stunned.

"Anna." Amilia caught her attention. "It is Anna, isn't it?"

The woman nodded, unable to take hear eyes off Modina.

"The empress is moving to a bedroom on the fifth floor. Run and get linens and pillows."

"Ah—but Edith told me to scrub the—"

"Forget Edith."

"She'll beat me."

"No, she won't," Amilia said, and thought for a moment. With sudden authority she continued, "From now on, you are working for the empress—her personal chambermaid—from now on you report directly to me, do you understand?"

Anna looked shocked.

"What do you want to do?" Amilia asked. "Defy Edith Mon or refuse the empress? Now get those linens and get the best room on the fifth floor in order."

"Yes, your eminence," she addressed Modina, "right away."

They climbed the stairs, moving quickly by the fourth floor. In the east wing, the fifth floor was a single long hall with five doors. Light entered from a narrow slit at the far end, revealing a dust-covered corridor.

Amilia looked at the doors for a moment. Shrugging, she opened one and motioned for them to wait as she entered. When she returned, she grimaced and said, "Let's wait for Anna."

They did not have to wait long. The chambermaid returned with an armload of linens, chased by two young boys with rags, a broom, a mop, and a bucket. Anna panted for breath and her brow glistened. The chambermaid traversed the corridor and selected the door at the far end. She and the boys rushed in. Amilia joined them. Before long, the boys raced back out and returned hauling various items: pillows, a blanket, more water, brushes. Modina and Gerald waited in the hallway, listening to the grunts and bumps and scrapes. Soon Anna exited, covered in dirt and dust, dragging armloads of dirty rags. Then Amilia reappeared and motioned for Modina to enter.

Sunlight. She spotted the brilliant shaft spilling in, slicing across the floor, along a tapestry-covered wall, and over a massive bed covered in satin sheets and a host of fluffy pillows. There was even a thick carpet on the floor. A mirror and a washbasin sat on a small stand. A little writing desk stood next to a fireplace, and on the far wall was the open window.

Modina walked forward and looked out at the sky, breathing in the fresh air she fell to her knees. It was narrow, but Modina could peer down into the courtyard below or look up directly into the blue of the sky—the real sky. She rested her head on the sill, reveling in the sunshine like a drought victim douses themselves with water. Until that moment, she had not noticed how starved she was for fresh air and sunlight. She thought Amilia had spoken to her, but she was too busy looking at the sky.

Smells were a treat. A cool breeze blew in, tainted by the stables below. For her, this was a friendly familiar scent, hearty and comforting. Birds flew past. A pair of swallows darted and dove in aerial acrobatics as they chased each other. They had a nest in a crevice above one of the other windows that dotted the exterior wall.

She did not know how long she knelt there. At some point, she realized she was alone. The door behind her had closed, a blanket draped over her shoulders. Eventually she heard voices drifting up from below.

"We've spent more than enough time on the subject, Archibald. The case is closed." It was Ethelred's voice, coming from one of the windows just below hers.

"I know you are disappointed," she recognized the fatherly tone of Bishop Saldur. "Still, you have to be mindful of the big picture. This isn't just some wild land grab; this is an Empire we are building."

"Two months at the head of an army and he acts as if he were a war-hardened general!" Ethelred laughed.

Another voice spoke, too softly or too distant from the window for her to hear. Then she heard the earl once again. "I've taken Glouston and the Rilan Valley through force of arms and thereby secured the whole northern rim of Warric. I think I've proved my skill."

"Skill? You let Marquis Lanaklin escape to Melengar and you failed to secure the wheat fields in Rilan, which burned. Those crops would have fed the entire Imperial Army for the next year, but now they are lost because you were preoccupied with taking an empty castle."

"It wasn't empty..." There was more said but too faint to hear.

"The marquis was gone. The reason for taking it went with him," the bellowing voice of Ethelred thundered. The regent must be standing very near the window, as she could hear him the best.

"Gentlemen," Saldur intervened, "water under the bridge. What's past is past. What we need to concern ourselves with is the present and the future, and at the moment both go by the same name—Gaunt."

Again, there were other voices speaking too faintly, their sounds fading to silence. All Modina could hear was the hoeing of servants weeding the vegetable garden below.

"I agree," Ethelred suddenly said. "We should have killed that bastard years ago."

"Calm yourself, Lanis," Saldur's voice boomed. Modina wasn't certain if he was using Ethelred's first name or addressing someone else whose voice was too distant for her to catch. "Everything has its season. We all knew the Nationalists wouldn't give up their freedom without a fight. Granted we had no idea Gaunt would be their general, or that he would prove to be such a fine military commander. We had assumed he was nothing more than an annoying anarchist, a lone voice in the wilderness like our very own Deacon Thomas. His transformation into a skilled general was—I will admit—a bit unexpected. Nevertheless, his successes are not beyond our control."

"And what does that mean?" someone asked.

"Luis Guy had the foresight to bring us a man who could effectively deal with the problems of Delgos and Gaunt and I present him to you today. Gentlemen, let me introduce Merrick Marius." His voice began to grow faint. "He's quite a remarkable man…been working for us these…on a…" Saldur's voice drifted off, too far from the window.

There was a long silence, then Ethelred spoke again, "Let him finish, you'll see."

Again the words were too quiet for her to hear.

Modina listened to the wind as it rose and rustled distant leaves. The swallows returned and played again, looping in the air. Below in the courtyard somewhere out of her sight she could hear the harsh shouts of soldiers in the process of changing guards. She had nearly forgotten about the conversation from below when abruptly she heard a communal gasp.

"You're not serious?" an unknown voice asked in a stunned tone.

More quiet murmurings.

"…and as I said, it would mark the end of Degan Gaunt and the Nationalists forever," Saldur's voice returned.

"But at what cost, Sauly?" another voice floated in. Normally too far it was now loud and clear.

"We have no other choice," Ethelred put in. "The Nationalists are marching north toward Ratibor. They must be stopped."

"This is insane. I can't believe you are even contemplating it!"

"We've done much more than contemplate. Nearly everything is in place. Isn't that so?" Saldur asked.

Modina strained to hear, but the voice that replied was too faint.

"We'll send it by ship after we receive word that all is set," Saldur explained. There was another pause, and then he spoke again, "I think we all understand that."

"I see no reason to hesitate any longer," Ethelred said. "We are all in agreement then?"

A number of voices spoke their acknowledgement.

"Excellent. Marius, you should leave immediately…"

"There's just one more thing…" She had not heard this voice before and he faded, no doubt walking away from the window.

Saldur's voice returned. "You have? Where? Tell us at once!"

More muffled conversation.

"Blast, man! I can assure you you'll get paid," Ethelred said.

"If he's led you to the heir, he is no longer of any use. That's right, isn't it Sauly? You and Guy have a greater interest in this, but unless you have an objection I say be done with him at your earliest convenience."

Another long pause.

277

"I think the Nyphron Empire is good for it, don't you?" Saldur said.

"You're quite the magician, aren't you Marius?" said Ethelred again. "We should have hired your services earlier. I'm not a fan of Luis Guy or any of the Patriarch's sentinels, but it seems his decision to employ you was certainly a good one."

The voices drifted off, growing fainter until it was quiet.

Most of what she heard held no interest for Modina, too many unknown names and places. She had only the vaguest notions of the terms Nationalist, Monarchist, and Imperialist. Tur Del Fur was a famous city, she heard of before—some place south, but Degan Gaunt was only a name. She was glad the talking was over. She preferred the quiet sounds of the wind, trees, and the birds. They took her back to an earlier time, a different place. As she sat looking out at her sliver of the world, she found herself wishing she could still cry.

Chapter 14
THE EVE

Gill had a hard time seeing anything clearly in the pouring rain, but he was certain that a man was walking right at him. He felt for the horn hanging at his side and regretted trapping it underneath his rain smock that morning. On thirty watches, he had never needed it. He peered through the gray curtain—no army, just the one guy. He was dressed in a cloak that hung like a soaked rag, his hood cast back, his hair slicked flat. No armor or shield, but two swords hung from his belt, and Gill spotted an additional sword—the two-handed pommel of a great sword—on his back. The man walked steadily through the muddy field. He seemed to be alone and could hardly pose a threat to the nearly one thousand men bivouacked on the hill. If he sounded the alarm, he would never hear the end of it. Gill was confident he could handle one guy.

"Halt!" Gill shouted over the drumming rain as he pulled his sword from its sheath and brandished it at the stranger. "Who are you, and what do you want?"

"I am here to see Commander Parker," the man said, not showing any signs of slowing. "Take me to him at once."

Gill laughed. "Oh, aren't you the bold one," he said, extending the sword. The stranger walked right up to the tip as if he meant to impale himself. "Stop or I'll run—"

Before Gill could finish, the man hit the flat face of the sword. The vibration ran down the blade, breaking Gill's grip. A second later the man had the weapon and was pointing it at him.

"I gave you an order, picket," the stranger snapped. "I am not accustomed to repeating myself to my troops. Look sharp or I'll have you flogged."

Then the man returned his sword, which only made matters worse.

"What's your name, picket?"

"Gill, ah, sir," he said, adding the *sir* unsure if this man was an officer or not.

"Gill, in future, when standing watch, arm yourself with a crossbow and never let even one man approach to within one hundred feet without putting a hole through him, do you understand?" The man did not wait for an answer. He walked past him and continued striding up the hill through the tall wet grass.

"Umm, yes, sir, but I don't have a crossbow, sir," Gill said as he jogged behind him.

"Then you had best get one, isn't that right?" the man called over his shoulder.

"Yes, sir." Gill nodded even though the man was ahead of him. The man walked past scores of tents, heading toward the middle of the camp. Everyone was inside away from the rain, and no one saw him pass. The tents were a haphazard array of rope and stick-propped canvas. No two were alike, as they scrounged supplies as they moved. Most were cut from ship sails grabbed at the port in Vernes and again in Kilnar. Others made do with nothing but old bed linens and, in a few rare cases, actual tents were used.

The stranger paused at the top of the hill. When Gill caught up he asked, "Which of these tents belongs to Parker?"

THE EVE

"Parker? He's not in a tent, sir. He's in the farmhouse down that way," he said, pointing.

"Gill, why are you off your post?" Sergeant Milford growled at him as he came out of his tent, blinking as the rain stung his eyes. He was wrapped in a cloak, his bare feet showing pale beneath it.

"Well, I—" Gill began, but the stranger interrupted.

"Who is this now?" the stranger walked right up to Milford and stood with his hands on his hips, scowling.

"This here is Sergeant Milford, sir," Gill answered, and the sergeant looked confused.

The stranger inspected him and shook his head. "Sergeant, where in Maribor's name is your sword?"

"In my tent, but—"

"You don't think it necessary to wear your sword when an enemy army stands less than a mile away and could attack at any minute?"

"I was sleeping, sir!"

"Look up, sergeant!" the man said. The sergeant tilted his head up, wincing once more as rain hit his face. "As you can see, it is nearly morning."

"Ah—yes, sir. Sorry, sir."

"Now get dressed and get a new picket on Gill's post at once, do you understand?"

"Yes, sir. Right away, sir!"

"Gill!"

"Yes, sir!" Gill jumped.

"Let's get moving. I'm late as it is."

"Yes, sir!" Gill set off following once more, offering the sergeant a flummoxed shrug as he passed.

The main body camped on what everyone called Bingham Hill, apparently after farmer Bingham, who grew barley and rye in the fields below. Gill heard there was quite the hullabaloo when Commander Gaunt informed Bingham the army would be using his farm and

Gaunt was taking his house for a headquarters. The pastoral home with thatched roof and wooden beams found itself surrounded by a sea of congested camps. Flowers that once lined the walkway were crushed beneath a hundred boots. The barn housed the officers, and the stable provided storage and was used as a dispensary and tavern for those with rank. Everywhere there were tents and a hundred campfires burnt rings into the ground.

"Inform Commander Parker I am here," the stranger told the guard on the porch.

"And who are you?"

"Marshall Lord Blackwater."

The sentry hesitated only a moment then disappeared inside. He remerged quickly and held the door open.

"Thank you, Gill. That will be all," the stranger said, as he stepped inside.

"You're Commander Parker?" Hadrian asked the portly man before him who was sloppily dressed in a short black vest and dirty white britches. An up-turned nose sat in the middle of his soft face, which rested on a large wobbly neck.

He was seated before a rough wooden table littered with candles, maps, dispatches, and a steaming plate of eggs and ham. He stood up, pulling a napkin from his neck, and wiped his mouth. "I am, and you are Marshall Blackwater? I wasn't informed of—"

"Marshall *Lord* Blackwater," he corrected with a friendly smile and handed over his letter of reference.

Parker took the letter, roughly unfolding it, and began reading.

Wavy wooden beams edged and divided the pale yellowing walls. Along these hung pots, sacks, cooking tools, and what Hadrian guessed to be Commander Parker's sword and cloak. Baskets, pails, and jugs huddled in corners stacked out of the way on a floor that listed downhill toward the fireplace.

After reading the letter, Parker returned to his seat and tucked his napkin back into his collar. "You're not really a lord are you?"

Hadrian hesitated briefly. "Well, technically I am, at least for the moment."

"What are you when you're not a lord?"

"I suppose you could call me a mercenary. I've done a lot of things over the years."

"Why would a princess of Melengar send a mercenary to me?"

"Because I can win this battle for you."

"What makes you think I can't win it?"

"The fact that you're still in this farmhouse instead of the city. You are very likely a good manager and quartermaster, and I am certain a wonderful bookkeeper, but war is more than numbers and ledgers. With Gaunt gone, you might be a bit unsure of what to do next. That's where I can help you. As it happens, I have a great deal of combat experience."

"So you know about Gaunt's disappearance."

Hadrian did not like the tone in his voice. There was something there, something coy and threatening. Aggression was still his best approach. "This army has been camped here for days, and you've not launched a single foray at the enemy."

"It's raining," Parker replied. "The field is a muddy mess."

"Exactly," Hadrian said. "That's why you should be attacking. The rain will give you the upper hand. Call in your captains and I can explain how we can turn the weather to our advantage, but we must act quickly—"

"You'd like that, wouldn't you?" There was that tone again. This time more ominous. "I have a better idea, how about you explain to me why Arista Essendon would betray Degan?"

"She didn't. You don't understand, she's—"

"Oh she most certainly did!" Parker rose to his feet and threw his napkin to the floor as if it were a gauntlet of challenge. "And you needn't lie any further. I know why. She did it to save her miserable little kingdom." He took a step forward and bumped the table. "By destroying Degan, she hopes to curry favor for Melengar. So what are your real orders?" He advanced pointing an accusatory finger. "To gain our confidence? To lead this army into an ambush like you did with Gaunt? Was it you? Were you there? Were you one of the ones that grabbed him?"

Parker glanced at Hadrian's swords. "Or is it to get close enough to kill me?" he said, staggering backward. The commander knocked his head on a low-hanging pot that fell with a brassy clang. The noise made Parker jump. "Simms! Fall!" he cried, and the two sentries rushed in.

"Sir!" they said in unison.

"Take his swords. Shackle him to a stake. Get him out of—"

"You don't understand, Arista isn't your enemy," Hadrian interrupted.

"Oh, I understand perfectly."

"She was set up by the Empire just as Gaunt was."

"So she's missing too?"

"No, she's in Ratibor right now planning a rebellion to aid your attack."

Parker laughed aloud at that. "Oh please, sir! You do need lessons in lying. A *princess* of Melengar organizing an uprising in Ratibor? Get him out of here."

One of the soldiers drew his sword. "Remove your weapons now!"

Hadrian considered his options. He could run, but he would never get another opportunity to persuade them. Taking Parker prisoner would require killing Simms and Fall, and destroying any hope of gaining their trust. With no other choice, he sighed and unbuckled his belt.

THE EVE

~

"Exactly how confident are you that Hadrian will succeed in persuading the Nationalists to attack tomorrow morning?" Polish asked Arista as they sat at the Dunlaps' table, while outside it continued to storm.

"I have the same level of confidence in his success as I do in ours," Arista replied.

Polish smirked. "I keep forgetting you're a diplomat."

Eight other people sat around the little table where the city lay mapped out using knickknacks borrowed from Mrs. Dunlap's shelves. Those present were handpicked by Hadrian, Doctor Gerand, Polish, or Emery, who was back on his feet and eating everything Mrs. Dunlap put under his nose.

With Royce and Hadrian gone, Arista spent most of her time talking with the young Mr. Dorn. While no longer stumbling over using her first name, the admiration in his eyes was unmistakable, and Arista caught herself smiling self-consciously. He had a nice face—cheerful and passionate, and while he was younger even than Alric, she thought him more mature. Perhaps that came from hardship and struggle.

Since he regained consciousness she had babbled on about the trials that brought her there. He told her about his mother's death giving him life and growing up as a soldier's son. They both shared stories of the fires that robbed them of the ones they loved. She listened as he poured out his life's story of being an orphan with such intensity that it filled her eyes with tears. He had such a way with words, a means of inciting emotion and empathy. She realized Emery could have changed the world if only he were born noble. Listening to him, to his ideals, to his passion for justice and compassion, she realized this was what she could expect from Degan Gaunt. A common man with the heart of a king.

"You must understand it is not entirely up to me," Polish told them. "I don't issue policy in the guild. I simply don't have the authority to sanction an outright attack, particularly when there is nothing to be gained. Even if victory were assured, instead of a rather wild gamble, my hands would still be tied."

"Nothing to be gained?" Emery said stunned. "There is a whole city to be gained! Furthermore, if the Imperial Army is routed from the field, it is possible that all Rhenydd might fall under the banner of the Delgos Republic."

"I would also add," Arista said, "that defeating the Imperials here would leave Aquesta open for assault by the remainder of the Nationalists, Melengar, and possibly even Trent—if I can swing their alliance. Once Aquesta falls, Colnora will be a free city and certain powerful merchants could find themselves in legitimate seats of power."

"You are good. I'll grant you that, my lady," Polish replied. "But there are many *ifs* in that scenario, and the Monarchists won't allow Colnora to be ruled by a commoner. Lanaklin would assume the throne of Warric and likely appoint his own duke to run the city."

"Well, the Diamond's position will certainly continue to decline if you fail to aid us and the Empire's strength grows," Arista shot back.

Polish frowned and shook his head. "This is far beyond the bounds of my mandate. I simply can't commit without orders from the Jewel. The Imps leave the Diamond alone, for the most part. They see us as inevitable as the rats in any sewer. As long as we don't make too much of a nuisance, they leave us to our scurrying. But if we do this, they will declare war. The Diamond will no longer be neutral. We'll be a target in every Imp city. Hundreds could be imprisoned or executed."

"We could keep your involvement a secret," Emery offered.

Polish laughed. "Even if that were possible—which it's not—as the winner chooses which secrets are kept, you would have to prove you are going to win before I could help you and, clearly by then you would not need my assistance. I am sorry, my rats will do what we can, but joining in the assault is not possible."

"Can you at least see that the armory door is unlocked?" Emery asked.

Polish thought a moment and nodded. "That I can do."

"Can we get back to the plan?" Doctor Gerand asked.

Before leaving, Hadrian outlined the details for a strategy to take the city. Emery's idea was a good one, but an idea simply was not the same as a battle plan and they were all thankful for Hadrian's advice. He had explained that surprise was their greatest tool and catching the armory unaware was their best tactic. After that, things would be more difficult. Their greatest adversary would be time. It was essential they secure the armory quickly in order to prepare for the attack by the garrison.

"I will lead the men into the armory," Emery declared. "If I survive, I will take my place in the square with the men at the weak point of the line."

Everyone nodded grimly.

Hadrian's plan further called for the forming of two straight lines—one before the other—outside the armory and to purposely leave a gap as a weak point. Professional soldiers would look for this kind of vulnerability so the rebels could predetermine where the attack would fall the hardest. He warned that the men stationed there would have the most casualties, but it would also allow them to fold the line and generate a devastating envelopment maneuver, which would take advantage of their superior numbers.

"I will lead the left flank," Arista said, and everyone looked at her, stunned.

"My lady," Emery began, "you understand I hold you in the highest esteem, but a battle is no place for a woman and I would be sorely grieved should your life come into peril."

"My life will be in peril no matter where I am, so I may as well be of some use. Besides, this is all my idea. I can't stand by while all of you risk your own lives."

"You need fear no shame," Doctor Gerand told her. "You have already done more than we can hope to repay you for."

"Nevertheless," she said resolutely, "I will stand with the line."

"Can you wield a sword too?" Perin the Grocer asked. His tone was not mocking or sarcastic, but one of expectant amazement, as if he anticipated she would reply that she was a master swordfighter of some renown.

The miraculous survival of Emery was only one of the rallying points of the rebellion. Arista had overlooked the power of her own name. Emery pointed out that she and her brother were heroes to those wishing to fight the Empire. Their victory over Percy Braga, immortalized in the traveling theater play, had inspired many all across Apeladorn. All the recruiters had to do was whisper that Arista Essendon had come to Ratibor and that she stole Emery from the clutches of the Empire, and most people simply assumed victory was assured.

"Well," she said, "I certainly have just as much experience as most of the merchants, farmers, and tradesmen that will be fighting alongside me."

No one said anything for a long while, and then Emery stood up.

"Forgive me, Your Highness, but I cannot allow you to do this."

Arista gave him a harsh, challenging stare and Emery's face cringed, exposing that a mere unpleasant glance from her was enough to hurt him.

"And how do you plan to stop me?" she snapped, recalling all the times her father or brother, or even Count Pickering, shooed her out of the council hall insisting she would spend her time more productively with a needle in her hand.

THE EVE

"If you insist on fighting, I will not," he said simply.

Doctor Gerand stood up. "Neither will I."

"Nor I," Perin said, also rising.

Arista scowled at Emery. Again her glare appeared to hurt the man, but he remained resolute. "Alright. Sit down. You win."

"Thank you, my lady," Emery said.

"Then I will lead the left flank, I suppose," Perin volunteered. He was one of the larger men at the table, stocky and strong.

"I will take the right flank," Doctor Gerand said.

"That is very brave of you, sir," Emery told him, "But I will ask Adam the Wheeler to take that responsibility. He has fighting experience."

"And he's not an old man," the doctor said bitterly.

Arista knew the helplessness that he was feeling. "Doctor, your services will be required to tend to the injured. Once the armory is taken, you and I will do what we can for those that are wounded."

They went over the plan once more from beginning to end. Arista and Polish came up with several potential problems: What if too few people came? What if they could not secure the armory? What if the garrison did not attack? They discussed and made contingency plans until they were certain everything was accounted for.

As they concluded, Doctor Gerand drew forth a bottle of rum and called for glasses from Mrs. Dunlap. "Tomorrow morning we go into battle," he said. "Some of us at this table will not survive to see the sunset again." He lifted his glass. "To those who will fall and to our victory."

"And to the good lady who made it possible," Emery added, and they all raised their glasses to her and drank.

Arista drank with the rest, but found the liquor to have a bitter taste.

Nyphron Rising

୬

The princess lay awake in the tiny room across the hall from Mrs. Dunlap's bedroom. It was smaller than her maid's quarters in Medford, with only a small window and a tiny shelf to hold a candle. There was so little room between the walls and the bed that she was forced to crawl over the mattress to enter. She could not sleep. The battle to take the city would start in just a few hours and she was consumed by nervous energy. Her mind raced through precautions, running a checklist over and over again.

Have I done all I can to prepare?

Everything was about to change. For good or ill.

Will Alric forgive me if I die? She gave a bitter laugh. *Will he forgive me if I live?*

She stared at the ceiling, wondering if there was a spell to help her sleep.

Magic.

She considered using it in the coming battle. She toyed with the idea while tapping her feet together, anxiously listening to the rain patter the roof.

If I can make it rain what else can I do? Could I conjure a phantom army? Rain fire? Open the earth to swallow the garrison?

She was certain of only one thing—she could boil blood. The thought sobered her.

What if I lose control? What if I boiled the blood of our men…or Emery?

When she boiled the water in Sheridan, the nearby clothing had sizzled and hissed. Magic was not so easy. Perhaps with time she could master it, but already she sensed her limitations. It was clear now why Esrahaddon had given her the task of making it rain. Previously she thought it an absurd challenge to attempt such an immense feat.

THE EVE

Now she realized that making it rain was easy. The target was broad as the sky and the action was natural—the equivalent of asking a marksman to throw a rock and try and hit the ground. The process would be the same, she guessed, for any spell, the drawing of power, the focus, and the execution through synchronized movement and sound, but the idea of pin-pointing such unruly force to a specific target was daunting. She realized with a shudder that if Royce and Hadrian had been on the hill that night, they, too, would have died along with the seret. There was no doubt she could defeat the garrison, but she might kill everyone in Ratibor in the process. It could be possible to use the Art to draw down lightning or summon fire to consume the soldiers, but it would be like asking a first-year music student to compose and orchestrate a full symphony.

No, I can't take that risk.

She turned her mind to more practical issues. Did they have enough bandages prepared? She had to remember to get a fire going to have hot coals for sealing wounds. Was there anything else she could do?

She heard a soft rapping and pulled the covers up, as she wore only a thin nightgown borrowed from Mrs. Dunlap. "Yes?"

"It's me," Emery said. "I hope I didn't wake you."

"Come in, please," she told him.

Emery opened the door and stood at the foot of the bed, wearing only his britches and an oversized shirt. "I couldn't sleep and I thought maybe you couldn't either."

"Who would have guessed that waiting to see if you will live or die would make it so hard to sleep?" She shrugged and smiled.

Emery smiled back and looked for a means to enter the room.

She sat up and propped two pillows behind her. "Just crawl on the bed," she told him, folding her legs and slapping the covers. He looked awkward but took her offer and crawled to sit at the foot of the mattress, which sank with his weight.

"Are you scared?" she inquired, and realized too late that it was not the kind of question a woman should ask of a man.

"Are you?" he parried, pulling his knees up and wrapping his arms around them. He was barefoot and his toes shone pale in the moonlight.

"Yes," she said. "I'm not even going to be on the line and I'm terrified."

"Would you think me a miserable coward if I said I was frightened too?"

"I would think you a fool if you weren't."

He sighed and let his head rest on his knees.

"What is it?"

"If I tell you something do you promise to keep it a secret?" he asked, keeping his head down.

"I am an ambassador. I do that sort of thing for a living."

"I've never fought in a battle before. I've never killed a man."

"I suspect that is the case for nearly everyone fighting tomorrow," she said, hoping he would assume she included herself in that statement. She could not bear to tell him the truth. "I don't think most of these people have ever used a sword."

"Some have." He lifted his head. "Adam the Wheeler fought with Ethelred's army against the Ghazel when Lord Rufus won his fame. Renkin Pool and Forrest the silversmith's son also fought. That's why I have them as leaders in the line. The thing is, everyone is looking to me like I am a great war hero, but I don't know if I will stand and fight or run like a coward. I might faint dead away at the first sight of blood."

Arista reached out, taking his hand in hers. "If there is one thing I am certain of," she looked directly in his eyes, "it is that you will stand and fight bravely. I honestly don't think you could do anything else. It just seems to be the way you're made. I think that is what everyone sees in you. Why they look up to you—and I do too."

THE EVE

Emery bowed his head. "Thank you, that was very kind."

"I wasn't being kind, just honest." Feeling suddenly awkward, she released his hand and asked him, "How is your back?"

"It still hurts," he said, raising his arm to test it. "But I'll be able to swing a sword. I really should let you get to sleep." He scrambled off the bed.

"It was nice that you came," she told him and meant it.

He paused. "I will only have one regret tomorrow."

"And what is that?"

"That I am not noble."

She gave him a curious look.

"If I were even a lowly baron and survived the battle, I would ride to Melengar and ask your brother for your hand. I would pester him until he either locked me up or surrendered you. I know that is improper. I know you must have dukes and princes vying for your affections, but I would try just the same. I would fight them for you. I would do anything...if only."

Arista felt her face flush and fought an urge to cover it with her hands. "You know, a common man whose father died in the service of his king, who was so bold as to take Ratibor and Aquesta, could find himself knighted for such heroics. As ambassador, I would point out to my brother that such an act would do well for our relationship with Rhenydd."

Emery's eyes brightened. They had never looked so vibrant or so deep. There was a joy on his face. He took a step back toward the bed, paused, then slowly withdrew.

"Well, then," Emery said at last, "I shall need my sleep if I am to be knighted."

"You shall indeed, *Sir* Emery."

"My lady," he said, and attempted a sweeping bow but halted partway with a wince and a gritting of his teeth. "Good night."

After he left her room, Arista discovered her heart was pounding and her palms moist. How shameful. In a matter of hours, men would die because of her. By noon, she could be hanging from a post, yet she was flushed with excitement because a man showed an interest in her. How horribly childish...how infantile...how selfish...and how wonderful. No one had ever looked at her the way he just had. She remembered how his hand felt and the rustle of his toes on her bed covers—what awful timing she had.

She lay in bed and prayed to Maribor that all would be well. They needed a miracle, and immediately she thought of Hadrian and Royce. Isn't that what Alric always called them...his miracle workers? Everything would be all right.

Chapter 15
THE SPEECH

Amilia sat biting her thumbnail, or what little was left of it. "Well?" she asked Nimbus. "What do you think? She seems stiff to me."

"Stiff is good," the thin man replied. "People of high station are known to be reserved and inflexible. It lends an air of strength to her. It's her chin that bothers me. The board in her corset fixed her back, but her chin—it keeps drooping. She needs to keep her head up. We should put a high collar on her dress, something stiff."

"A little late for that now," Amilia replied irritated. "The ceremony is in less than an hour."

"A lot can be done in that time, your ladyship," he assured her.

Amilia still found it awkward, even embarrassing to be referred to as *ladyship*. Nimbus, who always followed proper protocol, insisted on referring to her this way. His mannerisms rubbed off on the other members of the castle staff. Maids and pages, who only months earlier laughed and made fun of Amilia, took to bowing and curtsying. Even Ibis Thinly began addressing Amilia as *her ladyship*. It was flattering, but also fleeting. Amilia was only a noble in name—a title she could lose just as easily as it was won—and that is exactly what would happen in less than an hour.

"Alright, wait outside," she ordered. "I'll hand you the dress to take to the seamstress. Your eminence, can I please have the gown?"

Modina raised her arms as if in a trance and two handmaidens immediately went to work undoing the numerous buttons and hooks.

Amilia's stomach churned. She had done everything possible in the time allotted. Modina had been surprisingly cooperative and easily memorized and repeated the speech Saldur provided. It was short and easy to remember. Modina's role was remarkably simple. She would step onto the balcony, repeat the words, and withdraw. It would only be a few minutes, yet Amilia was certain disaster would follow.

Despite all the preparations, Modina simply was not ready. The empress had only recently showed signs of lucidity and managed to follow directions, but no more than that. In many ways, she reminded Amilia of a dog. Trained to sit and stay, a pup would do as it was told when the master was around, but how many could maintain their composure when left on their own? A squirrel passing by would break their discipline and off they would go. Amilia was not permitted on the balcony, and if anything unexpected happened there was no telling how the empress would react.

Amilia took the elaborate gown to Nimbus. "Make it quick. I don't want to be here with an empress clad only in her undergarments when the bell strikes."

"I will run like the wind, milady," he said with a forced smile.

"What are you doing out here?" Regent Saldur asked. Nimbus made a hasty bow then ran off with the empress' gown. The regent was lavishly dressed for the occasion, which made him even more intimidating than usual. "Why aren't you in with the empress? There is less than an hour before the presentation."

"Yes, your grace, but there are some last minute prep—"

Saldur took her angrily by the arm and dragged her inside

the staging room. Modina was wrapped in a robe and the two handmaidens fussed with her hair. They both stopped abruptly and curtsied.

Saldur took no notice. "Must I waste my time impressing on you the importance of this day?" he said while roughly releasing her. "Outside this palace, all of Aquesta is gathering, as well as dignitaries from all over Warric and even ambassadors from as far away as Trent and Calis. It is paramount that they see a strong, competent empress. Has she learned the speech?"

"Yes, your grace," Amilia replied with bowed head.

Saldur examined the empress in her disheveled robe and unfinished hair. He scowled and whirled on Amilia. "If you ruin this—if she falters, I will hold you personally responsible. A single word from me and you'll never be seen again. Given your background, I won't even have to create an excuse. No one will question your disappearance. No one will even notice you're gone. Fail me, Amilia, and I will see you deeply regret it."

He left, slamming the door behind him and leaving Amilia barely able to breathe.

"Your ladyship?" the maid Anna addressed her.

"What is it?" she asked, weakly.

"It's her shoe, my lady, the heel has come loose."

What else could go wrong?

On any ordinary day, nothing like this would happen, but today, because her life depended on it, disasters followed one upon another. "Get it to the cobbler at once and tell him if it isn't fixed in twenty minutes I'll—I'll—"

"I will tell him to hurry, my lady." Anna ran from the room, shoe in hand.

Amilia began to pace. The room was only twenty-feet long, causing her to turn frequently and making her dizzy, but she did it anyway. Her body was reacting unconsciously while her mind flew over every aspect of the ceremony.

NYPHRON RISING

What if she leaps off the balcony?

The thought hit her like a slap. As absurd as it seemed, it was possible. The empress was not of sound mind. With the noise and confusion of thousands of excited subjects, Modina could become overwhelmed and simply snap. The balcony was not terribly high, only thirty feet or so, it might not kill her if she landed well. Amilia, on the other hand, would not survive the fall.

Sweat broke out on her brow as her pacing quickened.

It was too late to put up a higher rail.

Perhaps a net at the bottom? No, that won't help. It was not the injury; it was the spectacle.

A rope? She could tie a length around Modina's waist and hold it from behind. That way if she made any forward movement she could stop her.

Nimbus returned, timidly peeking into the room. "What is it, milady?" he asked, seeing her expression.

"Hmm? Oh, everything. I need a rope and a shoe—but never mind that. What about the dress?"

"The seamstress is working as fast as she can. Unfortunately, I don't think there will be time for a test dressing."

"What if it doesn't fit? What if it chokes her so she can't even speak?"

"We must think positively, milady."

"That's easy for you to say, your life isn't dangling by a thread—perhaps literally."

"But surely, your ladyship, isn't in fear of such a thing merely from a dress alteration? We are civilized people after all."

"I'm not certain what civilization you're from Nimbus, but this one can be harsh to those who fail."

Amilia looked at Modina sitting quietly, oblivious to the importance of the speech she was about to give. They would do nothing to her. She was the empress and the whole world knew it.

THE SPEECH

If she disappeared there would be an inquiry and the people would demand justice for the loss of their god-queen. Even people as well placed as Saldur could hang for such a crime.

"Shall I bring the headdress?" Nimbus asked.

"Yes, please. Anna fetched it from the milliners this morning and likely left it in the empress' bedroom."

"And how about I bring a bite for you to eat, milady? You haven't had anything all day."

"I can't eat."

"As you wish. I will be back as soon as I can."

Amilia went to the window. From this vantage point she could just see the east gate, where scores of people poured through. Men, women, and children of all classes entered the outer portcullis. The gathering throng emitted a low murmur like some gigantic beast growling just out of sight. There was a knock at the door and in stepped the seamstress with the gown in her arms as if it were a newborn baby.

"That was fast," Amilia said.

"Forgive me, your ladyship, it's not quite done, but the royal tutor just stopped by and said I should finish up here where I can size it to her eminence's neck. It's not how things are done, you see. It's not right to make the great lady sit and wait on me like some dress dummy. Still, the tutor said if I didn't do as he said he—" She paused and lowered her voice to a whisper. "He said he'd have me horse whipped."

Amilia put a hand over her mouth to hide a smile. "He was not serious about the whipping, I can assure you, but he was quite right, this is too important to worry about inconveniencing her eminence. Get to work."

They dressed her once more in the gown and the seamstress worked feverishly, stitching in the rest of the collar. Amilia had begun to resume her pacing when there was another knock on the door. With the seamstress and maids occupied, Amilia opened it herself and was startled to find the Earl of Chadwick.

"Good evening, Lady Amilia," he said, bowing graciously. "I was hoping for a word with her eminence prior to the commencement."

"This is not a good time, sir," she said. Amilia could hardly believe she was saying "no" to a noble lord. "The empress is indisposed at the moment. Please understand."

"Of course, my apologies. Perhaps I could have a word with you then?"

"Me? Ah, well—yes, of course." Amilia stepped outside, closing the door behind her.

Amilia expected the earl would make his issue known right then, but instead he began to walk down the corridor and it took a moment for her to realize he expected her to follow.

"The empress is well I trust?"

"Yes, my lord," she said, glancing back at the door to the dressing room that was getting farther away.

"I am pleased to hear that," the earl said, then with sudden alarm added, "How rude of me. How are *you* feeling, my lady?"

"I am as well as can be expected, sir."

If Amilia was not so consumed with thoughts of the empress, she would have found it funny that an earl was embarrassed by not immediately inquiring about her own health.

"And it is beautiful weather for the festivities today, is it not?"

"Yes, sir, it is," she forced her voice to remain calm.

Nimbus, Anna, and the cobbler all appeared and rushed down the hall. Nimbus paused briefly, giving her a worried look before entering the dressing room.

"Allow me to be blunt," the earl said.

"Please do, sir." Amilia's anxiety neared the breaking point.

"Everyone knows you are the closest to the empress. She confides to no one but you. Can you—have you—does the empress ever speak of me?"

The Speech

Amilia raised her eyebrows in surprise. Under ordinary circumstances, the earl's hesitancy could have seemed quaint and even charming, but at that moment, she prayed he would just get it out and be done with it.

"Please, I know I am being terribly forward, but I am a forward man. I would like to know if she has ever thought of me, and if so, is it to her favor?"

"My lord, I can honestly say she has never once mentioned you to me."

The earl paused to consider this.

"I'm not sure how I should interpret that. I am certain she sees so many suitors. Can you do me a favor, my lady?"

"If it is in my power, sir."

"Could you speak to her about gracing me with a dance this evening at the ball after the banquet? I would be incredibly grateful."

"Her eminence won't be attending the banquet, sir. She never dines in public."

"Never?"

"I am afraid not, sir."

"I see."

The earl paused in thought as Amilia rapidly drummed the tips of her fingers together. "If you please, sir, I do need to be seeing to the empress."

"Of course, forgive me for taking up your valuable time. Still if you should perhaps mention me to her eminence and let her know I would very much like to visit with her."

"I will, your lordship. Now, if you will excuse me."

Amilia hurried back and found that the seamstress had finished the collar. It was tall and did indeed keep her chin up, although it looked horribly uncomfortable. Modina, of course, didn't seem to care. The cobbler, however, was still working on her shoe.

"What's going on here?" she asked.

"The new heel he put on was taller than the other," Nimbus told her. "He tried to resize, but in his haste he overcompensated and now it is shorter."

Amilia turned to Anna, "How long do we have?"

"About fifteen minutes," she replied gloomily.

"What about the headdress? I don't see it."

"It wasn't in the hall, or the bedroom, milady."

Anna's face drained of color. "Oh, dear Maribor forgive me. I forgot all about it!"

"You forgot? Nimbus!"

"Yes, milady?"

"Run to the milliner and fetch the headdress, and when I say run, I mean sprint do you hear me?"

"At once, milady, but I don't know where the milliner shop is."

"Get a page to escort you."

"The pages are all busy with the ceremony."

"I don't care! Grab one at sword point if necessary. Find one who knows the way and tell him it is by order of the empress and don't let anyone stop you, now move!"

"Anna!" Amilia shouted.

"Yes, my lady." The maid was trembling in tears. "I am so sorry, my lady, truly I am."

"We don't have time for apologies or tears. Go to the empress' bedroom and fetch her day shoes. She'll have to wear them instead. Do it now!"

Amilia slammed the door behind them and gave it a solid kick in frustration. She leaned her forehead against the oak as she concentrated on calming down. The gown would cover the shoes. No one would know the difference. The headdress was another matter. They worked on it for weeks and the regents would notice its absence. The milliner's shop was out in the city proper, and she had left it to Anna to pick it up. She could really only blame herself. She should have asked about it earlier and was furious at her incompetence. She kicked the door once more then turned around and slumped to the floor, her gown ballooning about her.

The ceremony began in minutes but there was still time. Modina's speech was last and Amilia was certain she would have at least another twenty, perhaps even thirty, minutes while the others addressed the crowd. Across from her, Modina sat stiff and straight in her royal gown of white and gold, her long neck held high by the new collar. There was something different about Modina she was watching Amilia with interest. She was actually studying her.

"Are you going to be alright?" she asked the empress.

Immediately the light in her eyes vanished and the blank stare returned.

Amilia sighed.

Regent Ethelred spoke on the colorfully bunted balcony for nearly an hour, though Amilia hardly heard a word of it. Something about the grandness and might of the New Empire and how Maribor had ordained it would unite all of humanity once again. He spoke of the Empire's military successes in the north and the bloodless annexation of Alburn and Dunmore. He followed this with the news of an expected surplus in wheat and barley and an end to the elven problem. They would no longer be allowed to roam free and instead of turning them into useless slaves they would simply disappear. The Empire was gathering wayward elves from all over the realm. How they would be disposed of he did not say. The massive crowd below cheered their approval and their combined voices roared.

Amilia sat in the staging room, her arms wrapped about her waist. She could not even pace now. The empress herself appeared unconcerned by the approaching presentation and sat calmly as ever in her shimmering gown and massive headdress that mimicked a fanning peacock.

Nimbus managed excellent time reaching the milliner, although he apparently terrified a young page, having brandished his rapier at the lad. They also had good fortune in that the ceremony started late due to a last-minute dispute as to the order of speakers. Amilia managed to secure the headdress on Modina just minutes before the first started.

The Chancellor spoke first, then Ethelred, and finally Saldur. With each word, Amilia felt it harder and harder to breathe. Finally, Ethelred's speech concluded and Saldur stepped forward for the formal introduction. The crowd hushed, as they knew the expected moment was at hand.

"Nearly a thousand years have passed since the breaking of the great Empire of Novron," he told the multitude below. "We stand here today as witnesses to the enduring power of Maribor and his promise to Novron that his seed will reign forever. Neither treachery nor time can break this sacred covenant. Allow me to introduce to you proof of this. Here now welcome the once simple farm maid, the slayer of the elven beast, the Heir of Novron, the High Priestess of the Nyphron Church, her most serene and Royal Grand Imperial Majesty, the Empress Modina Novronian!"

The crowd erupted in cheers and applause. Amilia could feel the vibration of their voices even where she sat. She looked at Modina, pleading and hopeful. The empress' face was calm as she stood up straight and gracefully walked forward, the train of her dress trailing behind her.

When she stepped upon the balcony—when the people finally saw her face—the noise of the crowd did the impossible. It exploded. The unimaginably boisterous cheering was deafening, like a continuous roll of thunder that vibrated the very stone of the castle. It went on and on and Amilia wondered if it would ever stop.

In the face of the tumult surely Modina could not endure. What effect would this have on her fragile countenance? Amilia wished

THE SPEECH

Saldur had allowed her to use the rope or accompany her onto the balcony. Amilia's only consolation was knowing that Modina was likely frozen. Her mind retreating to that dark place she had so long lived in, the place she crawled to hide from the world.

Amilia prayed the crowd would quiet. She hoped Ethelred or Saldur would do something to silence them, but neither moved and the crowd continued to roar with no end in sight. Then something unexpected happened. Modina slowly raised her hands, making a gentle quieting motion, and almost immediately the crowd fell silent. Amilia could not believe her eyes.

"My beloved and cherished loyal subjects," she spoke with a loud, clear, almost musical voice that Amilia had not heard at practice. "It is wonderful to finally meet you."

The crowd roared anew even louder than before. Modina allowed them to cheer for a full minute before raising her hands and silencing them again.

"As some of you may have heard, I have not been well. The battle with Rufus' Bane left me weakened, but with the help of my closest friend, the Grand Imperial Secretary Lady Amilia of Tarin Vale, I am feeling much better."

Amilia stopped breathing at the sound of her name. That was not in the speech.

"I owe Amilia the greatest debt of gratitude for her efforts on my behalf, for I should not be here at all if not for her strength, wisdom, and kindness."

Amilia closed her eyes and cringed.

"While I am feeling better, I am still easily exhausted and I must keep my strength in order to devote it to ensuring our defense against invaders, a bountiful harvest, and our return to the glory and prosperity that was Novron's Empire," she finished with an elaborate wave of her hand, turned, and left the balcony with elegant grace and poise.

The crowd erupted once more into cheers and continued long after Modina returned inside.

"I swear I didn't tell her to say that." Amilia pleaded with Saldur.

"By publicly naming you as her friend and the hero of the realm, you've become famous." Saldur replied. "It will now be almost impossible for me to replace you—*almost*. But don't worry," he continued thoughtfully. "With such a fine display I would be a fool to do anything other than praise you. I am once more impressed. I wouldn't have expected this from you. You're more clever than I thought, but I should have guessed that already. I will have to remember this. Good work, my dear. Good work indeed."

"Yes, that was excellent!" Ethelred said. "We can now put the fiasco of the coronation behind us. I can't say I approve of the self-aggrandizement, Amilia, but seeing what you've done with her, I can't begrudge you a little recognition. In fact, we should consider rewarding her for a job well done, Sauly."

"Indeed," he replied. "We'll have to consider what that should be. Come, Lanis, let's proceed to the banquet." The two of them left, talking back and forth about the ceremony as they went.

Amilia moved to the empress' side, took her hand, and escorted her back to her quarters. "You'll be the death of me yet," she told her.

Chapter 16
THE BATTLE OF RATIBOR

Hadrian sat in the rain. Heavy chains shackled his ankles and wrists to a large metal stake driven into the ground. All day he waited in the mud, watching the lazy movements of the Nationalist Army. They were just as slow to decide his fate as they were to attack. Horses walked past, meals were called, and men grumbled about the rain and the mud. The gray light faded into night and regret consumed him.

He should have escaped, even if it meant shedding blood. He might have been able to save Arista's life. He could have warned her that the Nationalists would not cooperate and have her call off the attack. Now, even if she succeeded, the victory would be short-lived and she would face the gallows or a beheading.

"Gill!" he shouted as he saw the sentry walking by in his soaked cloak.

"Ah yes!" Gill laughed, coming closer with a grin. "If it isn't the *grand marshall*. Not so grand now, are you?"

"Gill, you have to help me," he shouted over the roar of the rain. "I need you to get a message to—"

Gill bent down. "Now why would I help the likes of you? You

made a fool out of me. Sergeant Milford weren't too pleased neither. He has me running an all-night shift to show his displeasure."

"I have money," Hadrian told him eagerly. "I could pay you."

"Really? And where is this money, in some chest buried on some distant mountain, or merely in another pair of pants?"

"Right here in the purse on my belt. I have at least ten gold tenents. You can have it all if you just promise me to take a message to Ratibor."

Gill looked at Hadrian's belt curiously. "Sure," he said. Reaching down he untied the purse. He weighed it in his hands, the bouncing produced a jingle. He pulled open the mouth and poured out a handful of coins. "Whoa! Look at that. You weren't joshing; there's really gold in here. One, two, three...damn! Well thank you, marshall." He made a mock salute. "This will definitely take the sting out of having to stand two watches." He started to walk away.

"Wait!" Hadrian told him. "You need to hear the message."

Gill kept walking.

"You need to tell Arista not to attack," he shouted desperately, but Gill continued on his way swinging the purse around his finger until his figure was obscured by the rain.

Hadrian cursed and kicked the stake hard. He collapsed on his side, lost in a nightmare of frustration. He remembered the look on Arista's face, how hopeful. It never crossed her mind that he would fail. When he first met the princess, he thought her arrogant and egotistical—like all nobles—grown up brats, greedy and self-centered.

When did that change?

Images flooded back to him. He remembered her hanging out her wet things in Sheridan. How stubbornly she slept under the horse blanket that first night outside, crying herself to sleep. He and Royce were both certain she would cancel the mission the next day. He saw her sleeping in the skiff that morning drifting down the Bernum and how she had practically announced her identity to everyone when drunk in Dunstan's home. She had always been their patron and their princess, but somewhere along the way she became more than that.

As he sat, pelted with rain, and helpless in the mud, he was tormented with visions of her death. He saw her lying face down in the filthy street, her dress torn, her pale skin stained red with blood. The Imperials would likely hoist her body above Central Square, or perhaps drag it behind a horse to Aquesta. Maybe they would cut her head off and send it to Alric as a warning.

In a flash of anger and desperation, he began digging in the mud, trying to dislodge the stake. He dug furiously, pulled hard, then dug again—wrenching the stake back and forth. A guard spotted him and used a second stake on the chains connected to his wrists, to stretch him out flat.

"Still trying to get away and cause mischief are ya?" the guard said. "Well, that taint gonna happen. You killed Gaunt. You'll die for that, but until then you'll stay put." The guard spit in his face, but the effect was hardly what he sought as the rain rinsed it away. It crushed Hadrian knowing it was Arista's rain washing him clean. Lying there, he saw the first sign of dawn lightening the morning sky and his heart sank further.

Emery could see the horizon as the faint light of dawn separated sky from building and tree. Rain still fell and the sound of crickets was replaced by early morning stirrings. Merchants appeared on the street far earlier than usual pushing carts and rolling wagons toward the West End Square then, neglectfully, left them blocking the entrances from King's Street and Legends Avenue. Other men came out of their homes and shops. Emery watched them appear out of the gray morning rain, coming one and two at a time, then gathering into larger groups as they wandered aimlessly around the square, drifting slowly, almost hesitantly, toward the armory. They wore heavy clothes and carried hoes, pitchforks, shovels, and axes. Most had knives tucked into their belts.

A pair of city guards working the end of the night shift—dressed only in light summer uniforms—had just finished their last patrol circuit. They stopped and looked around at the growing crowd with curious expressions. "Say there, what's going on here?"

"I dunno," a man said, and then moved away.

"Listen, what are you all doing here?" the other guard asked, but no one answered.

Barefoot and dressed in a white oversized shirt and a pair of britches that left his shins bare, Emery strode forward feeling the clap of the sword at his side. "We are here to avenge the murder of our lord and sovereign, King Urith of Rhenydd!"

"It's him. It's Emery Dorn!" the guard shouted. "Grab the bastard."

As the guards rushed forward they were too late to realize their peril as the groups closed around them, sweeping together like a flocks of birds.

The soldiers hastily drew their swords swinging them.

"Back! Get back! All of you! Back or we'll have the lot of you arrested!"

Hatred filled the faces of the crowd and excitement crept into their eyes. They jabbed at the soldiers with pitchforks and hoes. The guards knocked them away with swords. For several minutes the crowd taunted with feints and threats, and then Emery drew his blade. Mrs. Dunlap found the sword for him. It had once belonged to her husband. In all the years of service, Paul Dunlap, carriage driver for King Urith, never had occasion to draw it. The steel scraped as Emery pulled the blade from the metal sheath. With a grim expression and a set jaw, he pushed his way through the circle and faced the guards.

THE BATTLE OF RATIBOR

They were sweating. He could see the wetness on the upper lip of the closest man. The guard lunged, thrusting. Emery stepped to the side and hit the soldier's blade with his own, hearing the solid *clank* and feeling the impact in his hand. He took a step forward and swung. It felt good. It felt perfect, just the right move. The tip of his sword hit something soft and Emery watched as he sliced the man, cutting him across the chest. The soldier screamed, dropping his sword. He fell to his knees, his eyes wide in shock, clutching himself as blood soaked his clothes. The other guard tried to run, but the crowd held him back. Emery pushed past the wounded man and with one quick thrust stabbed the remaining guard through the kidney. Several cheered and began beating the wounded men, hacking them with axes and shovels.

"Enough," Emery shouted. "Follow me!"

The guards' weapons were taken and the crowd chased Emery to the flagstone building with the iron gate. By the time they arrived, Carat was already picking the lock. They killed those on duty only to discover most of the rest were still in their beds. A few got to their feet before the mob arrived. They stabbed the first confused man through the ribs with a pitchfork that he took with him when he fell. Emery stabbed another and an axe took a third's shoulder partway off, lodging there so that the owner had to kick his victim to pull the axe free. Swords and shields lined the walls or lay in pine boxes. Steel helms and chain hauberks sat on shelves.

The mob grabbed these as they passed, discarding their tools of trade for tools of war. Only ten men guarded the armory and all died quickly, most beaten to death in their beds. The men cheered when they realized they took the armory without a single loss of life to their side. They laughed, howled, and jumped on tables, breaking plates and cups and whatever else they could find as they gleefully tested out their new weapons.

All around him Emery could see the wild looks in the eyes of the men and realized he must wear a similar expression. His heart was pounding, his lungs pumping air. He felt no pain at all from his back now. He felt powerful, elated, and a little nauseous all at the same time.

"Emery! Emery!" He turned to see Arista pushing through the men. "You're too slow," she screamed back at him. "The garrison is coming. Get them armed and formed up in the square."

As if pulled from a dream, Emery realized his folly. "Everyone out!" he shouted. "Everyone out now! Form up on the square!"

Arista had already begun organizing those men who remained outside into two lines with their backs to the armory and their faces to the square.

"We need to get weapons!" Perin shouted at the princess.

"Stay in line!" she barked. "We'll have them brought out. You have to maintain the lines to stop the garrison from charging."

The men who stood in line holding only farm tools looked at her terrified as across the square the first of the soldiers struggled to push away the wagons and carts that had been rutted in the mud. Soon the men Emery had shooed out began taking their place in front of the line.

"Form up!" Emery shouted. "Two straight lines."

Arista ran back into the armory and began grabbing swords and dragging them out. She spotted Carat stealing coins from a dead man's purse and shoved him against a wall. "Help me carry swords and shields out!"

"But I'm not allowed to," he said.

"You're not allowed to fight, but you can carry some swords damn it. Just like you unlocked the door. Now do it!"

Carat seemed like he would say something then gave in and started pulling shields down from the walls. Doctor Gerand entered carrying bandages but discarded them quickly to help deliver weapons. On her way out, Arista saw a woman running in. Her dress soaked from the rain, her long blonde hair pasted to her face so that she could hardly see. She stopped abruptly at her approach.

"Let me help," she said to Arista. "You get more while I pass these out."

Arista nodded and handed over the weapons then ran back inside.

Carat handed her the stack of shields he was carrying and she ran them down to the young woman, who in turn took them to the waiting line. When Arista came out again she found a line of older men and some women had formed up and were passing the weapons like a bucket brigade with the young blonde adding more to the line.

"More swords!" Arista shouted. "Helms and mail last."

Carat assembled weapons into manageable piles for the others to grab.

"No more swords!" The call soon came. "Send shields!"

The bell in Central Square began to ring, its tone sounding different that morning than any other, perhaps due to the heavy rain or the pounding of blood in her ears. Most men on the line only held a sword. Arista could see fear in every face.

She could hear Emery's voice drifting above the rain with each delivery. "Steady! Dress those lines. Tighten that formation," he barked the orders like a veteran commander. "No more than a fist's distance between your shoulders. Those with spears or pikes to the rear line, those with shields to the front. Wait! Halt!" he shouted. "Forget that. Back in line. Just pass the spears back and hand the shields forward."

With the next delivery of weapons Arista paused at the armory doorway and looked out across the square. The garrison had cleared the wagons from King's Street and a few soldiers entered. They looked briefly at the lines of townsfolk then went to work to clear the other carts.

Emery stood in front of the troops. Everyone had a sword or spear but most did not know how to wield them properly. Nearly all the men in the front row had a wooden shield, but most simply held them in their hands. In at least one man's case, he had his shield upside down.

"Adam the Wheeler, front and center!" Emery shouted and the middle-aged wheelwright stepped forward. "Take the left side and see that the men know how to wear their shields and hold their swords." Emery likewise called Renkin Pool and Forrest the silversmith's son into action and set them to dressing the line.

"Keep your shield high," Adam was shouting. "Don't swing your sword—thrust it instead. That way you can maintain tighter formations. Keep the line tight, the man next to you is a better shield than that flimsy bit of wood in your hands! Stay shoulder to shoulder!"

"Don't let them turn the flank!" Renkin was shouting on the other side of the line. "Those on the ends turn and hold your shields to defend from a side assault. Everyone must move and work together!"

Helms and hauberks were coming out now and there were a few in the front row hastily pulling chain mail netting over their heads.

A surprising number of imperial soldiers already formed themselves into rows on the far side of the square. Each one impeccably dressed in hauberk, helm, sword, and shield. They stood still, straight, and confident. Looking at Emery's men, Arista saw nervous movements and fear-filled eyes.

Four knights rode into the square. Two bore the imperial pennant at the end of tall lances. On the foremost horse rode Sheriff Vigan. Beside him came Trenchon, the city's bailiff, splashing through the puddles. Hooked to Vigan's belt, in addition to his sword, was the whip. Vigan's face was stern and unimpressed by the hastily assembled slightly skewed lines of peasants. He rode up and down, trotting menacingly, his mount throwing up clods of mud into the air.

"I know why you are here," Vigan shouted at them. "You are here because of one man." He pointed at Emery. "He has incited you to perform criminal acts. Normally, I would have each one of you executed for treason, but I can see it is the traitor Emery Dorn and not you who has caused this. You are victims of his poison, so I will be lenient. Put down those stolen weapons, return to your homes, and I will only hang the leaders that led you astray. Continue this and you will be slaughtered to the last man."

"Steady men," Emery shouted. "He's just trying to frighten you. He's offering you a deal because he's scared—scared of us because we stand before him united and strong. He's scared because we do not cower before his threats. He's scared, because for the first time he does not see sheep, he does not see slaves, he does not see victims to beat, but men. Men! Tall and proud. Men who are still loyal to their king!"

Vigan raised his hand briefly then lowered it. There was a harsh crack followed immediately by a muffled *thwack!* Emery staggered backward. Blood sprayed those near him. A crossbow bolt was lodged in his chest. An instant later the fiery red-haired boy fell into the mud.

The line wavered at the sight.

"No!" Arista screamed and shoved through the men and collapsed in the mud beside Emery. Frantically she struggled to turn him over, to pull his face out of the muck. She wiped the mud away while blood vomited from his mouth. His eyes rolled wildly. His breath wheezed in short halting gasps.

Everyone was silent. The whole world stopped.

Arista held Emery in her arms. She could see a pleading in his eyes as they found hers. She could feel his breath shortening with each wretched gasp. With each jerk of his body she felt her heart breaking.

This can't be happening!

She looked into his eyes. She wanted to say something—to give a part of herself to take with him—but all she could do was hold on. As she squeezed him tightly he stopped struggling. He stopped moving. He stopped breathing.

Arista cried aloud, certain her body would break.

Above her the sheriff's horse snorted and stomped. Behind her the men of the rebellion wavered. She heard them dropping weapons, discarding shields.

Arista took in a shuddering breath of her own and turned her face toward the sky. She raised one leg, then the other, pushing herself—willing herself—to her feet. As her shaking body rose from the mud, she drew Emery's sword in a tight fist and lifted the blade above her head and glared at the sheriff.

She cried in a loud voice, "Don't—you—dare—break! HOLD THE LINE!"

Chained and stretched out in the mud on his back, a shadow fell across Hadrian's face and the rain stopped hitting him. He opened his eyes, and squinting, saw a man outlined in the morning light.

"What in Maribor's name are you doing here?"

The voice was familiar and Hadrian struggled to see the face lost in the folds of a hooded robe. All around him rain continued to pour, splashing the mud puddles and grass, forcing him to blink.

The figure standing over him shouted, "Sergeant! Explain what goes on here. Why is this man chained?"

Hadrian could hear boots slogging through the mud. "It's

Commander Parker's orders, sir." There was nervousness in his voice.

"I see. Tell me sergeant, do you enjoy being human?"

"What's that, sir?"

"I asked if you liked the human form. Having two legs, two eyes, two hands for example."

"I ah—well, I don't think I quite understand your meaning."

"No, you don't, but you will if this man isn't freed immediately."

"But, Lord Esrahaddon, I can't, Commander Parker—"

"Leave Parker to me. Get those chains off him, get him out of that mud, and escort him to the house immediately, or I swear you will be walking on all fours within the hour, and for the rest of your life."

"Wizards!" the sergeant grumbled after Esrahaddon had left him. He pulled a key from his belt and struggled to unlocked the mud caked locks. "Up you go," he ordered.

The sergeant led Hadrian back to the house. The chains were gone but his wrists were still bound by two iron manacles. He was cold, hungry, and felt nearly drowned, but only one thought filled his mind as he saw the rising sun in the east.

Is there still time?

"And what about the wagons on the South Road?" Esrahaddon growled as Hadrian entered. The wizard stood in his familiar robe that was, at that moment, gray and perfectly dry despite the heavy rain. Esrahaddon looked the same as he did in Dahlgren except for the length of his beard, which now reached to his chest giving him a more wizardly appearance.

Parker was seated behind his table, a napkin tucked into his collar, another plate of ham and eggs before him.

Does he have the same meal brought to him each morning?

"It's the mud. They can't be moved, and I don't appreciate—" He paused when he spotted Hadrian. "What's going on? I ordered this man staked. Why are you bringing him here?"

"I ordered it," Esrahaddon told him. "Sergeant, remove those restraints and fetch his weapons."

"You?" Parker replied, stunned. "You are here only as an adviser. You forget I am in command."

"Of what?" the wizard asked. "A thousand lazy vagabonds? This was an army when I left. I come back and it's a rabble."

"It's the rain. It doesn't stop."

"It's not supposed to stop," Hadrian burst out in frustration. "I tried to tell you. We need to attack Dermont now. Arista is launching a rebellion this morning in Ratibor. She'll seal the city so he can't retreat. We have to engage and defeat Dermont before he is reinforced by Sir Breckton and the Northern Imperial Army. They will be here any day now. If we don't attack, Dermont will enter the city and crush the rebellion."

"What nonsense." Parker pointed an accusing finger. "This man entered the camp claiming to be a Marshall-at-Arms who was taking command of *my* troops."

"He is, and he will," the wizard told him.

"He will not! He and this princess of Melengar are both responsible for the treachery that probably cost Degan his life. And we have had no news of any Northern—"

"Degan is alive, you idiot. Neither Hadrian nor Arista had anything to do with his abduction. Do as this man instructs or everyone will likely be dead or captured by the Imperium in two days. You, of course," the wizard glared at Parker, "will die much sooner."

Parker's eyes widened.

"I don't even know who he is!" Parker exclaimed. "I can't turn over command to a stranger I know nothing about. How do I know he's capable? What are his qualifications?"

"Hadrian knows more about combat than any living man."

"And am I to take your word? The word of a—a—sorcerer?"

"It was on my word that this army was formed—my direction that produced its victories."

"But you've been gone. Things have changed. Degan left me in charge and I don't think I can—"

Esrahaddon stepped toward the commander. As he did his robe began to glow. A blood red radiance filled the interior of the house, making Parker's face look like a plump beet.

"Alright! Alright!" Parker shouted abruptly to the sergeant. "Do as he says. What do I care!"

The sergeant unlocked Hadrian's hands then exited.

"Now, Parker, make yourself useful for once," Esrahaddon said. "Go round up the regiment captains. Tell them that they will now be taking their orders from Marshall Blackwater, and have them gather here as soon as possible."

"Marshall *Lord* Blackwater," Hadrian corrected him with a smile.

Esrahaddon rolled his eyes. "Do it now."

"But—"

"Go!"

Parker grabbed up his cloak, his sword, and pulled his boots from under the table. He retreated out the door still holding them.

"Is he going to be a problem?" Hadrian asked, watching the ex-commander hop into the rain, grumbling.

"Parker? No. I just needed to remind him that he's terrified of me. Esrahaddon looked at Hadrian. "Marshall *Lord* Blackwater?"

"*Lord* Esrahaddon?" he replied rubbing feeling back into his wrists.

The wizard smiled and nodded. "You still haven't said what you are doing here."

"A job—for Arista Essendon. She hired us to help her contact the Nationalists."

"And now she has you seizing control of my army."

"Your army? I thought this was Gaunt's."

"So did he, and the moment I'm away Degan gets himself captured after putting that thing in charge. Royce with you?"

"Was—Arista sent him to contact Alric about invading Warric."

While eating Parker's ham and eggs Hadrian provided Esrahaddon with further details about the rebellion and his plans for attacking Dermont. Just as he had finished the meal there was a knock on the door. Five officers and the harried-looking sergeant, carrying Hadrian' swords, entered.

Esrahaddon addressed them. "As Parker no doubt informed you, this is Marshall Lord Blackwater, your new commander. Do anything he says as if he were Gaunt himself. I think you will find him a very worthy replacement for your general."

They nodded and stood at attention.

Hadrian got up, walked around the table, and announced, "We will attack the imperial position immediately."

"Now?" one said astonished.

"I wish there was more time, but I've been tied up elsewhere. We will launch our attack directly across that muddy field where the Imps' three hundred heavy cavalry can't ride, and where their longbow archers can't see in this rain. Our lightly armored infantry must move quickly to overwhelm them. We will close at a run and butcher them man to man."

"But they'll—" started a tall gruff-looking soldier with a partial beard and mismatched armor, then stopped himself.

"They'll what?" Hadrian asked.

"I was just thinking. The moment they see us advance, won't they retreat within the city walls?"

"What is your name?" Hadrian asked.

The man looked worried but held his ground. "Renquist, sir."

"Well, Renquist, you're absolutely right. That's exactly what they will try to do. Only they won't be able to get in. By then our allied forces will own the city."

"Allied forces?"

"I don't have time to explain. Don't strike camp, and don't use horns or drums to assemble. With luck there's a good chance we can catch them by surprise. By now, they probably think we will never attack. Renquist, how long do you estimate to have the men assembled and ready to march?"

"Two hours," he replied with more confidence.

"Have them ready in one. Each of you form up your men on the east slope out of their sight. Three regiments of infantry in duel lines, senior commanders located at the center, left, and right flanks in that order. And I want light cavalry to swing to the south and await the call of the trumpet to sweep their flank. I want one contingent of cavalry—the smallest—that I will command and hold in reserve to the north near the city. At the waving of the blue pennant begin crossing the field as quietly as possible. When you see the green relay the signal and charge. We move in one hour. Dismissed!"

The captains saluted and ran back out into the rain. The sergeant handed over Hadrian's weapons and started to slip out quietly.

"Wait a moment," Hadrian halted him. "What's your name?"

The sergeant spun. "I was just following orders when I chained you up. I didn't know—"

"You've just been promoted to adjutant-general," Hadrian told him. "What's your name?"

The ex-sergeant blinked. "Bently...sir."

"Bently, from now on you stick next to me and see that my orders are carried out, understand? Now, I'll need fast riders to work as messengers—three should do, and signal flags—a blue and a green one—as big as possible. Mount them on tall sticks and make certain all the captains have identical ones. Oh, and I need a horse!"

"Make that two," the wizard said.

"Make that three," Hadrian added. "You'll need one too, Bently."

The soldier opened his mouth, closed it, then nodded and stepped out into the rain.

"An hour," Hadrian muttered as he strapped on his weapons.

"You don't think Arista can hold out that long?"

"I was supposed to take control of this army yesterday. If only I had more time...I could have...I just hope it's not too late."

"If anyone can save Ratibor, it's you," the wizard told him.

"I know all about being the guardian to the heir," Hadrian replied.

"I had a feeling Royce would tell you."

Hadrian picked up the large spadone sword and looped the baldric over his head. He reached up and drew it out, testing the position of the sheath.

"I remember that weapon." The wizard pointed to the blade. "That's Jerish's sword." He frowned then added, "What have you done to it?"

"What do you mean?"

"Jerish loved that thing—had a special cloth he kept in his gauntlet that he used to polished it—something of an obsession really. That blade was like a mirror."

"It has seen nine hundred years of use," Hadrian told him and put it away.

"You look nothing like Jerish." Esrahaddon said then paused when he saw the look in Hadrian's face. "What is it?"

"The heir is dead—you know that don't you? Died right here in Ratibor forty years ago."

Esrahaddon smiled. "Still, you hold a sword the same way Jerish did. Must be in the training somehow. Amazing how much it defines both of you. I never really—"

"Did you hear me? The bloodline ended. Seret caught up to them. They killed the heir—his name was Naron by the way—and they killed his wife and child. My father was the only survivor. I'm sorry."

"My teacher, old Yolric, used to insist the world has a way of righting itself. He was obsessed with the idea. I thought he was crazy, but after living for nine hundred years you perceive things differently. You see patterns you never knew where there. The heir isn't dead, Hadrian, just hidden."

"I know you'd like to think that, but my father failed and the heir died. I talked to a member of the Theorem Eldership who was there. He saw it happen."

Esrahaddon shook his head. "I've seen the heir with my own eyes, and I recognize the blood of Nevrik. A thousand years cannot mask such a linage from me. Still, just to be sure, I performed a test that cannot be faked. Oh yes, the heir is alive and well."

"Who is it then? I'm the guardian, aren't I? Or I'm supposed to be. I should be protecting him."

"At the moment anonymity is a far better protection than swords. I cannot tell you the heir's identity. If I did, you would rush off and be a beacon to those watching." The wizard sighed. "And trust me, I know a great deal about being watched. In Gutaria they wrote down every word I uttered. Even now, at this very moment, every word I say is being heard."

"You sound like Royce." Hadrian looked around. "We're alone, surrounded by an army of Nationalists. Do you think Saldur or Ethelred have spies pressing an ear against this farmhouse?"

"Saldur? Ethelred?" Esrahaddon chuckled. "I'm not concerned with the Imperial Regents. They are pawns in this game. Have you never wondered how the Gilarabrywn escaped Avempartha? Do you think Saldur or Ethelred managed that trick? My adversary is a tad more dangerous and I am certain spends a great deal of time listening to what I say no matter where I am. You see, I do not have the benefit of that amulet you wear."

"Amulet?" Hadrian touched his chest, feeling the metal circle under his shirt. "Royce said it prevents wizards like you from finding the wearer."

The wizard nodded. "Preventing clairvoyant searches was the

primary purpose, but they are far more powerful than that. The amulets protect the wearers from all effects of the Art and has a dash of good fortune added in. Flip a coin wearing that, and it will come up the way you need it to more often than not. You've been in many battles and I'm sure in plenty of dangerous situations with Royce. Have you not considered yourself lucky on more than one occasion? That little bit of jewelry is extremely powerful. The level of the Art that went into making it was beyond anything I'd ever seen."

"I thought you made it."

"I did, but I had help. I could never have built them on my own. Yolric showed me the weave. He was the greatest of us. I could barely understand his instructions and wasn't certain I had performed the spell properly, but it appears I was successful."

"Still, you're the only one left in the world who can really do magic, right? So there's no chance anyone is magically listening."

"What about this rain? It's not *supposed* to stop? It would seem I am not the only one."

"You're afraid of Arista?"

"No, just making a point. I am not the only wizard in the world and I have already been far too careless. In my haste I took chances that maybe I should not have, drawing too much attention, playing into others' hands. With so little time left—only a matter of months—it would be foolhardy to risk more now. I fear the heir's identity has already been compromised, but there is a chance I am wrong and I will cling to that hope. I'm sorry Hadrian. I can't tell you just yet, but trust me I will."

"No offense, but you don't seem too trustworthy."

The wizard smiled. "Maybe you *are* Jerish's descendent after all. Very soon I'll need Riyria's help with an extremely challenging mission."

"Riyria doesn't exist anymore. I've retired."

The wizard nodded. "Nevertheless, I will require both of you, and as it concerns the heir, I presume you'll make an exception."

"I don't even know where I'll be."

"Don't worry, I'll find you both when the time comes. But for now, we have the little problem of Lord Dermont's army to contend with."

There was a knock at the door. "Horses ready, sirs," the new adjutant-general reported in.

As they stepped out, Hadrian spotted Gill walking toward him with the fighter's purse. "Good morning, Gill," Hadrian said, taking his pouch back.

"Morning, sir," he said, looking sick but making an effort to smile. "It's all there, sir."

"I'm a bit busy at the moment, Gill, but I'm sure we'll have a chance to catch up later."

"Yes, sir."

Hadrian mounted a brown-and-white gelding Bently held for him. He watched as Esrahaddon mounted a smaller black mare by hooking the stub of his wrist around the horn. Once in the saddle the wizard wrapped the reins around his stubs.

"It's strange. I keep forgetting you don't have hands," Hadrian commented.

"I don't," the wizard replied coldly.

Overhead, heavy clouds swirled as boys ran about the camp spreading the order to form up. Horses trotted, kicking up clods of earth. Carts rolled, leaving deep ruts. Half-dressed men darted from tents, slipping in the slick mud. They carried swords over their shoulders, dragged shields, and struggled to fasten helms. Hadrian and Esrahaddon rode through the hive of soggy activity to the top of the ridge where they could see the lay of the land for miles. To the north, the city with its wooden spires and drab walls stood as a ghostly shadow. To the south lay the forest, and between them a vast plain stretched westward. What was once farmland was now a muddy soup. The field was shaped like a basin, and at its lowest point a shallow pond formed. It reflected the light of the dreary gray sky like a steel mirror. On the far side, the hazy encampment of the Imperial Army was just visible through a thick curtain of rain. Hadrian stared but could only make out faint shadowy shapes. Nothing indicated they knew what was about to happen. Below them on the east side of the slope, hidden from imperial view, the Nationalist Army assembled into ranks.

"What is it?" Esrahaddon asked.

Hadrian realized he was grimacing. "They aren't very good soldiers," he replied, watching the men wander about creating misshapen lines. They stood listless, shoulders slumped, heads down.

Esrahaddon shrugged. "There are a few good ones. We pulled in some mercenaries and a handful of deserters from the Imperials. That Renquist you were so taken with, he was a sergeant in the imperial forces. Joined us because he heard nobility didn't matter in the Nationalist Army. We got a few of those, but mostly they're farmers, merchants, or men who lost their homes or families."

Hadrian glanced across the field. "Lord Dermont has trained foot soldiers, archers, and knights—men who devoted their whole lives to warfare and trained since an early age."

"I wouldn't worry about that."

"Of course *you* wouldn't. I'm the one who has to lead this ugly rabble. I'm the one who must go down there and face those lances and arrows."

"I'm going with you," he said. "That's why you don't need to worry about it."

Bently and three other young men carrying colored flags rode up beside them. "Captains report ready, sir."

"Let's go," he told them and trotted down to take his place with a small contingent of cavalry. The men on horseback appeared even less capable than those on foot. They had no armor and wore torn rain-soaked clothes. Except for the spears they held across their laps, they looked like vagabonds or escaped prisoners.

"Raise your lances!" he shouted. "Stay tight, keep your place, wheel together, and follow me." He turned to Bently. "Wave the blue flag."

Bently swung the blue flag back and forth until the signal was mimicked across the field, then the army began moving forward at a slow walk. Armies never moved at a pace that suited Hadrian. They crept with agonizing slowness when he was attacking, but when defending seemed to race at him. He patted the neck of his horse who was larger and more spirited than old Millie. Hadrian liked to know his horse better before a battle. They needed to work as a team in combat and he did not even know this one's name.

With the wizard riding at his right side and Bently on his left, Hadrian crested the hill and began the long descent into the wet field. He wheeled his cavalry to the right, sweeping toward the city, riding the rim of the basin and avoiding the middle of the muck, which he left to the infantry. He would stay to the higher ground and watch the army's northern flank. This would also place him near the city gate, able to intercept any imperial retreat. After his company made his turn, he watched as the larger force of light-mounted lancers broke and began to circle left, heading to guard the southern flank. The swishing tails of their horses soon disappeared into the rain.

The ranks of the infantry came next. They crested the hill, jostling each other, some still struggling to get their helms on and shields readied. The lines were skewed, broken and wavy, and when they hit the mud, whatever mild resemblance they had to a formation was lost. They staggered and slipped forward as a mob. They were at least quiet. He wondered if it was because most of them might be half-asleep.

Hadrian felt his stomach twist.

This will not go well. If only I had more time to drill the men properly they would at least look like soldiers.

Success or failure in battle often hinged on impressions, decided in the minds of men before the first clash. Like bullies casting insults in a tavern, it was a game of intimidation—a game the Nationalists did not know how to play.

How did they ever win a battle? How did they take Vernes and Kilnar?

Unable to see their ranks clearly, he imagined the Imperials lined up in neat powerful rows waiting, letting his troops exhaust themselves in the mud. He expected a wall of glistening shields peaked with shinning helms locked shoulder to shoulder, matching spears foresting above. He anticipated hundreds of archers already notching shafts to string. The knights, Lord Dermont would hold back. Any fool could see the futility of ordering a charge into the muck. With their pennants fluttering from their lances, and heavy metal armor, the knights probably waited in the trees and perhaps around the wall of the city—hidden until just the right moment—it is what he would do. When they tried to flank, Hadrian and his little group would be all that stood in the way. He would call the charge and hope those behind him followed.

They were more than halfway across the field, when he was finally able to see the imperial encampment. White tents stood in neat lines, horses corralled, and no one was visible.

"Where are they?"

"It's still very early," the wizard said, "and in a heavy rain no one likes to get up. It's so much easier to stay in bed."

"But where are the sentries?"

Hadrian watched, shocked as the mangled line of infantry cleared the muddy ground and closed in on the imperial camp, their lines straightening out a bit. He saw the heads of his captains. There was no sign of the enemy.

The Battle of Ratibor

"Have you ever noticed," Esrahaddon said, "how rain has a musical quality about it sometimes? The way it drums on a roof? It's always easier to sleep on a rainy night. There's something magical about running water that is very soothing, very relaxing."

"What did you do?"

The wizard smiled. "A weak, thin enchantment. Without hands it is very hard to do substantive magic anymore, but—"

They heard a shout. A tent flap fluttered, then another. More shouts cascaded, and then a bell rang.

"There, see," Esrahaddon sighed, "I told you. It doesn't take much to break it."

"But we have them," Hadrian said stunned. "We caught them sleeping! Bently, the green flag. Flag the charge. Flag the charge!"

Sheriff Vigan scowled at Arista. Behind her, men picked up weapons and shuffled back into position.

"I told you to lay down your arms and leave," the sheriff shouted. "Not more than a few of you will be punished in the stocks, and only your leaders will be executed. The first has already fallen. Will you stand behind a woman? Will you throw away your lives for her sake?"

No one moved. The only sound was that of the rain, the sheriff's horse, and the jangling of his bridle.

"Very well," he said. "I will execute the leading agitators one at a time if that is what it takes." He glanced over his shoulder and ominously raised his hand again.

The princess did not move.

She stood still and tall with Emery's sword above her head, his blood on her dress, and the wind and rain lashing her face. She glared defiantly at the sheriff.

Thwack!

The sound of a crossbow.

Phhump!

A muffled impact.

Arista felt blood spray her face, but there was no pain. Sheriff Vigan fell sideways into the mud. Polish stood in front of the blacksmith shop, an empty crossbow in his hands.

Renkin Pool grabbed Arista by the shoulder and jerked her backward. Off balance, she fell. He stood over her, his shield raised. Another telltale *thwack* and Pool's shield burst into splinters. The bolt continued into his chest. The explosion of blood and wood rained on her.

Another crossbow fired, this one handled by Adam the Wheeler. Trenchon screamed as the arrow passed through his thigh and continued into his horse which collapsed, crushing Trenchon's leg beneath it. Another bow fired, then another, and Arista could see that during the pause the blonde woman had hauled crossbows out of the armory and passed them throughout the ranks.

The garrison captain promptly assumed command of the Imperials. He gave a shout and the remainder of their bowmen fired across the square. Men in the line fell.

"Fire!" Adam Wheeler shouted and rebel bows gave answer. A handful of imperial soldiers dropped in the mud.

"Tighten the line!" Adam shouted. "Fill in the gaps where people fall!"

They heard a shout from across the field then a roar as the garrison drew their swords and rushed forward. Arista felt the vibration of charging men. They screamed like beasts, their faces wild. They struck the line in the center. There was no prepared weak point—Emery and Pool were dead, the tactic lost.

She heard cries, screams, the clanging of metal against metal, and the dull thumps of swords against wooden shields. Soldiers pushed forward and the line broke in two. Perin was supposed to lead the left flank in a folding maneuver. He lay in the mud, blood running down his face. His branch of the line disconnected from the rest and quickly routed. The main line also failed, disintegrated, and disappeared. Men fought in a swirling turmoil of swords, broken shields, blood, and body parts.

Arista remained where she fell. She felt a tugging on her arm and looked up to see the blonde woman again. "Get up! You'll be killed!" She had a hold on her wrist and dragged Arista to her feet. All around them men screamed, shouted, and grunted, water splashed, mud flew, and blood sprayed. The hand squeezing her wrist hauled her backward. She thought of Emery lying in the mud and tried to pull away.

"No!" The blonde snapped jerking her once more. "Are you crazy?" The woman dragged her to the armory entrance, but once she reached the door Arista refused to go in any farther and remained at the opening, watching the battle.

The skill and experience of the garrison guards overwhelmed the citizens. They cut through the people of Ratibor and pushed them against the walls of the buildings. Every puddle was dark with blood, every shirt and face stained red. Mud and manure mixed and churned with severed limbs and blood. Everywhere she looked lay bodies. Dead men with open, lifeless eyes and those writhing in pain lay scattered across the square.

"We're going to lose," Arista said. "I did this."

The candlemaker, a tall thin man with curly hair, dropped his weapons and tried to run. Arista watched as six inches of sword came out of his stomach. She did not even know his name. A young bricklayer called Walter had his head crushed. Another man she had not met lost his hand.

Arista still held Emery's sword in one hand and clutched the doorframe with the other as the world spun around her. She felt sick and wanted to vomit. She could not move or turn away from the carnage. They would all die. It was her fault. "I killed us all."

"Maybe not." The blonde caught Arista's attention and pointed at the far end of the square. "Look there!"

Coming up King's Street Arista saw a rush of movement and heard the pounding of hooves. They came out of the haze of falling rain. Riding three and four abreast, horsemen charged into the square. At their head were two riders. One carried the pennant of the Nationalists—the other brandished a huge sword. She recognized him instantly.

Throwing up a spray of mud, Hadrian crossed the square. As he closed on the battle, he led the charge into the thickest of the soldiers. The garrison heard the cry and turned to see the band of horsemen rushing at them. Out front, Hadrian came like a demon, whirling his long blade, cleaving a swath through their ranks, cutting them down. The garrison broke and routed before the onslaught. When they found no retreat, they threw down their weapons and pled for mercy.

Spotting Arista, Hadrian leapt to the ground and ran to her. Arista found it hard to breathe, and the last of her strength gave out. She fell to her knees, shaking. Hadrian reached down, surrounding her in his arms and pulled her up.

"The city is yours, Your Highness," he said.

She dropped Emery's sword, threw her arms around his neck, and cried.

Chapter 17
DEGAN GAUNT

The rain stopped. The sun so long delayed returned full face to a bright blue sky. The day quickly grew hot as Hadrian made his way around the square though the many mud-covered bodies, searching for anyone that was still alive. Everywhere seemed to be the muffled wails and weeping of wives, mothers, fathers, and sons. Families pulled their loved ones from the bloody mire and carried them home to wash them for a proper burial. Hadrian stiffened when he spotted Doctor Gerand gently closing the lifeless eyes of Carat. Not far from him, Adam the Wheeler sat slumped against the armory. He looked as if he had merely walked over and sat down for a moment to rest.

"Over here!"

He spotted a woman with long blonde hair motioning to him. Hadrian quickly crossed to where she squatted over the body of an imperial soldier.

"He's still alive," she said. "Help me get him out of the mud. I can't believe no one saw him."

"Oh, I think they saw him," Hadrian replied as he gripped the soldier under his back and knees and lifted him.

He carried the man to the silversmith's porch and laid him down gently as the woman ran to the well for a bucket of clean water.

Hadrian shed his own bloodstained shirt. "Here," he said, offering the linen to the woman.

"Thank you," she replied. She took the shirt and began rinsing it in the bucket. "Are you certain you don't mind me using this to help an imperial guard?"

"My father taught me that a man is only your enemy until he falls."

She nodded. "Your father sounds like a wise man," she said, and wrung the excess water from the shirt, then began to clean the soldier's face and chest, looking for the wound.

"He was. My name is Hadrian by the way."

"Miranda," she replied, "pleased to meet you. Thank you for saving our lives. I assume the Nationalists defeated Lord Dermont?"

Hadrian nodded. "It wasn't much of a battle. We caught them sleeping."

Pulling up the soldier's hauberk and tearing back his tunic, she wiped his skin and found a puncture streaming blood.

"I hope you aren't terribly attached to this shirt," she told Hadrian as she tore it in two. She used half as a pad, and the other half to tie it tight about the man's waist. "Let's hope that will stop the bleeding. A few stitches would help, but I doubt a needle could be spared for him right now."

Hadrian looked the man over. "I think he'll live, thanks to you."

This brought a shallow smile to her lips. She dipped her blood-covered hands in the bucket and splashed the clean water on her face. Looking out across the square she muttered, "So many dead."

Hadrian nodded.

Her eyes landed on Carat, a hand went to her mouth and her eyes started to tear. "He was such a help to us," she said. "Someone said he was a thief, but he proved himself a hero today. Who would have thought that thieves would stick out their necks? I saw their leader, Polish, shoot the sheriff."

Hadrian smiled. "If you ask him, he'll tell you you're mistaken."

"Thieves with hearts, who'd have thought," she said.

"I am not so sure I would go that far."

"No? Then where are the vultures?"

Hadrian looked up at the sky, then realizing his own stupidity, shook his head. "You mean the looters?" He looked around. "You're right. I didn't even notice until now."

She nodded. Sunlight reflected off Hadrian's medallion. Miranda pointed. "That necklace, where did you get it?"

"My father."

"Your father? Really? My older brother has one just like it."

Hadrian's heart raced. "Your brother has a necklace like this?"

She nodded.

Hadrian looked around the square, suddenly concerned. "Is he…"

She thought a moment. "I don't think so," she said. "At least my heart tells me he's still alive."

Hadrian tried to control his racing thoughts. "How old is your brother?"

"I think he'd be about forty now, I guess."

"You guess?"

She nodded. "We never celebrated his birthday, which was always kind of strange. You see, my mother adopted him. She was the midwife at his birth and…" She hesitated. "Things didn't go well. Anyway, my mother kept an amulet just like yours and gave it to my brother as his inheritance the day he left home."

"What do you mean things didn't go well with the birth?" Hadrian asked.

"The mother died—that sort of thing happens, you know. Mothers die all the time in childbirth. It's not at all uncommon. It just happens. We should probably look for other wounded—"

"You're lying," Hadrian shot back.

She started to stand but Hadrian grabbed her arm. "This is very important. I must know everything you can tell me about the night your brother was born."

She hesitated but Hadrian held her tight.

"It wasn't her fault. There was nothing she could do. They were all dead. She was just scared. Who wouldn't be?!"

"It's okay. I'm not accusing your mother of anything. I just need to know what happened." He held up his amulet. "This necklace belonged to my father. He was there that night."

"Your father, but no one..." He saw realization in her eyes. "The swordsman covered in blood?"

"Yes," Hadrian nodded. "Does your mother still live in the city? Can I speak to her?"

"My mother died several years ago."

"Do you know what happened? I have to know. It is very important."

She looked around and, when she was sure no one could overhear, she said, "A priest came to my mother one night looking for a midwife and took her to the Bradford Boarding House where a woman was giving birth. While my mother worked to deliver the baby, a fight started on the street. My mother had just delivered the first child—"

"First child?"

Miranda nodded. "She could see another was on the way, but men in black broke into the room. My mother hid in a wardrobe. The husband fought, but they killed his wife, child, and another man who came to help. The father took off his necklace—like the one you wear—and put it around the neck of the dead baby. There was still fighting on the street out front and the husband ran out of the room.

"My mother was terrified. She said there was blood everywhere, and the poor woman and her baby...but she summoned the courage to slip out of the wardrobe. She remembered the second child and knew it would die if she didn't do something. She picked up a knife and delivered it.

"From the window she saw the husband die and the street filled with dozen of bodies. A swordsman covered in blood was killing everyone. She didn't know what was happening. She was terrified. She was certain he would kill her, too. With the second child in her arms she took the necklace from the dead baby and fled. She pretended the baby was hers and never told anyone what really happened until the night she died—when she told me."

"Why did she take the necklace?"

"She said it was because the father meant it for his child."

"But you don't believe that?"

She shrugged. "Look at it." She pointed at his amulet. "It's made of silver. My mother was a very poor woman. But it's not like she sold it. In the end she did give it to him."

"What is your brother's name?"

She looked puzzled. "I thought you knew. I mean you were with the Nationalists."

"How would being with—"

"My brother is the leader of the Nationalist Army."

"Oh," Hadrian's hopes sank. "Your brother is Commander Parker?"

"No, no, my name is Miranda Gaunt. My brother is Degan."

She had not fought or taken blows, but Arista felt battered and beaten. She sat in what, until that morning, had been the viceroy's office. A huge gaudy chamber, it contained all that had survived the burning of the old royal palace. Night had fallen, heralding a close to the longest day she could recall. Memories of that morning were already distant, from another year, another life.

Outside, the flicker of bonfires bloomed in the square where they sentenced Emery to die. Die he did, but his dream survived, his promise fulfilled. She could hear them singing, see their shadows dancing. They toasted him with mugs of beer, and celebrated his victory with lambs on spits. A decidedly different gathering than the one the sheriff had planned.

"We insist you take the crown of Rhenydd," Doctor Gerand repeated, his voice carrying over the others.

"I agree," Perin said. Since the battle, the big grocer who was designated to lead the failed left flank and was wounded in the fight, became a figure of legend. He found himself thrust into the ad hoc city council hastily comprised of the city's most revered surviving citizens.

Several other heads nodded. She did not know them, but guessed they owned large farms or businesses—commoners all. None of the former nobility remained after the Imperial takeover and all the Imperials were either dead or imprisoned. Viceroy Androus, evicted from his office, was relocated to a prison cell along with the city guards that surrendered. A handful of other city officials and Laven, the man who had words with Emery in The Gnome, prepared to stand trial for crimes against the citizenry—a new law.

After the battle ended, Arista helped organize the treatment of the wounded. Soon people returned to her, asking what to do next. She directed them to bury the bodies of those without families outside the city. There was a brief ceremony presided over by Monsignor Bartholomew.

The wounded and dying overwhelmed the armory, and makeshift hospitals were created in the Dunlaps' barn and rooms commandeered at The Gnome. People also volunteered their private homes, particularly those with beds recently made empty. With the work of cleaning up the dead and wounded underway, the question of what to do with the viceroy and the other imperial supporters arose, along with a dozen other inquiries. Arista suggested they form a council and decide together what should be done. They did, and their first official act was to summon her to the viceroy's old office.

It was unanimous. The council voted to appoint Arista ruling queen of the Kingdom of Rhenydd.

"There is no one else here of noble blood," Perin said wearing a blood-stained bandage around his head. "No one else who even knows how to govern."

"But Emery envisioned a republic," Arista told them. "A self-determining government like they have in Delgos. This was his dream—the reason he fought, the reason he died."

"But we don't know how to do that." Doctor Gerand said. "We need experience, and you have it."

"He's right," Perin spoke up again. "Perhaps in a few months we could hold elections, but Sir Breckton and his army are still on their way. We need action. We need the kind of leadership that won us this city, or come tomorrow we'll lose it again."

Arista sighed and looked over at Hadrian, who sat near the window. As commander of the Nationalist Army, he also received an invitation.

"What do you think?" she asked.

"I'm no politician."

"I'm not asking you to be. I just want to know what you think."

"Royce once told me two people can argue over the same point and both can be right. I thought he was nutty, but I'm not so sure anymore, because I think you're both right. The moment you become queen, you'll destroy any chance of this becoming the kind of free republic Emery spoke of, but if someone doesn't take charge—and fast—that hope will die anyway. And they're right. If I were going to choose anyone to rule, it would be you. As an outsider, you have no bias, no chance of favoritism—you'll be fair. And everyone already loves you."

"They don't love me. They don't even know me."

"They think they do, and they trust you. You can give directions and people will listen. And right now, that's what is needed."

"I can't be queen. Emery wanted a republic, and a republic he will have. You can appoint me temporary mayor of Ratibor and steward of the Kingdom of Rhenydd. I will administer only until a proper government can be established, at which time I will resign and return to Melengar." She nodded more to herself than any of them. "Yes, that way I will be in a position to ensure it gets done."

The men in the room muttered in agreement.

"Tomorrow we can address the city. Is there anything else?"

The council filed out of City Hall into the square, leaving her and Hadrian alone. Outside the constant noise of the crowd grew quiet, and then exploded with cheers.

"You're very popular, Your Highness," Hadrian told her.

"Too popular. They want to commission a statue of me."

"I heard that. They want to put it in the West End Square, one of you holding up that sword."

"It's not over yet. Breckton is almost here, and we don't even know if Royce got through. What if he never made it? What if he did and Alric doesn't listen? He might not think it possible to take Ratibor and refuse to put the kingdom at risk. We need to be certain."

"You want me to go?"

"No," she said. "I want you here. I *need* you here. But if Breckton lays siege, we will eventually fall and by then it will be too late for you to get away. Our only hope is if Alric's forces can turn Breckton's attention away from us."

He nodded and his hand played with the amulet around his neck. "I suppose it doesn't matter where I go for awhile."

"What do you mean?"

"Esrahaddon was in Gaunt's camp. He's been helping the Nationalists."

"Did you tell him about the heir?"

Hadrian nodded. "And you were right. The heir is alive. I think he's Degan Gaunt."

DEGAN GAUNT

"Degan Gaunt is the heir?"

"Funny, huh? The voice of the common man is also the heir to the imperial throne. There was another child born that night. The midwife took the surviving twin. No one else knew. I have no idea how Esrahaddon figured it out, but that explains why he's been helping Gaunt."

"Where is Esrahaddon now?"

"Don't know. I haven't seen him since the battle started."

"You don't think..."

"Hmm? Oh, no. I'm sure he's fine. He hung back when we engaged Dermont's forces. I suspect he's off to find Gaunt and will contact me and Royce once he does." Hadrian sighed. "I wish my father could have known he didn't fail after all.

"Anyway, I'll take care of things tonight before I leave. I'll put one of the regiment captains in charge of the army. There's a guy named Renquist who seems intelligent. I'll have him see to the walls, patch up the stone work, ready gate defenses, put up sentries, guards, and archers. He should know how to do all of that. And I'll put together a list of things you'll want to do, like bring the entire army and the surrounding farmers within the city walls and seal it up. You should do that right away."

"You'll be leaving in the morning then?"

He nodded. "Doubt I'll see you again before I go, so I'll say goodbye now. You've done the impossible, Arista—excuse me—Your Highness."

"Arista is just fine." she told him. "I'm going to miss you." It was all she could say. Words were too small to express gratitude so immense.

He opened his mouth, but hesitated. He smiled then and said, "Take care of yourself, Your Highness."

Nyphron Rising

ℒ

In her dream Thrace could see the beast coming for her father. He stood smiling warmly at her, his back to the monster. She tried to scream for him to run, but only a soft muffled moan escaped. She tried to wave her arms and draw his attention to the danger, but her limbs were heavy as lead and refused to move. She tried to run to him, but her feet were stuck, frozen in place.

The beast had no trouble moving.

It charged down the hill. Her poor father took no notice, even though the beast shook the ground as it ran. It consumed him completely with a single swallow, and she fell as if pierced through the heart. She collapsed onto the grass, struggling to breathe. In the distance the beast was coming for her now, coming to finish the job, coming to swallow her up—his legs squeaking louder and louder as he advanced.

She woke up in a cold sweat.

She was sleeping on her stomach in her feather bed with the pillow folded up around her face. She hated sleeping. Sleep always brought nightmares. She stayed awake as long as possible, many nights sitting on the floor in front of the little window, watching the stars and listening to the sounds outside. There was a whole symphony of frogs that croaked in the moat and a chorus of crickets. Fireflies sometimes passed by her tiny sliver of the world. But eventually sleep found her.

The dream was the same every night. She was on the hill. Her father unaware of his impending death, and there was never anything she could do. However, tonight's dream had been different. Usually it ended when the beast devoured her, but this time she woke early. Something else was different. When the beast came it made a squeaking sound. Even for a dream that seemed strange.

DEGAN GAUNT

She heard it then. The sound entered through her window.
Squeak!

There were other noises, too, sounds of men talking. They spoke quietly but their voices drifted up from the courtyard below. She went to the window and peered out. As many as a dozen men with torches drew a wagon whose large wooden wheels squeaked once with each revolution. The wagon was a large box with a small barred window cut in the side, like the kind that would hold a lion for a traveling circus. The men were dressed in black and scarlet armor. She had seen that armor before in Dahlgren.

One man stood out. He was tall and thin with long black hair and a short, neatly trimmed beard.

The wagon came to a stop and the knights gathered.

"He's chained, isn't he?" she heard one of them say.

"Why? Are you frightened?"

"He's not a wizard," the tall man scolded. "He can't turn you into a frog. His powers are political, not mystical."

"Come now, Luis, even Saldur said not to underestimate him, legends speak of strange abilities. He's part god."

"You believe too much in church doctrine. We are the protectorate of the faith. We don't have to wallow in superstition like ignorant peasants."

"That sounds blasphemous."

"The truth can never be blasphemous so long as it is tempered with an understanding of what is good and right. The truth is a powerful thing, like a crossbow. You wouldn't hand a child a loaded crossbow and say 'run and play' would you? People get hurt that way, tragedies occur. The truth must be kept safe, reserved only for those capable of handling it. This—this sacrilegious treasure in a box—is one truth above all that must be kept a secret. It must never again see the light of day. We will bury it deep beneath the castle. We will seal it in for all time and it will become the cornerstone on which we will build a new and glorious Empire that will eclipse the previous one and wash away the sins of our forefathers."

She watched as they opened the rear of the wagon and pulled out a man. A black hood covered his face. Chains bound his hands and ankles. Nevertheless, the men treated him carefully, as if he could explode at any minute.

With four men on either side, they marched him across the courtyard out of the sight of her narrow window.

She watched as they rolled the wagon back out and closed the gate behind them. Thrace stared at the empty courtyard for more than an hour, until at last she fell asleep again.

The carriage bounced through the night on the rough hilly road, following a sliver of open sky between walls of forest. The jangle of harnesses, thudding of hooves, and the crush of wheels dominated this world. The night's air was heavily scented with the aroma of pond water and a skunk's spray.

Arcadius, the lore master of Sheridan University, peered out the open window and hammered on the roof with his walking stick until the driver brought the carriage to a halt.

"What is it?" the driver shouted.

"This will be fine," the lore master replied, grabbing up his bag and, finding the strap, slipped it over his shoulder.

"What is?"

"I'm getting out here." Arcadius popped open the little door and carefully climbed out onto the desolate road. "Yes, this is fine." He closed the door and lightly patted the side of the carriage as if it were a horse.

The lore master walked to the front of the coach. The driver sat on the raised bench with his coat drawn up around his neck, a formless sack-hat pulled down over his ears. Between his thighs he trapped a small corked jug. "But there's nothing here, sir," he insisted.

"Don't be absurd, of course there is. You're here, aren't you, and so am I." Arcadius pulled open his bag. "And look, there are some nice trees and this excellent road we've been riding on."

"But it's the middle of the night, sir."

Arcadius tilted his head up. "And just look at that wonderful starry sky. It's beautiful, don't you think? Do you know your constellations, good man?"

"No, sir."

"Pity." He measured out some silver coins and handed them up to the driver. "It's all up there, you know. Wars, heroes, beasts, and villains, the past and the future spread above us each night like a dazzling map." He pointed. "That long, elegant set of four bright stars is Persephone and she of course is always beside Novron. If you follow the line that looks like Novron's arm you can see how they just barely touch—lovers longing to be together."

The driver looked up. "Just looks like a bunch of scattered dust to me."

"It does to a great many people. Too many people."

The driver looked down at him and frowned. "You sure you want me to just leave you? I can come back if you want."

"That won't be necessary, but thank you."

"Suit yourself. Goodnight." The carriage driver slapped the reins and the coach rolled out, circled in a field, and returned the way it came. The driver glanced up at the sky twice, shaking his head each time. The carriage and the team rode away, the horses clopping softer and softer until they faded below the harsh shrill of nightly noises.

Arcadius stood alone observing the world. It had been some time since the old professor had been out in the wild. He had forgotten how loud it was. The high-pitched trill of crickets punctuated the oscillating echoes of tree frogs that peeped with the regular pace of a human heart. Winds rustled a million leaves, fashioning the voice of waves at sea.

Arcadius walked along the road, crossing the fresh grooves of the carriage wheels. His shoes on the dirt made a surprisingly large amount of noise. The dark had a way of drawing attention to the normally invisible, silent, and ignored. That was why nights were so frightening, without the distraction of light, the doors to other senses were unlocked. As children, the dark spoke of the monster beneath the bed, as adults the intruder, and as old men, the herald of death on its way.

"Long, hard, and rocky, is the road we walk in old age," he muttered to his feet.

He stopped when he reached a post lurching at a crossroad. The sign declared *Ratibor* to the right and *Aquesta* to the left. He stepped off the road into the tall grass and found a fallen log to sit on. He pulled the shoulder strap of the sack over his head and set it down. Rummaging through it he found a honeyed muffin, one of three he had pilfered from the dinner table at the inn. He was old, but his sleight of hand was still impressive. Royce would be proud; less so if he knew he paid for the meal, which included the muffins. Still, the big swarthy fellow at his elbow would have poached them if he had not acted first. Now it looked as if they would come in handy as he had no idea when—

He heard hoof beats long before he saw the horse. The sound came from the direction of Ratibor. As unlikely as it was for anyone else to be on that road, the lore master's heart nevertheless increased until at last the rider cleared the trees—a woman rode alone in a dark hood and cloak. She came to a stop at the post.

"You're late," he said.

She whirled around, relaxing when she recognized him. "No, I'm early. You are just earlier."

"Why are you alone? It's too dangerous. These roads are—"

"And who would you suggest I trust to escort me? Have you added to our ranks?"

She dismounted and tied her horse to the post.

"You could have paid some young lad. There must be a few in the city you trust."

"Those I trust would be of no aid, and those that could help I don't trust. Besides, this isn't far. I couldn't have been on the road for more than two hours. And there's not much between Ratibor and here." Before reaching him he started to rise. "You don't have to get up."

"How else can I give you a hug?" He embraced her. "Now tell, me how have you been? I was very worried."

"You worry too much. I'm fine." She drew back her hood, revealing long blonde hair that she wore scooped back.

"The city has been taken?" Arcadias asked.

"The Nationalists have it now. They attacked and defeated Lord Dermont's forces in the field and the princess led a revolt against Sheriff Vigan in the city. Sir Breckton and the Northern Imperial Army arrived too late. With the city buttoned-up and Dermont gone, Breckton's Army turned around and headed north."

"I passed part of his supply train. He's taking up a defensive position around Aquesta, I think. Hadrian and Arista? How are they?"

"Not a scratch on either," she replied. "Hadrian turned command of the Nationalist Army over to a man named Renquist—one of the senior captains—and left the morning after the battle. I'm not sure where to."

"Did you have a chance to talk with him?"

She nodded. "Yes, I told him about my brother. Arcadius, do you know where Degan is?"

"Me?" He looked surprised. "No. The seret have him, I am certain of that, but where is anyone's guess. They have gotten a whole lot smarter recently. It's like Guy has sprouted another head, and this one has a brain in it."

"Do you think they killed him?"

"I don't know," the wizard paused, regretting his curt words and looked at her sympathetically. "It's hard to fathom the imperial mind. We can hope they want him alive. Now that we've unleashed Hadrian, there's a good chance that he and Royce will save him. It could even be that Esrahaddon will connect the dots and send them."

"Esrahaddon already knows," Miranda said. "He's been with Degan for months."

"So, he found out. Excellent. I thought he might. When he visited Sheridan it was obvious he knew more than he let on."

"Maybe he and Hadrian are looking together—planned a place to meet up after the battle?"

The wizard stroked his chin thoughtfully. "Possible…probable even. So those two are off looking for your brother. What about Arista? What is she doing?"

Miranda smiled. "She's running the city. The citizens of Ratibor were ready to proclaim her queen of Rhenydd, but she settled for mayor pro tem until elections can be held. She intends to honor Emery's dream of a republic in Rhenydd."

"A princess establishing the first republic in Avryn." Arcadius chuckled. "Quite the turn of events."

"The princess has cried a lot since the battle. I've watched her. She works constantly, settling disputes, inspecting the walls, appointing ministers. She falls asleep at her desk in City Hall. She cries when she thinks no one is looking."

"All that violence after so privileged a life."

"I think she might have been in love with a young man who was killed."

"In love? Really? That's surprising. She's never showed an interest in anyone. Who was he?"

"No one of note—the son of the dead bodyguard to King Urith."

"That's too bad," the wizard said sadly. "For all her privilege, she's not had an easy life."

"You didn't ask about Royce," she noted.

"I know about him. He arrived back in Medford not long before I set out. The next day Melengar's army crossed the Galewyr. Alric has enlisted every able-bodied man and even a good deal of the boys. He's put Count Pickering, Sir Ecton, and Marquis Lanaklin in command. They broke through the little imperial force and at last report were sweeping south, causing a great deal of havoc. Another obstacle I had to travel around. Getting back to the university will take a month I expect."

The wizard sighed and a look of concern passed over his face. "Two things still trouble me. First, Aquesta is threatened by an enemy army resting in Ratibor, and they aren't negotiating or evacuating. Second, there's Marius."

"Who?"

"Merrick Marius, also known as Cutter."

"Isn't he the one who put Royce in Manzant?"

"Yes, and now he is working for the Empire. He's a wildcard I had not expected." The old man paused. "You're certain that Hadrian believed everything you said?"

"Absolutely. His eyes nearly fell out of his head when I told him who the heir was." She sighed. "Are you sure we—"

"I'm sure, Miranda. Make no mistake we are doing what is absolutely right and necessary. It is imperative that Royce and Hadrian never find out the truth."

Books in the Riyria Revelations

The Crown Conspiracy

Avempartha

Nyphron Rising

*The Emerald Storm**

*Forthcoming

THE RIYRIA REVELATIONS

If you enjoyed this novel, you will be happy to learn that…

Nyphron Rising is the third in a six book series entitled the Riyria Revelations. This saga is neither a string of sequels nor a lengthy work unnaturally divided. Instead, the Riyria Revelations was conceived as a single epic tale told through six individual episodes. While a book may hint at building mysteries or thickening plots, these threads are not essential to reach a satisfying conclusion to the current episode—which has its own beginning, middle, and end.

Eschewing the recent trends in fantasy toward the lengthy, gritty, and dark, the Riyria Revelations brings the genre back to its roots. Avoiding unnecessarily complicated language and world building for its own sake; this series is a distillation of the best elements of traditional fantasy—great characters, a complex plot, humor, and drama all in appropriate measures.

While written for an adult audience the Riyria Revelations lacks sex, graphic violence, and profanity making it appropriate for readers thirteen and older.

About the Author

Born in Detroit Michigan, Michael J. Sullivan has raised in Novi. He has also lived in Vermont, North Carolina and Virginia. He worked as a commercial artist and illustrator, founding his own advertising agency in 1996, which he closed in 2005 to pursue writing full-time. His first published novel The Crown Conspiracy was released in October 2008. He currently resides in Fairfax, Virginia with his wife and three children.

Awards for Riyria Books

2009 National Indie Excellence Award Finalist

2008 ReaderViews Literary Award Finalist

2007 Foreword Magazine Book of the Year Finalist

Fantasy Sites Recognition

Named one of the Notable Fantasy Books of 2009
—Fantasy Book Critic

Named one of the top 5 Fantasy Books of 2009
—Dark Wolf's Fantasy Reviews

Named a Notable Indie of 2008—Fantasy Book Critic

Websites

Author's Homepage: www.michaelsullivan-author.com

Author's Blog: www.riyria.blogspot.com

Social Networking Groups

www.goodreads.com/group/show/10550

www.facebook.com/group.php?gid=26847461609

www.shelfari.com/groups/30879/about

Contact

Twitter: twitter.com/author_sullivan

Email: michael.sullivan.dc@gmail.com

4593599

Made in the USA
Lexington, KY
09 February 2010